PRAISE FOR
MY BEST FRIEND'S EXORCISM

"Grady Hendrix's *My Best Friend's Exorcism* is a little bit 666, a little bit *Sixteen Candles*—a traum-com that's as much about the rites of teenage friendship as it is about the rituals of Satan-usurping."

—*Wired*

"*My Best Friend's Exorcism* is sharply written in all the ways that are most important—namely, the ebbs and flows and insecurities of adolescence, and depicting the messy emotional conflagrations that inevitably arise as youthful friends grow up and (potentially) grow apart."

—*A.V. Club*

"Hendrix nails the stagnant air of suburbia and gets right to the dark heart of dysfunction that lies beneath so many teenage-girl friendships. Readers who thought *Heathers* wasn't quite dark enough will find this humorous horror tale—filled with spot-on '80s pop-culture references—totally awesome."

—*Booklist* (starred review)

"My favorite book of the year, hands-down, is Grady Hendrix's *My Best Friend's Exorcism*—think *Mean Girls* with demonic possession, set in 1988 Charleston. It's funny, it's heart-wrenching, it's even a little spiritual, in a very strange way."

—*Southern Living Magazine*

"Hendrix revels in making insane, improbable, sometimes ludicrous premises and sequences believable, yet neither *Horrorstör* nor *My Best Friend's Exorcism* are pure carnival slapstick. The horror and gore are legit."

Fangoria

"A riveting and poignant story of an enduring friendship. I'll admit it, I got a little weepy! But don't worry, there's plenty of good, clean, horror fun." —Sarah Langan, author of *Audrey's Door*

"A huge win. It works as an exorcism thriller but feels like more than that, steeped in that particular coming-of-age sadness, feverishness, and joy."

—Austin Grossman, author of *Soon I Will Be Invincible* and *You: A Novel*

"From the author of the acclaimed *Horrorstör*, this book packs all the magic of a summer horror flick." —*Bustle*

"Take *The Exorcist*, add some hair spray and wine coolers, and enroll it in high school in 1988—that'll give you *My Best Friend's Exorcism*. When Abby's friend Gretchen turns super moody and super mean, Abby begins to suspect it's not just the typical high school drama. (The hundreds of dead birds in Gretchen's yard support that theory). Campy. Heartfelt. Horrifying."

—*Minnesota Public Radio News*

"As with the haunted-store setting of *Horrorstör*, this novel's reimagining of the possession tale in an '80s high school is far more than a gimmick. Hendrix stylishly delivers the scenario with humorous and ghoulish aplomb, with the scares often creeping out at the most unexpected of times, culminating in a few truly macabre scenes, including a sequence that may leave some readers never wishing to touch a milkshake again."

—*New York Journal of Books*

"*My Best Friend's Exorcism* marks a diabolically gleeful (and wholly original) entry in something of a new wave of possession tales. Proudly wearing its bloody heart on its rayon sleeve, this nostalgic tale of teen angst, friendship, and unholy possession is as surprisingly touching as it is grisly, making for one of the most unique reads of 2016."

—*New York Journal of Books*

"Fast-paced and witty, the novel balances moments of true horror with a portrait of true friendship and the lengths to which one friend will go for another."

—John Langan, author of *House of Windows* and *Mr. Gaunt and Other Uneasy Encounters*

"The book is sure to tug on the heartstrings of Gen-X'ers, but with nuanced character writing and solid storytelling, Hendrix will exceed expectations for a silly '80s flashback. This is a story about the power of friendship. Satirical, intense and surprisingly heartwarming, *My Best Friend's Exorcism* is, like, totally the perfect summer reading choice—if you don't mind some gore."

—*Charleston Gazette-Mail*

MY BEST FRIEND'S EXORCISM

MY BEST FRIE

ND'S EXORCISM

a novel by Grady Hendrix

QUIRK BOOKS
PHILADELPHIA

This is a work of fiction. All names, places, and characters are products of the author's imagination or are used fictitiously. Any resemblance to real people, places, or events is entirely coincidental.

First paperback edition, Quirk Books, 2017.
Originally published by Quirk Books in 2016.

Library of Congress Cataloging in Publication Number: 2015947003 (hardcover edition)

ISBN: 978-1-59474-976-6

Printed in the United States of America

Typeset in Futura, Sabon and ITC Benguiat

Cover designed by Doogie Horner
Cover illustration by Hugh Fleming
Production management by John J. McGurk

Quirk Books
an imprint of Andrews McMeel Publishing
a division of Andrews McMeel Universal
1130 Walnut Street, Kansas City, Missouri 64106
quirkbooks.com

The authorised representative in the EEA is Simon and Schuster Netherlands BV, Herculesplein 96 3584 AA Utrecht, Netherlands. (info@simonandschuster.nl)

20 19 18

FSC
www.fsc.org
MIX
Paper | Supporting responsible forestry
FSC™ C008955

For Amanda,
*Who knows the reasons why.**

*But if she doesn't, I would suggest she have her attorney consult both protective orders filed against her, the criminal complaint which outlines these reasons in great detail, and maybe also her conscience because disclosing the whereabouts of the bodies will finally bring some kind of closure for my family.

DON'T YOU FORGET ABOUT ME

The exorcist is dead.

Abby sits in her office and stares at the email, then clicks the blue link. It takes her to the homepage of the paper she still thinks of as the *News and Courier*, even though it changed its name fifteen years ago. There's the exorcist floating in the middle of her screen, balding and with a ponytail, smiling at the camera in a blurry headshot the size of a postage stamp. Abby's jaw aches and her throat gets tight. She doesn't realize she's stopped breathing.

The exorcist was driving some lumber up to Lakewood and stopped on I-95 to help a tourist change his tire. He was tightening the lug nuts when a Dodge Caravan swerved onto the shoulder and hit him full-on. He died before the ambulance arrived. The woman driving the minivan had three different painkillers in her system—four if you included Bud Light. She was charged with driving under the influence.

"Highways or dieways," Abby thinks. "The choice is yours."

It pops into her head, a catchphrase she doesn't even remember she remembered, but in that instant she doesn't know how she ever forgot. Those highway safety billboards covered South Carolina when she was in high school; and in that instant, her office, the conference call she has at eleven, her apartment, her mortgage, her divorce, her daughter—none of it matters.

It's twenty years ago and she's bombing over the old bridge in a crapped-out Volkswagen Rabbit, windows down, radio blasting UB40, the air sweet and salty in her face. She turns her head to the right and sees Gretchen riding shotgun, the wind tossing her blond hair, shoes off, sitting Indian-style on the seat, and they're singing along to the radio at the top of their tuneless lungs. It's April 1988 and the world belongs to them.

For Abby, "friend" is a word whose sharp corners have been worn smooth by overuse. "I'm friends with the guys in IT," she might say, or "I'm meeting some friends after work."

But she remembers when the word "friend" could draw blood. She and Gretchen spent hours ranking their friendships, trying to determine who was a best friend and who was an everyday friend, debating whether anyone could have two best friends at the same time, writing each other's names over and over in purple ink, buzzed on the dopamine high of belonging to someone else, having a total stranger choose you, someone who wanted to know you, another person who cared that you were alive.

She and Gretchen were best friends, and then came that fall. And they fell.

And the exorcist saved her life.

Abby still remembers high school, but she remembers it as images, not events. She remembers effects, but she's gotten fuzzy on the causes. Now it's all coming back in an unstoppable flood. The sound of screaming on the Lawn. The owls. The stench in Margaret's room. Good Dog Max. The terrible thing that happened to Glee. But most of all, she remembers what happened to Gretchen and how everything got so fucked up back in 1988, the year her best friend was possessed by the devil.

WE GOT THE BEAT

1982. Ronald Reagan was launching the War on Drugs. Nancy Reagan was telling everyone to "Just Say No." EPCOT Center was finally open, Midway released Ms. Pac-Man in arcades, and Abby Rivers was a certified grown-up because she'd finally cried at a movie. It was *E.T. the Extra-Terrestrial*, and she went back to see it again and again, fascinated by her own involuntary reaction, helpless in the grip of the tears that washed down her face as E.T. and Elliott reached for each other.

It was the year she turned ten.

It was the year of The Party.

It was the year everything changed.

One week before Thanksgiving, Abby marched into Mrs. Link's fourth-grade classroom with twenty-one invitations shaped like roller skates and invited her entire class to Redwing Rollerway on Saturday December 4 at 3:30 p.m. to celebrate her tenth birthday. This was going to be Abby's moment. She'd seen *Roller Boogie* with Linda Blair, she'd seen Olivia Newton-John in *Xanadu*, she'd seen shirtless Patrick Swayze in *Skatetown, U.S.A.* After months of practice, she was as good as all three of them put together. No longer would she be Flabby Quivers. Before the eyes of everybody in her class she would become Abby Rivers, Skate Princess.

Thanksgiving break happened, and on the first day back at

school Margaret Middleton walked to the front of the classroom and invited everyone to her polo plantation for a day of horseback riding on Saturday, December 4.

"Mrs. Link? Mrs. Link? Mrs. Link?" Abby waved her arm wildly from side to side. "That's the day of my birthday party."

"Oh, right," Mrs. Link said, as if Abby had not thumbtacked an extra-large roller skate with her birthday party information right in the middle of the classroom bulletin board. "But you can move that."

"But . . ." Abby had never said "no" to a teacher before, so she did the best she could. "But it's my birthday?"

Mrs. Link sighed and made a reassuring gesture to Margaret Middleton.

"Your party isn't until three thirty," she told Abby. "I'm sure everyone can come to your party after riding horses at Margaret's."

"Of course they can, Mrs. Link," Margaret Middleton simpered. "There'll be plenty of time."

On the Thursday before her birthday, Abby brought the classroom twenty-five E.T. cupcakes as a reminder. Everyone ate them, which she thought was a good sign. On Saturday, she forced her parents to drive to Redwing Rollerway an hour early so they could set up. By 3:15 the private party room looked like E.T. had exploded all over the walls. There were E.T. balloons, E.T. tablecloths, E.T. party hats, snack-sized Reese's Pieces next to every E.T. paper plate, a peanut butter and chocolate ice cream cake with E.T.'s face on top, and on the wall behind her seat was Abby's most treasured possession that could not under any circumstances get soiled, stained, ripped, or torn: an actual E.T. movie poster her dad had brought home from the theater and given to her as a birthday present.

Finally, 3:30 rolled around.

No one came.

At 3:35 the room was still empty.

By 3:40 Abby was almost in tears.

Out on the floor they were playing "Open Arms" by Journey and all the big kids were skating past the Plexiglas window that looked into the private party room, and Abby knew they were laughing at her because she was alone on her birthday. She sunk her fingernails deep into the milky skin on the inside of her wrist, focusing on how bad it burned to keep herself from crying. Finally, at 3:50, when every inch of her wrist was covered in bright red half-moon marks, Gretchen Lang, the weird new kid who'd just transferred from Ashley Hall, was pushed into the room by her mom.

"Hello, hello," Mrs. Lang chirped, bracelets jangling on her wrists. "I'm so sorry we're— Where is everybody?"

Abby couldn't answer.

"They're stuck on the bridge," Abby's mom said, coming to the rescue.

Mrs. Lang's face relaxed. "Gretchen, why don't you give your little friend her present?" she said, cramming a wrapped brick into Gretchen's arms and pushing her forward. Gretchen leaned back, digging in her heels. Mrs. Lang tried another tactic: "We don't know this character, do we, Gretchen?" she asked, looking at E.T.

She had to be kidding, Abby thought. How could she not know the most popular person on the planet?

"I know who he is," Gretchen protested. "He's E.T. the . . . Extra-Terrible?"

Abby could not even fathom. What were these crazy lunatics talking about?

"The extra*terrestrial*," Abby corrected, finding her voice. "It means he comes from another planet."

"Isn't that precious," Mrs. Lang said. Then she made her excuses and got the hell out of there.

A deadly silence poisoned the air. Everyone shuffled their feet. For Abby, this was worse than being alone. By now, it was completely clear that no one was coming to her birthday party, and both of her parents had to confront the fact that their daughter had no friends. Even worse, a strange kid who didn't know about extraterrestrials was witnessing her humiliation. Gretchen crossed her arms over her chest, crackling the paper around her gift.

"That's so nice of you to bring a present," Abby's mom said. "You didn't have to do that."

Of course she had to do that, Abby thought. It's my birthday.

"Happy birthday," Gretchen mumbled, thrusting her present at Abby.

Abby didn't want the present. She wanted her friends. Why weren't they here? But Gretchen just stood there like a dummy, gift extended. With all eyes on Abby, she took the present, but she took it fast so that no one got confused and thought she liked the way things were going. Instantly, she knew her present was a book. Was this girl totally clueless? Abby wanted E.T. stuff, not a book. Unless maybe it was an E.T. book?

Even that small hope died after she carefully unwrapped the paper to find a Children's Bible. Abby turned it over, hoping that maybe it was part of a bigger present that had E.T. in it. Nothing on the back. She opened it. Nope. It really was a Children's New Testament. Abby looked up to see if the entire world had gone crazy, but all she saw was Gretchen staring at her.

Abby knew what the rules were: she had to say thank you and act excited so nobody's feelings got hurt. But what about *her* feelings? It was her birthday and no one was thinking about her at all. No one was stuck on the bridge. Everyone was at Margaret

Middleton's house riding horses and giving Margaret all of Abby's presents.

"What do we say, Abby?" her mom prompted.

No. She would not say it. If she said it, then she was agreeing this was fine, that it was okay for a weird person she did not know to give her a Bible. If she said it, her parents would think that she and this freak were friends and they'd make sure she came to all of Abby's birthday parties from now on and she'd never get another present except Children's Bibles from anyone ever.

"Abby?" her mom said.

No.

"Abs," her dad said. "Don't be like this."

"You need to thank this little girl right now," her mom said.

In a flash of inspiration, Abby realized she had a way out: she could run. What were they going to do? Tackle her? So she ran, shoulder-checking Gretchen and fleeing into the noise and darkness of the rink.

"Abby!" her mom called, and then Journey drowned her out.

Super sincere Steve Perry sent his voice soaring over smashing cymbals and power-ballad guitars that pounded the rink walls with crashing waves as cooing couples skated close.

Abby wove between big kids carrying pizza and pitchers of beer, all of them rolling across the carpet, shouting to their friends, then she crashed into the ladies' room, burst into a stall, slammed the orange door behind her, collapsed onto the toilet seat, and was miserable.

Everyone wanted to go to Margaret Middleton's plantation because Margaret Middleton had horses, and Abby was a stupid moron if she thought people wanted to come see her skate. No one wanted to see her skate. They wanted to ride horses, and she was stupid and stupid and stupid to think otherwise.

"Open Arms" got louder as someone opened the door.

"Abby?" a voice said.

It was what's-her-name. Abby was instantly suspicious. Her parents had probably sent her in to spy. Abby pulled her feet up onto the toilet seat.

Gretchen knocked on the stall door.

"Abby? Are you in there?"

Abby sat very, very still and managed to get her crying down to a mild whimper.

"I didn't want to give you a Children's Bible," Gretchen said, through the stall door. "My mom picked it out. I told her not to. I wanted to get you an E.T. thing. They had one where his heart lit up."

Abby didn't care. This girl was terrible. Abby heard movement outside the stall, and then Gretchen was sticking her face under the door. Abby was horrified. What was she doing? She was wriggling in! Suddenly, Gretchen was standing in front of the toilet even though the stall door was closed, which meant privacy. Abby's mind was blown. She stared at this insane girl, waiting to see what she'd do next. Slowly, Gretchen blinked her enormous blue eyes.

"I don't like horses," she said. "They smell bad. And I don't think Margaret Middleton is a nice person."

That, at least, made some sense to Abby.

"Horses are stupid," Gretchen continued. "Everyone thinks they're neat, but their brains are like hamster brains and if you make a loud noise they get scared even though they're bigger than we are."

Abby didn't know what to say to that.

"I don't know how to skate," Gretchen said. "But I think people who like horses should buy dogs instead. Dogs are nice and they're smaller than horses and they're smart. But not all dogs.

We have a dog named Max, but he's dumb. If he barks while he's running, he falls down."

Abby was starting to feel uncomfortable. What if someone came in and saw this weird person standing in the stall with her? She knew she had to say something, but there was only one thing on her mind, so she said it: "I wish you weren't here."

"I know," Gretchen nodded. "My mom wanted me to go to Margaret Middleton's."

"Then why didn't you?" Abby asked.

"You invited me first," Gretchen said.

A lightning bolt split Abby's skull in two. Exactly! This was what she had been saying. Her invitation had been first! Everyone should be HERE with HER because she had invited them FIRST and Margaret Middleton COPIED her. This girl had the right idea.

Maybe everything wasn't ruined. Maybe Abby could show this weirdo how good she was at skating, and she'd tell everyone at school. They'd all want to see, but she'd never have another birthday party again, so they'd never see her skate unless they begged her to do it in front of the whole school, and then she might do it and blow everyone's minds, but only if they begged her a lot. She had to start by impressing this girl and that wouldn't be hard. This girl didn't even know how to skate.

"I'll teach you how to skate if you want," Abby said. "I'm really good."

"You are?" Gretchen asked.

Abby nodded. Someone was finally taking her seriously.

"I'm *really* good," she said.

After Abby's dad rented skates, Abby taught Gretchen how to lace them super tight and helped her walk across the carpet, showing her how to pick up her feet high so she wouldn't trip. Abby led Gretchen to the baby skate zone and taught her some basic turns, but after a few minutes she was dying to strut her stuff.

"You want to go in the big rink?" Abby asked.

Gretchen shook her head.

"It's not scary if I stay with you," Abby said. "I won't let anything bad happen."

Gretchen thought about it for a minute.

"Will you hold my hands?"

Abby grabbed Gretchen's hands and pulled her onto the floor just as the announcer said it was Free Skate, and suddenly the rink was full of teenagers whizzing past them at warp speed. One boy lifted a girl by the waist in the middle of the floor and they spun around and the DJ turned on the mirror ball and stars were gliding over everything, and the whole world was spinning. Gretchen was flinching as speed demons tore past, so Abby turned around and backskated in front of her, pulling her by both soft, sweaty hands, merging them into the flow. They started skating faster, taking the first turn, then faster, and Gretchen lifted one leg off the floor and pushed, and then the other, and then they were actually skating, and that's when the drums started and Abby's heart kicked off and the piano and the guitar started banging and "We Got the Beat" came roaring over the PA. The lights hitting the mirror ball pulsed and they were spinning with the crowd, orbiting around the couple in the center of the floor, and they had the beat.

Freedom people marching on their feet
Stallone time just walking in the street
They won't go where they don't know
But they're walking in line
We got the beat!
We got the beat!

Abby had the lyrics 100 percent wrong, but it didn't matter. She knew, more than she had ever known anything in her entire life, that she and Gretchen were the ones the Go-Go's were singing about. They had the beat! To anyone else watching, they were two kids going around the rink in a slow circle, taking the corners wide while all the other skaters zoomed past, but that's not what was happening. For Abby, the world was a Day-Glo Electric Wonderland full of hot pink lights, and neon green lights, and turquoise lights, and magenta lights, and they were flashing on and off with every beat of the music and everyone was dancing and they were flying so fast their skates were barely touching the ground, sliding around corners, picking up speed, and their hearts beat with the drums, and Gretchen had come to Abby's birthday party because Abby had invited her first and Abby had a real E.T. poster and now they could eat the entire cake all by themselves.

And somehow Gretchen knew exactly what Abby was thinking. She was smiling back at Abby, and Abby didn't want anyone else at her birthday party now, because her heart was beating in time with the music and they were spinning and Gretchen shouted out loud:

"This! Is! Awesome!"

Then Abby skated into Tommy Cox, got tangled up in his legs, and landed on her face, driving her top tooth through her lower lip and spraying a big bib of blood all down her E.T. shirt. Her parents had to drive her to the emergency room, where Abby received three stitches. At some point, Gretchen's parents retrieved their daughter from the roller rink, and Abby didn't see her again until homeroom on Monday.

That morning, her face was tighter than a balloon ready to burst. Abby walked into homeroom early, trying not to move her swollen lips, and the first thing she heard was Margaret Middleton.

"I don't understand why you didn't come," Margaret snipped, and Abby saw her looming over Gretchen's desk. "Everyone was there. They all stayed late. Are you scared of horses?"

Gretchen sat meekly in her chair, head lowered, hair trailing on her desk. Lanie Ott stood by Margaret's side, helping her berate Gretchen.

"I rode a horse and it took a high jump twice," Lanie Ott said.

Then the two of them saw Abby standing in the door.

"Ew," Margaret said. "What happened to your face? It looks like barf."

Abby was paralyzed by the righteous anger welling up inside her. She had been to the emergency room! And now they were being mean about it? Not knowing what else to do, Abby tried telling the truth.

"Tommy Cox skated into me and I had to get stitches."

At the mention of Tommy Cox's name, Lanie Ott opened and closed her mouth uselessly, but Margaret was made of sterner stuff.

"He did not," she said. And Abby realized that, oh my God, Margaret could just say Abby was a liar and no one would ever believe her. Margaret continued, "It's not nice to lie and it's rude to ignore other people's invitations. You're rude. You're *both* rude."

That's when Gretchen snapped her head up.

"Abby's invitation was first," she said, eyes blazing. "So *you're* the rude one. And she's not a liar. I saw it."

"Then you're both liars," Margaret said.

Someone was reaching over Abby's shoulder and knocking on the open door.

"Hey, any of you little dudes know where—aw, hey, sweetness."

Tommy Cox was standing three inches behind Abby, his curly blond hair tumbling around his face. The top button of his shirt was undone to show a gleaming puka shell necklace, and he was smiling with his impossibly white teeth. Heavy gravity was coming off his body in waves and washing over Abby.

Her heart stopped beating. Everyone's hearts stopped beating.

"Dang," he said, furrowing his brow and examining Abby's lower lip. "Did I do that?"

No one had ever looked so closely at Abby's face before, let alone the coolest senior at Albemarle Academy. She managed to nod.

"Gnarly," he said. "Does it hurt?"

"A little?" Abby managed to say.

He looked unhappy, so she changed her mind.

"No biggie," she squeaked.

Tommy Cox smiled and Abby almost fell down. She had said something that made Tommy Cox smile. It was like having a superpower.

"Coolness," he said. Then he held out a can of Coke, condensation beading on the surface. "It's cold. For your face, right?"

Abby hesitated then took the Coke. You weren't allowed to go to the vending machines until seventh grade, and Tommy Cox had gone to the vending machines for Abby and bought her a Coke.

"Coolness," she said.

"Excuse me, Mr. Cox," Mrs. Link said, pushing through the door. "You need to find your way back to the upper school building before you get a demerit."

Mrs. Link stomped to her desk and threw down her bag. Everyone was still staring at Tommy Cox.

"Sure thing, Mrs. L," he said. Then he held up a hand. "Gimme some skin, tough chick."

In slow motion Abby gave him five. His hand was cool and strong and warm and hard but soft. Then he turned to go, took a step, looked back over his shoulder, and winked.

"Stay chill, little Betty," he said.

Everyone heard it.

Abby turned to Gretchen and smiled and her stitches ripped and her mouth filled with salt. But it was worth it when she turned and saw Margaret Middleton standing there like a dummy with no comeback and nothing to say. They didn't know it then, but that's when everything started, right there in Mrs. Link's homeroom: Abby grinning at Gretchen with big blood-stained teeth, and Gretchen smiling back shyly.

THAT'S WHAT FRIENDS ARE FOR

Abby took that Coke can home and never opened it. Her lip healed and the stitches came out a week later, leaving an ugly fruit jam scab that Hunter Prioleaux said was VD but that Gretchen never even mentioned.

As her scab was healing, Abby decided there was no way her new friend hadn't seen *E.T.* Everyone had seen *E.T.* And so one day she confronted Gretchen in the cafeteria.

"I haven't seen *E.T.*," Gretchen repeated.

"That's impossible," Abby said. "*60 Minutes* says even the Russians have seen *E.T.*"

Gretchen stirred her lima beans and then made up her mind about something.

"You promise not to tell anyone?" she asked.

"Okay," Abby said.

Gretchen leaned in close, the tips of her long blond hair trailing across her Salisbury steak.

"My parents are in the Witness Protection Program," she whispered. "If I go to the movies, I might get kidnapped."

Abby was thrilled. Gretchen would be her dangerous friend! Life was finally getting exciting. There was only one problem:

"Then how could you come to my birthday party?" she asked.

"My mom thought it would be okay," Gretchen said. "They

don't want being criminals to keep me from having a normal life."

"Then ask her if you can see *E.T.*," Abby said, getting back to the important subject. "If you want to have a normal life, you have to see *E.T.* People are going to think you're weird if you don't."

Gretchen sucked the gravy off the tips of her hair and nodded.

"Okay," she said. "But your parents will have to take me. If my parents and I are seen in public together, a criminal might recognize them."

Abby exhausted her parents into agreement, despite the fact that her mom believed seeing a movie more than once was a waste of time, money, and brain cells. The next weekend, Mr. and Mrs. Rivers dropped off Abby and Gretchen at Citadel Mall to see the 2:20 showing of *E.T. the Extra-Terrestrial* while they went Christmas shopping. Because she lived a sheltered life in the Witness Protection Program, Gretchen was clueless about how to buy tickets or popcorn. It turned out she'd never even been to a movie on her own before, which was bizarre to Abby, who could ride her bike to the Mt. Pleasant 1–2–3 and see the $1 afternoon matinees. Gretchen may have had criminals for parents, but Abby felt a lot more worldly.

The lights went down and at first Abby was worried she wouldn't love *E.T.* as much as all the other times she'd seen it, but then Elliott called Michael penis-breath and she laughed and the government came and Elliott reached for E.T. through the plastic wall and she cried, reminding herself once more that this was the most powerful motion picture in the world. But as Elliott and Michael stole the van right before the big chase at the end, Abby had a horrible thought: What if Gretchen wasn't crying? What if the lights came on and Gretchen was sitting there sucking on her braids like this was an ordinary movie? What if she hated it?

These thoughts were so stressful, they kept Abby from enjoying the ending. As the credits rolled, she sat in the dark, miserable, staring straight ahead, too scared to look at Gretchen. Finally, she couldn't stand it anymore, and as the credits thanked Marin County for its assistance she turned her head and saw Gretchen staring at the screen, her face totally blank. Abby's heart cramped and then, before she said anything, she saw the light from the screen reflecting off Gretchen's wet cheeks, and Abby's heart unclenched and Gretchen turned to her and said, "Can we see it again?"

They could. Then they had dinner at Chi-Chi's and Abby's dad pretended it was his birthday and the waiters came out and put a giant sombrero on his head and sang him the Mexican birthday song and gave them all fried ice cream.

It was the greatest day of Abby's life.

"I have to tell you something serious," Gretchen said.

It was the second time she'd slept over. Abby's parents were out at a Christmas party, and so the two of them had eaten frozen pizzas during *The Powers of Matthew Star* and now *Falcon Crest* had just ended. *Falcon Crest* wasn't as good as *Dynasty*, but *Dynasty* came on Wednesday nights, a school night, so Abby wasn't allowed to watch it. Gretchen wasn't allowed to watch anything. Her parents had strict TV rules, and they didn't even have cable because it was too dangerous to have their names on the bill.

Three weeks into their friendship and Abby was used to all the strange rules of the Witness Protection Program. No movies, no cable, barely any TV, no rock music, no two-piece swimsuits, no sugary breakfast cereals. But there was something Abby knew about the Witness Protection Program from movies, and it scared her: sometimes, with no warning, the people under protection disappeared overnight.

And now that Gretchen had something important to say, Abby knew exactly what it was.

"You're moving," she said.

"Why?" Gretchen asked.

"Because of your parents," Abby said.

Gretchen shook her head.

"I'm not moving," she said. "You can't hate me. You have to promise not to hate me."

"I don't hate you," Abby said. "You're cool."

Gretchen kept picking at the plaid sofa, not looking at Abby, and Abby started getting worried. She didn't have a lot of friends, and Gretchen was definitely the coolest person she'd ever met, after Tommy Cox.

"My parents aren't really in the Witness Protection Program," Gretchen said, clenching her hands in her lap. "I made it up. They won't let me see PG- or R-rated movies. They'll only let me see G-rated movies until I'm thirteen. I didn't tell them I was going to *E.T.* I told them we went to see *Heidi's Song* instead."

There was a long silence. Tears slipped down her nose and dripped onto the sofa.

"You hate me," Gretchen said, nodding to herself.

Actually, Abby was thrilled. She'd never totally believed the whole Witness Protection Program story anyway because, like her mom said, if something seemed too good to be true then it probably was. And if Gretchen's parents treated her like a baby, that made Abby the cool one. Gretchen needed her if she was ever going to see a PG movie or keep up with *Falcon Crest*, so they'd always have to be friends. But Abby also knew that Gretchen might stop being her friend now that Abby knew a secret about her, so she decided to give her a secret back.

"You want to see something gross?" she asked.

Tears splatted onto the couch as Gretchen shook her head.

"I mean really gross," Abby explained.

Gretchen kept crying, clenching her hands until her knuckles turned white. So Abby got a flashlight out of the kitchen drawer, pulled Gretchen off the sofa, and forced her upstairs into her parents' bedroom, listening for their car pulling into the driveway the entire time.

"We shouldn't be in here," Gretchen said in the dark.

"Shhhh," Abby said, leading her past the trunk at the foot of the bed and into her dad's closet. Inside, behind his pants, there was a suitcase. Inside the suitcase was a black plastic bag, and inside the black plastic bag was a big cardboard box containing a videotape. Abby switched on the flashlight and shone it on the VHS box.

"*Bad Mama Jama*," she said. "My mom doesn't know he has it."

Gretchen wiped her nose on her sleeve and took the box from Abby with both hands. On the front cover, an extremely large black woman was bent over, dressed in nothing but a string bikini, spreading her fanny wide open. She was looking back over her shoulder, wearing orange lipstick that matched her nail polish, smiling like she was thrilled two little girls were looking up her butt. The caption under the photo read: "Mama's got *supper* in the *oven*!"

"Ew!" Gretchen squealed, throwing the tape at Abby.

"I don't want it!" Abby shouted, throwing it back at her.

"It touched me!" Gretchen said.

Abby wrestled her onto the bed and straddled Gretchen's squirming body, rubbing the tape all over her hair.

"Ew! Ew! Ew!" Gretchen screamed. "I'm going to die!"

"You're going to get pregnant!" Abby said.

That was the moment. When Gretchen stopped lying to Abby about the Witness Protection Program, when Abby showed Gretchen her dad's secret sex fetish for large black women, when Abby wrestled with Gretchen on her parents' bed. Starting that night, they were best friends.

Everything happened over the next six years. Nothing happened over the next six years. In fifth grade they had separate homerooms, but over lunch Abby told Gretchen everything that had happened on *Remington Steele* and *The Facts of Life*. Gretchen wanted Mrs. Garrett to be her mom, Abby thought Blair was usually right about everything, and they both wanted to grow up to run their own private detective agency where Pierce Brosnan had to do whatever they said.

Gretchen's mom got a speeding ticket with the girls in the car and said "Shit" out loud. To bribe them into not telling Mr. Lang, she took them to the Swatch store downtown and bought them brand new Swatch watches. Abby got a Jelly and used her own money to get one green and one pink Swatch guard that she twisted together; Gretchen got a Tennis Stripe and matching green and pink Swatch guards. After playing outside, they'd sniff each other's watch bands and try to figure out what they smelled like. Abby said hers smelled like honeysuckle and cinnamon and Gretchen's smelled like hibiscus and rose, but Gretchen said they both just smelled like sweat.

Gretchen slept over six times at Abby's house in Creekside before Abby was finally allowed to spend the night at Gretchen's house in the Old Village, the la-di-da part of Mt. Pleasant where all the houses were dignified and either overlooked the water or had enormous yards, and if anyone saw a black person walking down the street who wasn't Mr. Little, they would pull their Volvo over and ask if he was lost.

Abby loved going to Gretchen's. The Langs' house sat on Pierates Cruze, a dirt road shaped like a horseshoe where the house numbers went in the wrong order and the street name was spelled wrong because rich people could do whatever they wanted. Their house was number eight. It was an enormous gray cube that looked out over Charleston harbor through a back wall that was a two-story high window made of a single sheet of glass. Inside, it was as sterile as an operating theater, all hard right angles, sheer surfaces, gleaming steel, and glass that was polished twice a day. It was the only house in the Old Village that looked like it was built in the twentieth century.

The Langs had a dock where Abby and Gretchen swam (as long as they wore tennis shoes so they wouldn't cut their feet on oysters). Mrs. Lang cleaned Gretchen's room every other week and threw out anything she didn't think her daughter needed. One of her rules was that Gretchen could have only six magazines and five books at a time. "Once you've finish reading it, you've finished needing it" was her motto.

So Abby got all the books that Gretchen bought at B. Dalton's with her seemingly unlimited allowance. *Forever...* by Judy Blume, which they knew was all about them (except for the gross parts at the end). *Jacob Have I Loved* (secretly Abby believed that Gretchen was Caroline and she was Louise). *Z for Zachariah* (which gave Gretchen nuclear war nightmares), and the ones they had to sneak into the Langs' house hidden in the bottom of Abby's bookbag, all of them by V. C. Andrews: *Flowers in the Attic*, *Petals in the Wind*, *If There Be Thorns*, and, most scandalous of them all, *My Sweet Audrina*, with its endless parade of sexual perversion.

But mostly, for six years, they stayed in Gretchen's room. They made endless lists: their best friends, their okay friends, their worst enemies, the best teachers and the meanest teachers, which teachers should get married to each other, which school bathroom was their favorite, where they would be living in six years, in six months, in six weeks, where they'd live when they were married, how many babies their cats would have together, what their wedding colors would be, whether Adaire Griffin was a total slut or just misunderstood, whether Hunter Prioleaux's parents knew their son was the spawn of Satan or if he fooled them, too.

It was an endless *Seventeen* quiz, an eternal process of self-classification. They traded scrunchies, they pored over *YM* and *Teen* and *European Travel and Life*. They fantasized about Italian counts, and German duchesses, and Diana, Princess of Wales, and summers in Capri, and skiing in the Alps. In their shared fantasies, dark European men were constantly escorting them into helicopters and flying them to hidden mansions where they tamed wild horses.

After they snuck into *Flashdance*, Abby and Gretchen would slip off their shoes at the dinner table and grab each other's crotches with sock-covered feet. Abby would wait until Gretchen was lifting a forkful of peas, then stick her foot in Gretchen's crotch, making her fling food everywhere and sending her dad into a tirade.

"Wasting food is no joke!" he'd shout. "That's how Karen Carpenter died!"

Gretchen's parents were uptight Reagan Republicans who spent every Sunday at St. Michael's downtown, praising God and social climbing. When *The Thorn Birds* came on, Abby and

Gretchen were dying to watch it on the big TV, but Mr. Lang was dubious. He'd heard that the content was questionable.

"Dad," Gretchen said. "It's just like *The Winds of War*. It's basically a sequel."

Herman Wouk's dry-as-dust, fourteen-hour miniseries about World War II was Mr. Lang's favorite television event of all time, so invoking its name meant they automatically received his blessing. While they were watching episode one of *The Thorn Birds*, he came home and stood in the door of the TV room long enough to realize that this was no *Winds of War*. His face turned dark red. Abby and Gretchen were too caught up in the steamy Outback love scenes to notice, but sixty seconds after he left the room, Mrs. Lang came in and turned off the TV. Then she marched them into the living room for a lecture.

"The Roman church can glorify foul language and half-naked priests rutting like animals," Mr. Lang told them. "But not in this house. Now, there's no more television tonight and I want you girls to go upstairs and wash your hands. Your mother's got supper in the oven."

Halfway up the stairs, they couldn't hold it in anymore and Abby laughed so hard she peed.

Sixth grade was the bad year. After he'd gone on strike back in '81, Abby's dad had lost his job as an air traffic controller and been hired as assistant manager at a carpet cleaner. Eventually they had cutbacks, too. The Rivers family had to sell their place in Creekside and move into a sagging house on Rifle Range Road. Four giant pine trees loomed over their brick shoebox and showered it with spider webs and sap while completely blocking out the sun.

That was when Abby stopped inviting Gretchen over to spend the night and started inviting herself over to the Langs' house every weekend. Then she started showing up on weeknights, too.

"You're always welcome here," Mr. Lang said. "We think of you as our other daughter."

Abby had never felt so safe. She started leaving her pajamas and a toothbrush in Gretchen's room. She would have moved in if they'd let her. Their house always smelled like air-conditioning and carpet shampoo. Her house had gotten wet a long time ago and never dried. Winter or summer, it stank of mold.

In 1984, Gretchen got braces, and Abby got politics when Walter Mondale declared Geraldine Ferraro his running mate. It never occurred to Abby that anyone could possibly object to electing the first female vice president, and her parents were too caught up in their own economic drama to notice when she put a Mondale/Ferraro bumper sticker on their car. Then she put one on Mrs. Lang's Volvo.

She and Gretchen were in the TV room watching *Silver Spoons* when Mr. Lang came in after work shaking with rage, the shreds of the bumper sticker waving from one hand. He tried to throw the pieces on the floor, but they stuck to his fingers.

"Who did this?" he demanded, voice tight, face red behind his beard. "Who? Who?"

That's when Abby knew she was going to get expelled from the Langs' house forever. Without even realizing it, she'd committed the greatest sin of all and made Mr. Lang look like a Democrat. But before Abby could confess and accept her exile, Gretchen spun around on the couch and drew herself up onto her knees.

"She'll be the first female vice president ever," Gretchen said, gripping the back of the sofa with both hands. "Don't you want me to feel proud of being a woman?"

"This family is loyal to the president," Mr. Lang said. "You'd better hope no one saw that . . . *thing* on your mother's car. You're too young for politics."

He made Gretchen take a razor blade and peel off the rest of the sticker while Abby watched, terrified she was going to get in trouble. But Gretchen never told. It was the first time Abby had ever seen her fight with her parents.

Then came the Madonna Incident.

For the Langs, Madonna was totally and completely out of the question. But when Gretchen's dad was at work and her mom was taking one of her nine billion classes (Jazzercise, power walking, book club, wine club, sewing circle, women's prayer circle), Gretchen and Abby would dress up like the Material Girl and sing into the mirror. Gretchen's mom had a jewelry box devoted entirely to crosses, so it was basically like she was inviting them to do it.

With dozens of crosses strung around their necks, they stood in front of Gretchen's bathroom mirror and teased their hair big, tying huge floppy bows in it, cutting the arms off of T-shirts, painting their lips bright coral, shadowing their eyes bright blue, dropping makeup on the white wall-to-wall carpet and accidentally stepping on it, holding up a hair brush and a curling iron as microphones and singing along to the "Like a Virgin" Cassingle on Gretchen's peach boombox.

Abby had just decided to draw on a beauty spot and was hunting for eyeliner in the makeup carnage on the counter while Gretchen was singing "Like a vir-ir-ir-ir-gin/With your heartbeat/Next to mine . . ." when suddenly Gretchen's head was yanked backward and Mrs. Lang was between them, tearing the bow out of her daughter's hair. The music was so loud, they hadn't heard her come home.

"I buy you nice things!" she screamed. "This is what you do?"

Abby stood there stupidly while the Cassingle looped and Gretchen's mom chased her daughter between the twin beds, hitting her with a hairbrush. Abby was terrified that Mrs. Lang would notice her, and a part of her brain knew she should hide, but she simply stood there like a dummy as Mrs. Lang followed Gretchen down to the ground between the two beds. Gretchen curled up on the carpet, making a high-pitched sound, while Madonna sang, "You're so fine, and you're mine/I'll be yours/Till the end of time . . ." and Mrs. Lang's arm worked up and down, raining blows on Gretchen's legs and shoulders.

"Make me strong/Yeah, you make me bold . . . ," Madonna sang.

Gretchen's mom walked to the boombox and jammed down on the buttons, prying open the door and yanking out the Cassingle while it was still playing, leaving big loops of magnetic tape drooling everywhere. In the sudden silence, Abby heard the motor whine as the gears jammed. The only other sound was Mrs. Lang breathing hard.

"Clean up this mess," she said. "Your father will be home."

Then she stormed out and slammed the door.

Abby crawled across the bed and looked down on the floor at Gretchen. She wasn't even crying.

"Are you okay?" Abby asked.

Gretchen raised her head and looked at her bedroom door.

"I'm going to kill her," she whispered. Then she wiped her nose and looked up at Abby. "Don't ever tell I said that."

Abby remembered a day the summer before when she and Gretchen had tiptoed into Gretchen's parents' room and opened the drawer on her dad's bedside table. Lying inside, under an old issue of *Reader's Digest*, was a stubby black revolver. Gretchen took it out and pointed it at Abby and then at the pillows on the bed, first one, then the other.

"Bang . . ." she whispered. "Bang."

Abby remembered those whispered "bangs," and now she looked at Gretchen's dry eyes and she knew that something was happening that was truly dangerous. But she never told. Instead, she helped Gretchen clean up, then she called her mom and asked her to come pick her up. Whatever else happened that night when Gretchen's dad got home, Gretchen never talked about it.

A few weeks later it had all blown over, and the Langs took Abby with them to Jamaica for a ten-day vacation. She and Gretchen got cornrows in their hair that clicked everywhere they walked. Abby got sunburned. They played Uno every night and Abby won almost every game.

"You're a card sharp," Gretchen's dad said. "I can't believe my daughter brought a card sharp into our family."

Abby ate shark for the first time. It tasted like steak made out of fish. They had their first big fight because Abby kept playing Weird Al's "Eat It" on the cassette player in their room, until the second to the last day when she found pink nail polish spilled all over her tape.

"I'm sorry," Gretchen said, enunciating each word like she was royalty. "It was an accident."

"It was not," Abby said. "You're selfish. I'm the fun one, and you're the mean one."

They were always trying to figure out which one of them was which. Recently, Abby had been designated the fun one and Gretchen the beautiful one. Neither of them had ever been the mean one before.

"You just tag along with my family because you're poor," Gretchen snapped back. "God, I'm sick of you." Gretchen's braces hurt all the time and Abby's braids were too tight and gave her headaches. "You know which one you are?" Gretchen asked. "You're the dumb one. You play that stupid song like it's cool, but it's for little kids. It's immature, and I don't want to hear it anymore. It's stupid. It makes YOU stupid."

Abby locked herself in the bathroom, and Gretchen's mom had to coax her out for supper, which she ate alone on the balcony while the bugs chewed her up. That night, after the lights went out, she felt someone crawl into her bed, and Gretchen slid up next to her.

"I'm sorry," she whispered, filling Abby's ear with her hot breath. "I'm the stupid one. You're the cool one. Please don't be mad at me, Abby. You're my best friend."

Seventh grade was the year of their first slow-dance make-out party, and Abby tongue-kissed Hunter Prioleaux as they rocked back and forth to "Time after Time." His enormous stomach was harder than she thought it would be and he tasted like Big League Chew and Coke, but he was also really sweaty and smelled like burps. He followed Abby around for the rest of the night trying to get to third base, until she hid in the bathroom while Gretchen ran him off.

Then came a day that changed Abby's life forever. She and Gretchen were returning their lunch trays, talking about how they needed to stop getting hot lunch like little kids and start bringing healthy food to school so they could eat outside with everyone else, when they saw Glee Wanamaker standing by the tray window, hands twisting, her fingers squirming and pulling at each other, eyes red and shining, staring into the big garbage can. She'd put her retainer on her tray and then dumped it in the trash, and now she wasn't sure which garbage bag it was in.

"I'll have to look in all of them," she sobbed. "This is my third retainer. My dad's going to kill me."

Abby wanted to go but Gretchen insisted they help, and so William, the head of the lunch room, took them out back and showed them the eight bulging black plastic bags full of warm milk, half-eaten pizza squares, fruit cocktail, melted ice cream, wet shoestring fries, and curdled ketchup. It was April and the sun had been cooking the bags into a rank stew. It was the worst thing Abby had ever smelled.

She didn't know why they were helping Glee. Abby didn't have a retainer. She didn't even have braces. Everyone else did, but her parents wouldn't pay for them. They wouldn't pay for much of anything, and she had to wear the same navy corduroy skirt twice a week, and her two white shirts were turning transparent because she washed them so much. Abby did her own laundry because her mom worked as a home nurse.

"I do laundry for other people all day," Abby's mom told her. "Your arms aren't broken. Pull your weight."

Her dad had been working as the dairy department manager at Family Dollar, but they let him go because he accidentally stocked a bunch of expired milk. He'd put up a sign at Randy's Model Shop to do small engine repairs on people's remote control planes, but after customers complained that he was too slow, Randy made him take down the sign. Now he had a sign up at the Oasis gas station on Coleman Boulevard saying he'd fix any lawn mower for $20. He had pretty much stopped talking, and he'd started filling their yard with broken lawn mowers.

Abby was beginning to feel like everything was too much. She was beginning to feel like nothing she did made any difference.

She was beginning to feel like her family was sliding down a hill and they were dragging her down after them and at the bottom of that hill was a cliff. She was beginning to feel like every test was a life-or-death challenge and if she failed even one of them, she'd lose her scholarship and get yanked out of Albemarle and never see Gretchen again.

And now she stood behind the cafeteria in front of eight steaming bags of fresh garbage, and she wanted to cry. Why was she the one helping Glee, whose dad was a stockbroker? Why wasn't anyone helping *her*? She never knew what caused it, but at that moment, Abby changed. Something inside her head went "click" and the next second she was thinking differently.

She didn't have to be poor. She could get a job. She didn't have to help Glee. But she could. She could decide how she was going to be. She had a choice. Life could be an endless series of joyless chores, or she could get totally pumped and make it fun. There were bad things, and there were good things, but she got to choose which things to focus on. Her mom focused only on the bad things. Abby didn't have to.

Standing there behind the cafeteria in the stink of an entire school's worth of putrid garbage, Abby felt the channels change, the world brighten as the sunglasses came off her brain. She turned to Gretchen and said, "Mama's got supper in the oven!"

Then she untied the nearest bag, took out a slice of half-chewed pizza, and frisbeed it onto the roof before plunging elbow-deep into an ocean of greasy, slimy, used food. By the time they found Glee's retainer, strings of congealed cheese stuck in their hair, gobs of fruit cocktail stuck to their shirts, they were laughing like maniacs, throwing handfuls of limp lettuce at one another and flicking French fries against the wall.

Eighth grade was the year of Max Headroom and Spuds Mackenzie. The year that Abby's dad started watching Saturday morning cartoons for hours and sleeping on a cot in his shed in the backyard. It was the year that Abby got Gretchen to sneak out of her house so they could ride bikes across the Ben Sawyer Bridge to Sullivan's Island. Halley's Comet was passing and everyone had gone to the beach in the middle of the night to see it. They found a deserted spot and lay on their backs in the cold sand, looking up at millions of stars.

"So let me get this straight," Gretchen said in the dark. "It's a dirty snowball shaped like a peanut floating through space and that's why everyone's so excited?"

Gretchen was not very romantic about science.

"It only comes around once every seventy-five years," Abby said, straining to see if the speck of light she saw was moving or if she was only imagining it. "We might never see it again."

"Good," Gretchen said. "Because I'm freezing and I have sand in my underwear."

"Do you think we'll still be friends the next time it comes around?" Abby asked.

"I think we'll be dead," Gretchen said.

Abby did the math in her head and realized they'd be eighty-eight years old.

"People are going to live longer in the future," she said. "We might still be alive."

"But we won't know how to set the clocks on our VCRs and we'll be old and hate young people and vote Republican like my parents," Gretchen said.

They had just rented *The Breakfast Club*, and turning into adults felt like the worst thing ever.

"We won't wind up like them," Abby said. "We don't have to be boring."

"If I stop being happy, will you kill me?" Gretchen asked.

"Totally," Abby said.

"Seriously," Gretchen said. "You're the only reason I'm not crazy."

They were quiet for a moment.

"Who said you're not crazy?" Abby asked.

Gretchen hit her.

"Promise me you'll always be my friend," she said.

"DBNQ," Abby replied.

It was their shorthand for "I love you." Dearly But Not Queerly.

And they lay there on the freezing sand and felt the earth turn beneath their backs, and they shivered together as the wind blew off the water, and a frozen ball of ice passed by their planet, three million miles away in the cold distant darkness of deep space.

PARTY ALL THE TIME

"You guys want to freak the fuck out?" Margaret Middleton asked.

Blood-warm water slopped against the hull of the Boston Whaler. It had been quiet for almost an hour as the four girls drifted in the creek; Bob Marley played low on the boombox, their eyes closed, legs up, sun warm, heads nodding. They'd been waterskiing on Wadmalaw, but after Gretchen wiped out hard, Margaret cruised them into an inlet, cut the engine, dropped the anchor, and let them float. For an hour, the loudest sounds were the occasional spark of a lighter as someone lit a Merit Menthol or the ripe pop as someone cracked a lukewarm Busch. Underneath it all was the endless hiss of marsh grass rustling in the wind.

Abby faded up from her nap to see Glee rattling a beer out of the cooler. Glee made her "Want one?" face and Abby stretched out an arm, dried salt cracking on her skin, and took a slug of the warm watery wonderful Busch. It was their drink of choice, mostly because the old lady who ran Mitchell's would sell them a case for forty dollars without asking for ID.

Abby was overflowing with a sense of belonging. Out here, there was nothing to worry about. They didn't have to talk. They didn't have to impress anyone. They could fall asleep in front of one another. The real world was far away.

The four of them were best friends, and while some of the kids called them bops, or mall maggots, or Debbie Debutantes, the four of them didn't give a tiddly-fuck. Gretchen was number two in their class, and the other three were in the top ten. Honor roll, National Honor Society, volleyball, community outreach, perfect grades, and, as Hugh Horton once said with great reverence, their shit tasted like candy.

It didn't come easy. They cared hard. They cared about their clothes, they cared about their hair, they cared about their makeup (Abby especially cared about her makeup), and they cared about their grades. Abby, Gretchen, Glee, and Margaret were going places.

Margaret was sitting in the driver's seat, legs up on the hydroslide, blowing out big plumes of mentholated smoke, rich as shit, loaded with old Charleston money, American by birth, Southern by the grace of God. She was Maximum Margaret, a giant blond jock whose sprawling arms and legs took up half the boat. Everything about her was too much: her lips were too red, her hair was too blond, her nose was too crooked, her voice was too loud.

Glee yawned and stretched. The total opposite of Margaret, she was a tiny, tanned girl version of Michael J. Fox who still had to buy her shoes in the children's department. In the summer her skin turned chestnut and her belly button darkened to black. Her hair was highlighted seven different shades of brown, and despite having a koala nose and sad puppy-dog eyes, she always attracted too much male attention because she'd developed early, and way out of proportion to her height. Glee was also scary smart, a baby yuppie down to the bone. Her little red Saab wasn't from her daddy: she'd made the down payment with money she'd earned on the stock market. The only thing daddy did was put in her trades.

Gretchen lifted her head from where she was lying facedown

on a towel in the prow and took a sip of her Busch. Gretchen: treasurer of the student vestry, founder of the Recycling Club, founder of the school's Amnesty International chapter, and, if the bathroom walls were to believed, the hottest girl in tenth grade. Long, lean, lanky, and blond, she was a Laura Ashley princess in floral print dresses and Esprit tops—a stark contrast to Abby, who barely reached Gretchen's shoulders and whose big hair and thick makeup made her look like she should be waiting tables in a truck-stop diner. Abby tried very hard not to think about the way she looked, and most days, especially days like this, she succeeded.

As they lit their cigarettes, as they opened their beers, as they came blinking back into the world, Margaret pulled a black plastic film canister out of her bag, held it up, and asked:

"You guys want to freak the fuck out?"

"What is it?" Abby asked.

"Acid," Margaret said.

Bob Marley suddenly sounded very mellow, indeed.

Gretchen twisted around on her towel. "Where'd you get it?"

"Stole it from Riley," Glee lied.

Margaret was the only girl in her enormous family, and her second-oldest brother, Riley, was a notorious burnout who alternated between doing semesters at the College of Knowledge and rehab at Fenwick Hall, where Charleston's richest alcoholics went to rest. He was famous for slipping drugs into girls' drinks at the Windjammer, and then, after they passed out, he'd have sex with them in the backseat of his car. It came to an end when one of the girls woke up, broke his nose, and ran down the middle of Ocean Boulevard with no top on, screaming her lungs out. The judge encouraged the girl's parents not to press charges because Riley came from a fine family and had his whole future ahead of him. Ultimately, all that happened was he was required to live at home for a year. So now he moved between different Middleton houses—from Wadmalaw, to Seabrook, to Sullivan's Island, to downtown—staying out of reach of his dad, supposedly going to AA meetings but mostly selling drugs.

That said, Riley was a known quantity. If Margaret and Glee told Gretchen where they'd really gotten the acid, she'd never ingest it; and if these girls were going to trip, it would be all of them at once or nobody at all. That's how they did everything.

"I don't know," Gretchen said. "I don't want to wind up like Syd Barrett."

Syd Barrett, the original lead singer for Pink Floyd, had done so much acid in the sixties that his brain melted, and now, twenty years later, he lived in his mom's basement and sometimes, on good days, managed to ride his bike to the post office. He collected stamps. Gretchen believed that if she did acid, it was one hundred percent guaranteed she'd pull a Syd Barrett and never be normal again.

"My brother said Syd put out an album last year but all the songs were about stamp collecting," Glee said.

"What if that's me?" Gretchen asked.

Margaret blew out a dramatic plume of smoke.

"And you don't collect stamps," she said. "What the fuck are you going to sing about?"

"I'll do it if you promise to drive all the recycling club's cans to the recycling center," Gretchen said to Margaret.

Margaret flicked her butt into the creek.

"Recycle that, you hippie."

"Glee?" Gretchen asked.

"Those bags leak," Glee said. "I get wasps in my car."

Gretchen stood up, raised her arms over her head, and her fingertips brushed the sky.

"As always," she said. "Thank you for your support."

Then she stretched out one long leg, stepped off the prow, and dropped into the water without a splash. She didn't come back up. Big whoop. Gretchen could hold her breath forever and she liked to wallow in the freezing cold at the bottom of the river. That was the good thing about Gretchen. As much as she wanted to save the planet, she was pretty casual about it.

"Tell her where we got it and I'll break your face," Margaret said to Abby.

Summer of '88 had been the most amazing summer ever. It was the summer of "Pour Some Sugar on Me" and "Sweet Child O' Mine," and all of Abby's money went for gas because she'd finally gotten her license and could drive after dark. Every night at 11:06, she and Gretchen popped their screens, slipped out of their windows, and just cruised around Charleston. They went night swimming at the beach, they hung out with the James Island kids at the Market, they smoked cigarettes in the parking lot in front of the Garden and Gun club and watched Citadel ca-dicks pick fights. One night they'd just driven north on 17, making it almost all the way to Myrtle Beach, smoking an entire pack of Parliaments and listening to Tracy Chapman sing "Fast Car" and "Talkin' Bout a Revolution" over and over before heading home just as the sun was coming up.

Meanwhile, most of Margaret and Glee's summer had been spent sitting in Glee's car waiting for drug deals to materialize. No one except the most maximum mutants in their class had ever done acid, so it was important to Margaret that they be the first normal people to trip; the same as they were the first girls to bring a note to sit out gym class because of their periods, the same as they were the first four to go to a live concert (Cyndi Lauper), the same as they were the first four to get their driving permits (except for Gretchen, who had problems telling her left from her right).

Margaret and Glee spent months on the acid project, but every single deal fell apart. Abby started feeling sorry for Glee, and she offered to employ the Dust Bunny on yet another of Margaret's long drug drives to nowhere. Abby's offer infuriated both Glee and Margaret.

"Hell, no," Margaret said. "You are not driving. We went to lower school in a building named after my granddaddy."

"My father's firm manages the school's portfolio," Glee added.

"If we get busted, we'll get suspended," Margaret said. "That's a free fucking vacation. If you get busted, you'll get expelled. I'm not being friends with a high school dropout who works at S-Mart."

As far as Abby was concerned, that was a needlessly negative view of the situation. Yes, she had stayed in school by getting a scholarship that came with dozens of strings attached, but Albemarle Academy was definitely not looking for an excuse to get rid of her. Her grades were totally awesome. But you couldn't argue with Margaret, so instead Abby offered to pay for Glee's gas and was secretly relieved when Glee turned her down.

Their most recent drug safari had taken Glee and Margaret to the parking lot of a bait shop on Folly Beach, where they sat in Glee's car for two hours in the pouring rain before Margaret got on the pay phone and discovered that their connection was not simply waiting a crazy long time to signal them. He'd been busted. They went to his room at the Holiday Inn, because what else were they going to do, and discovered that the cops not only had left the door wide open but had also totally failed to find his stash hidden underneath the mattress. Margaret and Glee did not make the same mistake.

Now there's always a chance that if you find acid hidden underneath a mattress in a Holiday Inn, left there by two guys you've never met, who were hiding it from the police and who are now in jail, it might be spiked with strychnine or something worse. But there was also a chance that it might *not* be spiked with strychnine or something worse, and Abby preferred to look on the bright side.

Gretchen popped up out of the water and spat Margaret's cigarette butt into the boat. It stuck to Margaret's massive thigh.

"Oh my God," Margaret said. "How did you even know that's mine? AIDS!"

Gretchen sprayed a mouthful of water into the boat.

"That's not how you get AIDS," she said. "As we all know, you get AIDS by sucking face with Wallace Stoney."

"He does not have AIDS," Margaret said.

"Duh!" Glee said. "You get cold sores from herpes."

Margaret looked pissed.

"What does it taste like?" Gretchen asked, grabbing onto the side of the boat and chinning herself up to look into Margaret's eyes. "Do his herp lips taste like true love?"

The two of them stared at each other.

"For your information, they're not cold sores, they're zits," Margaret said. "And they taste like Clearasil."

They laughed and Gretchen pushed herself away from the boat and floated on her back.

"I'll do it," she said to the sky. "But you have to promise I won't get brain damage."

"You've already got brain damage," Margaret said, jumping into the water, almost flipping the boat, and landing on Gretchen, one arm around her neck, dragging her beneath the surface. They came up sputtering and laughing, hanging onto each other. "Killer!"

They piloted the boat back to Margaret's dock, the air getting colder as the sun set. Abby wrapped a flapping towel around her shoulders and Gretchen let the wind catch her cheeks and blow them out like a balloon. Three dolphins breached off to port and paced them for a couple hundred yards, then peeled away and headed back out to sea. Margaret made gun fingers and pretended to shoot them. Gretchen and Abby turned and watched them dive and rise, flickering through the waves, disappearing in the distance, as gray as the chop.

They tied up at Margaret's dock and started lugging the skis up into the backyard, but Gretchen lingered with Abby down by the boat, cupping her elbows.

"Are you going to do it?" she asked.

"Hell, yeah," Abby said.

"Are you scared?" she asked.

"Hell, yeah," Abby said.

"So why?"

"Because I want to know if *Dark Side of the Moon* is actually profound."

Gretchen didn't laugh.

"What if it opens the doors of perception and I can't get them closed again?" Gretchen worried. "What if I can see and hear all the energy on the planet, and then the acid never wears off?"

"I'd visit you in Southern Pines," Abby said. "And I bet your parents would get, like, the lobotomy wing named after you."

"That would be choice," Gretchen agreed.

"It'll be crazy fun," Abby said. "We'll stick together like swim buddies at camp. We'll be trip buddies."

Gretchen pulled some strands of hair around to her mouth and sucked salt water off the tips.

"Will you promise to remind me to call my mom tonight?" she asked. "I have to check in at ten."

"I will make it my mission in life," Abby vowed.

"Cool beans," Gretchen said. "Let's go fry my brains."

Together the four of them heaped all their gear into a big pile in the backyard and hosed it down. Then Abby sprayed the hose up Margaret's butt.

"Cleansing enema!" she yelled.

"You're confusing me with my mother," Margaret shouted, running for the safety of the house.

Abby turned on Glee, but Gretchen was crimping the hose. Things were devolving rapidly when Margaret came out on the back porch carrying one of her mother's silver tea trays.

"Ladies," she sing-songed. "Tea time."

They gathered around the tray underneath a live oak. There were four china saucers, each with a little tab of white paper in the middle. Each tiny tab was stamped with the head of a blue unicorn.

"Is that it?" Gretchen asked.

"No, I decided to bring you guys some paper to chew on," Margaret said. "Doy."

Glee reached out to poke her tab, but pulled her finger back before she made contact. They all knew you could absorb acid through your skin. There should have been more of a ceremony; they should have showered first or eaten something. Maybe they shouldn't have been out in the sun all day drinking so much beer. They were doing this all wrong. Abby could feel everyone losing their nerve, herself included, so just as Gretchen was taking a breath to make an excuse, Abby grabbed her tab and popped it in her mouth.

"What's it taste like?" Gretchen asked.

"Nuttin' honey," Abby said.

Margaret took hers, and so did Glee. Then, finally, Gretchen.

"Do we chew it?" she lisped, trying not to move her tongue.

"Let it dissolve," Margaret lisped back.

"How long?" Gretchen asked.

"Chill, buttmunch," Margaret lisped around her paralyzed tongue.

Abby looked out at the bright orange sunset burning itself off over the marsh and felt something final: she'd taken acid. It was irreversibly in her system. No matter what happened now she had to ride this out. The sunset glowed and throbbed on the horizon, and Abby wondered if it would look so vivid if she hadn't just dropped acid. Reflexively she swallowed the little bit of paper, and that was that: she'd done something that couldn't be undone, crossed a line that couldn't be uncrossed. She was terrified.

"Is anyone hearing anything?" Glee asked.

"It takes hours to kick in, retard," Margaret said.

"Oh," Glee said. "So you normally have a pig nose?"

"Don't be mean," Gretchen said. "I don't want to have a bad trip. I really don't."

"Do y'all remember Mrs. Graves in sixth grade?" Glee asked. "With the Mickey Mouse stickers?"

"That was so bone," Margaret said. "Y'all got that, right? Her lecture about how, at Halloween, Satan worshippers drive around giving little kids stickers with Mickey Mouse on them, and when the kids lick the stickers they're coated in LSD and they have bad trips and kill their parents."

Gretchen covered Margaret's mouth with both hands.

"Stop . . . talking . . . ," she said.

So they laid around the backyard as it got dark, smoking cigarettes, talking about nice things, like what was up with Maximilian Buskirk's weird butt and that year's volleyball schedule, and Glee told them about some new kind of VD she'd read about that Lanie

Ott almost definitely had, and they discussed whether they should get Coach Greene an Epilady for her upper lip, and if Father Morgan was *Thorn Birds* hot, regular hot, or merely teacher hot. And the whole time, all of them were secretly trying to see if their smoke was turning into dragons or if the trees were dancing. None of them wanted to be the last one to hallucinate.

Eventually, they lapsed into a comfortable silence, with only Margaret humming some song she'd heard on the radio while she cracked her toe knuckles.

"Let's go look at the fireflies," Gretchen said.

"Cool," Abby said, pushing herself up off the grass.

"Oh my God," Margaret said. "You guys are so queer."

They ran through the yard and into the long grass in the field between the house and the woods, watching the green lightning bugs hover, butts glowing, as the air turned lavender the way it does when it gets dark in the country. Gretchen ran over to Abby.

"Spin me around," she said.

Abby grabbed her hands and they spun, heads tipped back, trying to make their trip happen. But when they fell into the grass, they weren't tripping, just dizzy.

"I don't want to see Margaret pinch off firefly butts," Gretchen said. "We should buy the plot next door and turn it into a nature preserve so no one else can ruin the creek."

"We totally should," Abby said.

"Look. Stars," Gretchen said, pointing at the first ones in the dark blue sky. "You have to promise not to ditch me."

"Stick with me," Abby said. "I'll totally be your lysergic sherpa. Wherever you go, I'm there."

They held hands in the grass. The two of them had never been shy about touching, even though in fifth grade Hunter Prioleaux had called them homos, but that was because no one had ever loved Hunter Prioleaux.

"I need to tell you—" Gretchen started to say.

Margaret loomed up out of the dark, pinched-off firefly butts smeared into two glowing lines underneath her eyes.

"Let's go in," she said. "The acid's coming up!"

THE NUMBER OF THE BEAST

Four hours later, Abby watched the digits on the clock radio flip from 11:59 to 12:00, and the acid was definitely not coming up. Spread out across Margaret's massive bedroom, they weren't tripping. They were bored.

"I think I see tracers!" Abby said, twinkling her fingers optimistically.

"You're not seeing tracers," Margaret sighed. "For the nine millionth time."

Abby shrugged and went back to flipping through Margaret's shoebox of tapes, trying to find something to play.

"Are you seriously doing homework?" Margaret barked at Glee, who was sitting against her bed and seriously doing homework.

"This is boring," Glee said.

"What about the Proclaimers?" Abby asked.

"No!" Margaret snapped.

"That one song is good?" Abby ventured.

Margaret flopped back in her armchair.

"This blows," she groaned. "Seriously, I'm not feeling anything. Do you guys want to get buzzed? Glee, stop doing your homework or I'm going to hurt you."

Abby looked down the room. Gretchen was at the far end,

staring out the window, putting braids in her hair, then taking them out. Abby went over and stood next to her.

"What're you looking at?" she asked.

"Fireflies," Gretchen said.

Abby looked down into the side yard. The only light in the bedroom came from a few candles, so it was dim enough to see out the windows and all the way across the yard to the black treeline.

"What fireflies?" she asked.

"They stopped," Gretchen said.

"I've got a ouija board," Margaret volunteered. "Y'all want to talk to Satan?"

"Did you know that Crest toothpaste is satanic?" Glee asked, looking up from her Trapper Keeper.

"Glee . . . ," Margaret said.

"It is," Glee said. "If you look at the side of the tube, there's a picture of an old man with two horns and the hair in his beard makes an upside-down 666. And he's got thirteen stars around him. Ouija boards are made by Parker Brothers, who make Trivial Pursuit."

"So?" Margaret sighed.

"So," Glee said. "If you want to communicate with Satan, you'd be better off brushing your teeth than doing ouija."

"Thanks, nerd," Margaret said.

The dim room got quiet. Gretchen hid a yawn in the crook of her elbow. Someone had to rescue the night. As usual, it was Abby.

"Let's go skinny dipping," she said.

"Fuck that," Margaret said. "Too cold."

"Just for a minute," Abby said.

The idea of being outside sounded nice.

"I'll go," Gretchen said, pushing herself up off the window sill.

"Let me finish this trig," Glee said.

Margaret walked over to Glee and clapped her notebook shut.

"Come on, spazmo," she said. "Don't chap my rooster."

The four of them rumbled down the three flights of stairs, flipped on the yard lights, and spilled out into the backyard.

"Turn out the lights," Gretchen said. "So we can see the stars."

"Abby," Margaret said, "the switch is by the back door."

Abby tromped back up the stairs, found the switch behind the microwave, and the backyard went dark again. Instantly, the sky got lighter and the crickets got louder. A fat orange moon hung on the horizon, right above the treeline. The night felt like it was listening to them as Abby tiptoed back down the stairs.

"So pretty," Gretchen was saying.

They watched the moon for a second, each of them willing herself to trip, but the moon just hung there being a moon. Then Gretchen pulled off her T-shirt.

"Bodacious ta-tas!" she shouted, and then she ran into the darkness headed for the dock, shedding clothes, reaching behind her back to unhook her bra, her long legs taking leaps that ate up the grass as she disappeared into the shadows.

"Hold up!" Margaret called. "It's low tide."

Gretchen didn't slow down. They heard her feet thumping fast along the wooden dock.

"Gretchen!" Abby yelled. "Don't jump!"

They ran after her, Margaret and Abby in the lead, stepping on Gretchen's shorts and underwear in the grass. Ahead of them came the sound of a shallow splash.

"Shit," Margaret said.

In the moonlight, they saw that the tide had gone out and the creek had been reduced to a tarnished ribbon of silver water that ran between two high mud banks. For a moment, Abby saw Gretchen hitting the pluff mud and shattering her kneecaps, or landing in three feet of water and slashing her face open on a hidden oyster bed.

"Gretchen?" Abby called.

No answer.

She and Margaret had reached the railing at the end of the dock. Glee trotted up behind them.

"Where's Gretchen?" she asked.

"She jumped," Abby said.

"Shit," Glee said. "Is she okay?"

They looked up and down the creek but Gretchen was gone. They called her name a few times, their voices echoing across the water.

Abby bounced down the ramp to the floating dock.

"There's alligators," Margaret warned.

"Gretchen?" Abby called across the creek.

No answer. Abby realized she was going to have to go in.

"Do you have a flashlight?" she called up to Margaret. "We should put in the boat."

"And run over her head?" Margaret said. "Genius."

"Then, what?" Abby asked.

"She can hold her breath like a bone," Margaret said. "Wait for her to come up."

The water oozed around the floating dock, rocking it up and down.

"What if she hit her head?" Abby said.

"Are there really alligators?" Glee asked.

Something moved in the marsh grass and Abby jerked. Was it an alligator? What did an alligator sound like? Were alligators nocturnal? She didn't know. Why didn't school teach them anything useful?

Abby scanned the creek one more time, hoping to spot Gretchen because she really didn't want to jump in the water. Across the creek, something moved again in the marsh grass. Abby strained her eyes and saw a shadow separate itself from the darkness and drag itself toward the water. She stared hard. A shape that wasn't human slithered through the pluff mud, making a dead *plop* as it slipped into the black flowing river that led out to the sea. A sharp wind blew off the water. Summer was over. It was getting cold.

"Gretchen!" Glee shouted.

"Where?" Abby asked.

"Down there," she said. "Where I'm pointing."

"I can't see you pointing in the dark."

"To the left," Glee said. "Where it curves."

Abby looked downstream, using her hand to block out the bright orange moon. Far down, where the creek bent toward the ocean and disappeared around a curving bank of marsh grass, was a pale shape, long like Gretchen, picking its way through the pluff mud toward the treeline. Abby cupped her hands around her mouth.

"Gretchen!" she shouted.

The figure kept moving.

"How do we get down there?" Abby called up to Margaret.

She heard a lighter snap above her and smelled menthol.

"See," Margaret said. "She's fine."

But Abby knew she wasn't fine. Gretchen probably didn't know how to get back to the house. She had zero sense of direction, and she was naked. She might have kept her sneakers on, but Abby had her clothes.

"Do you have a flashlight?" Abby asked.

"Spaz down," Margaret said. "She'll be back in five minutes."

"I'm going to get her," Abby said, heading up the ramp. "Give me one of those."

Margaret slid a cigarette out of the pack and handed it over. Orange light flared in Abby's face and then she was seeing spots and sucking menthol. She didn't want to tell them, but her heart was hammering.

"I'll be right back," Abby said.

"Watch out for snakes," Margaret called after her helpfully.

Abby picked her way through the long grass and plunged into the trees. Instantly, the woods cut her off from the house, from the stars, from the sky, and she was buried beneath dark branches. All she could hear were the cicadas shrieking, the sound of her own footsteps crunching leaves, and the occasional close-up whine of a mosquito in her ear. She had the feeling that something was listening to her walk. She moved as quietly as possible and stayed close to the river. To her left, the woods were pitch black.

By the time Abby emerged into the little clearing where the river bent, her Merit had burned down to the filter. She tossed the butt in the water, hoping it would bring Gretchen running out to tell her she was hurting Mother Nature.

Nothing.

"Gretchen?" Abby whisper-called into the darkness.

No answer.

"Gretchen?" she tried again, slightly louder.

A path of crushed marsh grass and churned-up pluff mud showed where Gretchen must have crawled out of the water. Abby lined herself up at the top of the bank, where Gretchen would have emerged, and looked into the black woods. Leaves sighed as a high wind blew through the treetops. The cicadas kept screaming. Far off there was a single hollow knock that made Abby's heart squeeze tight.

"Gretchen!" she said in her normal voice.

The woods didn't answer.

Before she could wimp out, Abby walked into the trees, following a straight line, pretending she was Gretchen. Where would she have gone? Which way would she have turned? Within seconds she was deep in darkness. Her eyes had nothing to hold on to and they were spazzing out, her vision sliding helplessly over the shadows, trying to force them into shapes. Keeping one hand in front of her face so she didn't walk into a tree and break her nose, Abby made her way deeper into the woods.

Up ahead, the trees thinned and moonlight shone dull gray on something square and black planted in the ground. Abby slowed as she walked into the clearing. It was a ruined blockhouse, just a simple one-room rectangle, its thick tabby walls burned black, the roof collapsed. A single blind window stared out, and it was impossible to shake the sense that something was looking out at her. That's when she saw the darkness inside the blockhouse start to move. That's when Abby realized the cicadas had stopped screaming.

Her heart shifted into fourth gear. She didn't know where she was. She had never heard about any buildings back here. There couldn't be anything inside it, but something in there was moving and Abby couldn't look away. The darkness inside was deeper. She could see it through the window, twisting around itself, squirming, rolling, undulating. And something was buzzing, a sinister sizzle she could feel through her feet, humming deep underground. Abby tightened her grip on Gretchen's shorts and shirt. She heard the sound of a far-off hunting horn.

This had to be the acid. It was finally kicking in, after all. She just needed to turn around and walk away. Nothing was going to hurt her. It was a powerful drug, but it had never caused any harm to anyone except maybe Syd Barrett. All she had to do was turn around and go. There was nothing to worry about because none of this was real.

That's when a man called her name.

"Abby," a voice said from inside the house.

It came out of the darkness—no weird sound effects, nothing scary, just a normal man, saying her name in a normal voice.

Her hands went cold; something snapped inside her brain and Abby ran. She panicked, she stumbled, she ran face-first into a tree because *someone was right behind her* and any minute she would feel him grab her T-shirt and drag her back to that dark house. So she kept running.

Abby steered toward the lighter part of the woods, spinning off tree trunks, tripping over logs, stumbling through bushes. She ran as thorns hacked at her shins, as branches whipped at her eyes, as something caught her hair and yanked her backward. But she kept running and she felt her hair rip at the roots. Up ahead, the darkness was thinning. She could see where the trees ended. She was close. A whine rose up in her throat, and a light smashed into her face.

"Whoa!" Margaret said.

Abby fell out of the woods and landed on her hands and knees. Margaret and Glee were standing in the waist-high field. They were far from the river, farther than Abby had realized.

"Behind me!" she said, pushing herself up off the cold grass.

Margaret whipped her light off Abby's face and ran it over the wall of tree trunks that were dirty and small and not scary at all in the flashlight beam.

"Did you see someone?" Margaret asked.

"Where's Gretchen?" Glee asked.

"She's not with y'all?" Abby asked, panting.

"Shit," Margaret said.

Margaret and Glee started walking up and down the edge of

the woods, shining their light into the trees, calling Gretchen's name. Abby realized that she only had Gretchen's shorts in her hand. She must've dropped the T-shirt somewhere in the woods, and that made her feel inexplicably sad, like she'd broken something expensive that couldn't be replaced. But there was no way she was going back to find it. There was no way she was going back in those woods for any reason whatsoever.

After a while her panic passed, and soon she started to walk the treeline with Glee and Margaret. And then they thought maybe Gretchen was at the house, and Abby didn't want to split up, so all three of them went back but it was empty. They picked at pasta salad, and smoked, and tried to figure out if they should call the police. Then they found batteries for two more flashlights and went back outside.

"Gretchen!" they called, walking the property. "Gretchen? Greeeetch-ennnnn!"

When the sky started to soften and every step was like walking through concrete they decided to bite the bullet. They had to call the police.

"I'm so fucked," Margaret said.

"She might be dead," Abby said. "Or kidnapped."

"It could be a cult," Glee suggested. "Like Satan worshippers."

"Shut the fuck up, Glee," Margaret moaned. "Before I ruin my life, we're going to search the woods."

Even with dawn turning everything gray, Abby couldn't handle the idea of going back into the woods.

"No way," she said. "We should call the police. Someone might have taken her."

"Who?" Margaret asked, switching off her flashlight. It was light enough to see their faces without it. "Who would want her? No one fucking took her. Before we call the police and I'm grounded for the rest of my life, we're going to look one last time."

Margaret had a way of making you feel like a stupid baby, so Abby meekly followed her and Glee out of the safe, open field and back into the maze of trees.

"We're not going to a party," Margaret said. "Spread out."

"This is how they always get in trouble on *Scooby-Doo*," Glee said, but she obeyed and, reluctantly, so did Abby. The three of them spread out through the woods, but Abby kept her flashlight on, even as the sky lightened. At first she tried to stay near the treeline, but the thought of Margaret cursing her out for being a coward, coupled with the thought of Gretchen lying injured and unconscious somewhere, forced her to go deep. The loblolly and palmetto trunks kept her from walking in a straight line, lured her in, turned her around, pulled her farther from the treeline. When they finally led her to the concrete bunker again, she wanted to scream.

Instead she took a deep breath and forced herself to be cool. In the grimy morning light the blockhouse looked depressing, covered in graffiti where kids had carved their initials and weird symbols that might be pictures of perverted sex: "Eat Fuk Preps," "The Uncalled Four," and "Nuke the Killer Whales." Abby felt the pressure of someone watching her, and she spun around.

Nothing but tree trunks. She turned back to the building and saw a pale figure standing in the window, staring at her. It had shadowy holes for eyes and a ragged black rip for a mouth. Abby's flashlight thumped to the ground.

"What time is it?" Gretchen asked.

Her throat was scratchy, her voice was raw. Then she disappeared from the window and came around the side of the house, stark naked except for her sneakers, smeared up to her thighs with scales of pluff mud, filth streaked over the rest of her body, hands black, leaves in her hair. She stepped into the light and the rising sun was reflected in her eyes. For a moment they were cold silver discs.

"Where were you?" Abby asked.

Gretchen brushed past her, heading out of the woods.

"Gretchen?" Abby called, then hurried after her. "Are you okay?"

"I'm peachy," Gretchen said. "I'm cold, I'm naked, I'm starving, I spent all night in the fucking woods."

The reply threw Abby. Gretchen never cussed. She held out Gretchen's shorts.

"I found these," she said. "But I lost your shirt."

Snatching them from Abby's hand, Gretchen stepped into her shorts, her joints cold and stiff. She pulled them up and then crossed her arms over her chest, tucking her hands into her armpits.

"We thought you were lost," Abby explained. "We've been looking for you since you jumped off the dock. Margaret was about to call the police."

Gretchen leaned over, arms hiding her breasts, skin rough with goose pimples, and she kept bending until she was crouched like she was going to pee, and then she froze, hair hanging over her face. It took Abby a second to realize she was crying, and then Abby crouched beside her, wrapping her arms around Gretchen's ice-cold back.

"Shh, shh, shh," she said, rubbing Gretchen's back. "It's okay."

Gretchen leaned into her awkwardly, and snuffled and shook for a full minute before she made a complicated noise in her throat.

"What?" Abby asked.

"I want to go home," Gretchen repeated.

"We are," Abby said.

She stood up, pulling Gretchen with her, turning them around, trying to walk. But Gretchen's legs were too stiff to do more than stumble.

"Glee!" Abby yelled. "Mar-ga-ret!"

Seconds later, the girls came crashing through the woods.

"Thank fucking God," Margaret said.

Then Glee and Margaret were all over Gretchen, leading her out of the clearing, Margaret pulling off her own big T-shirt and sliding it over Gretchen's head because at least Margaret was wearing a bra. Abby stood and watched them go, relief flooding her limbs. She looked back at the blockhouse and saw something modern poking around its corner. Leaning over, she got a better look. A big metal box was planted in the dirt. Dusty green, it squatted in the woods, a white number 14 stenciled on the side. She picked her way over and laid a hand on top. It was buzzing. A Southern Bell logo was stamped on a padlocked hatch on the side, and she realized that the humming last night came from some kind of phone equipment.

Mystery deflated, she turned again to the blockhouse and realized it didn't look evil now, just filthy. Half the ceiling had collapsed and big chunks of broken tabby lay piled on the ground. The inside walls were scratched deep from top to bottom with more obscene graffiti, every inch thick with shaky symbols, unreadable words, weird letters that might have been numbers, band names hacked over sex drawings scratched over wannabe satanic designs. The ground was carpeted with empty wine-cooler bottles and cigarette butts.

One slab of tabby lay in the center, as big and round as a dinner table, tipped up on one side to present its face to the window. Watery morning light shone on half of it. Smeared across its surface was a handful of something red that could have been fresh paint. Abby backed away slowly from the window and got out of the woods.

It was just paint, she told herself. That's all it was.

SUNDAY BLOODY SUNDAY

Everyone was starving but the only items in Margaret's fridge were half a grapefruit, a curl of cheddar cheese in a Ziploc bag, a case of Perrier, and a box of Fleet laxative suppositories, because Margaret's mom was watching her weight again.

Glee was jazzed up on no sleep, telling no one in particular the blow by blow of how they'd spent all night looking for Gretchen and how worried she'd been the whole time. Margaret was a space cadet, standing in front of the coffee maker, watching it fill. The girls stank. Abby's shins seethed with scratches, her arms felt like solid bruises, and her scalp ached where she'd lost some hair. She kept trying to get Gretchen out the door, but Gretchen was moving in circles. First she wanted to go look for her T-shirt in the woods, then she couldn't find her wallet, then her house keys weren't in her bag. Margaret kept waiting for them to go, but after Gretchen put down her bag and couldn't find it for the third time, Margaret stomped off to the shower and slammed the bathroom door. Finally, finally, *finally* they loaded up the Dust Bunny and backed out way too fast.

"We should've waited for Margaret," Gretchen mumbled, slumped against the passenger side window.

"We'll see her on Monday," Abby said. "Right now we need to get home before your parents."

She bounced the Dust Bunny hard down the oak-lined dirt road.

"Ow," Gretchen moaned as her head knocked against the window.

Old Charleston families loved their big country houses, and they loved their long driveways, and the worse condition they kept them in, the more they felt like they were the right kind of people. The Middletons were exactly the right kind of people. Just as her shock absorbers couldn't take any more damage, Abby hung a right and the Dust Bunny hauled itself onto the two-lane blacktop that cut through the deep pine forest out of Wadmalaw and toward Charleston; she pressed the gas. The Bunny's little sewing machine engine hummed like crazy.

"Do you have twelve dollars I can borrow?" Abby asked.

Gretchen just fiddled with the radio.

"Gretchen?" Abby said.

No answer. Abby decided to go for the long explanation. "They shorted me at TCBY this week but they're making it up on my next paycheck. We're not going to make it home if I don't get some gas."

There was a long pause, then:

"I can't remember anything about last night," Gretchen said.

"You got lost," Abby said. "And spent the night in that building. There's a gas station in Red Top."

Gretchen thought about this.

"I don't have any money," she decided.

"They take cards," Abby said.

"I have a card?" Gretchen asked hopefully.

"In your wallet," Abby said.

Abby knew that Gretchen's dad had given her a credit card for emergencies. Except for Abby, all the girls had gas cards and credit cards and allowances, because no one's dad wanted his daughter to be stranded somewhere without enough money to get home. Except for Abby's dad. He didn't much care about anything except lawn mowers.

Gretchen hauled her bag onto her lap and began pawing through it until she found her wallet, fumbled it open, and froze.

"How much do you have?" Abby asked.

Nothing but the hum of the Dust Bunny's engine.

Abby risked a look over.

"Gretchen?" she asked. "How much?"

Gretchen turned to Abby, and in the morning sun Abby could see that her eyes were swimming with tears.

"Sixteen dollars," she said. "That's enough for gas and a Diet Coke, right? That's okay if I have a Diet Coke?"

"Of course," Abby said. "It's your money."

The light sparkled on tears as they slid down Gretchen's cheeks.

"Gretchen?" Abby asked, suddenly worried.

Sunlight flickered through the trees as they drove, turning strong and solid as they left the pine forest behind. Tomato fields lay flat and fallow for acres on either side of the two-lane blacktop. Gretchen inhaled so deep, it turned into a shuddering sob.

"I just really, really . . . ," Gretchen broke off, overcome. She tried again. "I need everything to be normal right now."

Abby reached over, took her hand, and squeezed. Gretchen's skin was cold, but the inside of the car was warming from the sun.

"You're going to be okay," Abby said. "I promise."

"You're sure?" Gretchen asked.

"Totally positive," Abby said.

By the time they rolled into Red Top, they were running on fumes and Gretchen was starting to come down.

They were silent the rest of the ride home. Exhausted, Gretchen leaned way back in her seat, picking at her hair, her mud-caked legs stretched out in front of her. The closer they got to Mt. Pleasant, the happier Abby felt. They were headed up onto the first span of the bridge when Bobby McFerrin started whistling; Abby turned up the volume on "Don't Worry, Be Happy" and mellow radio reassurance filled the car. Everyone was in church, so there was no bridge traffic. The sun was sparkling off the waves in the harbor, and there wasn't a thing in the world that couldn't be fixed by a good night's sleep.

Where the Oasis gas station split Coleman Boulevard in two, Abby hung a right and rolled through the Old Village at a stately twenty-five miles per hour. Live oaks formed tunnels over every street, occasionally exploding out of the middle of the road and forcing the asphalt to split around them. There was nothing suburban about the neighborhood; it felt as if they were driving through a forest full of farmhouses. They passed the brick Sweet Shoppe with its basketball courts, then the mossy Confederate cemetery on the hill, the pinprick police station, the tennis courts. They drove past house after house, and every one of them comforted and calmed Abby.

There were red houses with white trim. Magnolia yellow Southern mansions with wraparound porches and giant white columns. Neat little saltbox cottages with mossy slate roofs. Rambling two-story Victorians wreathed in drooping verandas. Looking up, you couldn't see the sky, just the underside of an endless green and silver canopy of leaves dripping Spanish moss. Every lawn was clipped, every house was freshly painted, every power walker waved hello and Abby always waved back.

The only flaw in the Old Village's perfection were big orange stains splashed up the sides of houses where the sprinklers hit. City water was expensive and, even worse, full of fluoride. That might be fine for your children, but God forbid you use it to hydrate your Alhambra Hall Yard-of-the-Month flowerbeds. So everyone sunk wells for their outdoor hoses and (because the Mt. Pleasant water table was loaded with iron) the sprinklers stained everything orange: driveways, sidewalks, porch railings, wood siding. After enough years of sprinkler splash, your property looked jaundiced, and then the neighbors complained, and then you had to repaint your house. But that's the price you paid to live in paradise.

The Dust Bunny rumbled onto Pierates Cruze, where live oak branches raced low over lawns and hung close enough to the road to scrape the Bunny's roof. Rocks pinged off the undercarriage as they rolled down the dirt road, the tires kicking up a lazy beige cloud as Abby pulled to a stop in front of Gretchen's house, which sat close to the street with only a square of asphalt for parking. She yanked the emergency brake (the Bunny had a tendency to roll) and turned to give Gretchen a hug.

"Are you okay?" Abby asked.

"I'm in so much trouble," Gretchen said.

Abby looked at the digital clock glued to her dashboard: 10:49. Gretchen's parents were usually home from church by 11:30 these days. There was plenty of time for her to hose off her shoes, get inside, clean herself up, and get her head together but she needed to start moving. Instead, she sat there staring out the windshield. She needed a pep talk.

"I know you're seriously freaked out," Abby said. "But I promise you that things are not as bad as they seem. Nothing you're feeling right now is permanent. But you have to get inside and get cleaned up and get normal or your parents are going to kill you."

She leaned over and gave Gretchen a hug.

"Eye of the Tiger," Abby said.

Gretchen looked down at the gearshift and nodded. Then she nodded again, more definitely. "Okay," she said. "Eye of the Tiger."

She pushed open the door with her shoulder, then heaved herself up out of the car, slamming the door behind her and stumbling up the driveway to her house. Abby hoped she remembered to leave her shoes outside.

Gretchen was cold. Gretchen was tired. Gretchen had spent all night alone in the woods. They'd hang out later that night, Abby told herself. They'd rent a movie or something. Nothing was wrong here. Don't worry. Be happy.

The Old Village was in Abby's rearview mirror as she crossed back over Coleman Boulevard and headed up Rifle Range Road, driving toward a neighborhood where no one ever told you to repaint your trim. In Abby's neighborhood, telling someone their trim looked a little orange could get you shot.

She passed the Kangaroo gas station across the street from the guy who sold boiled peanuts and garden statuary out of a shack surrounded by hundreds of concrete birdbaths. Then she passed the Ebenezer Mount Zion A.M.E. church, which marked the boundary of Harborgate Shores, a bland cookie-cutter subdivision that ran for miles; after that, the houses got smaller and the yards were mostly full of boat trailers and dirt. Abby passed a thicket of brick ranchers with fake colonial columns holding up vestigial front porches, then it was all roadside shacks, tin-roofed cinder-block bunkers, and, finally, Abby's driveway.

She pulled up in front of her sad, sagging house, with its broken spine and huffing window-unit air conditioners and the army of busted lawn mowers sprouting from the weeds, which were the only things growing in their yard. Despite owning close to three hundred lawn mowers, Abby's dad never cut the grass.

When Abby entered Gretchen's house, it was like opening the pressurized airlock of a gleaming spaceship and walking into a sterile environment. When she entered her own house, it was like forcing open the waterlogged door of a hillbilly's shack and walking into a moldy cave. Boxes were still piled along the walls and pictures were stacked down the hall because even four years after the move from the larger Creekside house, Abby's mom still hadn't unpacked.

Mr. Rivers sat on the worn couch, shirt off, hairless belly resting in his lap, holding a Styrofoam cereal bowl, his feet resting on their scratched-up coffee table. He had the TV on.

"Hey, Dad," Abby said, crossing the living room and kissing him on the cheek.

His eyes didn't move from the screen.

"Mm," he said.

"What're you watching?" Abby asked.

"Gobots," he said.

Abby stood to the side and watched mopeds transform into grinning robots, and fighter jets shoot lasers out of their tires. She waited for a conversation to materialize. It didn't.

"What're you doing today?" she asked.

"Fixing mowers," he said.

"I've got TCBY," Abby said. "I might go over to Gretchen's after. What time's Mom home?"

"Late," he said.

"You want me to get you a real bowl?" she tried.

"Mm," he shrugged.

Based on past experience, this was about all she could expect from him, so Abby headed into the kitchen, grabbed a green apple, and walked quickly through the drab house to her bedroom. She opened and closed her door as fast as possible, so that none of the poison gas that made her parents so depressing could follow her.

No one was allowed inside Abby's room. It belonged to a different house, one she'd built herself, with her own money and hard work. Diagonal pink and silver wallpaper lined the walls, and a carpet of black and white circles with a large red triangle cutting across them covered the floor. There was a JC Penney two-deck stereo sitting on a milk crate she'd draped in silver shimmer fabric, the touch-tone Mickey Mouse phone she'd gotten one Christmas sat next to her bed, and her 19-inch Sampo color TV sat on a glass coffee table.

A shiny pink and black vanity stood against one wall. Its round mirror bordered with layer upon layer of snapshots: Gretchen in bed with the covers pulled up to her chin that time she had mono, Gretchen and Glee at the beach looking hot in their neon green and black bikinis, Margaret catching air on the hydroslide, the four of them posed for a photo at the ninth-grade semiformal, Gretchen and Abby with their cornrows in Jamaica.

Abby's bed was a high, soft nest, held together on three sides by curly white metal railings that rattled whenever she got in. It was piled deep with comforters and blankets, six huge pink pillows, and a mound of her old stuffed animals: Geoffrey the Giraffe, Cabbage Head, Wrinkles the Pound Puppy, Hugga Bear, Sparks, and Fluffy the Fluppy Puppy. She knew it was childish, but what was she going to do? She couldn't stand to see the hurt in their beady plastic eyes if she put them in the trash.

Everything in this room had been paid for by Abby, or bought by Abby, or hung by Abby, or painted by Abby, and it was the one place where she felt as comfortable as she did at Gretchen's. She dropped Duran Duran's *Arena* into her stereo and cranked up the volume. Gretchen had given it to her for her birthday three years ago, and it always made her feel like summer in the car with the windows down. She crept down the hall, blasted away the crud with a boiling hot shower, wrapped a towel around herself, and then retreated back to her room. It was getting close to 1 p.m, which meant it was time to put on her face and go to work.

Back in seventh grade, Abby had woken up one day with a huge blast of zits across her cheeks, forehead, and chin. They were moving out of Creekside at the time and she was so upset and nervous about every single thing in her life that she'd started picking at them. Within a week her face was a mass of oozing scabs and angry, infected craters. She'd begged her parents to let her go to the dermatologist, like Gretchen did, but only got a chorus of her mother's favorite number-one hit single, "We Can't Afford It."

Can we have a dog? "We Can't Afford It."

Can I get biology tutoring? "We Can't Afford It."

What about summer school, so I can graduate early? "We Can't Afford It."

Can I go on the Greece trip with Mrs. Trumbo's art class? "We Can't Afford It."

Can I go to a doctor so my face doesn't look like scab pizza? "We Can't Afford It."

Abby had tried Seabreeze, Noxzema, and St. Ives mud masks. Everything advertised in *Seventeen*, everything she saw in *YM*. There was even one misguided moment when she'd rubbed mayonnaise into her chin and forehead in a fight-fire-with-fire approach she'd read about in *Teen*. The results weren't pretty. No matter what she did, the zits got bigger. It had taken just five days for them to appear, but nothing she did made them go away.

Then she stopped touching her face, and cut out Coke and chocolate, and maybe changing hormones helped, too, because after three months of humiliation her face started to clear up. Not entirely, but at least it was a cease-fire. But the war left her skin ravaged with scars. There were deep ones on her cheeks, shallow wide ones in the middle of her forehead, enormous black holes jabbed into her nose, and deep red marks outlining her chin.

"You can only see them when the light hits at a certain angle," Gretchen reassured her, but it was too late. Abby was heartbroken because she had ruined her face and never even gone out with a boy. She stayed in her room for an entire weekend that summer; then on Monday, Gretchen took her to the Book Bag on Coleman Boulevard and they went through all the beauty magazines, and finally Gretchen shoplifted a makeup book. Back home, they studied it more closely than they'd ever studied anything at school, made a list, and drove to Kerrisons, where Gretchen bought her eighty-five dollars' worth of makeup. It took Abby a couple weeks of experimenting, but by Labor Day she had a face she could live with.

Sometimes a clueless dork would ask why she looked like a clown, and in bright sunlight she could be confused for a Miss America contestant in full stage makeup, but Abby diverted the attention by being cheerful all the time. When there was a joke to be made, she made it. When there was something nice to do, she did it. And by eighth grade, when people started reinventing their looks in preparation for high school, everyone just accepted that this was the way Abby looked.

The downside was that it took her a solid half hour in the morning to sponge, powder, and poke her face into submission.

She had to put down a base layer of foundation, then blend, and smooth, and powder, and draw on her eyebrows and do her lips and do her blush for color, and get everything perfectly in balance so that she didn't look like Tammy Faye Bakker. But as long as she woke up early enough, it was actually kind of relaxing to watch her acne scars disappear underneath her real face as she got prettier and prettier, section by section.

Her shift started in twenty minutes, so she finished her makeup, sprayed her bangs up high, put on her green and white uniform, pulled her ponytail through the back of her baseball cap, resprayed her bangs, and got everything situated.

She drove to the strip mall on Coleman, and for the next six hours Abby stood in the cold glass cube of TCBY, marinating in the sour vanilla stink of frozen yogurt. It didn't bother her. Every hour she spent chilling in this giant freezer was another four dollars in her bank account.

It was a pretty uneventful shift until around four thirty, when the telephone rang.

"TCBY, how may I help you?" Abby said.

"Blood," Gretchen said. "Everything's covered in blood."

IT'S THE END OF THE WORLD AS WE KNOW IT (AND I FEEL FINE)

Abby turned her back to the line of customers and dropped her voice. She heard sloshing in the background. "Where are you?" she asked.

"I took a bath," Gretchen said. "And I decided to shave my legs but the water turned bright red and I don't know if it's my blood, or a flashback, or if it's real, or if I'm freaking out."

The background sound dropped away and Abby heard a high-pitched buzzing.

"Help me," Gretchen whispered.

"How much is there?" Abby asked.

"A lot."

"Okay, stand up. Get out of the tub, and stand in front of the mirror. Stand on a white towel."

Dee Dee tugged Abby's sleeve.

"We've got a line," she said.

"One sec," Abby mouthed, waving Dee Dee away, because frozen yogurt was really not a priority right now. She heard splashing over the receiver, then dripping, then silence.

"Are you looking?" Abby asked. "Is there blood on the towel?"

A long pause.

"No," Gretchen said, relief in her voice.

"You're sure? The towel's fine?"

"Yes. God, I'm losing my mind."

"Watch TV and I'll talk to you tonight," Abby said. "Don't forget to call me."

"I'm sorry I bugged you," Gretchen said. "Go work."

Abby hung up and, having solved a major crisis, she happily pulled vanilla cones and spooned Heath bar crunch over them until nine o'clock, when she and Dee Dee locked up. When Abby got home she turned on the tail end of *The Jerry Lewis Telethon*, got into bed, and held one finger on the cradle of her Mickey Mouse phone until exactly 11:06. This was her nightly phone date with Gretchen. She could never call Gretchen's house this late, and technically Gretchen wasn't supposed to call either, but as long as Abby kept her finger on the cradle and let go the moment the ringer vibrated, her parents never had a clue.

But that night, the phone never rang.

Seven twenty on Monday morning and mist clung to the Old Village, creeping up from the harbor, forming a white scrim that hovered over the ground, blurring all the hard lines. Abby pulled onto Pierates Cruze and rolled to a stop in front of Gretchen's house, singing along to Phil Collins because nothing put her in a better mood. In the back seat was a tray of rice krispie treats to give Gretchen a soft landing after the hard weekend.

Gretchen usually waited for Abby on the street, but this morning there was only Good Dog Max. He'd tipped over Dr. Bennett's garbage can and was up to his shoulders in trash. When Abby put on the parking brake he started and spun around, standing stiff-legged, staring at the Dust Bunny until she opened her door, at which point he leapt over the white trash bags, caught his front legs, and face-planted into them. Abby ran to the front door while he flailed around.

Instead of a sleepy Gretchen ready for her Diet Coke infusion, the glass door unsealed and Mrs. Lang stood there in her housecoat.

"Gretchen won't be coming to school today," she said.

"Can I go up?" Abby asked.

She heard a rumble as Gretchen avalanched down the stairs, dressed for school, bookbag over one shoulder. "Let's go," she said.

"You hardly slept," Mrs. Lang said, grabbing Gretchen's bookbag and dragging her to a halt. "I'm the mother and I say you're staying home."

"Get OFF me," Gretchen yelled, twisting away.

Abby's skin felt hot and clammy. Their fighting always embarrassed her. She never knew how to make it clear whose side she was on.

"Tell her, Abby," Gretchen said. "It's vital to my education that I go."

Mrs. Lang looked in Abby's direction, forcing Abby to stumble over her words.

"Well," she said. "Um . . ."

Mrs. Lang's face fell.

"Oh, Max," she said.

Abby looked behind her. Good Dog Max had trotted up the path and was staring at the three of them as if he'd never seen them before. A stained Maxipad was stuck to his muzzle.

"Gross," Abby said, laughing. She grabbed Max's collar and pulled him toward the door.

"No, Abby!" Mrs. Lang said. "He's covered in yuck." She took hold of the collar, and in the confusion Gretchen slipped from her grip and broke for the Dust Bunny, dragging Abby along in her wake.

"Bye, Mom," she called over her shoulder.

Mrs. Lang looked up.

"Gretchen—" she said, but by then they were at the end of the driveway.

Dr. Bennett was squatting by his garbage cans; he looked up as they ran by.

"Keep that dern dog out of my yard," he said. "I've got my air rifle."

"Morning, Dr. Bennett," Gretchen said with a wave as the two of them slammed into the Dust Bunny and Abby pulled out.

"Why didn't you call last night?" Abby asked.

"I was on the phone with Andy," Gretchen said.

She handed Abby two sweaty quarters and reached between the seats to pull out the Diet Coke that Abby always brought her.

Abby was annoyed. Gretchen had come back from Bible camp talking about nothing but Andy, her great summer love. Andy was so cool. Andy was so studly. Andy was so living in Florida and Gretchen was so going to go visit him. By the first week of July she'd forgotten about him, and Abby assumed it was over. Now here he was again.

"Great," Abby said.

She hated that she sounded sour, so she put on a smile and cocked her head like she was interested. Abby hadn't seen any pictures of Andy ("Andy says that taking pictures is like clinging to the past," Gretchen said, sighing) and she hadn't talked to him on the phone ("I'm writing him letters," Gretchen crooned. "They're so much more meaningful."), but Abby could picture him perfectly. He was a gimpy hunchback with one eyebrow and braces. Maybe headgear.

"He's done acid before," Gretchen said. "And he told me that the thing in my bathtub was totally normal. A lot of people have had that happen, so I'm not Syd Barrett."

Abby was gripping the steering wheel so hard her fingers ached.

"I told you it was fine," she said, smiling.

Gretchen leaned forward, rifled through Abby's tapes, and popped in their awesome summer mix. By the time they roared into the student parking lot in a cloud of white dust, they were both screaming along with Bonnie Tyler, having Total Eclipses of the Heart. Abby cruised into an empty space at the far end, put the Dust Bunny in park, and yanked the emergency brake. They were facing the sports fields that led to the headmaster's house, where five of the stray dogs that made their home in the marsh were chasing one another through the mist.

"Ready for AA?" Abby asked Gretchen.

Gretchen flinched, then turned to check the backseat.

"I'm having flashbacks," Gretchen said.

"What?" Abby said.

"Someone keeps touching the back of my neck," Gretchen said. "It kept me up all night."

"Wowzers," Abby said. "You *have* turned into Syd Barrett."

Gretchen flipped her the bird.

"Come on," she said. "Let's go to AA."

They got out of the Dust Bunny and headed into school. On the way, Abby brushed her hand against the back of Gretchen's neck and Gretchen jumped.

"Stop," she said. "You wouldn't like it if I did it to you."

Albemarle Academy sat at the end of Albemarle Pointe on the Ashley River, bordered by marsh on two sides and by the Crescent subdivision on the third. Albemarle was expensive and intensive, and everyone who went there thought they were better than everyone else in Charleston.

"Uh-oh," Gretchen said.

She nodded ahead and Abby looked as they crossed Albemarle Road, which separated the student parking lot and the sports fields from the school buildings. That enormous wall of meat, Coach Toole, was crossing in the opposite direction, wearing obscenely tight weightlifting pants.

"Ladies," he said, nodding as he passed.

"Coach," Gretchen said, swinging her bookbag around and reaching inside. "You want some nuts? My mom gave me a bag."

"No, thanks," he said, still walking. "I've got my own nuts."

The two girls looked at each other, incredulous, and then ran away laughing, racing up the sidewalk by the drop-off lanes where Trey Sumter, already behind on his homework this early in the year, was sitting on the bench by the flagpole, begging them as they passed. "Did y'all do those earth science questions?"

"Igneous rock, Trey," Gretchen said. "It's always igneous rock."

Then Abby and Gretchen turned the corner into the breezeway, with the front office on one side and the glass doors leading into the upper school hallway on the other, the vast green Lawn spread out before them, the bell tower rising on the other side, and they were in the thick of it, surrounded by the student body of Albemarle Academy.

"Oh, God, spare me," Gretchen said. "We're all so pathetic."

They were the children of doctors and lawyers and bank presidents, and their parents owned boats and horses, plantations in the country and beach houses on Seabrook, and they lived in gracious homes in Mt. Pleasant or in historic houses downtown. And every single one of them was exactly the same.

The Albemarle student handbook was the Bible, and the dress code was clear: you dressed like your parents. The kids saved their big hair, big colors, and big shoulderpads for the weekends. During the week the dress code was all New England prep academy. The girls dressed like "young ladies," the boys like "young gentlemen" and if you didn't know what that meant, then you didn't belong at Albemarle.

The boys had it the worst. They shopped at M. Dumas, the shabby chic store on King Street where their moms picked one look for them in seventh grade, and they stuck with it for the rest of their lives: khakis, long-sleeved Polo shirts in winter, short-sleeved Izod shirts in spring. After college they added a navy sportscoat, a seersucker suit, and an array of "fun" ties to wear to their first jobs at local law firms or their fathers' banks.

The girls tried. Occasionally, a rebel like Jocelyn Zuckerman showed up wearing cornrows, which, although not explicitly banned by the dress code, were considered outrageous enough to get her sent home. But for the most part they kept their self-expression inside the dress code through elaborate workarounds. White turtlenecks were for girls who wanted to draw attention to their chests without showing forbidden cleavage. Girls who thought they had good butts wore stirrup pants that clung to their assets. Subdued animal prints (leopard, tiger, zebra) were popular with girls who were trying to project unique personalities. But no matter how hard they tried, they all still looked the same.

Because it wasn't just their clothes. Albemarle taught grades one through twelve but there were only seventy-two students in Abby's class, and most of them had been going to Albemarle together since first grade. They had carpooled to Brownies together, and gone to Cotillion together, and their mothers belonged to the

Hibernian Society together, and their dads did business and went dove hunting together.

It was a school where everyone complained about the work load, but ragged on public schools for being "too easy." Where everyone hated the dress code, but snickered at the "rednecks" who roamed Citadel Mall in stonewashed denim and mullets. Where everyone was desperate to be an individual, but they all were terrified to stand out.

The first bell rang and they headed to class, and all day long Abby distributed rice krispie treats wherever she went: Intro to Computing, where the new teacher, Mr. Barlow, told them there was no eating around his computers. Then Geometry with Mrs. Massey, who confiscated them, ate two, and returned the tray to Abby at the end of class. U.S. History, where Abby made sure to give everyone treats before the second bell rang and the intolerable Mr. Groat appeared and made everyone throw them in the garbage.

As soon as the bell rang for lunch, Abby met up with Gretchen and they headed for the Lawn. Framed by the front office and the breezeway on one side and the auditorium on the other, the Lawn existed in the shadow of the bell tower. Set next to the auditorium entrance, the tower was a four-story rectangular monolith made of rust-colored bricks hammered into the heart of the school like a stake. On the side facing the Lawn, large metal letters spelled out the school motto: "Faith & Honor."

They found Glee and Margaret sitting on one of the Charleston benches in the sun near the bocce players. Abby and Gretchen plonked down on the grass, broke out their green apples and yogurt cups, and soon they were talking about Saturday night like they were old pros who'd been dropping acid since Woodstock.

"Are y'all getting flashbacks?" Abby asked.

"Yeah," Margaret said. "I saw your face on a dog's butt."

"That's barely even funny," Abby said. "Gretchen got flashbacks."

They all looked at Gretchen, who shrugged.

"I was just tired," she said.

That didn't sound right to Abby. Normally Gretchen loved sharing drama.

"What happened?" Glee asked.

"The acid didn't work," Margaret explained. "So nothing happened."

"I thought I cut my legs shaving," Gretchen said. "It's no biggie."

"That is grotesque," Glee said. "Were you in the tub? Did you think you were bleeding to death?"

Gretchen ripped out bits of grass until Abby came to her rescue.

"I heard stuff in the woods when I was looking for her," Abby said.

"What kind of stuff?" Glee asked, leaning forward.

"Weird noises," Abby said. "And I saw some old building."

"Oh, yeah. That thing," Margaret said, barely interested. "It's totally like some historic landmark we can't tear down. It's so tainted."

Abby turned back to Gretchen. "Do you remember anything that happened?"

Gretchen wasn't listening. She was hunched forward, and while Abby watched, her shoulders twitched and she flinched again.

"Earth to Space Ace," Margaret said. "What happened when you were naked in my backyard?"

"Who was naked?" a voice asked, and suddenly Wallace Stoney was among them.

Instantly, the mood changed. The girls could relax around one another, but Wallace Stoney was a senior, and a boy, and a football player. He thought friendships were emotional, and emotions were weakness, and weakness must be stomped.

"Gretchen was," said Margaret, scooting over on the bench.

"You should have done 'shrooms," he said, sitting beside her and squeezing out Glee. She stood up and joined Abby and Gretchen on the grass.

Wallace Stoney had a harelip scar, and Abby was always fascinated that it hadn't made him a nicer person. In fact, he was a giant jackass, and they only tolerated him because he was a senior and he was going out with Margaret, and Margaret only put up with him because he did whatever she said.

He put an awkward arm around Margaret and hauled her legs onto his lap. "Lovemaking is intense when you're shrooming," he said, gazing into her eyes.

"Make me barf now," Glee said. "I'm going to the computer lab."

"Nerd," Margaret called after her.

"I'm coming with," Gretchen said, getting up.

"What's the matter?" Wallace leered. "Did I make the virgins uncomfortable?"

Gretchen stopped, turned, and looked at Wallace for a full second.

"It takes one to know one," she said and took off after Glee.

Abby got up to follow. "I'll leave y'all to your face-sucking."

By the time she caught up with Gretchen, the bell was ringing and so she didn't see her again until volleyball practice. Their first game was coming up and it would be totally humiliating if they lost. Last year they'd beaten Ashley Hall 12–0, but now the JV team's power players had moved up to varsity and Coach Greene was not enthusiastic about their chances.

"You ladies are the most undermotivated, underachieving bunch of playing-to-lose girls I've ever seen," she told them. "Go home and think about if you even want to be playing JV this year. Because if you're not fired up, I don't want y'all on the court."

"Thanks, Coach," Margaret said on their way out. "Truly inspirational."

"I'm not your parents, Middleton," Coach Greene said. "It's time you girls woke up and joined the real world."

Margaret and Abby rolled their eyes at each other, and then Margaret went to watch Wallace's band practice while Abby and Gretchen walked out to the parking lot. Abby noticed Gretchen flinch again.

"What's going on?" she asked.

"The flashbacks are getting worse," Gretchen said.

"Didn't Andy say that was totally normal?" Abby asked.

"Andy doesn't know what he's talking about," Gretchen said, and Abby's heart soared. "It's been like someone's touching the back of my neck all day long. And it's happening more. Every second it's, like, touch-touch-touch."

They crossed the street and walked between the mossy oaks that guarded the gate to the student parking lot, kicking rocks, the sharp white gravel poking through the soles of their shoes. Most of the cars were already gone, and the Bunny sat at the end, all alone.

"Like this?" Abby asked, extending one finger and poking Gretchen in the shoulder. Poke.

"It's not funny," Gretchen said. "I couldn't sleep last night. The second I got tired, hands started touching my face and pulling on my legs. I turned on the lights and they stopped, then I started falling asleep and they were touching me again."

"It'll wear off soon," Abby assured her. "It's been less than forty-eight hours. This stuff can't stay in your system forever." She managed to sound confident, as if she was an expert on the half-life of hallucinogenic drugs.

Gretchen hitched her bookbag strap higher on one shoulder. “If I don’t get some sleep tonight, I’m going to go nuts. My entire face hurts.”

Abby poked her in the shoulder again, and Gretchen swatted her hand away.

It was just another Monday to Abby.

She didn’t know it was the beginning of the end.

ONE THING LEADS TO ANOTHER

"Some of you seniors may have seen this at parties," said Coach Greene, standing at the podium in front of the upper school assembly, holding a green glass bottle. "The manufacturer calls it 'Bartles and Jaymes wine cooler,' but the Charleston County Police Department calls it 'rape juice.'"

Sitting next to Abby, Gretchen jerked forward, flinching. She turned to see who had touched her, but of course nobody had. Hushed whispering and snickers broke out behind them: Wallace Stoney and his football buddy sidekicks, John Bailey and Malcolm Zuckerman (who had taken to calling himself Nuke for some unknown reason).

"It tastes sweet," Coach Greene continued. "It costs about a dollar, and in hot weather, if you're not careful, you'll drink three or four of them without even noticing. But do not be fooled. Each one of these contains more alcohol than a can of beer. If you're a young woman, these make it very easy to put yourself in a situation where that which is most precious to you could be permanently ruined. Y'all know what I'm talking about."

She took a dramatic pause and scanned the audience, daring a single student to make a single joke. Laughter was lethal when you were being told something For Your Own Good.

"Some things that are broken cannot be fixed," Coach Greene

said. "Sometimes it only takes one mistake to ruin what cannot be repaired, be it your reputation, your family's good name, or your . . . most . . . valuable . . . gift."

Abby wanted to lean over and whisper it to Gretchen in solemn tones: Your . . . Most . . . Valuable . . . Gift. It had the potential to become something they said to each other all the time, like "Nik Nak Woogie Woogie Woogie," the love cry of the Koala Bear, or "Hefty, Hefty, Hefty . . . wimpy, wimpy, wimpy" from the television commercial. But ever since she'd dropped into the shotgun seat of the Dust Bunny that morning, Gretchen had been bleary-eyed and miserable, all herking, jerking raw nerves.

Invisible hands had been touching her all night, she'd told Abby. Touching her face, tapping her shoulders, stroking her chest. She'd laid in her bed for hours, holding completely still, praying the flashbacks would stop while tears ran down her temples and pooled in her ears. Around 2 a.m., Gretchen snuck the cordless phone into her bedroom, called Andy, and talked to him for two hours until she finally fell asleep. When she woke at dawn, she was excited that she'd managed to sleep for two solid hours. Then she felt a hand brush her stomach and she ran into the bathroom and threw up.

"I cannot tell you the number of students who come into my office crying," Coach Greene said from the podium on the big blond-wood stage at the front of the auditorium. "You don't know how valuable something is until it's gone."

Abby wondered if maybe Gretchen was exaggerating. How long could flashbacks really last? But it seemed real. Earlier that morning, Gretchen had fallen asleep in U.S. History, which made Mr. Groat rap on her desk and moan through his mustache that maybe she'd find the front office more interesting.

"This is your future I'm talking about, people," Coach Greene shouted. "A little bit of carelessness and you could ruin it permanently. Like that!"

She snapped her fingers and they sounded like bones breaking. Coach Greene paused to let the import of her remarks sink in. A sheen of sweat coated her upper lip.

The massive air-conditioning system rumbled on and shoved cold air out the ceiling vents. Someone on the other side of the auditorium coughed. In the silence, Gretchen jerked forward again, making her chair rattle. Abby shot her a look. Gretchen's right shoulder was twitching like someone was pushing it again and again, joggling it back and forth. Abby never prayed in chapel but right now she prayed that Coach Greene didn't notice the disruption.

"Stop it," Gretchen said, under her breath.

Cold sweat ran down Abby's ribs.

"Shh," she whispered.

"One gift," Coach Greene repeated, waving the green bottle dramatically. "And you can only give it away one time, and that should be to the person you love, not—"

"Stop it!" Gretchen shouted, standing up and turning around, face flushed.

Every head in the auditorium whipped in her direction, every student leaned forward, everyone suddenly focused on Gretchen, her face bright red, arms tense, body quivering.

"I didn't do anything," Wallace Stoney said, leaning back, holding up his hands in the "I surrender" position.

"May I help you, Miss Lang?" Coach Greene asked.

"Gretchen," Abby whispered out the side of her mouth. "Sit. Down."

"Is there a problem, Miss Lang?" Coach Greene repeated, landing hard on each word.

"Someone keeps touching me," Gretchen said.

"And then you woke up," Wallace Stoney murmured, getting a ripple of laughter from the boys sitting around him.

"Quiet!" Coach Greene shouted. "Am I boring you, Miss Lang? Because I can repeat this in Saturday School if you'd prefer. Or maybe you can hear it again when you're crying in my office after you've thrown your treasure in the gutter and shamed yourself, your family, and your school. Would you like that?"

Gretchen should have said "No, ma'am." She should have apologized. She should have sat down and taken her lumps. Instead, to Abby's horror, she argued.

"Wallace keeps touching the back of my neck."

"You wish!" Wallace said, and even Mrs. Massey sitting at the end of their row laughed before putting on her faculty face and leaning forward, extending a silencing finger at Wallace.

"Enough," she said.

"But I didn't do anything," Wallace protested.

"We saw him," Nuke Zuckerman said, jumping to his buddy's defense. "He was just sitting here. She's psycho."

Coach Greene pointed at Gretchen with the wine cooler bottle.

"Wait in the lobby, Lang," she said. "Better yet, march yourself to the front office and wait for Major. He'll have a better idea of how to deal with you."

"I didn't do anything!" Gretchen shouted.

"Outside, right now! March!"

"But—"

"Now!"

Abby looked down, studying her hands, twisting her fingers around themselves.

"S'not fair," Gretchen mumbled as she dragged herself over Abby's legs and stumbled down the row, exhausted and loose-jointed. Maybe she lost her footing, maybe somebody stuck out a leg, but when she reached the end she went sprawling into the big aisle that led to the exit doors and landed on all fours. And that was when the woo sound started.

No one knows how it happens, or who starts it, but it's the same sound that arises spontaneously when someone breaks a glass in the cafeteria. A long, low sound of chiding and shame that slipped softly out of three hundred throats and filled the auditorium: A-woooooo. As relentless and unchanging as an air-raid siren, it accompanied Gretchen on her long march up the aisle to the double doors while Abby sat ramrod straight, mortified, refusing to join in.

"Stop that!" Coach Greene shouted from the front of the auditorium. She clapped twice into the microphone. "Cut it out!"

Then she took the whistle hanging around her neck, leaned into the microphone, and blew a single sharp blast. The microphone shrieked feedback, the woo sound stopped, and students grabbed their ears in exaggerated pain.

"You think this is funny?" Coach Greene shouted. "There are people out there waiting for you to turn your head for a single second so they can put drugs in your Coca-Cola: GBH, LSD, PCP. You think I'm lying? Read a newspaper."

Which is when Major heaved himself up out of his chair in the first row and trundled to the podium, bulldozing Coach Greene aside.

"Settle," he mumbled in his clotted monotone. "Settle, everyone. Thank you, Coach, for that valuable information."

He brought his thick flippers together in a dull drumbeat that went on and on until the faculty took the hint and picked it up; finally students joined in with ragged applause.

"I would like to take this moment to convey my deepest disappointment in you all," Major rumbled. "The fundamental core values of Albemarle Academy are embodied in our motto: Faith and Honor. This morning you all have broken faith with me."

Major was always disappointed in everyone. It was his sole emotional state. He was thick-waisted and gray: gray hair, gray skin, gray eyes, gray tongue, gray lips. He had attended Albemarle as a boy and been either a teacher or the principal for more than three decades, and in all that time he'd been disappointed in every single student who'd passed through his doors.

"The school year has barely begun and already there are incidents of vandalism in the Senior Hut," he rumbled on, crushing all those who whispered before him. "There have been students parking in the senior lot without the proper sticker clearly visible in their windows. Students have been seen smoking on campus. Starting this afternoon, the Senior Hut is closed for the duration of the semester. I've spoken to the hut advisor, Mr. Groat, who agrees with my decision."

There was a pause. The air felt charged.

"Also," Major continued, "anyone found parking in the senior lot without the appropriate sticker on his or her vehicle will receive a suspension. Discipline . . ." Whispering was breaking out through the rows. Coach Greene moved up the aisle, writing down names. "Settle. Discipline is the training that makes punishment unnecessary. Let us now sing our alma mater."

Mrs. Gay scurried to the upright piano at the foot of the stage and started banging it out while Major, Coach Greene, and Father Morgan, the new chaplain, rose and sang. The faculty and student body hauled themselves to their feet and joined in. Abby was probably the only person in the auditorium who knew all the words, but she mumbled through the verses, the same as everyone around her. The room swelled with atonal chanting as the student body sang the praises of their school with all the joy of prisoners breaking rocks.

Abby, Glee, and Margaret regrouped immediately afterward. Everyone was abuzz, scattered in clumps across the Lawn. Rumors were flying that Major was going to cancel the homecoming dance, or Spirit Week, or tear down the Senior Hut, or he was going to murder everyone's parents and give them all Saturday School. No one could tell what he would do next. The man was insane.

The three girls, however, were worried about Gretchen. They'd gone directly to the front office the second that assembly ended, but Miss Toné, the upper school secretary, kicked them right back out again. They retreated to the Lawn and sat where they could see the office door. They watched it with so much attention, it was surprising it didn't burst into flames. They saw Major go inside. They saw him go into his office, with Gretchen. They saw him snap his venetian blinds shut. They stared at the front office door, barely talking. They needed to see Gretchen the second she emerged.

"What's up, space cadets?" Wallace Stoney said, dropping to the grass between Margaret and Glee and sticking his tongue down Margaret's throat.

"You guys," Glee said. "Gag me. For real."

Face still latched onto Wallace's mouth-hole, Margaret flipped Glee the bird while she put her legs over his lap and kept feeding him her tongue.

"Very mature," Glee said.

Abby was sure it was crazy awesome to have someone hot for your body all the time, but now wasn't the time to show off your killer romance by scrumping in the middle of the Lawn.

"What did you do to Gretchen?" she asked Wallace.

"You were right there," he said, detaching from Margaret. "Get the fucking makeup out of your eyes. She's clearly dreaming about me touching her, because she can't stop talking about it."

"She's been in there for half an hour because of you," Abby said. "You should tell what you did."

"You should mind your own fucking business," Wallace said calmly. "Your little bone buddy is a psycho, why's that my fault?"

They ignored him because Gretchen was finally coming out of the front office. She trudged over and plonked down next to Abby, not even looking at Wallace.

"What happened?" Glee asked. "You were in there for, like, three hours."

Margaret wiped Wallace's spit off her chin. Then she broke off half her Carnation breakfast bar and handed it to Gretchen. She was only too happy to give away solid food that contained actual calories.

"What did that buttmunch say to you?" she asked.

Gretchen started breaking Margaret's breakfast bar into crumbs, letting them fall on the grass. "He just talked," she said. "Mostly about faith and honor, and how there's a war in America for the souls of its children or something. I stopped listening. He wanted to know if I was on drugs."

"Yeah," Wallace said. "Stupid pills."

Everyone ignored him.

"What'd you say?" Margaret asked. She harbored an irrational fear that Gretchen might have narced on all of them.

"I told him Coach Greene didn't have anything to say that I needed to hear. Then he told me I needed to apologize to her before I could return to volleyball practice. Then I told him that was fine because I'm quitting the team."

The three of them stared at her in horror. When you got in trouble, you tried to make it better; you didn't make it worse. Wallace Stoney barked a seal laugh.

"You are so hosed!" he cackled.

"What did he do?" Abby asked.

"He gave me detention," Gretchen said. "For disrespect."

"Smooth move, Wretched." Wallace laughed again. "You really boned that up."

"For real?" Abby asked in disbelief. How could Gretchen just walk off the volleyball team and leave her behind? "If you quit the team, your parents are going to kill you."

Gretchen shrugged. Then Wallace came in again, commandeering the conversation, not even noticing that no one was laughing.

"Are you on the rag?" he asked. "Is that why you tried to get me in trouble?"

"Wallace," Gretchen said quietly, "stop being a pig."

Everyone held their breath for a minute, waiting for Margaret to react.

"Stop being a dumb whore," Wallace shot back, laughing, the big senior man swatting down the sophomore.

"You don't have to pretend to be tough with us," Gretchen said. "We all know about the first time you and Margaret did it. You didn't last five seconds."

She was staring at Wallace now, hands clenched around her shins, chin tucked behind her knees. No one was laughing, no one even dared to move. This was a total secret that Margaret had told them, and they all knew they were not supposed to ever repeat it ever. The scar over Wallace's upper lip turned white.

Margaret tore out a clump of grass and threw it at Gretchen. "What's your malfunction?" she snapped.

"I'm just being honest with Mr. Stud Muffin," Gretchen said. "He's a poser. He can't do it without being wasted, and he picks on Abby because she's too nice to fight back. I'm tired of being polite to him."

"At least I'm not an ice queen virgin bitch," Wallace snarled at Gretchen, sitting up straight, pushing Margaret's legs off his lap.

Gretchen didn't miss a beat.

"At least I don't sniff my sister's underwear."

Wallace lunged for her, hands outstretched. Glee and Abby screamed. Everyone on the Lawn looked over, and even the bocce players stopped tossing their balls to stare. Margaret jumped on Wallace's back and knocked him away from Gretchen, who propelled herself backward on the grass, crab-style.

"Fuck you, skank!" Wallace roared, standing up as best he could with Margaret hanging off him.

"You wish," Gretchen said.

Abby and Glee were frozen. *Wallace Stoney sniffed his sister's underwear?*

Gretchen stood up and got right in Wallace's face. He looked like he wanted to grab her, but even Wallace knew you didn't hit a girl in the middle of the Lawn.

"You aren't good enough for Margaret," Gretchen said. "You cheat, you lie, you say you love her but only so she'll do you. And you know what's most pathetic? The way you keep hitting on me. I'm not interested, Wimpy."

Gretchen's jaw was sticking out, her neck was corded, and her eyes were so wide you could see white all the way around. Abby felt like she should stop her, but things had gone too far. They were in a new territory that she didn't know how to navigate.

"Margaret should dump your ass," Gretchen said, "because—"

Then she leaned forward and threw up. Abby and Glee scuttled backward as a gallon of hot milky liquid spewed from Gretchen's mouth in a high-pressure stream, hosing the grass between Wallace's feet. Abby was barely out of the blast radius when Gretchen's stomach flexed again, pumping out another gallon of thick white fluid. In it were black strands that looked like worms. Abby leaned closer and realized they were feathers.

Wallace leapt backward, shrieking like a girl.

"These are new shoes!" he shouted.

He noticed that everyone was watching and stuck his chest out, pushing Margaret behind him like a real man, protecting his woman from the horrible threat of girl vomit. Gretchen stood there, bent over at the waist, hands on her knees, breathing hard. Everyone could hear the seagulls, creaking and wheeling overhead, flocking around this sudden abundance of food.

"Oh. My. God," Glee said.

"I—" Gretchen started, then she fell to her knees and unleashed another blast of white barf; when she'd finished, some of the feathers clung to her lower lip like spider legs. Abby saw Mr. Barlow running across the grass toward them; people were starting to move, and far off someone was giving a slow clap and whistle. Noise was breaking out across the Lawn, but Abby only had eyes for Gretchen. She raised her head and their eyes met. It looked like Gretchen was mouthing the words "help me."

Then Mr. Barlow was there, and everyone was talking, and he was pulling Gretchen up and leading her to the front office, handling her carefully. Wallace was going back to his friends, getting away from the scene of the crime, pulling Margaret along behind him.

People started approaching the site of the disaster, but before they could get close, Abby snatched the volleyball shirt out of her bag and covered the pile of throw up. As she dropped her jersey over the white puddle, she could have sworn she saw some of the black feathers squirming slowly and unfolding, curling around each other as if they were alive.

PARENTS JUST DON'T UNDERSTAND

When Gretchen got mono at the end of eighth grade, taking care of her was a team effort. Abby, Margaret, and Glee had all her classes covered. Every day Abby would drop off Gretchen's homework. On weekends the three of them would get together at Margaret's downtown house and call Gretchen, sharing the phone, two ears pressed to the receiver at a time, as they told her how unfair Mr. Vikernes's algebra exam was, and how all the seniors got in trouble for Senior Cut Day, and how Naomi White failed all her classes and was going to be held back.

That was the year Abby started weekday shifts at TCBY, and Mrs. Lang used to pick her up in the afternoon when she was finished. Abby would bring Gretchen vanilla in a cup with rainbow sprinkles and Oreo cookie crunch (once Gretchen's throat could handle it) and sit on the other bed in Gretchen's dark room and they'd do magazine quizzes and Abby would read to her: horrifying accounts of skiing accidents from Mrs. Lang's copies of *The Upper Room*, gruesome stories of ballet dancers disfigured in house fires from her copies of *Guideposts*, and the "It Happened to Me" columns from *Sassy* with titles like "My Mom's a Drug Addict" and "I Was Raped."

That was the year Abby and Margaret lobbied Mr. Lang to start paying for cable. When they all pulled together for six weeks to get Gretchen better.

This time, Abby was doing it alone.

Gretchen wasn't in school Thursday or Friday. Abby knew she hated skipping, so she kept calling Gretchen's house, desperate to find out what was wrong, but Gretchen could never come to the phone. Over the weekend, Abby tried to convince Margaret and Glee to drive over with her, but Margaret wasn't having it.

"She can call me and apologize or she can kiss my rooster," Margaret said. "Did you hear what she said about Wallace? Who even *thinks* shit like that?"

Also, she was going out in the boat that weekend.

"I can't come over," Glee said. "It's too upsetting."

"And you're going out in Margaret's boat this weekend," Abby said.

There was a long silence.

"Well, what am I supposed to do?" Glee asked. "Stay home?"

Abby kept calling Gretchen's house until finally Mrs. Lang got sick of it.

"Honestly, Abby, you have to stop calling. It's becoming inappropriate."

After that, she let the machine pick up.

On Monday morning, Mrs. Lang called Abby's house and explained that she would be driving Gretchen to school because they had a doctor's appointment. Abby was tempted to ask what kind of doctor but didn't want to be called inappropriate again—it was a polite way of saying she was tacky—so she kept her mouth shut.

A tropical storm was clawing its way up the coast, pushing massive thunderstorms toward Charleston. It was so dark that Abby drove to school with her headlights on. An angry gray wind ripped down the breezeway, and during first-period Intro to Programming it rattled the door all through class, then changed direction and started screaming through the cracks.

It wasn't until fifth-period Ethics that Gretchen finally arrived. Father Morgan taught the class and he was way too young and looked way too much like a blandly handsome TV weatherman to be taken seriously. So when Gretchen straggled in well after the second bell, holding a late slip, Abby had no problem waving to her while Father Morgan was talking.

"Every week for fourteen years," Father Morgan was saying, "we've been taken on a wonderful journey to a place called Lake Wobegon, a little town of five hundred souls somewhere in Minnesota."

Gretchen looked dully around the room, and Abby waved again.

"Gretchen!" she whisper-hissed.

"It's a town with—yes, Abby?" said Father Morgan.

Abby wilted under the attention of an interrupted teacher, even a lightweight like Father Morgan. "I saved Gretchen a seat," she explained.

"Wonderful," he said, grinning. "Now, while Lake Wobegon feels as real as Charleston, some of you will be surprised to discover that it exists only in the imagination of Garrison Keillor . . ."

Gretchen looked up and down the rows, and Abby waved again.

"Abby?" Father Morgan grinned. "Is this about Lake Wobegon?"

"No, sir," Abby said, dropping her hand.

Gretchen took an empty desk by the door. While Father Morgan went on about Lake Wobegon and the power of storytelling, and the wind rattled the windows, Abby tried to figure out what was wrong. Gretchen looked pale, her hair was lank, and she wasn't even wearing lip gloss. Something white and crusty was caked in the corner of her mouth. Abby worried she had mono again.

Thirty-nine interminable minutes later, the bell rang and everyone ran for the door, shoving their desks back and grabbing their books, overjoyed that they didn't have to listen to Father Morgan anymore. Abby caught up with Gretchen in the crush by the door as the class spilled out into the breezeway.

"What happened?" she asked. "I've been calling you all weekend."

Gretchen shrugged and tried to push her way through the bodies, but Abby would not be denied. She pulled Gretchen up the breezeway, past the waist-high brick wall and into the garden in front of the auditorium. The ground was paved in dark brown brick; the garden was screened from the breezeway by a wall of trees and scattered with benches for private reflection and making out. A cold wind rattled the crepe myrtle branches.

"Leave me alone," Gretchen said.

"What is going on?" Abby asked. "Where have you been?"

Gretchen rubbed her arm where Abby had grabbed it.

"Nothing," she said.

"Why haven't you called?" Abby asked.

"I don't know," Gretchen said, and she seemed genuine.

"Why'd your mom drop you off?" Abby asked.

Gretchen stared over Abby's shoulder.

"Doctor's appointment," she mumbled.

"What kind of doctor?"

The seconds ticked by.

"Did you ask about the flashbacks? Did you tell him you threw up?"

"It wasn't that kind of doctor," Gretchen said, and on the last word her face turned bright red and her forehead furrowed.

Abby didn't understand. "What kind of doctor was it?"

Gretchen sucked in a big whoop of air and began to cry. "To see if I was a virgin," she wailed, covering her mouth with the crook of her elbow to muffle her scream. Then she bit down hard on her arm, her teeth sinking into her sweater as tears slicked her face. Abby pulled Gretchen's arm out of her mouth and led her deeper into the chapel garden, getting her to a bench and sitting her down.

Gretchen slammed her feet on the ground. "Fuck them," she hissed. "Fuck them, fuck them, fuck them. I hate them."

"You *are* a virgin, right?" Abby asked.

Gretchen's eyes zoomed in on Abby.

"You're my best friend," she said. "How can you even say that?"

Abby looked away.

"Why'd they take you?" she asked.

Gretchen stared straight ahead and Abby turned to see where she was looking. Behind her was the auditorium garden, the brick walkway, the sidewalk, and the distant Lawn where fourth graders were filing outside with Mrs. Huddleson's turtles. Abby realized Gretchen wasn't seeing any of it.

"I had to put on a robe that didn't cover anything," Gretchen said. "Then the doctor made me put my feet up in stirrups so he could see everything, and then he stuck his fingers inside of me. They were freezing cold, and afterwards they gave me a tissue to wipe out the grease, but I can still feel it down there."

Gretchen's pupils were pinpoints. She was breathing hard.

"That's sick," Abby said.

"My mom said it's because of the noises," Gretchen whispered. "She and my dad can't sleep at night because of noises in my room."

"What noises?" said Abby.

Gretchen bit a hangnail off her little finger and spat it out. "Sex noises," she said.

Abby didn't understand.

"From your room? What are you doing?"

"Nothing!" Gretchen snapped. "I'm sleeping. I'm finally sleeping. They're liars. And they lied to the doctor, and now he thinks I'm having sex."

"Your mom's crazy," Abby said. "They can't do this. It's child abuse."

Gretchen wasn't listening to her anymore.

"They're going to tell everyone," she said. "They want to get rid of me. They want to send me to Southern Pines."

"Did they say that?" Abby asked.

Southern Pines was worse than Fenwick Hall. Southern Pines was where crazy kids went, and even Riley wasn't bad enough to wind up there. But it existed, somewhere out in North Charleston, the ultimate threat. Cause too much trouble, cross some invisible line, and your parents sent you, like Sweet Audrina in the V. C. Andrews book, to get electroshock therapy and lose your memory, one toasted brain cell at a time.

The fifth-period bell rang.

"The doctor has a file on me," Gretchen said, tears gathering along the bottoms of her eyes as she held up her thumb and forefinger two inches apart. "This thick. I'm not going to let them send me away. You can't let them."

The sky was thick with clouds and a strong wind pulled them to shreds. No one was sending Gretchen away. This kind of thing didn't happen to people like them. Abby found a ragged Kleenex in the bottom of her bag and wiped Gretchen's face.

"It's going to be okay," she said. "You're just tired."

Gretchen jerked her head away.

"If they send me away, I'll kill them both," Gretchen said. "I'll get my dad's gun and kill them both."

"You don't mean that," Abby said.

"I begged them to help me," Gretchen said. "I *begged* them. And they put my name in for prayers at church and—"

Gretchen couldn't go on. She dug her fingernails into her knees, squeezing so hard her wrists shook. Abby tried to pull on them, to make her relax, but Gretchen kept digging in.

"What happened?" Abby asked.

"It was an accident," Gretchen said, letting go of her knees and swiping tears off her face. "I threw up again."

"In church?" Abby asked.

Mute with shame, Gretchen met her eyes and nodded.

"They know you didn't mean it," Abby said.

"They made me eat oatmeal," Gretchen said. "I told them I didn't feel good, but they didn't listen. They decided I had to have breakfast. They decided that's what's good for me. They never ask me what's good for me."

"When's the last time you ate something?" Abby asked, taking Gretchen's left hand in hers.

"I can't," Gretchen said.

"It'll settle your stomach," Abby said. "I'll get you Donut Stix and ginger ale from the machines."

"No!" Gretchen said, pulling her hand away, her eyes wide. "Everything I eat tastes nasty and rotten. I'm so hungry and I'm so tired, I don't know what to do anymore."

Abby put her arm around Gretchen's shoulders and pulled her close while Gretchen buried her head against Abby's chest and hyperventilated. After a few minutes, Abby tried rocking her from side to side. A minute later, Gretchen held her palms out.

"We are the world," she whisper-sang, rocking into Abby from side to side. "We eat the children."

She exhaled sharply through her nose, and now they were both rocking from side to side all cheesy, singing their own private version of "We Are the World."

"We put butter on everything," they both whisper-sang. "And just start chewing."

In sixth grade, Mrs. Gay had made the lower school choir do a special lunchtime performance of "We Are the World." Gretchen had been Kim Carnes. Abby, who had no musical ability whatsoever, was relegated to playing Quincy Jones, standing in front of the choir and pretending to conduct. In blackface.

Now, sitting in front of the auditorium, late for class, they did the Cyndi Lauper part, and the Bob Dylan part, and by the time they'd re-created the Stevie Wonder/Bruce Springsteen duet, Gretchen was dry-eyed enough to clean up her face.

Abby got them both into their next classes with late notes from Miss Toné, and at lunch she bought Diet Cokes for Margaret and Glee and used everything she had to convince them to sit with her and Gretchen.

"She's totally sick," Abby told them. "She wants to apologize, but she feels awful."

Margaret remained unconvinced. Gretchen had made her look bad in front of her senior boyfriend, and she'd never forgive her. But Glee dreaded any kind of unpleasantness.

"It's supposed to be gross all week," Glee said. "Let's sit outside while we can."

"Exactly!" Abby agreed.

Together, they bullied Margaret into going, and for the rest of lunch they all huddled together on the Lawn, under gray skies, and the entire time Abby told herself that it wasn't so bad. But it was. The wind was freezing. Margaret sat on the bench, not talking. Gretchen sat on the grass, not talking. Margaret barely ate. Gretchen barely ate. Abby and Glee had to do enough talking and eating for all four of them.

"Did you do your notecards for *The Scarlet Letter*?" Abby asked Glee.

"Oh my God, it's so boring," Glee said. "And why are we supposed to feel sorry for Hester? She's a tramp."

Abby and Glee talked about the homecoming dance and PSATs and Spirit Week while Gretchen and Margaret stared into space. The conversation limped along until the bell rang and Margaret bolted without a glance back. Glee followed.

Gretchen stayed seated. Abby sat beside her as the Lawn emptied and everyone headed to class. The wind started up again, whipping their hair around. "Margaret's just being Margaret," Abby said. "Let's go."

"I hope she dies," Gretchen said in a low voice. "I hope Wallace gives her AIDS and she dies a slow, miserable death."

"You shouldn't say things like that," Abby said.

"I need you to buy me a phone," Gretchen said, getting up and brushing off her butt.

"Like, a phone phone?" Abby asked, not following.

"Go to a thrift store. You can get one for ten bucks," Gretchen said. "I'll pay you back."

She grabbed her bookbag, hefted its strap over one shoulder, and started walking. Abby tried to keep up. "I've got TCBY tonight," she said. "I don't get off until nine."

"My mom's having book club at our house," Gretchen said. "Just come over. She'll be drunk."

Abby was about to ask why she needed a phone when Gretchen suddenly leaned over and gave her a hug. Abby caught a whiff of something sour.

"No matter what happens," she said. "I'll never hurt you."

For the rest of the day, Abby wondered why Gretchen thought she needed to say that.

BROKEN WINGS

Mom cars spilled out of the Langs' driveway and lined Pierates Cruze—Volvos and Mercedes and Jeep Grand Cherokees parked fender to fender in front of the neighbors' houses. Abby spotted a space in front of Dr. Bennett's and pulled the Bunny onto his grass. Before she even turned off her ignition, the front porch lights came on and Dr. Bennett was standing outside, shaking his finger at her. Embarrassed, Abby drove around the block and parked in the Hunts' front yard instead.

The Cruze was dark. The air was heavy and the wind was wet. The bamboo grove next to Gretchen's house rustled and sighed. Abby was always welcome to walk into Margaret's and Glee's houses, but she had to ring the doorbell at Gretchen's. Because tonight was book club, she didn't know whether she should ring or just slip inside, but as she came up the walkway the sound of women laughing got louder and Mr. Lang came out the door.

"Hey, Mr. Lang," Abby said.

"Oh, Abby," he said, closing the door and muffling the raucous lady laughter. "That's a wild bunch."

"Yes, sir," Abby said.

They stood there. The wind changed direction. Another peal of laughter erupted inside.

"Can I go see Gretchen?" Abby asked.

"Is Gretchen all right?" Mr. Lang asked at the same time.

They both paused, caught off guard by their accidental jinx.

"Um, yes, sir," Abby said.

Over the years, Abby had engaged in very few adult conversations with Gretchen's dad, mostly because she'd learned to be wary of them. Usually they involved her being led through a series of rhetorical questions that ended with a lecture on trickle-down economics, the Evil Empire, or the real solution to the homeless problem.

"You can talk to me, Abby," Mr. Lang said. "Right? We understand each other?"

She thought about Mr. Lang looking through Gretchen's notebooks to see if she'd been doodling boys' names in the margins. She thought about the doctor telling him that his daughter's virginity was intact.

"We understand each other perfectly," Abby said.

"If something is happening with Gretchen, I'd like to think you'd tell me."

Behind him, heat lightning flickered on the horizon.

"Sure," Abby said. "Can I go upstairs?"

He considered her for a minute, trying to peer through Abby's skull with his lawyer eyes, then stepped aside. "Go on," he said. "I have to get the cat."

"What cat?" she asked, reaching for the door handle.

Mr. Lang started toward the back of the house.

"There's a dead cat on the lower level," he said.

"Whose is it?" Abby asked.

"We've got owls," he said. "They've been carrying off cats all week. Just snatching them up. It's a mess."

"Abby!" Gretchen said, exploding out of house. Talking and noise and laughter poured through the open door; Gretchen grabbed Abby's arm and pulled her inside. "Stop bothering my friend," she snapped at her dad.

The house was bright white and filled with the smell of flowers and the sound of happy women in the living room.

"Yoo-hoo!" Mrs. Lang called. "Is that Abby Rivers?"

Gretchen took the white carpeted stairs two at a time, pulling Abby behind her, turning back over her shoulder to shake her head. Abby paused at the top of the stairs and leaned over the rail.

"Hi, Mrs. Lang!" she called, and then she was in Gretchen's room and Gretchen was closing the door. The air-conditioning was on subzero, so Abby pulled her sleeves down over her hands.

"Did you get it?" Gretchen asked, plucking at Abby's bookbag.

Abby opened her bag and produced the beige Trimline phone she'd bought from First Baptist Mission for eleven dollars. There was a scuff mark on one end, and it was spattered with white paint. Gretchen snatched it, bounced over her twin beds, and crouched on the carpet to plug it into the jack behind her headboard. Then she lifted the receiver and grinned.

"Dial tone!" she whispered.

She unplugged the cord, wrapped it around the phone, and opened her closet. Max stood up stiffly and crawled out from underneath Gretchen's desk, yawning and stretching. While Gretchen buried the phone in her closet, the dog trotted over and stuck his cold nose into Abby's hand.

When Gretchen emerged, Abby noticed the dark circles under her eyes and that her skin was cloudy. Her jaw was tight and she was jumpy, but she didn't seem quite as exhausted as before.

"Come on," Gretchen said, heading into her bathroom. "I'm doing my hair."

Gretchen stood at the counter while Abby lowered herself into the empty bathtub and stretched out. She liked sitting in Gretchen's tub. It was her thing. Max settled himself in the doorway. He never came into the bathroom because he was scared of floor tiles.

"They took away my phone privileges," Gretchen said, focusing on her reflection, lifting a long section of hair straight up. "But I still need to call Andy."

"You need to call Margaret," Abby said, her feet propped against the wall.

Gretchen lifted the crimping iron. "I'm not apologizing. Everything I said was true, and Margaret knows it. That's why she's mad."

"Wallace totally deserves to be barfed on," Abby said. "But he is her boyfriend."

Gretchen squeezed the crimping iron and held it for five seconds. The bathroom filled with the smell of hot hair.

"Margaret's so far up his butt, she's lost her identity," Gretchen complained.

"What're you doing to your hair?" Abby asked.

"Andy told me I should embrace change."

A muffled burst of laughter rose through the floor. Abby wished she could go downstairs. She wanted to see the book club. She wanted to be around their jokes and their gossip. She wanted to see if Mrs. Lang had made those miniature quiches.

"I hope we still laugh like that when we're their age," Abby said.

"They're drunk," Gretchen said. "I'd rather die than turn into them."

More laughter filtered through the floor. At the sound, Gretchen tightened her lips; she released the crimping iron with a *clack*, sniffed her warm length of hair, and then moved on to the next section.

"Wallace is lame," Abby said. "But you need to be diplomatic if we're all going to stay friends."

Gretchen squeezed the crimping iron so hard her knuckles turned white.

"Maybe I don't want to be friends," she said.

Abby couldn't even process this. How do you decide you don't want to be friends anymore? How do you toss aside people you've known for years?

"But they're our *friends*," she said.

It was the best she could do.

"Listen to them," Gretchen spat as more laughter shook the floor. "They're giving me a headache. You should have heard my mom going on about her 'problem daughter.' How I'm 'troubled' and how she's 'crucified on the cross of my adolescence.' They're such hypocrites, it makes me sick."

She put down the crimping iron and turned her head from side to side in the mirror.

"Does this look hot? Or bizarre?"

"I liked your hair the way it was," Abby said.

She used the toe of her sneaker to raise and lower the lever that opened and closed the tub drain. Gretchen lifted another section of hair and kept crimping. Abby caught a whiff of that sour smell again.

"I'm so sick of my stupid hair," Gretchen said. "I'm so sick of it just hanging down, making me look like Pony and Grace's perfect daughter. 'Hello, I am the Gretchen Robot. Would you like to have two-point-five babies and move to the suburbs?'"

"Your parents aren't evil or anything," Abby said. "They're doing the best they can."

"You're so naive," Gretchen said. "Did you know Molly Ravenel was sacrificed to Satan?"

The abrupt change in conversation left Abby confused.

"I think she went to Davidson," she said. "Like, years ago. Isn't her brother in student vestry?"

Gretchen ignored the question. "When we were in seventh grade, a bunch of seniors were in a cult and Molly was spying on them in the woods. They caught her and cut out her tongue and her heart."

"That story's been around for ages," Abby said. "The first time I heard it was back in fourth grade. They used to say it about anyone who transferred senior year."

"It's not a joke," Gretchen said. "Even Andy knew about it. The school hushed it up because they didn't want enrollment to drop, and her parents got paid off to keep quiet. So Molly's body is buried out there in the woods and everyone acts like it's normal. Our parents don't actually care what happens to us unless it makes them look bad, and then they send us to Southern Pines to get reprogrammed."

Gretchen lifted another hank of hair and placed it in the crimping iron.

"That's unicorns," Abby said, moving her foot to the lever that switched from tub to shower.

"Like Glee was talking about Procter and Gamble," Gretchen said, not even listening. "They give money to satanic churches. And there was that preschool in California that was molesting little kids in tunnels underneath the classrooms. Everyone pretended it was normal for years. No one cares about their kids. They go to church and smile, but there's this dark evil inside of them. You really don't like it?"

Gretchen braced her hands on the sink and struck a dramatic pose, peering at her reflection through crimped bangs. Abby didn't like the way it looked at all. It made Gretchen look older, like she could get into clubs.

"It's okay." Abby shrugged, trying to mash the shower/tub lever with her toe.

Abby liked Gretchen's hair because it was thick and blond and full. Abby had bleached her hair so many times that it was wispy and thin, swirling around her head in a cotton candy cloud. Gretchen didn't know what she had, and when it was gone she was going to miss it.

"You shouldn't be obsessed with all this dark stuff," Abby said. She repositioned the ball of her sneaker on the shower/bath switch and started pressing it to the right.

"This stuff is important," Gretchen said, releasing the crimping iron and examining her hair from another angle. "You think all these shallow things matter? My mom's stupid book club, and good grades, and Glee having the hots for Father Morgan, and whether Margaret should break up with Wallace Stoney? Those are all distractions."

"From what?" Abby asked.

"From what's really going on," Gretchen said.

"DBNQ," Abby said. "But you used to think unicorns were real."

Gretchen turned around.

"Extinct," she said. "I thought they were extinct."

"They had to be real to become extinct," Abby said.

A foul odor rolled through the room. It was hot and squalid, sharp and bitter, worse than anything Abby had ever smelled.

"Max!" Gretchen said, hauling him out of the doorway by his collar.

As she did, he cut another dog fart. This one squeaked.

"That's what Max thinks!" Abby laughed, fanning a hand in front of her face.

Gretchen shut the door against Max and sprayed United Colors of Benetton perfume around the room. They were both cracking up.

"No," Gretchen said. "That's how he agrees with me."

"Max?" Abby called to the door, putting her toe on the shower lever again. "Does your air biscuit signify agreement or—wah!"

The lever moved unexpectedly and the shower head dumped cold water on Abby's crotch. Gretchen burst out laughing.

"Damn Sam!" she howled, then did Coach Greene's voice. "You must learn to protect your . . . Most . . . Precious . . . Gift."

Abby looked down at the wet spot on her uniform pants, then checked her Swatch.

"I should go," she said.

Gretchen grabbed her hair dryer and started hunting through the counter clutter for the plug. "Hold on," she said. "You're going to run the gauntlet down there. They'll think you wet your pants."

It took them almost half an hour to blow-dry Abby's crotch because they were laughing so hard, and by then it was after ten thirty and book club was breaking up. As Abby and Gretchen hugged, Abby caught another whiff of sour stink.

"Call me," Abby said, but she had a feeling Andy would get top priority.

As Abby walked down the steps, a crowd of tiny women with big blond hair clustered in the front hall, pecking at one another's cheeks and chirping like chickens.

"Abby Rivers!" a very tipsy and delighted Mrs. Lang said, spotting her. "You look adorable in your waitress uniform!"

Abby felt self-conscious as five pairs of eyes swiveled up to her, and widened.

"Isn't she precious!"

"That is too cute!"

The women all giggled, and Abby descended into their midst,

inhaling an eye-watering cloud of Liz Claiborne and Opium by Yves Saint Laurent.

"Let me just squeeze you," Mrs. Lang said, wrapping her arms around Abby, who went with it.

Mrs. Lang had to be pretty drunk because she generally wasn't a hugger. Mr. Lang came out of the TV room to say good-night to the ladies, his forefinger holding his place in *The Cardinal of the Kremlin*; Abby was gently bounced from one cooing southern lady to another as she made her way to the front door. Gretchen's singing cut through everything.

"Oh, I wish I was in the land of cotton!" Gretchen sang in a loud, clear voice, and everyone looked up.

She stood at the top of the stairs, one hand on the black metal bannister, chest out, chin raised. Abby always thought Gretchen had a beautiful voice, and now she was projecting, really pushing air through her diaphragm, filling the entire stairwell with clear tones. "Old times there are not forgotten! Look away! Look away! Look away! Dixie Land!"

Everyone paused because no one knew if they should be delighted or insulted. Was this sarcasm or a serenade?

"In Dixie Land where I was born!" Gretchen continued, getting louder, beating out time with the heel of her hand. "Early on one frosty morn! Look away! Look away! Look away! Dixie Land!"

"That's enough, Gretchen," Mr. Lang said.

"What have you done to your hair!" Mrs. Lang gasped.

The ladies were suddenly abuzz, flustered, bumping into one another in the crowded hall, realizing they were in the middle of a family squabble.

"I wish I was in Dixie!" Gretchen shouted, swinging her arms wide. "Hooray! Hooray!"

"Don't make me come up there," Mr. Lang warned, his face turning purple. "Enough."

"In Dixie Land I'll take my stand/to live and die in Dixie!" Gretchen shouted.

Mr. Lang pushed past Abby and headed up the stairs. Abby felt someone claw her shoulder, and she turned to face Mrs. Lang's wild eyes.

"Did you do that?" she demanded. Her lips were wet and her eyes glassy. She was loaded. "Did you ruin my daughter's hair?"

"Away! Away!" Gretchen shouted. "Away down south in Dixie!"

"I'm not her babysitter," Abby said, struggling out of Mrs. Lang's grip.

"Away! Away! Away down south in DIXIEEEE!"

The sound of scuffling and a smack came from the top of the stairs. The ladies gasped. Abby looked up and saw Gretchen holding her cheek and staring at her father.

"That's enough," he said, then turned an apologetic smile to the hallway full of women.

Gretchen started up again. "Hooray! Hooray! To live and die—"

Mr. Lang grabbed her arm, yanking her to one side. Gretchen straightened and somehow Mr. Lang lost his footing. He slipped off the top step, arms windmilling, and tumbled backward. It happened in an instant, but Abby was sure she'd seen Gretchen push him.

Mr. Lang thudded into the wall, his breath slapped out of his lungs in a single shout. He landed hard on his butt, then fell backward down the stairs, his legs cartwheeling over his head. He almost took out Abby when he smashed into the landing.

A moment of silence followed. Gretchen stood frozen at the

top of the stairs, her eyes blazing with wild triumph. Abby was white-knuckling the bannister with both hands. Mrs. Lang was opening and closing her mouth. The book club ladies were all frozen. No one dared to move.

Mr. Lang struggled into a seated position.

"I'm okay," he said. "I—"

BANG!

Everyone turned toward the living room. The wall at the far end was made of glass, and lying at its base was a flapping pigeon that had broken its neck. Just as Abby was about to turn away, another *BANG* sounded and a seagull hit the window, smearing blood on the glass. *TOK! TOK! TOK!* Three sparrows smacked into the glass, one after the other.

One of the ladies began to recite the Lord's Prayer as bird after bird flew into the window; within minutes the concrete walkway was littered with stunned seagulls wandering in circles, dragging broken wings, dead sparrows on their backs, talons slowly curling, twitching pigeons, a pelican in a heap, beak open unnaturally wide, slowly turning its head from side to side.

The house vibrated as birds dove into upstairs windows, the skylight, the side windows—one after the other without pause. It sounded as though invisible hands were knocking all over the house, saying, "Let me in, let me in." Three of the women held hands and prayed. Mrs. Lang raced to the enormous window at the end of the room and waved her arms, trying to shoo away the birds so they wouldn't fly into the glass, but they kept coming.

Two owls swooped out of the darkness and landed among the stunned and dying birds, their talons digging into soft bodies. They strutted through this morbid buffet, dipping their beaks into feathered breasts.

"Dear Jesus," one of the ladies said.

The two owls cornered the pelican, which put up a fight until a third owl dove out of the shadows, talons pinning the pelican's neck to the ground. It tried to get away, thrashing its wings, but the owls were pulling it to pieces. One of its wings streaked blood onto the huge window.

A scream ripped loose, high pitched and pained, making the air in the stairwell vibrate, drowning out the sound of birds hitting the house. As it drilled into Abby's eardrums, she looked up to see Gretchen on her knees at the top of the stairs, clutching both sides of her head, digging her fingers into her frizzy hair, screaming, "Make it stop! Make it stop! Make it stop!"

It didn't.

PARANOIMIA

The next morning was so dark that the streetlights were still on when Abby got in the Dust Bunny and drove to Gretchen's. She'd raced through putting on her face because she needed to hear what happened after Mr. Lang had limped up the stairs and pulled Gretchen's hands away from her ears. After he'd wrapped his arms around her. After he'd muffled her screams against his chest. After the book club ladies had run for their cars. After Mrs. Lang had noticed that Abby was still there and rushed her out of the house.

"Please," she'd said, closing the door in Abby's face. "We need some time."

Abby pulled onto Pierates Cruze, and the Bunny's headlights swept over three bulging trash bags piled at the end of the Langs' driveway. A whirl of stray feathers blew around them. The bags were lumpy and dimpled with talons and beaks.

Gretchen was waiting on the side of the driveway closest to Dr. Bennett's house, shoulders hunched, wind tossing around the stiff ends of her frizzy hair. She was wearing the same skirt from the day before. Abby pulled up and Gretchen slammed into the Bunny, and they took off.

"Are you okay?" Abby asked. "What happened? Did you get in trouble?"

Gretchen shrugged.

"I don't know," she said.

"But you pushed your dad!" Abby said, pulling onto Pitt Street. "I saw you."

Gretchen shook her head.

"I don't know," she said. "My head was killing me. I just remember getting angrier and angrier and then my brain went white. I tried to tell them how I can't sleep, but they never listen."

She started to gnaw on her nails.

"Did your dad have to clean up all the birds?" Abby asked.

Gretchen nodded, miserable.

"Dr. Bennett came over to help but they wound up fighting," Gretchen said. "My dad says there were more than a hundred. Every time I started to fall asleep, I heard them again."

They were driving on Coleman Boulevard now, approaching the last traffic light before the bridge.

"How much trouble are you in?" Abby asked, stopping as the light turned red.

Gretchen shrugged.

"We're going to have a 'family meeting' tonight," Gretchen said, making quote marks with her fingers. "I'm supposed to sit and listen while they tell me what my problems are."

Before Abby could ask anything else, the light changed and the Bunny shifted into the lane that went over the old bridge. The old bridge—a two-lane tightrope with no sidewalks—stretched over the Cooper River for three miles before dropping cars onto the crosstown express, which ran along the trashy northern edge of downtown, where all the fast food restaurants were.

It made everyone nervous. The lanes were too narrow; one four-inch drift and you'd knock off your side mirror on the steel rails that whipped past your ears. A newer, wider bridge ran parallel to the old one, with three lanes and actual shoulders and sidewalks, but only one of its lanes ran downtown, so it was bumper-to-bumper this early. Every morning you had to pick your poison: new and slow or old and fast. Today, Abby went with old and fast.

The wind howled, trying to shove the Dust Bunny into the other lane as Abby held on to the wheel for dear life. They were roaring down the backside of the first span, cars screaming by close enough to swap paint.

"I hear voices," Gretchen said.

"What?"

"They tell me things."

"Okay."

Abby couldn't say any more because they had reached the long curve at the bottom of the first span, where the worst accidents happened.

"They won't leave me alone," Gretchen said. "Someone's always whispering in my ear. It's worse than the touching."

Abby powered the Dust Bunny up the second span, wondering if this would be the day its engine finally exploded. Her foot mashed the accelerator all the way to the floor, but other cars kept passing them.

"What do they say?" Abby asked, shouting over the noise of the engine as they crested the peak of the second span.

The Bunny was in the homestretch, with Abby riding the brakes down the final drop onto the crosstown.

"They tell me things," Gretchen said. "About people. About Glee and Margaret. About Wallace and my parents. And you."

They leveled out on the crosstown, their speed dropping from fifty to thirty-five, and Abby was able to stop thinking about sudden death and focus on what Gretchen was saying.

"You already know everything about me," she said. "I'm stupid, Gretchen. I don't understand all these hints and riddles. If you want to tell me something, just say it."

Abby shifted gears. Gretchen dropped back in her seat.

"They told me you wouldn't understand," she said.

And that was the moment Gretchen started to pull away, and there wasn't a thing Abby could do to stop her.

It wasn't that Abby didn't try. She had three classes with Gretchen: Intro to Programming, U.S. History, and Ethics. She saw her at lunch. She saw her at fourth-period break. And every time, she made sure she told a funny story about a lame customer at TCBY or about something ridiculous that Hunter Prioleaux said in class. Anything to distract Gretchen, to get her mind off home, to make her laugh.

Nothing worked.

At lunch she tried to convince Glee and Margaret to sit with them.

"We're not talking to Gretchen," Margaret said.

"Anymore or right now?" Abby asked.

Margaret rested her shoulder blades against the wall as Glee rooted around inside her locker, hunting for her lunch.

"She's spastic," Margaret said. "You know that, right? She's gone fucking schizo."

Abby was shaking her head before Margaret even finished.

"There's something wrong with her," she said. "Like, for real. We can't ditch her now."

"We aren't ditching her," Margaret said. "She ditched us."

Margaret talked in a way that made Abby feel helpless. Everything was the way Margaret said it was, and if you didn't agree you were a moron. Arguing was useless.

"But we're her friends," Abby said.

"We're taking a Gretchen vacation," Margaret said. "So you can hang with us or hang with her. Come on if you're coming."

Then she pushed herself off the lockers and headed toward the Lawn.

Abby turned to Glee, who was pulling out her Tupperware lunchbox.

"She's your friend, too," Abby said.

"Sophomore year is the most important one on your transcript," Glee said. "So that's cool if you want to stick with Gretchen, but I'm staying out of it. I've got too much on my plate."

She closed her locker and spun the combination.

"You're already in it," Abby said.

"Not if I don't want to be," Glee said, and then she followed Margaret.

Abby couldn't entirely blame them. It was getting harder and harder to be seen with Gretchen. At first she'd just recycled the same calf-length gray skirt that she wore too often anyways because some senior once said it made her look hot. Then Abby noticed that Gretchen wasn't wearing makeup anymore. Her nails were always dirty and she was chewing them again.

Plus, she was starting to smell. This was no simple whiff of bad breath; it was a constant sour stink, like the boys after PE. Every morning Abby wanted to crack her window, but they had a rule: the Bunny's windows stayed up on school days. Otherwise, she'd have to respray her hair when they got to Albemarle.

"Did you step in something?" Abby asked one morning, trying to drop a hint.

Gretchen didn't answer.

"Can you check your shoes?" Abby said.

Gretchen was silent. It had gotten to the point where Abby wondered if she spoke at a pitch Gretchen couldn't hear. Some mornings Gretchen would pull out her daybook and scribble in it, not saying a word all the way to school. Other mornings she would pull it out and let it sit unopened in her lap. This morning was a scribbling day, and Abby was grateful to pull onto the old bridge so she could focus on something besides the sound of Gretchen scratching away in her book.

There were no more 11:06 phone calls because Gretchen never called anymore. Abby still called Gretchen's house, but Gretchen was always taking a nap or doing homework. Mrs. Lang would keep Abby on the phone, asking if Gretchen was seeing someone, or if she'd said she was feeling sick, or if she'd seemed a little funny recently. She burbled and chirped, circling around the question she couldn't bring herself to ask: What was wrong with her daughter? Abby wanted to ask the same thing: What were they doing to Gretchen? After the doctor, after the book club, Abby had a good idea that whatever was making Gretchen lose her mind was happening at home, behind closed doors. She was too polite to hang up on Mrs. Lang, so she faked conversation; when that got too hard, she stopped calling altogether.

PSATs were coming up, and Kaplan books started appearing underneath everyone's arms. Glee had already taken them once the year before, and Margaret had a tutor; normally, Abby would be studying with Gretchen, but now she sat alone in her room every night, burying herself in test prep, unable to focus on the practice questions; she was trying to think of how to get through to Gretchen.

Gretchen was still wearing the same skirt, and by the second week she had started recycling her blouse, too. It was a plaid Esprit top in electric blue, belted at the waist. After a few days, she stopped wearing the belt, which made it look like a shapeless sack. Worst of all, her skin started breaking out. Tiny inflamed pimples appeared all around her nose.

One morning while they were waiting at the stoplight on the crosstown, the minor-key piano opening of "Against All Odds" started playing on 95SX. They had a rule that whenever Phil Collins came on the radio, they had to stop everything and sing along. This morning, Abby was ready.

"Cow Chicken is eating all my hay," Abby sang to Gretchen, replacing the lyrics with rhyming nonsense. This never failed to crack Gretchen up. "And she's pecking at my face/I can't take this pecking anymore . . . can you . . . oooOOO/She's the only one/ Who ever pecks me at all."

Gretchen was supposed to pick up the second verse, but as the synthesizers swelled and the traffic light changed, no one was singing in the car except Phil. Abby couldn't stand it.

"Come on, ladies," she said, calling out like a cheesy piano player. "You know the words."

Gretchen looked out her window at the passing fast-food restaurants. Abby had no choice but to jump in on the chorus.

"So take a look at my cow/She's got a chicken face/And there's no one left here to remind me/That she comes from outer space."

Once Abby started she couldn't stop, so she kept up with the song all the way through the chorus, feeling like a dweeb for singing her heart out and being completely ignored. Then she stopped abruptly, as if she was never really planning to get much into the second verse anyway. The rest of the drive passed in silence.

Gretchen kept her sleeves rolled down no matter how warm the weather was. Some mornings she showed up with filthy Band-Aids on her fingertips. Her breath got worse. Her tongue became coated in a thick white film. The crimping had turned her hair into a frizzy nest barely controlled by a scrunchie, and her lips were always chapped. She looked beaten, exhausted, hunched over, wrung dry. Abby wondered how she made it past her mom every morning.

The first teacher to say something was Mr. Barlow. After Gretchen fell asleep twice in first period, he held her back after class. Abby waited until she came slouching out of his office.

"What'd he say?" she asked as Gretchen brushed past her.

Before she could answer, Mr. Barlow called Abby into his tiny office. The room reeked of Gretchen's sour sweat. Mr. Barlow was pounding on his window with the heel of his hand, trying to get it open.

"I don't know what's going on with Gretchen," he said, giving up on the window and turning on a desk fan. "But if you care about your friend, you need to get her off whatever she's on."

"What?" Abby asked.

"What?" Mr. Barlow mimicked. "I'm not an idiot. I know what drugs are. If you're really her friend, get her to stop."

"But, Mr. Barlow—" Abby said.

"Save it," he snapped, dropping into his chair and picking up a stack of test papers. "I said my piece, you heard me, and the next person I'll tell is Major. I'm giving you a chance to help your friend. Now get to class."

Abby realized that no one was going to do anything. For five years, Gretchen had been the perfect Albemarle student, and the faculty still saw what they were used to seeing—not what was really happening. Maybe they chalked it up to PSAT stress or problems at home. Maybe they figured that tenth grade was a tough transition. Maybe they were caught up in their own divorces and career dramas and problem kids, and if she still wasn't turning things around on Monday they'd say something. Or maybe the following Monday. Or the Monday after that.

Something was changing inside Gretchen. Maybe it was the acid, maybe it was Andy, maybe it was her parents, maybe it was something worse. Whatever it was, Abby had to keep trying. She couldn't abandon her friend because soon Gretchen would be ready to talk. Any minute now she'd look up from her daybook and say, "I have to tell you something serious."

The next day was Wednesday, and when Gretchen got into the Dust Bunny, Abby was relieved: she was still wearing the same clothes but didn't smell bad. Maybe Mr. Barlow had gotten through to her after all.

Then a new smell hit her: United Colors of Benetton perfume. Gretchen was drenched in it. She'd gotten a bottle from her parents two years ago, and it quickly became her signature scent. That morning, Gretchen reeked of it. Abby's eyes were still burning when she walked into first period.

Later that day, Abby went against her better judgment and appealed to a higher authority. She came back from TCBY and found her mother balancing the checkbook at the dining room table. Abby's mom took every shift that came her way, sleeping at patients' houses three times a week in case they woke up in the middle of the night and needed someone to change their Depends. Abby mostly saw her in passing or asleep on the sofa, or she heard her coughing behind a closed bedroom door. Clueless as to how to start a conversation, she hovered awkwardly by the couch until her mom noticed.

"What?" Mrs. Rivers said without looking up.

Abby dove in before she could second-guess herself.

"Do you ever have patients who hear voices?" she asked. "Like voices that talk to them all the time and tell them things?"

"Sure," her mom said. "Nutjobs."

"Well," Abby said, forging ahead, "how do they get better?"

"They don't," her mom said, tearing up a stack of voided checks. "We put them on pills, send them to the nuthouse, or hire someone like me to make sure they don't chug-a-lug the Drano."

"But there has to be something you can do," Abby said. "To make them like they used to be."

Abby's mom was exhausted but she wasn't stupid. She took a sip of her Diet Pepsi and looked at her daughter.

"If this is about Gretchen, and it usually is," she said, "then it's none of your beeswax. You worry about you and let Gretchen's parents worry about Gretchen."

"Something's wrong with her," Abby said. "You could talk to her parents, or we could go over there together. They'd listen to you."

"Families like that don't listen to other people," Mrs. Rivers said. "You get in the middle of whatever this is and you'll be giving them an excuse to blame you for everything."

Abby was reeling. Deep down she thought that, too, but it sounded so unfair coming out of her own mother's mouth. Her mom didn't know anything about the Langs.

"You're just jealous that I have friends," she shot back.

"I see the friends you have," Abby's mom said. "And they're of no consequence. You've got big things ahead of you, but these girls will wear you out and drag you down."

Abby's chest prickled with heat. Her mom had never expressed an opinion about Abby's friends—and she was horrified to hear how twisted and misguided it was. Her mom didn't know anything about her friends.

"You don't even have friends," Abby said.

"Where do you think they went?" Abby's mom asked. "Charleston people like the Langs, they only want easy times. The minute it rains, watch them run."

Words could not express the frustration Abby felt.

"You don't understand anything," she said.

Her mother looked genuinely surprised.

"Good God, Abby. Where do you think I grew up? I understand these people better than you."

"I shouldn't have said anything," Abby said.

Her mom massaged the bridge of her nose. She started talking while her eyes were still closed.

"When I was your age, I trusted the wrong people," she said. "I was silly when I should have been serious. I let myself get in over my head. Those girls are not the same as you. If they make a mistake, their parents can buy their way out of it. But people like us? We take one wrong step and it haunts us forever."

Abby wanted to say that her mom was wrong. She wanted to force her to see that they were nothing alike; but she was so angry, her throat couldn't form the words.

"I never should have talked to you!" she shouted and stormed off to her room.

On Monday, Abby pulled up in front of the Langs' house and saw that Max had knocked over the garbage cans again and pulled a bag into the center of Dr. Bennett's yard, where he was ripping it apart. When Abby pulled the emergency brake, Max yanked his nose out of the white plastic and ran away. That's when Abby saw that the bag was full of used Maxipads and tampons, a whole pile of them, saturated with clotted black blood.

Abby was debating whether to clean up the mess or honk the horn when Dr. Bennett came around the Cruze from the opposite direction. He was returning from his morning walk, swinging the cane he'd made out of a sawed-off broomstick, a rubber cap nailed to one end.

He saw the bloody garbage strewn across his grass at the exact moment Gretchen emerged from her house, looking dazed and still wearing the same outfit as the day before. From inside the Dust Bunny with the windows rolled up, the whole scene was like a silent movie, with Dr. Bennett shouting at Gretchen, punctuating his sentences by whacking the garbage bag with his stick. Gretchen replied by raising her middle finger, and Abby read her lips:

"Fuck you."

Abby's spine stiffened; she didn't know what to do. Get out? Stay in the car? Dr. Bennett was coming at Gretchen faster than Abby had ever seen him move, passing in front of the car's hood and swinging his stick at Gretchen's legs. Gretchen hit him with her bookbag, knocking him against Mrs. Lang's Volvo. He was shouting again, and then Mr. Lang was running out of the house, with Mrs. Lang right behind him in a pink sweatsuit.

Abby watched Mr. Lang mouth the words "Whoa, whoa, whoa, whoa!" as he put himself between Dr. Bennett and his daughter, and then the two men were tussling, grabbing each other's shirt collars.

Gretchen, forgotten for the moment, ran around the back of the Dust Bunny and yanked open the door, shouts filling the car as she dropped into her seat in a nostril-searing cloud of United Colors of Benetton.

"Go," she said.

Abby hit the accelerator, sending rocks spraying from underneath her tires. They flew through the Old Village. At the first stop sign Abby really looked at Gretchen, trying to see who was there, not just who had always been there before. Angry pimples were smeared across Gretchen's chin, infected whiteheads grew in the creases next to her nostrils, dry scabs were encrusted on her forehead. Her breath smelled bad. Her teeth were yellow. Crust was caked in the corners of her eyes. She stank of perfume.

Someone had to do something. Someone had to say something. Teachers weren't doing it. Her mom wasn't going to do it. The Langs wouldn't do it. That left Abby.

Traffic on the bridge was light because they were running late, so Abby veered left onto the new bridge. As they started to climb the first span, with the Bunny's engine having a heart attack underneath the hood, she finally said it.

"What's happening to you?" Abby asked.

At first she thought Gretchen wasn't going to say anything, but then she spoke, her voice hoarse.

"I need you to help me," Gretchen said.

Abby levitated.

"Anything," she said.

"You have to help me . . ." Gretchen repeated, her voice trailing off. She chewed her fingernails.

"Help you what?" Abby asked, riding the brakes downhill.

"You have to help me find Molly Ravenel," Gretchen said.

Abby's heart sank and then shattered into pure rage. She'd spent weeks worrying about what to do, and now Gretchen was talking about a stupid urban legend?

"I don't care about Molly Ravenel!" Abby shouted. "Why are you acting this way?"

"We have to dig her up and give her a Christian burial," Gretchen gabbled, leaning close. "She's underneath the blockhouse on Margaret's land in Wadmalaw, rotting in the dirt because Satan put her there, because he ate her soul. But if we can bury Molly, save Molly, if we can get Molly out—"

"Shut up!" Abby screamed as the Bunny wheezed up the second span. "Shut up! Shut up! Shut up! I'm the only friend you have left and I have stuck by you even though everyone says I shouldn't, and you finally talk to me and it's this crazy kindergarten junk? I don't know who you are anymore!"

"I'm me," Gretchen said. "Am I? Maybe I'm someone else? No, I'm still me; it hasn't happened yet, it can't have happened yet. I'm still me, I'm still myself. You have to believe I'm still me."

Abby decided that Gretchen needed a dose of reality. Everyone was tiptoeing around her and acting like nothing was wrong. Someone had to confront her.

"If you don't start talking normally," Abby said, "I will ditch you and I will never talk to you again, and then you'll be all alone and—"

Gretchen lunged across the gearshift and grabbed the wheel. They were in the downtown lane and Gretchen jammed the wheel hard to the left, sending the Bunny careening into oncoming traffic, steering straight into the grill of a navy-blue pickup truck.

"No!" Abby screamed.

Her instinct was to jam on the brakes, but the pickup was too close. Abby could see the driver: no shirt, mullet rippling in the wind, his cigarette falling out of his mouth, grabbing the top of his wheel with both hands. The car behind them laid on its horn. Abby cranked the wheel to the right, but Gretchen fought her. The Bunny's tires flickered and wobbled, and then Abby elbowed Gretchen hard in the ear. Gretchen snapped back in her seat, her head knocking into the window, and Abby hauled hard to the right, praying there wasn't a car where she wanted to go.

The Bunny dipped its hood dangerously low to the asphalt, then swerved back into the right-hand lane with a sickening lurch. Abby had overcorrected, and now she heard that sound in movies when tires squeal; she smelled burning rubber. The Bunny flew at the side of the bridge with its thin steel railing, and Abby saw the hood hitting the metal and her rear end lifting, and then the Bunny flipping end over end into space, falling, falling, hitting the water eighty feet below, hard as concrete.

And then they were back in their lane like nothing had happened, the Bunny doing a cool fifty-five miles per hour. A Creekside mom in a freshly washed station wagon honked as she flew past on the left. The back end of the navy-blue pickup was in the rearview mirror, disappearing toward Mt. Pleasant; Gretchen was leaning against her door, cradling one ear.

Abby's heart was banging against her ribcage as they rode over the next span and then got off the bridge. She took a left and pulled into the parking lot outside the old cigar factory and pried her hands off the wheel, one cramped finger at a time. Then she screamed so loudly, her voice bounced off the ceiling.

"What the hell is wrong with you?"

Gretchen buried her face in her hands and unleashed huge wracking sobs that made her shoulders twitch. Maybe she was crying, maybe she was laughing. Abby didn't care anymore. Her anger made her incandescent, screaming, jabbing her finger at Gretchen's shaking back.

"I'm done with you!" she shouted. "You just tried to kill us! I'm done! I'm never talking to you again!"

Gretchen's hand shot out and twisted itself in the sleeve of Abby's shirt.

"Don't," she begged. "Please don't leave me alone. If you leave, I can't do it anymore."

"Then tell me what's happening," Abby said, feeling the adrenaline drain, leaving her hungry and sick.

"I'm so tired," Gretchen said, leaning back in her seat, eyes closing. "I just want to sleep."

"Don't," Abby warned.

"You want to know what's happening?" Gretchen asked. "You want to know what's really happening?"

"What do you think?" Abby asked.

They sat in the Bunny for a long time without talking, and then Gretchen finally told Abby the truth.

KING OF PAIN

"You can't be involved," Gretchen said. "This can't touch you."

"I'm already involved. You almost killed us," Abby said, feeling her stomach tighten and her heart beat faster.

Gretchen wasn't listening. She was looking at Abby pleadingly.

"Can you promise me?" she asked. "Can you promise me that when this is all over, everything will go back to normal?"

"If you don't tell me what's going on right now, then no more phone calls," Abby said. "No more rides to school. Maybe later, after Christmas vacation, but right now I need a break."

"Promise me?" Gretchen demanded, tears slipping out of one eye. The other eye was pink and infected. "Promise me it's not too late for everything to go back to the way it was."

"Then tell me what's happening," Abby said.

Gretchen smeared her shirtsleeve across her face. It came away snotty.

"I've been having my period for two weeks," she said. "I think I'm bleeding to death but my mom won't listen. She buys me pads and I go through five or six a day."

"You have to go to the doctor," Abby said.

"I've been," Gretchen said.

"A different doctor," Abby said. "A real doctor. You could have a disease."

Gretchen's hollow laugh echoed in the Bunny.

"A disease," she repeated. "It's like a disease, sure. I caught it that night at Margaret's."

Abby felt her heart slow, her fists unclench. They were finally getting somewhere.

"What happened?" she asked.

"I'm not a virgin anymore," Gretchen said.

The statement hung in the air between them. It wasn't just that Gretchen had lied to her in front of chapel when she'd asked, but that they had promised not to do this without talking to each other; now Gretchen had crossed a threshold and left Abby behind with the little kids. On the heels of that thought came a more serious one. *That night at Margaret's.* Gretchen hadn't just lost her virginity. This was worse.

"Who was in the woods?" Abby asked.

Abby had read the stories in *Sassy*, she'd seen *The Burning Bed*, she and Gretchen had gone to *The Accused*. If this could happen to Gretchen . . . the thought couldn't fit inside her head. Who would hurt Gretchen? Who would twist her and tear her up and then dump her in the woods like garbage?

"I can't," Gretchen said.

The pieces fit. These were the warning signs in the *Cosmo* features. And if Gretchen couldn't say the name, then it was someone they knew.

"Who was it?" Abby asked.

Gretchen closed her eyes and dropped her chin to her chest. Abby reached out and rubbed her arm. Gretchen flinched. Faces from the yearbook flicked through Abby's head.

"Who?" Abby asked again. "Tell me his name."

"Every night," Gretchen said. "Again and again. He sits on my chest and I can't move. He watches me, and then he hurts me."

"Who?" Abby asked.

"I can't change clothes," Gretchen said. "I have to stay covered. I have to sleep in my clothes and I can't shower because when he sees my skin, he tears it. I can't give him a way in. I have to keep him out. Do you understand?"

Abby was lost. Everything was coming too fast.

"If you tell me his name, we can go to the police," she said.

"Every night . . . ," Gretchen began, then she unbuttoned her left sleeve and rolled it up over her elbow. Three deep vertical slashes ran down her forearm, from her elbow to her wrist. Abby had heard that this was the right way to slit your wrist if you wanted to kill yourself: up and down, not side to side.

She grabbed Gretchen's hand: her skin was ice cold. Abby turned Gretchen's arm backward and forward, then lifted it and looked close. These weren't cuts, they were gouges. Thick, black scabs scaled her skin, surrounded by yellow bruises. Something had dug in and torn out three trenches of flesh.

"What did you do?" Abby asked.

"I can make him stop," Gretchen said. "But I don't want to."

"Why?"

"Because what comes next is worse," Gretchen said, then she pulled her arm away and rolled down her sleeve.

"We need to call the police," Abby said.

"It was in the woods," Gretchen said. "He was waiting for me. It was dark and he was so much bigger . . . he was bigger than a person should be . . ."

So it was true. Someone had been in the woods and attacked Gretchen, and now she was hurting herself again and again as she relived the trauma, punishing herself just like *Seventeen* said. It all made so much sense that, insanely, Abby felt proud for having figured it out.

"We have to tell someone," she said.

Gretchen yawned, a big jaw-cracker, and shook her head.

"No one will believe me," she said.

"They'll believe both of us," Abby said.

Gretchen leaned back against the window, her eyelids heavy. She had delivered her secret to Abby, and now she was drained.

"I know how to stop it," Gretchen said, eyelids drooping. "But if it stops, that's when it starts. If it stops, you'll never see me again."

"I can fix this," Abby said. "I can make it stop. Do you trust me?"

Gretchen nodded, eyes closed.

"I'm so tired," she mumbled. "I don't know how much longer I can do this."

"I'll make it stop," Abby said. "And when it's over, I promise, things will go back to the way they were, okay?"

Gretchen was silent for a long time.

"Okay," she finally said. Then, in a little girl's voice: "I want to go home."

Abby turned the Bunny around and headed back over the bridge. They weren't skipping school; she was taking a sick friend home. She could tell Mrs. Lang what had happened and together they could figure out what to do. This was bad, but nothing was ruined.

She drove into Mt. Pleasant and through the Old Village, never going over twenty-five, her head buzzing with what she would say to Gretchen's mom. By the time they pulled up in front of the Langs' house, she was as ready as she'd ever be, but then she came up short. The driveway was empty.

"Where's your mom?" Abby asked.

"Supposed to be here," Gretchen mumbled.

Abby parked on the street. She grabbed Gretchen's bookbag and led her inside.

Gretchen's house was freezing. The cold cut through Abby's clothes and made her skin ripple with gooseflesh. The refrigerated air stank of Glade, and Lysol disinfectant, and potpourri, and Stick-Ups. Abby saw three Magic Mushroom air fresheners on the hall table, and underneath the chemical scent was something sour and earthy.

She helped Gretchen upstairs. As they neared the second floor, the stench of rotten meat overpowered the air fresheners. When she opened the door to Gretchen's room, Abby stopped in shock. The air fresheners didn't work in here. The stench oozed down the walls, raw and uncut, seeping up from the floor, coating Abby's tongue with grease, soaking into her clothes, burrowing into her hair. She breathed through her mouth and it turned her saliva rancid, dripping thick down the back of her throat. But it wasn't the smell that stopped her.

"Did your mom stop coming in here?" Abby asked.

Every other week, Gretchen's mom waited for her to go to school and then cleaned Gretchen's room, hunting for notes, digging through trash, searching the underwear drawer, hauling away big black garbage bags full of everything she'd decided Gretchen didn't need, leaving the space as sterile and impersonal as a furniture display in a department store. But now, Gretchen's room was a wreck.

Clothes drooled from open drawers, neither of the twin beds were made, the trash can was on its side, and a Diet Coke can lay in the middle of the wall-to-wall white carpet. The walls were scored with black marks. Through the open bathroom door Abby could see the counter thick with balls of used Kleenex, spilled hair product, scrunchies, Band-Aids, Maxipads.

Gretchen squirmed out of Abby's arms and collapsed on one of the unmade beds. She wrapped the comforter around herself and pulled it tight until only her face was showing. She yawned again.

The cold was seeping into Abby's bones. Her arms were shaking.

"Do you have a sweater?" she asked.

Gretchen nodded at her closet.

"There's some in there that he hasn't ruined," she said, thick-tongued.

Abby rumbled open the closet doors and pulled out a red Fair Isle sweater that was cleanish. She pulled the sleeves over her hands like gloves, then sat on the end of the bed, staring at three jagged furrows gouged into the drywall; they extended from just beneath the ceiling all the way down to the headboard. Abby couldn't believe something like that had been allowed to mar Mrs. Lang's perfect house.

Gretchen's eyes were closed, her breathing deep and regular. One filthy hand snaked out from beneath the blanket and clutched Abby's wrist in an ice-cold grip.

"Don't leave me," she mumbled.

After a few minutes, Gretchen's hand opened and fell away. Abby stood up, causing Gretchen's eyes to flicker open and then immediately droop closed again. Abby knew what she had to do. It was going to be the hardest thing she'd ever done in her life, but because it was so hard, it felt right.

She found Mr. Lang's office number on the contact cube next to the kitchen phone.

"Thurman, O'Dell, Huggins, and Krell," a woman said.

"I need to speak to Mr. Lang," Abby said. "It's . . . this is his daughter's friend. It's really important."

She'd crossed the barrier and now Gretchen's parents knew.

She couldn't come back.

"Abby?" Mr. Lang barked. "What happened?"

"I couldn't find Mrs. Lang," Abby said. "So I called you. Gretchen's home and—"

"I'll be right there," he said. "Don't move."

He hung up. Abby stood holding the phone and listening to the refrigerator hum. Then she went back upstairs to wait. Minutes dragged into hours. She found an issue of *Seventeen* and tried to do the "Is Your Best Friend Competing with You?" quiz, but her head was crawling with too many thoughts. She couldn't focus.

Gretchen snored lightly, the way she always did. Abby watched her sleep. When they'd first spent the night together, in fourth grade, Abby had noticed that Gretchen always smiled in her sleep. She'd told her about it the next morning.

"That's because I always have good dreams," Gretchen had said.

Gretchen wasn't smiling now. She looked dead. A wet patch spread across her collar where sweat trickled down her neck. Abby wanted to unwrap the blanket a little, but Gretchen was holding it too tight.

She waited. The phone rang at nine thirty and again at ten fifteen, but Abby didn't know if she should answer, so she let the machine pick up. The only sound in the house was cold air hushing through the vents and, downstairs, the crisp *tock-tock-tock* of the Langs' grandfather clock in the front hall. Gretchen slept, and Abby watched, and after a long while she heard the gravel crunch and car doors slam. Good Dog Max let out a single bark. The Langs were home.

Abby was coming down the stairs as they were walking up to the house. Mrs. Lang was turned away, reprimanding a delighted Max for getting into the garbage again. Mr. Lang was already talking as he opened the glass door.

"Abby, what—" he began.

"Shh," Abby said, putting her finger to her lips and pointing meaningfully upstairs. "She's sleeping."

"Why aren't you in school?" he stage-whispered.

Feeling very important, and a bit unsure of herself, Abby motioned for them to go into the TV room at the front of the house. It was dark in there, far from the stairwell, and way too small for the giant leather sofa that dominated the middle of the room.

"We got a call from the office that you two cut class," Mrs. Lang began.

"I have to tell you something," Abby said. "It's not good."

"We know Gretchen is very sick," Mr. Lang interrupted. "We know she hasn't been herself. We're already taking steps."

"She's in trouble," Abby said. "I think something bad happened."

Mr. Lang gave Mrs. Lang a look. Did they already suspect?

"Abby, what has Gretchen said to you?" Mr. Lang asked. Then, like a typical adult, he didn't wait for her answer. "What Gretchen is going through is very scary, and I don't blame you for backing off from your friendship a little. But we've talked to doctors and they tell us that what's happening is an unfortunate sickness of the mind and spirit that happens sometimes as girls grow up."

Abby knew what kind of doctors they went to.

"Have you seen her arm?" she asked.

Mr. Lang made his sad face.

"I'm sorry you had to see that," he said. "It's terrible when a young person hurts herself. But it can be a reaction to a lot of things. We've found someone in the church who Gretchen can speak to, and that's how she's going to start getting better."

"I know you're as alarmed by her behavior as we are," Mrs.

Lang said, smiling. "But we have everything under control."

Instantly, Abby was furious. How dare they act like they knew what was going on? They didn't know a thing.

"She was raped," Abby said.

Saying "rape" out loud sounded more melodramatic than she intended, but it also wiped the smiles right off their faces. The Langs exchanged another look, as if Abby was being difficult.

"Oh, Lord," Mrs. Lang said.

"You can't toss around those accusations," Mr. Lang said. "You have no idea what's going on here. You're a child."

Abby could tell by their faces that the door was slamming shut. Because they were adults and easily frightened, she had wanted to lay the case out for them one piece of evidence at a time, but now she knew she had to throw it all on the table at once.

"When we were at Margaret's house," she said, "three Saturdays ago. I forget the date." She should have remembered the date. "We took LSD—and I know we shouldn't have, but we'd never done it before, we were just experimenting. I know now that I should have taken better care of Gretchen, but it was our first time and it wasn't very strong. Gretchen got lost in the woods, and it was a few hours before we saw her again, and when we did she was different. I think she's hurting herself . . ." How did this make sense? But then Abby had it again and was galloping forward. "She's reliving the rape every night, like Vietnam veterans have flashbacks. It's my fault; I shouldn't have left her alone when we did the LSD, because that's when it happened. We all swore we wouldn't do it again. I promise."

"You were doing drugs?" Mrs. Lang asked. Abby was frustrated that she was reacting to the wrong thing. "At Margaret Middleton's house, you did drugs?"

"Someone attacked Gretchen," Abby said.

"Where did you get the drugs, Abby?" Mr. Lang said in a controlled voice.

Abby didn't want to tell on Margaret, so she decided to take the blame. Compared to what had happened in the woods, this was small beans.

"They were mine," Abby said. "But it was just an experiment."

Mrs. Lang started toward the door.

"I'm going to check on Gretchen," she said.

Mr. Lang grabbed her arm.

"Grace," he said, "Gretchen's fine. You haven't given her anything today, have you, Abby?"

Abby wanted to be honest, so she thought hard. She hadn't bought her a Diet Coke, or any food; they hadn't even stopped at Wendy's.

"No," she said. "She's asleep."

Mr. Lang steered his wife to the sofa and lowered her gently onto the leather.

"Abby," Mr. Lang said. "We welcomed you into our home. We treated you like family. And you gave our daughter poison."

"The drugs aren't important," Abby said. "I think Gretchen was . . ." But that sounded too qualified, too weak. They needed to know that she had no doubts about what had happened. "I *know* Gretchen was raped, Mr. Lang."

"I asked you if you knew what was happening," Mr. Lang said. "The night of the book club. I asked you to tell me the truth. And the way you lied to my face makes my blood run cold."

Mrs. Lang's eyes were wet as she took both of Abby's hands and held them tight.

"How long has this been going on?" she asked. "No, don't tell me. I know exactly." She raised her eyes to Mr. Lang, who was staring at Abby. "The bloodshot eyes, the messy room, sloppy appearance, loss of appetite, the bad smells. Right under our noses. Right in our own home."

Abby tried to pull away but Mrs. Lang gripped her hands tighter.

"No," she said, "you don't understand. Someone attacked Gretchen. Someone did this to her. The drugs, it was only one time. They're not important."

"Oh, Abby," Mrs. Lang said. "Don't you see? Her sickness starts with you. We've taken Gretchen to the doctor. There was no intercourse. You're the one who hurt Gretchen. You did it, not someone else. You gave her the drugs that made her this way. There's no 'one time' with drugs. And I bet this isn't the first time you've skipped school together."

Abby yanked her hands back and they slipped, sweat-slick, through Mrs. Lang's fingers.

"I'm her friend," she said. "I didn't hurt her. Somebody else did."

"Don't lie to us," Mr. Lang said. "We should have taken steps a long time ago. We thought being around Gretchen would be good for you. Not once did we imagine this is how you'd repay our kindness."

They were acting like they were the victims, and that's what made Abby's mouth start talking before her brain could slow it down.

"Why are you blaming me?" she heard herself say. "You're the ones who dragged her to that doctor who couldn't even tell she wasn't a virgin anymore. You're the ones who spy on her all the time. You did this to her. This is your fault. I'm trying to save her!"

"Is that what the drugs tell you?" Mrs. Lang said.

"I'm not on drugs," Abby shouted. "I'm the only person trying to help Gretchen! You two don't care about her! You just want to control her. You hit Gretchen! All you care about is that she doesn't embarrass you!"

She wasn't even aware of what was coming out of her mouth. She just threw words at them, hearing them only after they were echoing around the room. Mr. Lang cut her off.

"Get out, Abby," he said. "We have given you every chance, but you have poisoned our daughter and our family. If we had known what kind of girl you were, we *never* would have welcomed you into our home. You're lucky I'm not calling the police. I am giving you a very adult second chance right now. I am going to call your mother and let her deal with you, despite all the evidence that she has not done a very good job."

Abby was desperate. Someone had to do something.

"This happened!" she shouted. "You can't make it go away. She was raped!"

Mr. Lang's face turned to stone.

"Let me tell you something, young lady," he said. "If you repeat these vile allegations to anyone, then I will not hesitate to call the police and have you arrested for drugs. And that won't be the end of it. You do not want to see what my lawyer can do to your parents."

Tears spiked out of Abby's eyes. No adult had ever hated her before, and she was reeling. But how could they not believe their daughter had been raped when all the evidence was right there in front of them?

"Is it you?" Abby asked. "Are you protecting someone?" She looked at Mrs. Lang. "Is it him?"

In an instant, Mrs. Lang was off the couch and she had Abby by one arm and was marching her to the door. Abby tried to pull away, but Mrs. Lang dug in her claws, leaving bruises on the soft skin inside Abby's elbow.

“How dare you,” Mrs. Lang hissed, and then she kept hissing the words over and over all the way to the door. “Don’t come back, Abby. Do not come back. Not for a long time. Not ever.”

Then she shoved Abby outside and slammed the door. Through the glass, Abby watched her lock it. They were treating her like a criminal. They were locking their doors like she was some dangerous delinquent. As if she couldn’t just throw one of their stupid modern flowerpots right through the glass and get back inside if she wanted.

Abby walked to the street, the humid air thawing her as she went, and she realized that she was still wearing Gretchen’s sweater. It suddenly felt very precious.

When Abby got home, she saw that the answering machine light was blinking. One unplayed message. Her hand was shaking so hard, it took her three tries to press Play.

“Mary, this is Grace Lang,” Mrs. Lang’s tiny recorded voice said. Even though it was small, Abby could feel it filling her house with contempt. “I am calling because of what we have learned about Abby today—what she came to our house and admitted—and we are shocked. Please call us as soon as you get this message. This matter is very serious, and we hope there’s no need to get the police involved.”

Abby’s head felt light. A high-pitched whine rang in her ears as she pushed Erase, deleting Mrs. Lang’s message forever.

“I’ll save you, Gretchen,” Abby swore to herself. “They can’t stop me from saving you.”

JENNY (867-5309)

The next morning, Abby parked in the student lot and headed straight to the main office.

"Miss Toné," she said, "I need to speak with Major."

There was no emergency that Miss Toné hadn't seen, and since Abby wasn't visibly bleeding she made her wait until the first bell.

"I'll give you a late slip," Miss Toné said. "But you need to take a breath."

Abby kept an eye on the window, trying to see if Gretchen was going to walk into school, but she never appeared. The bell rang and Major came through the door. He liked to roam the halls before first period, handing out demerits for bare shoulders, bizarre fads and fashions, or any sartorial expression of personal identity that had no place at Albemarle Academy. He had just finished writing up Jumper Riley for a dress code violation (hair touching his collar) when he saw Abby and stopped short.

"I'm Abby Rivers," she said. "In tenth grade."

"She's been waiting to speak with you," Miss Toné explained.

Wordlessly, Major beckoned Abby into his office. It had the standard yellow-painted cinderblock walls and institutional furniture. The only decorations were an American flag in the corner, a large framed photo of President Reagan smiling off into the future, and a poster tacked to the back of the door. One half of the poster showed a football player smeared with mud and kneeling on the grass, bearing the words "I quit . . ." On the other half was a giant crucifix atop a hill backlit by the setting sun, saying, "He didn't."

Major settled his bulk behind his desk.

"Major," Abby said. "I need to tell you about something that happened with another student. My best friend? Gretchen Lang? I think a teacher needs to know."

He turned to a file cabinet behind him, withdrew a manila folder, set it in the center of his bare desk, and flipped through the pages. Eventually, he looked up.

"It says here that you're one of our scholarship students, Miss Rivers," Major said.

The digression threw Abby off guard.

"Yes, sir," she said. "I am."

Major nodded to indicate that this point was something they both agreed on.

"In fact, at this time, you're our most senior scholarship student," he rumbled. "That is a great responsibility, Miss Rivers. Our Albemarle family wants to reach down and find outstanding scholars among those less fortunate, then elevate them so that they might enjoy the opportunities of a well-rounded education. But first, you must help yourself."

Abby had no idea what he was talking about, but she did her best to be agreeable.

"Yes, sir," she said. "Exactly. And that's why I wanted to tell you about what happened to Gretchen Lang. She's not a scholarship student," she added lamely.

"No," Major agreed. "I am familiar with Miss Lang's situation. Now, school has already started and you're wasting valuable classroom time, so what is it you have to tell me, Miss Rivers?"

Confronted with having to say it out loud, Abby did her best.

"She was attacked?" Abby said, trying to keep emotion out of her voice. "We were staying at Margaret Middleton's house in Wadmalaw and Gretchen got lost in the woods, and while she was out there someone did something to her. She was gone all night, and now something's really wrong with her."

"She was attacked?" Major repeated.

"Yes, sir."

"By?"

"By . . . a boy?"

"A student?"

"I don't know," Abby admitted.

Major leaned back in his chair, steepled his fingers, and studied the poster on the back of his door for a long moment.

"So you believe that Miss Lang was sexually assaulted?"

Abby felt her heart start to beat again. He was taking her seriously. She nodded.

"Yes, sir," she said.

"And you believe that this crime happened when you were off campus at a slumber party in Wadmalaw on the Middleton family's property?" he asked.

Abby nodded, then followed up with a belated, "Yes, sir."

It felt good to get it off her chest.

"And why isn't Miss Lang here telling me this?" Major asked.

Abby thought about what Gretchen would say if she was sitting there, the star student, scabby and stinking of perfume, hunched over in her chair, mumbling about Molly Ravenel.

"She's a little bit confused," Abby said.

"It might interest you to know that before you arrived this morning, I received a telephone call," Major said. "Can you guess who it was? No? It was Gretchen Lang's mother. She was worried that you and her daughter had had a falling out. She thought you might try dragging her daughter's name through the mud. She told me she was concerned with the nature of your friendship with her daughter. The word she used, I believe, was 'inappropriate.' Do you understand what I'm saying?"

Abby's head felt hollow. She was suddenly self-conscious about how young she was. How young and how stupid.

"I do not currently have an opinion on the nature of your friendship with Miss Lang," Major rolled on. "But I am rapidly developing one. I noted your unexcused absence yesterday. I have noted the recent changes in Miss Lang's behavior. Do not think I am unaware of students on this campus who are selling and consuming narcotics, Miss Rivers. I have made it my mission to discover who those students are, and I have been watching Miss Lang very closely. And after this phone call from Mrs. Lang, I am now watching you very closely as well. A worried mother's allegations are not the same thing as proof, but if I find that you are in any way responsible for the change in Gretchen Lang's behavior, if I find that you are her 'dealer,' I will turn you over to the authorities. Needless to say, that will be the end of your academic career."

He closed Abby's file and rested his palm on its cover.

"I am going to do you a great favor, Miss Rivers," he said. "The Lang family has been an integral part of the Albemarle community for many years, and Frank Middleton is an active and generous alumnus of this institution. I have no wish to inconvenience them with your wild allegations, which I am assured by Mrs. Lang are baseless. I realize that attending Albemarle is a challenge for you, and while you have risen to face it in the past, that is no guarantee you will continue to do so in the future. This goes no further, but I have my eye on you, Miss Rivers."

Abby couldn't get enough air. She was stupid to think that she was smarter than Mrs. Lang. Of course she had called the school.

Abby wanted to go back and start over, to do this differently, but it was too late. She had blown her chance.

"Get to class," Major said. "I will not be writing you a late slip, and let us consider that your reprimand. Reflect on how you have repaid Miss Lang's friendship. Faith and Honor, Miss Rivers. Do you have them?"

For the rest of the morning, Abby was wrapped in cotton, floating through her classes in a daze. Mrs. Erskine called on her and she didn't know who wrote *Sinners in the Hands of an Angry God*. In Biology, Mrs. Paul passed out permission slips for the upcoming tour of the medical university's gross anatomy lab. She took one but didn't hear a word about what they'd be seeing.

At lunch, she sat on the Lawn with Margaret and Glee out of habit and listened to Wallace Stoney go on about how he had ditched his band the Dukes of Neon (now on their third name change) and how they would never go anywhere without him because he was the glue that held them together. Then he segued seamlessly into a monologue about the gross anatomy field trip, which was a rite of passage for every tenth-grade class.

"It's rad," he said. "I wrote a song about it."

"Is it really full of cadavers?" Glee asked.

"Dude," he said, "it was gnarly. There's all this nasty stuff like glass jars with two-headed babies in them, and there was even a pecker in a jar and the water was all green. It looked like pecker-flavored wine cooler."

"Foul," Glee said.

"Shut up," Margaret said, "or I'll never be able to drink wine coolers again."

"Aw, sugarbear," Wallace said, "the green stuff's nasty. The red stuff is what's righteous. You can drink ten bottles of that shit and never barf."

Abby robotically ate her carrot sticks and drank her Snapple. Everyone felt very, very far away. She didn't come to herself again until she was pulling out of the parking lot after school and found that she was turning left at the stoplight on Folly Road instead of right, headed toward Wadmalaw. She was driven by a powerful conviction: if the Langs didn't believe her about Gretchen's rape, if Major didn't believe her about Gretchen's rape, she'd make them believe. If something had happened to Gretchen, there might still be evidence at Margaret's, at that blockhouse buried in the woods.

But forty-five minutes and a quarter tank of gas later, as she stood in front of that rancid outbuilding, Abby saw that it contained nothing but the same stupid garbage—a water-swollen copy of *Oui*, a charred pair of men's tightie whities, a pile of Bartles and Jaymes Premium Blush empty bottles. It was covered with the same stupid graffiti—"Eat Fuk Preps" and "Dukes uf Neon world sexxx tour 88." It was a waste of time.

She walked around the building again. One second she was crawling over the broken slabs of tabby, staring at the graffiti, trying to find a clue like they always did on TV but realizing that she had nothing, and the next second she knew.

Dukes uf Neon. That was the name of Wallace's band, or it used to be, before they changed it for the third time. He'd just said so on the Lawn. All these empty bottles of Bartles and Jaymes (*The Charleston Police Department calls it rape juice*). In Abby's imagination, a picture began to form: Wallace coming to visit Margaret, waiting in the woods, hiding in the blockhouse until she could sneak away from her friends. And instead finding Gretchen in the darkness, lost, afraid, naked.

Wallace Stoney.

"I wouldn't," a man's voice said.

Abby jumped. Standing behind her was a big guy, cigarette

burning in one hand, belly hanging out beneath a stained Polo shirt, wearing M. Dumas khakis frayed at the cuffs. His unbrushed blond hair stuck up, his nose was crooked, and his eyes were dull. Riley Middleton.

"I'm a friend of Margaret's," Abby said. She didn't know what drugs he might be on. Then she wanted to laugh. The Langs thought she was some bigtime drug dealer, and here she was, scared of the real thing.

"I know," he said. "You're Glee."

"Abby," she said. "Glee's our other friend. What wouldn't you do?"

He took a step toward her and Abby stepped back. He had drugged girls. He had done things to them in the back of his car and no one knew she was out here. Riley stopped and took a showy drag off his cigarette.

"I wouldn't go in there," he said, exhaling a thick blue cloud of smoke. "If I were you."

Abby tried to glimpse the Bunny through the woods and realized that all she could see was more trees. All she could hear was the sound of frogs. She was alone with Riley. A plug opened behind her belly button and her courage drained away.

"Why not?" she asked, playing for time, trying to keep him talking, looking for an opening.

"Heavy shit went down here," he said. "Devil worship, slave torture, murder." He paused and smiled. "Rape."

Abby took another step backward and stumbled over a chunk of tabby. She could hear the telephone junction box humming in the silence, she could feel it hissing through the ground. Riley smiled again.

"You've got a nice body," he said. "How old are you?"

"Thanks," she said automatically. She wanted to run, but

Gretchen needed her. She packed her panic down tight. "Riley," she said, "do you know if anyone was out here on Labor Day weekend? Like any guys partying in the woods?"

"Probably," he said. "Why don't you ask Margaret?"

"I should do that," she said. Then, before he could react. "My mom's waiting for me. Bye."

She was moving before "bye" had even left her lips, walking as fast as she could, away from the buzzing junction box, away from Riley, around tree trunks and bushes and tangles of undergrowth. She started running when she emerged from the woods and saw the Dust Bunny. She fumbled for her keys, slid in, locked the doors, and slammed into gear, pushing the pedal to the floor, flying for Red Top.

When she got home it was almost eight. Abby closed her bedroom door and jammed her pink blanket against the crack at the bottom to keep the sound from leaking out. The last thing she wanted was her mom to hear anything she was about to say. Then she called Glee. It was impossible for her brain to make small talk, so she started in right off the bat.

"Do you remember the night with the acid? When Gretchen got lost?" she asked. "Do you think Wallace was there?"

"Why?" Glee asked.

"Because I need to know," Abby said. "Do you think it's possible he was out in the woods?"

"How should I know?" Glee asked.

"Glee," Abby said. "I have to tell you something and you have to promise not to tell anyone, especially not Margaret. Do you promise?"

"Totally," Glee said, and Abby could hear the excitement in her voice.

"A boy jumped Gretchen," Abby said. "Like, he raped her.

When we were out at Margaret's. When Gretchen was lost in the woods."

A long silence followed.

"And I think it was Wallace," Abby said.

A shorter silence and then Glee said, "Let me call you right back. My sister's home."

Five minutes later Mickey Mouse chirped "I'm Mickey!" Abby snatched the receiver out of his hand.

"What took you so long?" she asked.

"Sorry," Glee said. "My sister was being a total pig. Can you hear me okay? What were you saying about Wallace?"

Abby told Glee everything. She told her about Gretchen's confession, Gretchen's parents freaking out, driving to Wadmalaw when Margaret wasn't there and finding the wine cooler bottles and the Dukes of Neon graffiti. It was a relief to get it all out, and Glee was a good listener. If Abby hadn't been able to hear her breathing, she would have assumed Glee had hung up; she was so quiet, but that was Glee. Whenever you had a problem, you could count on her to focus.

Finally, Abby finished. Neither of them said anything for a minute.

"This is why she said those things about Wallace?" Glee asked.

"It's what happens, right?" Abby said. "You have someone do that to you, and then you kind of go crazy. She's not thinking right, Glee."

"But do you really think Wallace did it?" Glee asked. "He told Margaret he'd never cheat on her."

"I know," Abby said. "But boys lie all the time. If Margaret believes Wallace, then she's super naive. Wallace brags about other girls all the time."

"That's not nice," Glee said.

"But he does," Abby said. "You've heard him."

"No, he doesn't," Glee said, and that's when Abby should have known something was wrong.

"What are you going to do?" Glee continued.

"I have to tell someone," Abby said. "I thought I'd start with Wallace. See if he admits it. If not, I'll go to the police. And if they won't listen to me, I'll tell everyone at school."

"What about Margaret?" Glee asked.

"I don't know," Abby said. "That's the tricky part. Maybe I should tell her first?"

"No," Margaret said. "I don't think you should tell Margaret first."

Abby almost dropped the phone. Her stomach and head hollowed out and her hands turned numb. Glee had her on three-way calling.

"Don't you ever come near us again!" Margaret screamed. "You're jealous of Wallace, and you want to fuck up everything that's good in my life!"

Abby was trying to talk at the same time.

"Margaret!" she was yelling. "Margaret! Margaret! Margaret! You have to understand—"

"I don't have to understand shit, you slut!"

"You have to talk to Gretchen!"

"Fuck you!" Margaret snarled, and then she was screaming directly into the mouthpiece; her voice was louder than Abby's, blowing out the earpiece speaker. "Stay away from us! Stay the fuck away from us or I will fuck you up! You want to be pals with Gretchen—fine! You tell her your sick little lies. But if you look at us, if you talk to us, if you say anything to anyone near us, I will get my dad to sue the shit out of you!"

Margaret's line went dead. Abby sat there, her ear ringing, and then realized that Glee was still on the line.

"Glee . . ." she said.

"You're evil," Glee said.

And hung up.

TOTAL ECLIPSE OF THE HEART

Spirit Week was the school's annual festival of misrule.

Faculty hated it because they got through less material in class, the administration hated it because handbook violations increased, parents hated it because it threw carpool schedules out of whack—but Spirit Week was impossible to stop. It was Christmas in October. It was the carnival of chaos.

It was the worst week of Abby's life.

Monday was Twins Day. Last year, Abby and Gretchen showed up in matching outfits. This year Glee and Margaret were dressed alike and they refused to speak to Abby when she tried to apologize. Gretchen didn't show up at all.

Tuesday was Dress-Down Day, when everyone wore jeans and attended the Battle of the Bands at lunch. Last year, Abby and Gretchen had sat on the Lawn and watched Parish Helms play, bending over his bass, the sun burning his blond hair white. This year, Gretchen wasn't in school and Abby was wandering through the auditorium garden, looking for a place to have lunch, when a carton of milk exploded on the sidewalk at her feet. She looked up. Standing in front of her was Wallace Stoney, wearing his football jersey, face blank, breathing hard through his nose.

"You want to get stomped?" Wallace asked.

Abby looked around to see if anyone was nearby, but everyone was on the other side of the Lawn watching a Wallace-less Dukes of Neon play "Brown-Eyed Girl." She looked back at Wallace. His pupils were pinpricks, his nostrils were flaring.

She tried to walk around him. Wallace blocked her way.

"You think I would piss on Gretchen Lang if she was on fire?" he asked. "You think I'd stick my dick in that cooze if she begged me?"

Abby held very, very still. When she spoke, she chose her words carefully.

"I don't think anything, Wallace," she said, making sure to keep her eyes down.

Because she wasn't watching, she didn't see his hand swing until it was too late. He didn't hit her hard, but it took her by surprise and she stumbled to one side, dropping her books.

"No one spreads lies about me, bitch," he said, stepping up close.

Abby flinched and Wallace smiled, then he shoulder-checked her and walked away.

Abby needed to speak to Gretchen so bad. It wasn't just Wallace, it was everything. All the pent-up things she had to say clouded her brain, made her drunk, slowed her thinking, thickened her tongue. She said them to herself when she drove home from school, she tried to write them down, she told them to Geoffrey the Giraffe. Finally her fingers picked up the phone and dialed Gretchen's number by themselves.

"Hello?" Mr. Lang said. "Hello?"

Abby slammed down the receiver. It buzzed beneath her hand.

"Hi, I'm Mickey!" the phone said. "Hi, I'm Mickey!"

Slowly, Abby lifted the receiver.

"Abby," Mr. Lang said, "if you call our house one more time, I'm telephoning the police. You are not wanted here."

That night, she snuck out her window and drove to the Old Village and parked at Alhambra Hall. She walked the block down Middle Street to Pierates Cruze, and in the darkness she stood beneath Gretchen's bedroom window and threw rocks at the glass. They were tiny, but the sound echoed around the block.

"Gretchen!" Abby hissed. "Gretchen!"

When she finally gave up and turned to go, something swooped down out of the darkness. Abby threw herself to the ground, skinning her palms on the dirt road, barely holding back a scream. Looking up, she saw a great horned owl glaring at her from the branch of a live oak across the street. Abby picked herself up and got the hell out of there.

Wednesday was Nerd Day, when everyone pulled their pants up high, wore rainbow suspenders, and buttoned their top buttons. Everyone except Abby. She just kept her head down.

Thursday was Slave Day.

Five years later, Slave Day was gone as if it had never existed, but in 1988 no one dreamed that it could possibly be offensive. It was a tradition.

A clot of students was clustered around the front office window, where the Slave Market was posted. It was a giant piece of white butcher's paper, and the idea was that students could buy a slave for a set price. If the slave didn't beat the bid by one dollar, then they were "owned" by their master, who would make them do whatever she wanted during the lunchtime Slave Parade. The master might make the slave wear an ugly sweatshirt, or if she was feeling really evil, the slave would have to wear her bra on the outside of her clothes. Some guys would make a girl wear a leash and walk the Lawn on all fours like a dog. All the money raised went to the Alumni Fund, so that made it okay.

Miss Toné was out front with a marker writing down names

of slaves and owners. Abby gave the list a glance and then froze. It was right there in Miss Toné's rushed block letters.

OWNER: Gretchen Lang
SLAVE: Abigail Rivers

Gretchen was at school. She had to be to participate. It used to be that Abby always knew where Gretchen was and vice versa. They had memorized each other's class schedules; they each knew which bathroom the other preferred, which hidey-holes they'd retreat to when stressed (Abby: behind the chapel; Gretchen: rear carrel at the library). They planned what they were doing the next day on the phone every night. But all that was gone now. Mrs. Lang had insisted that Abby's class schedule be swapped so that she and Gretchen didn't share any classes, and Gretchen no longer talked to Abby on the phone. The part of her brain that kept track of Gretchen was broken.

But now she knew. Gretchen was here and all Abby had to do was find her.

"Hey, slave," Gretchen said.

Abby spun around. Gretchen was standing right behind her wearing the same sweat-stained clothes, her hair all wire bristle, her face a greasy mess, stinking of perfume.

"Where have you been?" Abby asked. "Are you okay?"

Gretchen giggled to herself.

"A slave doesn't get to ask questions," she said.

"Screw that," Abby said. "I'm really worried. No one—"

Gretchen put a filthy finger to Abby's lips, and Abby was torn between pulling away and being comforted that Gretchen was touching her again.

"Let's talk in the bathroom," Gretchen said. "Come on."

She turned and headed down the breezeway, and Abby followed as fast as she could. Gretchen preferred the bathroom in the fine arts building. Abby figured they had just enough time to get there and back before the first bell. She wasn't worried about being Gretchen's slave. They were friends. Gretchen wouldn't make her do anything bad.

"Wipe off your makeup," Gretchen said.

Abby kept smiling like an idiot, her back against the bathroom door. Gretchen was standing by the sink, her face so pasty it matched the tile walls behind her. The cold room reeked of United Colors of Benetton.

"It was Wallace Stoney, wasn't it?" Abby asked. "We have to tell or he'll do it to someone else."

Instead of answering, Gretchen opened her bookbag and took out a folded yellow hand towel from her mom's bathroom and a big tub of Ponds cold cream and set them on the edge of the sink.

"I'm the owner," she said, "and you're the slave. And the slave doesn't get to wear makeup."

Since seventh grade, only Gretchen had ever seen Abby without her face on, and she knew not to talk about it at school. No one talked about Abby's makeup.

"I'm not playing around," Gretchen said.

She unscrewed the lid of the jar.

"Take it off."

Abby's spine went weak. Her head was spinning from the perfume. Maybe if she played along for a bit, Gretchen would stop. Like, Abby would be about to put the cold cream on her face and then Gretchen would grab her hand and laugh and say "Just kidding!" and they'd be friends again.

"If you don't take off your makeup," Gretchen said, "I'll do it for you."

"We have to tell your parents about Wallace," Abby managed to say. "He attacked me, too."

Gretchen held out the jar of Ponds, gleaming soft and white in the fluorescents like a big tub of Crisco. Abby walked to the mirror on straw legs and looked at her reflection. Under the ugly bathroom lights her skin looked like poached shrimp, all pink and shiny. At some point in the next few seconds, Gretchen was going to see how ugly she was being.

"Do you really want this?" Abby asked, scooping up cold cream with two fingers.

"Duh," Gretchen said.

But Abby was physically incapable of bringing her fingers any closer to her face. Her hand was shaking. Gretchen rolled her eyes. The whites were inflamed with burst blood vessels.

"I'll do it for you," she said.

"Please," Abby said, her eyes suddenly aching, her throat closing tight. "It's my makeup, Gretchen."

Gretchen grabbed Abby's hand and smeared the cold cream onto Abby's face. The white goo mushed into her eye, then left a smear across the bridge of her nose. It was cold and greasy on her eyeball.

Abby lost it. She shoved herself away from the sink, knocked into Gretchen (who weighed next to nothing), and sent her reeling backward into the hand dryer. Abby scrabbled at her face and flung the gob of cold cream on the floor with a splat, then shoved her way out of the bathroom. Holding one hand over her right eye, not knowing how bad the damage was, she ran without looking until she got to the bathroom in the back hall behind the library, where the faculty offices were, and locked the door.

She didn't want to look in the mirror, but she finally forced herself to. She saw that her eye was bloodshot, but otherwise not too bad. She touched up her makeup, then made it to first period just before the second bell. All day she simmered; then after school she waited outside where parents picked up the middle schoolers until she saw Gretchen shuffling out, hugging her books to her chest. Abby went right for her, shoving her backward, not caring who saw.

"Stay the fuck away from me," Abby snarled, dimly aware of students stopping to watch. "I am your only friend. I am the one person who cared what happened to you. I am the one person who still talks to you, and you just lost me. You know exactly what you did and you know exactly why it matters, so get this through your rich-bitch skull: We are not friends. Not now. Not ever."

Gretchen didn't move. She just stood there, taking it.

"You don't need a ride to school? I'm too dirty for your parents? You want to treat me like dog crap? Then fuck you."

At TCBY, Abby shoved her arms into the ice machine until they went numb. She couldn't even feel it when she stuck the pin from her nametag through her skin. She wanted to be cold forever. She wanted to be made of ice. She went home and drank water, then turned on *The Equalizer*. At 11:06, her phone rang.

"Hi, I'm Mickey!" it shouted. "Hi, I'm Mickey!"

Abby snatched it off the hook.

"Hello?" she said.

A long moment of silence whistled down the wire.

"Please," Gretchen said, "don't hate me."

Out of habit, Abby almost said she didn't hate Gretchen, but she took a minute and remembered everything and put it all into her voice when she said, "Go away."

"Don't be mad at me, Abby. Please," Gretchen said.

All you really need to know is that I'm going to crack you wide open, Robert McCall said on the TV.

"I don't want to talk to you," Abby said.

"I don't understand," Gretchen said, totally bereft. "What did I do?"

That's when Abby knew: Gretchen was crazy. She had gone crazy and she was pulling Abby down with her. The longer they talked, the worse it would get.

"If I have to explain it to you, then we were never friends," Abby said.

"Don't leave me alone," Gretchen begged. "I can't do this on my own. I can't fight it by myself. I'm sorry for what I did, but he makes me. He's always whispering in my ear, telling me what to do, making me hurt people. He wants me to be all alone, with no one left but him. I'm sorry, Abby. I'm so, so, so sorry."

The whining, wheedling edge in Gretchen's cracked voice made Abby feel nothing but contempt.

"Goodbye, Gretchen," she said.

"But we're friends," Gretchen cried in a tiny voice inside the receiver, and a fist gripped Abby's heart and squeezed. "You're my best friend."

Abby was far away from her body, and all she had to do was stay out of the way as her hand floated to Mickey's arm and hung up the phone.

"It's over," her mouth said to no one in particular.

The phone rang again, but Abby picked up the receiver and dropped it. She didn't want to talk to Gretchen. Right now, she wanted to show Gretchen how much this pain hurt. Abby wanted her to feel what she felt. She wanted her to know this wasn't a game.

Friday was Spirit Day, and God's fist, made of angry black clouds, slammed down on Charleston with a vengeance. The wind kicked over garbage cans and sent trash skittering down the streets, whipping fine sand through the parking lot, lashing its grains against exposed ankles. By first period, everyone's hair was ruined—the girl's bathroom reeked of hairspray, the sinks were spattered with gobs of mousse. The breezeways became wind tunnels that blew up skirts and blasted faces red.

By the end of second period it was pitch dark outside the windows. Packs of football players gathered in the halls, muttering blackly about how their game had better not be canceled or there would be hell to pay. Something oppressive coiled around the school and squeezed. Five of the football players face-planted Dereck White into a garbage can. Someone shook up a Coke can and tossed it inside Carson Moore's locker.

The rain smashed down during Spanish 2. One second Mr. Romasanta was conjugating *asesinar*, the next second his voice was drowned out by a wave of static as the full fury of the sky was unleashed. Cold water misted through the windows, followed by a scramble as the suck-up students raced to close them and turn on the air-conditioners.

That night, Abby didn't eat anything except a bag of microwave popcorn in her room while she watched *Dallas*, *Miami Vice*, *Lifestyles of the Rich and Famous*—anything that turned off her brain. The rain kept up all day Saturday, turning streets into rivers and yards into lakes.

Abby's dad ran out to his shed early and stayed there all day. Abby hid in her room and distracted herself by cleaning out her closet. Normally the rain made her feel snug and cozy, but today it only made her feel cold.

She found her old Dukes of Hazzard lunch box where she kept

all her pictures, and she sat on the bed with her stuffed animals and went through them, dealing out a deck of cards from her past: she and Gretchen dressed for the punk rock party at Lanie Ott's house when they were all still friends; Gretchen in fifth grade showing off her moonwalk in the driveway. Gretchen asleep, covers pulled up to her chin, photographic evidence taken by Abby that she smiled when she slept (Gretchen still wasn't convinced).

So many pictures right before a moment or after a moment; pictures of each other when they weren't ready for the picture yet, or when one of them had her hat on when she meant to take it off or her sunglasses off when she meant to put them on. Abby talking, mouth in weird half-open shapes, Gretchen gesturing at unseen things Abby couldn't even remember anymore. Abby laughing. Lots and lots of pictures of Abby laughing.

The summer after sixth grade it had rained like this. Abby and Gretchen had put cots on the screened porch of the Langs' beach house on the Isle of Palms and slept outside every night, listening to the rain whisper as they fell asleep. For a week in August, Mr. Lang took off from work and stayed at the beach house, too. He spent the mornings on the phone, but at night they played Uno and Monopoly. During a lull in the rain, he took them shrimping to show them how to use a cast net, but it turned out he didn't have a clue. A black lady fishing on the beach had shown them how to hold it in their teeth, sucking in salt water, biting the lead weights along the edge, then twisting their upper bodies and hurling the net like a carpet. They caught exactly one shrimp. It was delicious.

At night they lay in the dark, listening to 95SX play "Russians" by Sting and "Take Me Home" by Phil Collins over and over again, and they talked about how they'd move in together after high school, and they'd each get a cat and they'd name them Matt Dillon and Mickey Rourke, and even if they had boyfriends, they wouldn't let boys get in the way of their friendship.

Now the rain came crashing down, and there was no one calling Abby and no one she wanted to call. She was completely alone, and she couldn't imagine a future where it wasn't raining.

She woke up Monday morning and decided she had to fix things. She took a hot shower and put on her face, then steered through the darkness, tires barely clinging to the old bridge, wind shoving the Dust Bunny from lane to lane; she vowed the whole way that by the time the day ended, she and Gretchen would be friends again.

Abby waited outside Mrs. Erskine's English room for Gretchen to show up. As the last echo of the second bell died, the stairwell door swung open and Gretchen entered the hall. Abby had her statement all planned out, and then she saw Gretchen and couldn't say a word.

Gretchen had cut her hair. The long blond frizz was gone, replaced by a tight halo of curls that hugged her scalp, showing off her neck, suddenly giving her cheekbones. There was a lump in Abby's throat—she would never make such a huge move without consulting Gretchen first, and Gretchen had gone and done it without talking to Abby at all. Even worse, it looked great.

Gretchen's skin wasn't perfect, but it was clearing up and makeup concealed the rest of the damage. Her eyes were bright. She was wearing black stirrup pants and black Capezios and a leopard print sweater with a black turtleneck underneath. Her posture was perfect, spine straight, shoulders back, and she'd done her nails with French tips. Most of all, she glowed. She was beaming. She was healthy. She was beautiful.

"What?" Gretchen asked, hand on the classroom door, noticing Abby for the first time. Her voice wasn't hoarse; it was thick and southern and sounded like normal.

"Are you all right?" Abby asked.

Gretchen wrinkled her brow.

"Why wouldn't I be?" she asked.

"All that stuff," Abby said. "Last week? Everything that was going on?"

Gretchen raised an eyebrow and gave a half smile.

"I don't know what you're talking about," she said. "I'm fine. But maybe something's wrong with you?"

NEW SENSATION

"No way is that dillweed sitting here," Margaret said.

It took Abby a second to realize that she was the dillweed in question.

Abby wanted to say "Up yours" or "I didn't want to sit with you anyways," but to her profound disappointment she found herself looking down at the grass, embarrassed, desperate to be allowed to sit at the picnic table.

The tropical storm had missed Charleston and veered out into the Atlantic, and Monday was humid and clear. It had rained the night before and the grass was still spongy. Margaret and Glee had commandeered the picnic table in the middle of the Lawn and there was plenty of room, but apparently it was for non-dillweeds only.

"It doesn't matter to me," Gretchen said. "I don't know why she's following me around."

"Whatever," Margaret said. "But I don't want that thing speaking."

Abby watched in shock as Gretchen sat down with Margaret and Glee and the three of them started talking as if she didn't exist. Too humiliated to leave, too uncomfortable to stay, desperately wishing she could make up her mind, Abby started to sit, then stopped. She looked at everyone walking across the Lawn, throwing Frisbees, running and sliding over the rain-slicked grass in their dress shoes, and then she looked back at the picnic table and finally decided to perch at the far end. So it was like she was sitting with them, but not close enough to make anyone angry. Was that okay for dillweeds?

"I need a faculty advisor for the Environmental Awareness Club," Gretchen said.

"Ask Father Morgan," Margaret said, then she lowered the green apple she'd been toying with for the past few minutes and looked at Glee. "Glee would have to join."

"Stop it," Glee said, blushing.

"Father Organ," Gretchen said, and she and Margaret collapsed onto each other's shoulders, laughing.

"Father Morgasm," Margaret said, and they laughed even harder.

"Father More-Than," Abby said.

They both stopped laughing and stared at her.

"What?" Gretchen asked.

are you driving away your best friend?

You both swore to study for the big English test together. Suddenly, she cancels. Do you:

- **A** Assume she got a better offer and spend the afternoon feeling rejected.
- **B** Blow it off. Sometimes these things happen.
- **C** Call her and demand she tell you the real reason why.
- **D** Give her the silent treatment. If she won't study with you, you won't talk to her.

In fifth grade, Elizabeth Root had peed her pants during the Founders Day concert. The theme was "The Roaring Twenties" and the elementary school chorus was right in the middle of a chanted song about Al Jolson and the stock market when Elizabeth just couldn't hold it anymore and the front of her gray skirt blossomed black. She tried to run offstage but the stage-left exit was blocked by the entrance of a giant papier-mâché Tin Lizzie. The stage-right exit was blocked by the boys' choir.

Mrs. Gay tried to cover by playing her upright piano louder. The more obedient chorus members sang along, and for sixty seconds the assembled parents watched as a little girl, blinded by tears, stumbled around in circles, trailing urine across the stage as an enormous Model T Ford rolled toward her.

Everyone talked about it for weeks afterward. People made "Pssss . . ." sounds whenever Elizabeth Root walked by in the halls. At lunch she was demoted to sitting with two very kind but deeply unpopular girls. The lower school headmaster finally sent home a note telling parents how to discuss Elizabeth's pants-peeing with their children. Two years later, when Elizabeth transferred to Bishop England, everyone knew it was because of that time she'd peed her pants.

On the other hand, there was Dr. Gillespie, a marriage counselor for half the divorced couples in Charleston. Last year he was found tied to one of his office chairs, dressed in women's clothing, beaten to death with a Pre-Columbian statue from his collection. Not a single story about it appeared in the newspaper. When people mentioned it at fundraiser receptions, they referred to it as a "terrible accident," and twelve months later you'd be hard pressed to find anyone who would admit to remembering Dr. Gillespie, let alone being one of his patients.

Turning eighteen doesn't determine when you become an

adult in Charleston; neither does registering to vote, graduating from high school, or getting your driver's license. In Charleston, the day you become an adult is the day you learn to ignore your neighbor's drunk driving and focus instead on whether he submitted a paint-color change proposal to the Board of Architectural Review. The day you become an adult is the day you learn that in Charleston, the worse something is, the less attention it receives.

At Albemarle, everyone was suddenly being very adult about Gretchen.

For almost a month, Gretchen had been shunned. Now she wasn't getting demerits, she was getting attention. People wanted to be near her, to sit where she sat, to talk to her before class, to get her opinion, to receive her attention. For three weeks, Gretchen had been an unmentionable. In three days, she'd soared to number one.

It scared Abby how quickly everything changed.

Your best friend says she's stressed-out and needs a break, so she's canceling your plans to double-date this Friday.

A What a relief! You didn't want to go either.
B This friendship is over!
C Cancel your date and go to her house instead. She must need to talk.
D Your poor date. Now what else are you going to talk about on Friday night?

The weather got hot. The sky was a cloudless silver dome.

Gretchen opened her thermos and poured a cup of thick white milkshake.

"What is that nastiness?" Margaret asked.

"This?" Gretchen asked. "I don't think you'd like it."

"How the fuck would you know?" Margaret asked.

Gretchen reached into her backpack and pulled out an unmarked white plastic canister with a black lid and handed it to Margaret.

"My mom got it from Germany," she said. "It's a diet supplement. One shake a day meets all your nutritional needs. It's got, like, eight hundred calories in it or something. I think it's full of speed. Anyhoo, the FDA totally won't approve it, but I stole one from her."

She pulled the canister out of Margaret's hand, who held onto it for a few seconds longer, then watched with deep longing as it went back into Gretchen's bookbag.

"Let me smell it," she said.

Gretchen handed her the cup. Margaret wafted it under her nose, then held it there.

"Vanilla," she said. "And bananas? Can I try?"

Gretchen raised her eyebrows and nodded.

Most people had Margaret pegged wrong. They thought she just wanted to party all the time, but Margaret was a big girl who wanted to be small, and she would do anything to melt her flesh, whether it was Jazzercise twice a week, the Cambridge Diet, the Rotation Diet, the F-Plan Fiber Diet, Scarsdale, Deal-a-Meal, Grapefruit 45. None of them worked, so she kept trying one after the other, suffering through the bloating, the fainting spells, the farts, the hunger pains, the headaches, the cramps. One of these regimes was bound to make her skinny. She had faith.

"It's not totally rank," Margaret said, putting down the cup and wiping the thick white mustache from her upper lip. "Do you have more?"

"Cases," Gretchen said, rolling her eyes.

"I'll buy one," Margaret said.

"No way, José," Gretchen said. "I'll give it to you. My mom doesn't even drink them anymore."

Your bestie shows up at school on Monday sporting a brand new 'do she didn't tell you about. It's radical, it's expensive, and it makes her look like a poodle. You:

- **A** Tell her it looks great. That's what friends are for.
- **B** Pretend nothing's happened. After all, if you can't say something nice . . .
- **C** Burst out laughing. At least it's not you!
- **D** Be brutally honest. Somebody's got to say it.

Abby couldn't put her finger on what had changed. All of Gretchen's clothes were new—blazers with rolled sleeves, a man's necktie with a beige vest, a diamond-print oversized sweater dress, blue-and-white striped sailor tees—but it wasn't the clothes. She had a new haircut, she was wearing more makeup, she was standing straighter and pushing out her chest, but none of those were it, either.

Gretchen was glowing. She was spotlit by a personal shaft of sunlight wherever she went. She was turned on, engaged, vibrant, kinetic. Every guy was watching her. More than once, Abby saw Mr. Groat turn to stare at Gretchen's butt when she walked down the hall.

No one watched Abby walk down the hall. She'd woken up on Tuesday, the day after Gretchen's miraculous return, and discovered a small red spot on her right cheek. It was the stress, she told herself. The next morning, the spot was bigger and darker. The morning after that, there were two more.

Abby stared at herself in the mirror and tried hard not to cry. There were three pink spots to the right of her nose, and the skin on her forehead was rough. No matter how much powder she applied, her chin stayed shiny. There was a sore spot on her neck, and when she pressed, she could feel something painful and swollen deep beneath the surface. No matter what she did, the spots kept ripening.

Gretchen was no longer in any classes with Abby, so it was days before she finally managed to speak with her privately. Abby caught her in the hall right as fourth-period break started; she was throwing books into her locker.

"Hey," Abby said, slowing down and playing it casual.

"Hey," Gretchen said, without stopping.

"You look a lot better," Abby said.

Gretchen zipped up her bookbag.

"As if you'd care," she said.

"That's all I care about," Abby said.

Gretchen slammed her locker shut and then rounded on Abby, hitching one strap of her bookbag over her shoulder. She was a few inches taller and Abby could see her nostrils flaring, her pupils dilating.

"If you cared, you would have helped," she said. "Not just talked about me behind my back."

"I tried to help," she said. "You know I did."

Gretchen blew out her bangs.

"Psh," she said. "You didn't do shit." Then she was smiling, her mouth wide, eyes sparkling, and Abby's heart leapt for a second because it was clearly a joke, and then Gretchen was saying over Abby's shoulder, "Hey, y'all!" and she was hugging Margaret and Glee, and the three of them were heading off down the hall, shoulder to shoulder, framed in the bright afternoon sunlight spilling through the glass doors, leaving Abby back in the shadows by the lockers, wishing she could go with them, or stay where she was, or at least be comfortable with either choice.

Everyone was Gretchen's buddy—everyone except Abby. Even Wallace Stoney had managed to forgive her. Mrs. Lang had recruited Wallace to drive Gretchen to school since he lived in Mt. Pleasant, too. One morning Abby saw them sitting in his truck ahead of her in traffic, waiting to make the light on Folly Road, Gretchen was talking and Wallace was laughing. When Wallace hung out with Gretchen and Margaret and Glee during fourth-period break, he mostly talked to Gretchen.

Abby wondered what Margaret thought about that.

You were grounded over the weekend. How do you catch up when you see her on Monday?

A I talk, she listens. So much has happened.
B She talks, I listen. She's always got the scoop.
C Chitchat for a minute before class, then take off. I have so much work to do.
D Compete for conversation time. Both of us have a lot to say.

Abby sat across from Father Morgan in his office. His curtains were closed and it was cool and dark and he was telling Abby that Gretchen was completely normal.

"I wouldn't take all the credit," he said. "But I spoke with her parents and it certainly seems to have helped get her back on track."

"That's the thing," Abby said. "She's not on track."

Father Morgan smiled.

"You can't judge a book by its cover," he agreed. "But the cover does give you a pretty good indication of what's inside. And I'd say Gretchen's cover looks a heck of a lot better than it did."

It had taken Abby a while to realize that there was one person who'd talk about Gretchen as much as she wanted: Father Morgan. He was way too involved in students' lives, he thought he knew everything, and all you had to do was make an appointment.

Now, sitting there in Father Morgan's office, she knew she'd made the right decision. White and brown nubby curtains were drawn over his only window, leaving the room dim and safe. The furniture was nice furniture from a house, not the harsh office furniture that filled the rest of the school. Instead of yellow-painted cinderblock walls, Father Morgan's office was lined with bookshelves filled with titles like *Understanding Your Teenager* and *Living a God-Focused Life*. And he loved to talk.

"Gretchen is happy and social," Father Morgan said. "She's been an absolute joy in all our interactions and there is no shadow upon her as far as I can tell. You know what that says to me, Abby?"

He waited for an answer, so she finally fed him his line.

"No, sir."

"You're scared of losing your friend," he said and then smiled.

Abby looked at her knee. She inhaled, shaking her head.

"When she was sick," Abby said, "she told me that people could look fine on the outside but be evil inside. Like satanists."

Or her parents.

Father Morgan's smile disappeared, and he stood up and came around his desk. He pulled a chair closer to Abby.

"Abby," Father Morgan said, "I know how it is to be a young

person. There are all these reports of satanic cults everywhere, sacrificing babies. Geraldo Rivera's doing a two-hour special on them next week. Of course you feel these things deeply, and they upset and influence you. But they're not real."

"Then what are they?" Abby asked.

"They're . . ." Father Morgan waved one hand around in the air. ". . . metaphors. Ways of dealing with information and emotions. Adolescence is a complicated time, and some really bright people think that when the adult emerges, it's like you're being taken over by a different person. Almost like being possessed. Sometimes parents, or friends, get hurt when a loved one changes. They look around for something to blame. Music, movies, satanism."

He leaned back and flashed a smile.

"So you think Gretchen is possessed?" Abby asked. "Like she has a demon inside of her?"

His smile flicked off.

"What?" he said. "No, it's a metaphor. Abby, do you know the story of the Gadarene madman?"

"Is he a satanist?" Abby asked.

"In the Bible," Father Morgan continued, "Jesus goes to Gerasa, and when he gets there a man approaches him who is possessed by demons. He's been shunned and forced to live in the graveyard, which is as bad as it gets in Bible times. And when Jesus asks him what's wrong, the man says he's possessed by an unclean spirit. Jesus asks its name and it says, 'My name is Legion.' Does that sound familiar?"

Abby shrugged. Her family didn't go to church, but she thought she'd heard something like that in a horror movie.

"So Jesus expels the demons and puts them in a bunch of nearby pigs," he says. "And the pigs run off a cliff and die and the man is cured. He's free. But everyone in the village is upset and they ask

Jesus to leave. You see?"

"Poor pigs," Abby said.

"Poor pigs," Father Morgan agreed. "But do you see the bigger point?"

"That no one ever thanks you for trying to save them?" Abby said.

"That the people in that village needed the Gadarene madman to be sick," Father Morgan said. "That way they could project all their problems onto him. They blamed him for everything: too much rain, too little rain, their kids staying out past curfew, cows dying. As long as he was sick, they could point to someone who wasn't them and say, 'That's his fault. He's possessed by Satan.' And when Jesus cured him, they didn't know what to do. They were at a loss."

Abby was not following this logic.

"You think there isn't anything wrong with Gretchen," she said.

"I'm saying maybe you *need* something to be wrong with Gretchen," Father Morgan said. "Sometimes the hardest thing for us is when the sick person gets better."

"Why?" Abby asked.

"Because then we have to deal with ourselves," he said, looking at her meaningfully and letting his words sink in.

A rap at the door broke the mood. Father Morgan put his hands on his knees and pushed himself up and opened the door. Gretchen stood there.

"Hi, Father M," she said, smiling.

"Come on in," he said. "I was just wrapping up with Abby."

"What are you doing here?" Abby asked, staring at Gretchen. Standing behind her was Glee.

"I'm in vestry," Gretchen said. "And Glee wants to join. What are you doing here?"

Before Abby could answer, Father Morgan answered for her.

"She's still worried about you," he said. "She just wanted to check in with me."

Gretchen stepped into the room.

"I feel great," she said, but her voice was too bright and hard.

"Now," Father Morgan said, "if I recall correctly, you two shouldn't be spending time together. So Abby, why don't you skedaddle."

As Abby got up to go, she eased past Gretchen in the door, and Gretchen made eye contact and smiled.

"I'd love to have been a fly on the wall," she said. "I can't imagine what you must be saying about me."

Your best friend doesn't have time for you anymore. Do you:

A Keep calling until she tells you why. You deserve an explanation.

B Respect her wishes. You don't want to be needy.

C Tell everyone you rejected her first. Who does she think she is?

D Refuse to accept it. This friendship is over when you say it's over.

The next day, the exorcist arrived.

MISSIONARY MAN

"When you're worried and stressed out, when you feel like everyone hates you and your parents just don't understand. When the world keeps coming at you and pushing you down and down, you'll finally hear a still, small voice inside your head. No, it doesn't mean you're ready for the funny farm. That voice is God, and he's speaking to you, and he's saying, 'Dude, I've got this.'"

Then the enormous young man lying shirtless on the stage floor gritted his teeth while his musclebound brother brought down a sledgehammer and smashed the cinderblock resting on his abs. It exploded into gray powder, and the football players in the audience cheered ironically.

"Praise God!" the shirtless guy shouted, leaping to his feet. "Sometimes God lets you hit rock bottom to show you that he is the *rock* at the *bottom*!"

Everyone in the auditorium hooted and cheered. Abby couldn't tell if the five guys onstage understood that they were being laughed at, or if they thought they were being laughed with. She sunk down lower in her seat. She just wanted assembly to be over.

The Lemon Brothers Faith and Fitness Show was the funniest thing ever to hit Albemarle Academy. Five enormous meat potatoes strutted across the plastic-covered stage, popping their biceps, striking poses, and praising God. In the audience, the utter insanity of it all was blowing everyone's minds.

Once a month, Wednesday assembly put on a barn-burner. One week it was a screening of "Black Ice, White Lines," about a bunch of high school seniors who did cocaine at parties ("flying high on the Devil's dust," the narrator intoned) and then drove home and hit a patch of black ice that sent them straight to hell.

There was the day the assistant football coach from the Citadel came and described in vivid detail the Passion of Christ, lingering over every wound in nauseating technical detail. There was a kid with no arms who played trumpet with his feet. But this? This was something truly special. Throughout the entire student body, not a single pair of pants was dry.

Elijah, the second-youngest brother, took center stage.

"Sometimes," he said, "when I'm shifting steel and sweating blood and I don't think I'm going to make the clean and jerk, or when I'm stuck on the hang and can't get the snatch, suddenly I'll feel lighter, like someone has taken my load. And that's when I look up and I say, 'That was you, God. Thank you! Thank you for taking my load!'"

People were laughing so hard, they thought they'd never return to normal. Father Morgan sat in the front row, looking up at the massive bodybuilders, all gleaming and glistening in the spotlights, with his mouth hanging open in awe. Major looked unreadable. The Lemon Brothers seemed to think the laughter meant they were on the right track.

Isaiah, the ringleader and MC, pointed to two enormous notched wooden beams leaning against the massive blank stage wall, one much shorter than the other. Jonah and Micah, his other brothers, heaved up the longer beam and brought it center stage.

"We want to invite any volunteers to come move this burden," Isaiah said, a smile breaking out across his mustached face. "Can you guys lift this lumber? Can you shift this weight? What about you? Young lady, would you like to try?"

Everyone laughed as Gretchen flexed her muscles in the audience.

Isaiah laughed and flexed his own back at her. Then he pointed next to her.

"How about you? You look strong?"

He was pointing at Wallace Stoney. No one wanted to get onstage and be embarrassed, but Wallace was too arrogant to refuse. He stood up and said something that Abby couldn't hear.

"You can bring people, sure," Isaiah said. "The more the merrier. Don't be shy."

Wallace said something fast to Gretchen, then he grabbed Nuke Zuckerman and the two Bailey brothers to go onstage with him. They were a big chunk of the football team's offensive line, and school pride swept the auditorium. The football players clapped for them first, and then everyone else joined in, eager to see these corny Christians get their challenge shoved back in their faces by the pride of Albemarle. Maybe these guys couldn't win a football game, but they were certainly able to pick up heavy things.

"Now come to the center," Isaiah said, leading them to the larger wooden beam. It was about fifteen feet long. "Can you lift this? Let me see some muscle. Show us your muscle."

The four boys struck exaggerated bodybuilding poses and the Lemon Brothers clapped for them.

"Now let's see you lift," Isaiah said. "Or are those just show muscles?"

Wallace bossed the other football players into position. He bent over one end of the log, with Nuke at the other and the Baileys in the center. On his count, they strained and managed to lift the chunk of wood to shoulder height. Faces reddening, arms shaking, they pushed and raised it over their heads. Major looked nervous, probably thinking of liability issues, but Isaiah was ecstatic.

"Give them a big round of applause," he cued the crowd. "But now, let's see the real challenge. Lift that . . . *and* this."

Micah and Jonah heaved the shorter beam off the back wall and brought it center stage, where they lowered it with a loud bang. It was only a third the length.

"Can we put this one down?" Wallace asked.

Isaiah made a "whatever works" gesture, and the football players dropped the long heavy log with a boom and began strategizing. First they tried to lift both beams at once, then they stacked them, piled them on top of each other, tried to balance them, but they couldn't make it work. Wallace was getting angrier and angrier. Finally, when it was clear they weren't getting anywhere, Isaiah intervened.

"That's okay," he said. "You tried."

Isaiah laid a hand on Wallace's shoulder, but Wallace flicked it off. He and his football buddies started to walk offstage angrily, but Isaiah planted himself in front of them.

"I've never seen volunteers raise it chest-high before, so another round of applause for these fine young men," he said as the audience obliged. "Wait here, don't go anywhere. What would you say if I said my brother can pick up both these logs all by himself?"

He held out the mic.

"I'd say you were lying," Wallace replied.

Isaiah cued his brothers, and Christian, the youngest one with the biggest muscles, walked over to the two massive pieces of lumber. He dragged the short one to the top of the long one and dropped it into place, locking the notches. Then he bent his knees, lifted the end of the longer beam, arms shaking, face red, neck corded, and he ducked underneath. Balancing it on his back, he lifted both logs at once. Notched together, they formed an enormous cross. Face sweating, Christian shifted his grip and the rear of the cross swung wildly, almost taking out the back wall of the auditorium; but then he had it and was pressing up and up and up. The cross was over his head. Slowly, he spun in a circle, his brothers ducking so they wouldn't get decapitated. The crowd went wild. Christian held the massive cross for two seconds before bending his elbows.

"Hup!" he cried, and his four brothers came and took the weight.

More applause.

"With the power of the cross," Christian crowed into his brother's microphone, breathing hard, "everything is possible."

He struck a bodybuilding pose, flexing his sculpted shoulders under his mesh tank top. Next, Jonah, who walked with a limp, placed a watermelon on a table.

With one blow, Christian shattered it with a fist.

"These are the problems that afflict this world," Christian said as the melon exploded into a shower of pink pulp. Jonah threw him two grapefruits. "Life may be tough, but my God is tougher."

Christian squeezed the fruits to dripping pulp with his bare hands. The show was moving into a final frenzy.

"These are the demons that haunt this world, destroyed through the faith and power that sustain me!"

"Wow," Dereck White muttered, sitting behind Abby. "If any rogue citrus attacks, he's got it covered."

The kids in the Environmental Awareness Club sitting on either side of him giggled. Onstage, Jonah picked up a stack of CDs.

"What do you think we're going to do with these?" he called, striding to the lip of the stage. "You want us to throw them out to you guys? We've got some Slayer, some Megadeth, some Anthrax. Does anyone want some Anthrax?"

Ironic cheering rose up around the auditorium, and Jonah stacked the CDs and squeezed them like an accordion. His massive chest muscles bounced as the stack exploded into shards of plastic.

"That's what we think of explicit lyrics!" he shouted. "That's what we think of backward masking!"

Behind him, Micah was bringing out a cinderblock and placing it in front of Christian.

"See what the Lord has given me!" Christian cried, shredding his mesh tank top and exposing his gleaming muscles.

"Take it off!" someone shouted.

"I do all things through Christ who strengthens me," Christian said.

His four brothers bowed their heads around the stage and began to pray, hands clasped and pressed to their foreheads, lips moving.

"I see this demon-haunted world," Christian said, flexing his enormous muscles behind the cinderblock. "I see shapes and shadows moving through it. The demon of anger, the demon of sloth, the demon of not respecting your parents, the demon of heavy-metal music, the demon of not keeping your promises."

He scanned the rows dramatically as if he were seeing the demons out there right now, shading his eyes, playing to the crowd.

"I challenge anyone who is in league with Satan," Christian called. "Any of his representatives, any of his emissaries here on earth, any of them, to get up on this stage right now and you pray to your God and I'll pray to mine and we'll see who's more powerful."

More ironic cheering, and then Christian stopped. He kept staring into the audience, and Abby realized he was looking right at Gretchen. He stared for a long minute, and everyone started to get uncomfortable. The happy buzz in the auditorium quieted.

When he finally spoke again, the room was silent.

"I see your demon, young lady," he said, taking the microphone from his brother. "I see the demon holding you down. I see it making you hurt the ones you love. I challenge it. You think you're strong, Demon? You think you're strong? Say it with me. You think you're strong, but my God is stronger. Demon, begone! You think you're tough, well my God is tougher! Demon, begone!"

With that, he drew back a fist and drove it into the cinderblock. It didn't crack—it exploded. A shower of gray sand bloomed and Christian shoved his arms into the air in a V for victory, his right hand bright red.

Everyone erupted into frenzied applause and ecstatic mayhem.

It was the craziest, weirdest, lamest, funniest assembly ever. As students gossiped on the way out about whether the Lemon Brothers had part-time jobs as Chippendale strippers, Abby made her way around the auditorium to the back, where the Lemon Brothers' van was parked in the dirt patch next to the side door.

The van's rear doors were open, and Christian was sitting on the bumper while Jonah rubbed Icy Hot on his red forearms and swollen hand. The other three brothers were packing their props into the van, carrying milk crates out of the auditorium, hauling out trash bags stuffed with the plastic dropcloth wrapped around the cinderblock fragments and watermelon pulp.

"Excuse me?" Abby said.

Jonah and Christian looked up. Jonah smiled big beneath his blond mustache.

"Are you here to dedicate your life to Christ?" he asked. "Or do you want an autograph? We've got a mailing list."

"Um," Abby said. "I wanted to talk to him?"

She pointed at Christian.

"I don't think I can sign anything," Christian apologized, holding out his right hand. His fist looked raw. "That last cinderblock did a number on me."

"No, I wanted to ask about what you said. About the girl with the demon? She's my best friend. I wanted to know what you saw."

"He didn't see anything," Elijah said, passing in front of her with two sledgehammers, one in each hand.

"I have the gift of discernment," Christian huffed.

"You couldn't discern your hand in front of your face," Elijah said, throwing the sledgehammers into the back of the van with loud bangs.

"He's just jealous," Christian said, turning back to Abby. "I saw a demon haunting your friend. A demon in the shape of a great owl, with his dark shadow obscuring her face."

"Show's over," Jonah said, stepping in front of Christian. "We've got to get out of here. They're not paying us to pack up. Here, have one of our pamphlets, and tell all your friends about the Lemon Brothers Faith and Fitness Show."

Abby took the Xeroxed flier and backed away, keeping her eyes on Christian for as long as possible.

I see the demon holding you down. I see it making you hurt the ones you love.

She wasn't alone anymore.

DANCING IN THE DARK

"Fifteen celery sticks," Margaret said, writing *15 Ce* in her spiral notebook. "Twelve carrot sticks," *12 Ca*. "Eight slices of apple," *8 A Sl*. "Twenty-five grapes," *25 Gr*. "Two milkshakes," *2 MS*.

Gretchen's German milkshakes had melted Margaret to a molten core of hotness. A knife had wicked away her soft curves and now she had dramatic cheekbones. Her hair was thicker, her eyes brighter.

"Wallace can't keep his hands off of me," she bragged, sitting Indian-style in the October sunshine on the Lawn.

Winter was late, and the grass was packed. Circles of girls ate their yogurts and the boys in Juggling Club flashed pins over their heads, making them squeal. Hacky sacks bounced between boys. Bocce players stood with their hands in their pockets, watching one another's bowls. Some seniors were down at the far end playing touch football in their T-shirts.

Sunglasses were on, sweaters were off, shirts were unbuttoned. Everyone was basking in the sun, growing tan and juicy. Humors were good, tolerance was high, laughter was easy, and Margaret was beautiful. Now she could pull off a black dress at winter semiformal, something only a few of the skinniest senior girls would ever dare. In Charleston, you wore solid colors or prints; black was considered too urban. If you were going to wear black, you really had to own it. Margaret could, and she owed it all to Gretchen.

"Seriously," Margaret said, closing her food notebook and stretching her legs in front of her, sunglasses aimed at the sky. "If he keeps dogging me, I'm going to be preggo by January."

"We'll all be so proud," Glee said.

"One day you'll grow up, too," Margaret said. "And then you'll experience the mature pleasures of boning."

"That reminds me," Gretchen said, sitting up.

She'd been lying on her back, *Wordly Wise* held in the air as she raced through the lessons. Their English class was on Chapter Four. Gretchen was doing the crossword puzzle at the end of Chapter Twenty-One. Her bookbag was shoved under her head as a pillow, the end unzipped, and when she raised herself on her elbows her books spilled out, the paisley daybook sliding to the edge of the jumble. Abby couldn't take her eyes off it.

"Here," Gretchen said, and she handed a folded piece of paper to Glee. "It's from Father Morgan. About vestry."

"Oo," Margaret said. "Bone note."

Glee ignored her and slipped it into her books.

"Do you have any more of that milkshake I could try?" Glee asked Gretchen.

Gretchen wrinkled her nose underneath her sunglasses.

"My dad got ticked my mom wasn't drinking them," she said. "He threw out the box."

"Is there—" Glee started.

"Mine," Margaret said. "Whatever's left is mine."

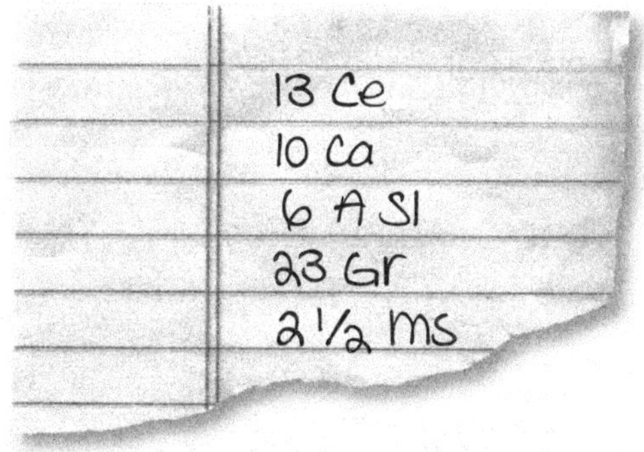

In Biology class, Abby raised her hand and asked to use the bathroom. She didn't have to go; she just needed to smell fresh air for a minute. They were dissecting fetal pigs, and the vinegar fumes made her queasy.

Voices droned behind each closed door as she passed them in the dim hall. The door to Madame Millicent's French classroom was open and she could hear chalk tapping the board as Madame explained something to students who didn't care. Abby didn't know where she was going until she stopped at Gretchen's locker.

Out of curiosity, she tried the combination. It had always been Abby's birthday, the same way Abby's locker combination had always been Gretchen's birthday. She spun the combination to 12-01-72 and lifted the latch. It didn't budge. Hurt, Abby decided she was going to make this work. Gretchen couldn't keep secrets from her.

She thought for a second, then spun the combination to 05-12-73, Gretchen's birthday. The latch lifted with a *clack*, the door swung open, and the first thing she saw was Gretchen's daybook sitting on top of her textbooks. Before she could reconsider, Abby grabbed it and ran for the parking lot.

Gretchen would guess her combination in a flash, so Abby's only hope was the Dust Bunny. She avoided classroom windows, reached her car in two minutes flat, and hid the book under the driver's seat. Then she raced back to class, caught her breath outside the door, and went back inside. Teachers never commented on how long girls stayed in the bathroom, especially when they took their purses.

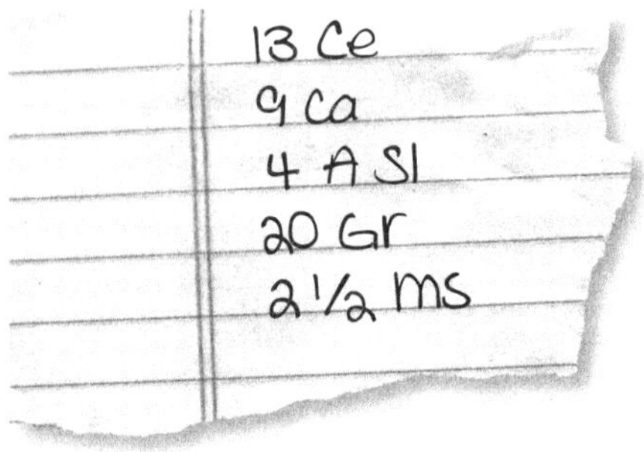

"It's like the Beverly Hills Diet," Gretchen said to Margaret. "Only all fruits and veggies. Combined with the milkshakes, you're going to lose ten pounds before the semiformal. Easy."

Gretchen and Margaret sat next to each other at the picnic table on the Lawn, elbows propped on the silver sun-warmed wood, going over Margaret's food diary. Gretchen's German textbook lay forgotten in front of her. Abby noticed that Gretchen was already on the second-to-last chapter.

Glee sat across from them, facing the auditorium, looking for something. Abby was perched at the far end of the table, trying to stay on top of her biology homework, listening to the conversation, wondering why Gretchen was so concerned with Margaret's diet.

Margaret looked like those skinny, pale girls in the Robert Palmer videos—complete with high forehead, sharp jawline, and dramatic cheekbones. She was buying new clothes every week as her old outfits got baggy and loose. Her mom was prouder of Margaret for losing weight than she'd ever been about anything in her daughter's life. She bragged that Margaret was finally having a second growth spurt and “filling out.” Her friends agreed. Margaret was turning into a real beauty, they said. Mr. Middleton didn’t notice because he hadn’t gotten his credit card bills yet.

“I’m barely even hungry anymore,” Margaret said.

“You don’t have a butt anymore,” Glee said.

“I’ll borrow some of yours,” Margaret said.

Frisbees and seagulls floated through the air. Teachers were holding grass class out on the Lawn, and all the classroom windows were open.

“Oh, by the way,” Gretchen said, reaching into her bag. She pulled out a sealed envelope. “Father Morgan is using me as his delivery service again. I’m going to start charging.”

Glee hesitated then took the envelope, stacked her books, and marched off in the direction of the auditorium, taking the turn around the bell tower that led to chapel. Abby was surprised that Margaret wasn’t saying anything. What kind of note was a teacher sending a student that had to be sealed in an envelope?

“You know she’s doing vestry all the time,” Gretchen said, watching Glee go. “I feel bad for getting her involved. I think she’s spreading herself too thin.”

“You can never be too thin,” Margaret said, then pointed to something in her food diary. “Look, see last Monday? *20 Ce*. I’m already cutting it in half. I hate all this water weight.”

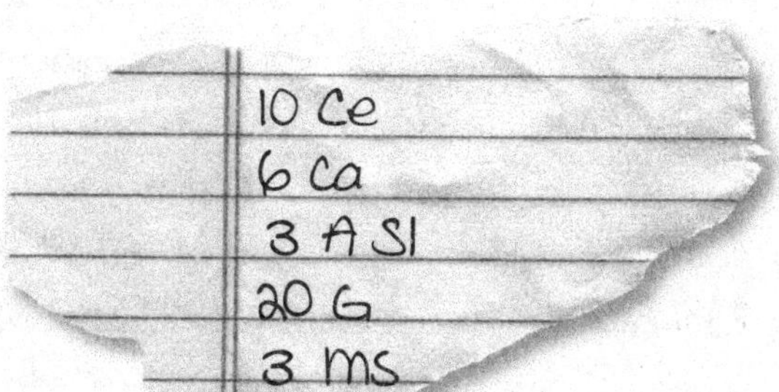

Abby sat on her bed and opened Gretchen's daybook. The first page was devoted to Andy's phone number, written in bubbly blue digits, each letter in his name outlined in yellow highlighter: Andy Solomon. Abby turned the page. For a few pages it was Gretchen's homework assignments written in different colored pens, back when they'd still had some of the same classes:

Intro to Program – *basic shapes*
English – *poss. test*
US History – *think of topic for research paper*
Ethics – *do questions for Thurs news articles*
German – *read vocab*
Biology – *graph for friday*
Geometry – *pg 28, 32 #1–8 (I understand it!! Sort of?)*

Bright splashes of color marked birthdays, school letting out early, volleyball games. Then the schedule stopped, the colors disappeared, and the next page was packed with cramped handwriting from top to bottom, curling back up the side, a tiny crazy monologue. The same with the next page, and the next. Abby tried to read it, but it was either nonsense about angels and demons or chains of random words.

Then the drawings began. At first they were between the words, but then they grew until they pushed the words off the page, were written on top of them, red scrawls of marker forming spirals and bars, pictures of crying sad faces, flowers dripping tears, funnels inside mouths, crude insects, bugs, worms, cockroaches, spiders.

Near the back, Abby found the pages that would get Gretchen a one-way ticket to Southern Pines if anyone ever saw them. The pages that read: *Kill them all. I want to die. Kill me. Make it stop make it stop make it stop.* Reading them made Abby's breath come fast and shallow and high in her chest. It made her feel lightheaded. White scratches dotted her vision.

The next morning, she woke up to find her forehead almost solid with scabs, and the zits around her nose had filled with yellow pus. Abby used two Q-tips to squeeze them dry before she pancaked and powdered her face into uneven, lumpy order and went to school. The first thing she did when she got there was find Gretchen. It was time they had a talk.

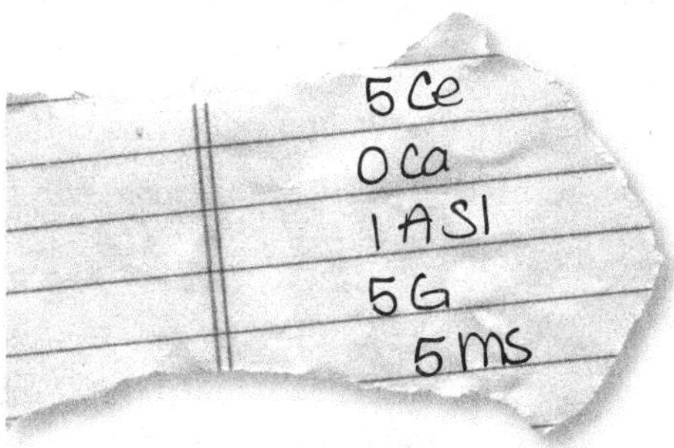

Gretchen's hand raced down the pages of her spiral notebook, answering the end-of-chapter German questions.

"I can help you," Abby said, planting herself directly in front of Gretchen's desk.

They were in Mrs. Erskine's English room before the first bell. People were slowly drifting in, finding desks or frantically finishing the previous night's homework, racing through the assigned reading.

Gretchen looked up, blinking. She glanced around to see who else was in the room.

"You're not in this class," she said. "Did you transfer?"

"No," Abby said, relieved that Gretchen was at least talking to her. "I can help you with whatever is going on."

Abby had been stressing all night over how to say this, but now it was going better than she thought.

Gretchen gave her a vague smile.

"What's going on?" she asked, bemused and confused.

"I know you're not happy," Abby said, sitting down backward at the desk in front of Gretchen, arms on the back, being earnest. "Just talk to me. Tell me what happened. We're still friends."

Gretchen bent back over her German book.

"Of course we're still friends," she said. "Why else do you think I let you sit with us at lunch? I know Margaret's being a giant pill, but that's Margaret. Maybe when she loses some weight, she'll be happier."

Abby put a hand flat on Gretchen's notebook, blocking her pen.

"Why are you doing that with Margaret?" she asked.

This time, Gretchen looked at her seriously.

"The same reason I got Glee into vestry," she said. "Because it makes her happy. You're so negative lately. I don't know what happened between y'all, and I know it's stressful, but it'll work out, Abby. Actually, the person I worry about most is you. I want all my friends to be happy, and something's definitely wrong with you. I didn't want to say anything, but your skin is acting up again."

Something nudged the side of Abby's hand and she looked down to see that Gretchen's right hand was still moving on the page, frantically scrawling jagged print across her notebook.

Abby looked up quickly.

Gretchen was still staring at her, totally unaware of what her right hand was doing, a sweet expression of concern on her face.

"What's bothering you, Abby?" she asked. "Why don't you tell me?"

Gretchen's hand stopped moving, and Abby couldn't help herself: she looked down. Rushed letters were written upside down so that the words faced her.

not me not me help me not me

Abby looked away, but not fast enough. Suddenly Gretchen tore the page from the notebook, her face filled with fury. She crumpled it up and was about to say something when Wallace Stoney appeared beside them.

"How's it hanging, G-meister?" he asked.

She beamed up at him.

"Hey, Wallace," she said. "Is everyone still going to Med Deli after?"

"Only if you figure out my Deutsch," he said. "I should never have signed up for Nazi."

"It's easy," Gretchen said. "Give it here."

He started to sit in Abby's chair, as if she were invisible. Abby flinched and got up, careful not to touch him.

"See you later, Abby," Gretchen said. "Think about what I said."

Then she and Wallace bent their heads over his German book. As Abby left, she could hear Gretchen explaining to Wallace Stoney just how easy everything was.

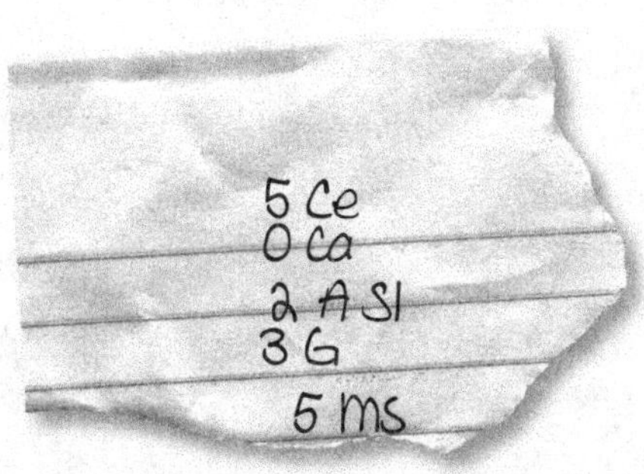

"It's Julie Slovitch," Margaret said during lunch. "God, that pig is delusional. She fantasizes about humping him all the time."

Christ, Laura Banks agreed, Julie Slovitch was so gross. She's definitely the person who must have had that bouquet of white roses delivered to Wallace during fourth-period break that morning.

"Now look at him," Margaret said. "Acting like he's King Stud."

Abby sat with her back against the lamppost on the Lawn, next to the dark green Charleston bench where Margaret was ranting at Laura Banks. Glee didn't sit with them anymore. At lunch she went to Chapel and took Communion instead. Gretchen was spending her lunches on the benches outside the now-shuttered Senior Hut with all the upperclassmen. Margaret dismissed Glee as a "Jesus freak" and ignored her defection, but she couldn't ignore the fact that she was losing Wallace. It ate away at her from the inside.

Indian summer was making everyone slap-happy. Wallace worked the Lawn, passing out his white roses to all the girls, bestowing them with courtly bows and kissing their hands. Eventually, he wandered over to Margaret, Laura, and Abby and offered Margaret a rose.

"Here," he said. "You looked so lonely, and you know, I have so many flowers because I'm such a stud."

Margaret regarded him for a moment.

"Why don't you shut up about your fucking flowers?" she finally suggested.

"Jealous much?" Wallace asked.

"I feel sorry for you," Margaret snapped. "Julie Slovitch is a dog. If you loved me, you'd dump those in the trash."

Abby knew exactly what Wallace was going to say before he said it.

"Who says I love you?" he asked.

Then he realized what he'd said. A single second of silence passed, and then Margaret laughed, harsh and braying. The sound echoed to the breezeway.

"You did," she said. "When I almost dumped you and you begged me on the phone to stay with you."

"I never begged shit," Wallace said.

"You begged me like a little girl," Margaret said, darting her face forward.

Her cheeks were bright red and the tendons in her neck popped. Her forehead was bony, bisected by a single pulsing vein, and the muscles along her jaw twitched beneath her translucent skin. Her knuckles were huge. On the volleyball court it was clear that her knees were wider than her thighs. The flesh was melting from her bones.

"You're a bitch," Wallace said. "Even Julie Slovitch has a better body than you. My dog has a better body than you."

"Then why don't you fuck your dog," Margaret snapped.

That's when Gretchen appeared, and instead of sitting with them, she put her hand on Wallace's shoulder.

"Come on, Wallace," she said. "You're just chapping Margaret's rooster. Why don't you go?"

To Abby's surprise, he left.

But not before getting in the final word.

"Fucking Skeletor," he said.

Then he was off, high-fiving Owen Bailey, handing out the rest of his roses. The next afternoon it was written on one of the mirrors in the girl's upper school bathroom:

"Skeletor gives good bone."

Margaret had a new nickname.

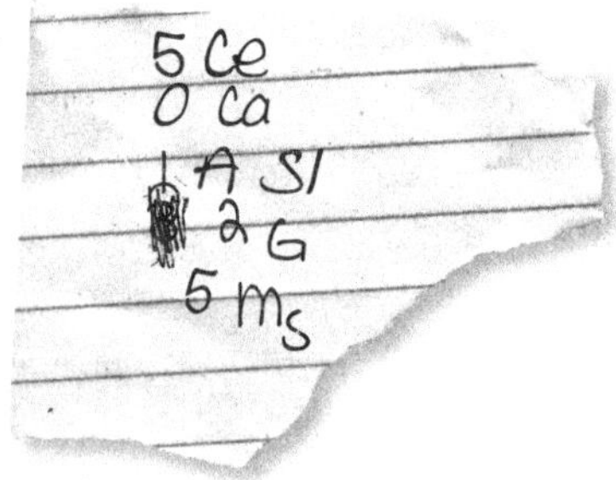

There was one last person Abby hadn't tried. As much as she hated to admit it, one other person might know Gretchen the way she did. So on Saturday night she finished her TCBY shift, and the second she got home she slammed her bedroom door, laid the pink blanket along the bottom, and opened Gretchen's daybook. There was Andy's phone number. She reached for Mickey Mouse and dialed.

The phone rang, short and shrill, twice, three times, then the click of someone picking up.

"Hello?" Abby said.

Silence. Outside her bedroom window, a moth batted against the screen.

"Is this Andy?" Abby asked. "I'm Abby Rivers. I'm a friend of Gretchen Lang?"

Silence. The fiber-optic ball on her dresser faded from purple to red.

She heard a mechanical echo down the line, wind blew static through a metal pipe. Her digital clock read 11:06.

"Abby?" a faint voice said.

Even furred with distortion, Abby recognized it instantly. This was the voice that reached down her throat and wrapped its fingers around her heart.

"Gretchen?" Abby said.

There was a series of clicks as solenoids snapped into place somewhere in the darkness of the phone company switching center. Deep space pops flew down trunk lines buried underground.

"Abby?" Gretchen said again, clearer. "Please?"

"Where are you?" Abby asked, her voice dry. "What number is this?"

A wall of static washed across the line. When it had passed, Gretchen was already talking.

". . . need you," Abby heard her say.

"I can fix this," Abby said. "All you have to do is talk to me. Tell me how to fix this."

"It's too late," Gretchen said, and her voice peaked and distorted. "I think? What time is it?"

"Are you home?" Abby asked. "I'll meet you at Alhambra."

"It's dark," Gretchen said, her voice drifting away. "He tricked me . . . he switched places with me and now I'm here and he's there."

"Who?" Abby asked.

"I think I'm dead," Gretchen said.

Abby was suddenly very aware of the phone in her hand, her body on the bed, the thinness of the walls, how her window wasn't locked, of the darkness pressing against the glass.

She imagined the phone lines running underground, through the dirt, past Molly Ravenel's grave. She knew it was an urban legend but she imagined Molly hugging the Southern Bell cable tightly to her bony chest, clutching it with her hard fingers, throwing one leathery leg around it and drawing it close to the dry, insect-heavy center of herself, pressing her skeleton lips to the line, the clips and clicks echoing behind her grinning teeth.

"This is me," Gretchen said, suddenly loud and clear. Then

the sound of a tuning radio buzzed in Abby's ear. "That isn't me. That's . . ." Metal crunched hard around the next few words. "You have to stop her. I mean me. I mean her. This is so hard, Abby. I can't think clearly and it hurts to do this for long, but you have to stop her. She's going to hurt everybody."

"Who?" Abby asked.

"What time is it there?" Gretchen asked.

"11:06," Abby said.

"What time?" Gretchen repeated with idiotic simplicity. "What time is it there? What time is it there? What time is it there?"

Abby tried to appease her.

"It's Thursday night," she said. "October 27."

"Halloween is coming," Gretchen said. "You have to be careful, Abby. She's been planning something for you. She wants to hurt you most of all."

"Why?" Abby asked.

"Because you're my only friend," Gretchen said.

The last word dissolved into a metallic echo, and then something thick and plastic snapped in Abby's ear and the line was clear.

"Gretchen?" Abby whispered into the receiver.

Gretchen was gone.

Abby called the number back but the phone just rang.

Monday was the start of the blood drive, and during fourth-period break Margaret went out to the Red Cross Winnebago parked in front of the school to give blood. When she got up off the couch afterward, she seemed unsteady, then she said, "Mom?" and passed out. It happened all the time, but the Red Cross nurse was alarmed at how thin Margaret was and insisted they send her home.

Something was happening. Abby thought about the phone call with Gretchen, and how she was putting Glee in vestry and helping Margaret lose weight, and how she seemed to be dating Wallace. Something was going on, and Abby needed to stop it, but she couldn't do it alone.

She would find a way to talk to Glee, even if it meant going to Communion during lunch, because Glee was spending all her time doing vestry, which was a very un-Glee thing to do. She'd talk to Margaret, too. Maybe even Father Morgan. If they didn't believe her, she had the daybook, but that was a last resort. A school administrator would see that and put Gretchen directly in Southern Pines. She couldn't show it to anyone until she was sure.

But first, there were the dead bodies.

SHE BLINDED ME WITH SCIENCE

Abby had been dreading this moment since ninth grade. Everyone knew it was coming, and the only thing you could do was pray it wasn't as bad as you'd heard.

On Thursday morning, the school loaded all the tenth graders onto Albemarle's one yellow school bus, put the ones who couldn't fit inside the red sports van, and carted them over the West Ashley Bridge to downtown Charleston. It was time for that most feared and anticipated rite of passage: the gross anatomy lab field trip.

Gretchen and Glee made sure they were in the red van because it was being driven by Father Morgan, but Abby didn't even try to join them. She sat on the big yellow bus with everyone else, crammed against the rear window next to Nikki Bull. All around her, students were nervous or scared or excited, and they talked nonstop. Mostly they were talking about Geraldo Rivera.

His two-hour special *Exposing Satan's Underground* had aired the night before during prime time on NBC. It sent Geraldo up against the forces of satanism, talking to serial killers (and Ozzy Osbourne) as he proved (or strongly implied) that a secret network of over one million satanists was responsible for murdering fifty thousand children a year. The special made Abby feel corroded. It was streaked with dirt from shallow graves, smeared with blood from crime scene photos, splattered with hot saliva from possessed men in white sweaters foaming at the mouth as they snarled "Get out of here" at crosses being waved in their faces during exorcisms. Geraldo stood in front of a wall of TV screens, sickened by what he heard: women identified as "breeders" calmly explaining that their babies were born to be eaten in satanic communions, their tiny corpses burned, buried in concrete, hacked into pieces, and scattered at sea.

The next day, satanism was all anyone could talk about.

"There was a senior last year," Nikki Bull said, "she had a baby, and devil worshippers made her drown it behind the school. The marsh is full of dead babies. Sometimes their bones wash up but the administration says they're seagull bones, and the maintenance staff burns them in the incinerator."

"The custodians know what's going on, but they're too scared to say anything," Eric Frey added.

"My uncle's in law enforcement and he says you couldn't pay him a million dollars to go to Northwoods Mall this time of year," Clyburn Perry said. "Right before Halloween, they walk around with a needle hidden under their watchbands, and it's got a tiny bit of AIDS blood on it. They scratch the back of your hand as you walk by and you don't think it's a big deal but then six months later you've got AIDS."

"Who's 'they'?" Dereck White asked, turning around in his seat. "Who's this mysterious 'they' doing all these terrible things?"

Everyone felt sorry for him because it was so obvious.

"Satanists," Nikki Bull said. "It was on TV."

The bus rumbled into downtown Charleston and cars stacked up behind it, the drivers too polite to honk their horns. Abby listened to low-hanging branches scrape the roof as they pulled into the medical university's parking lot. As they were packed into the enormous elevator to go up to the fifth floor, Nikki Bull was still talking about satanists.

"So the last headmaster? Some satanists broke into the graveyard and stole his mom's body. Then they went to the haunted house he always put up in his front yard at Halloween, and they dressed her corpse up as a witch and hung it from a tree by a noose. He thought it was one of his decorations and left it up there for three days. When he went to take it down, he saw that it was his mom and he went insane."

"Can it, Bull," Mrs. Paul said from the other side of the elevator.

The elevator cage rattled once, hard, and then the doors slammed open and the students spilled out on a floor that was cold and smelled like pickle juice. Up ahead was the first bunch of kids, giggling and nervous and jostling one another. Abby's group got sandwiched between the students ahead and those coming in behind as more kids piled off the elevator and squeezed into the narrow corridor, trying to stay as far away as possible from the door to the gross anatomy lab. Now that the hall was full, they all lapsed into expectant silence. Everyone knew what was coming next.

"Hello," the doctor said. He had a chicken-skin neck and a vulture's bald head covered with liver spots. He wore a white lab coat with loaded pockets that sagged halfway down his thighs, and he was thrilled to be there. "I'm Dr. Richards and I run the Medical University of South Carolina's Gross Anatomy Lab. Today, you are about to see what's eventually going to happen to every single one of you. So let's dive right in and meet your future."

The students shuffled and pushed and shoved through the double doors after him, flooding into the vast room; then they saw what lay inside and jammed up in the doorway, pressing themselves to the wall. The room stretched into the distance, with green marbled linoleum on the floor and plastic tiles on the walls. Down the center were sixteen steel tables, each one a hard bed on which lay a single partially peeled cadaver.

"The first class that new medical students take is Gross Anatomy," Dr. Richards said, grinning. "They're split into groups of four and assigned a donor. The donor is anonymous, and while in the old days we might get the occasional uncle or friend of the family popping up on the table, we haven't had a surprise like that since 1979. All the donors are carefully screened. In the spring, when class is over, the students gather at the chapel and have a memorial service for their donors, because it is a great thing to leave your body to science. I hope some of you will choose to do so after today. It would be a pleasant change to get some younger donors into the rotation."

The doctor was relaxed and easy around these jigsaw bodies. They made him happy.

"But between the first day of class and the memorial service," Dr. Richards continued, "the students work each donor down to the bone and learn what makes them tick."

Kids were giggling and shoving each other, and the smell of pickles drove all the oxygen out of the room. Abby forced herself to look at the dead bodies. Their skin was covered in bristles and their toenails were thick and yellow. Their dusty gray skin was peeled back to reveal layers of beef jerky muscles and a fruit basket of internal organs. Mottled gray lungs, dark red hearts, glistening links of lavender intestines, brown livers, a cornucopia of meaty fruit piled up inside.

Dr. Richards kept talking, full of macabre observations and corny jokes. When a cadaver's hand slipped off a table and dropped into his pocket, he mugged a startled reaction.

"Get out of there," he said, chuckling, and he plucked out the dead hand by its hairy wrist and dropping it back on the table. Everyone laughed too hard as he said, "I think he was going for my wallet."

Dr. Richards was eager to give the students his best stories: a balloon of cocaine found inside a stomach cavity, a donor whose feet were mysteriously crossed every morning when they opened the lab, a donor who was the class valedictorian's long-lost aunt. Abby saw Gretchen and Glee standing behind Father Morgan on the other side of the circle, whispering to each other. Before she could start to feel left out, Dr. Richards changed the subject.

"And this," he said, leading them to the wooden shelves in the back of the room, "this is our little cabinet of curiosities."

It was exactly as Wallace had advertised. Floating inside jars of yellow pickle juice were a disembodied breast, a two-headed baby with its sternum laid open so they could see its bifurcated spinal column, a tongue distended by a tumor the size of a baseball, a severed hand with six fingers.

"Hey, Abby," Hunter Prioleaux said over her shoulder, "you dropped your lunch."

Abby looked down and nearly tripped over a white plastic ten-gallon bucket. It was sitting on the floor and overflowing with gray fetuses. They were pressed from the same mold: skin smooth, eyes closed, mouths open, tiny hands bunched into fists. Piled in the bucket without rhyme or reason, they looked like hairless kittens, heavy and sleek.

Abby swore she wouldn't be the first one to go out to the hall. Her vision swam and blurred around the edges. She looked up and locked eyes with Gretchen. They stared at each other for a second and then Gretchen smiled, and though Abby thought the smile looked mean, she instinctively smiled back. She couldn't help it. Gretchen stopped smiling and whispered something in Glee's ear and the two of them giggled. Abby flicked her eyes away. All she could think was, *Why on the floor? Couldn't they at least put them on a table?*

On the drive back to school, Abby could still smell pickles clinging to her clothes. In front of her, Dereck White and Nikki Bull continued talking about some kid named Jonathan Cantero who'd stabbed his mom to death in Tampa. Abby couldn't stop seeing their muscles moving beneath their skin as they talked. She imagined what their mouths would look like with no lips.

"He was a Dungeons and Dragons geek," Nikki said. "That's why he killed his mom. The game made him do it."

"You're insane," Dereck said. "A game can't make anyone do anything."

"It's a satanic game," Nikki said, and she rolled her eyes. "You're so naive."

Abby peeled the skin back from everyone on the bus, which became a metal can on wheels full of wide-eyed skeletons with clacking jaws. Their muscles jerked and danced like puppet strings, raising and lowering their arm bones and leg bones, and they were all just bones and meat and they all looked exactly the same.

Through the window, Abby saw the red school van pull up alongside them on the West Ashley Bridge. Father Morgan honked, and Abby watched as Glee and Gretchen looked out the window. They saw her, and Gretchen locked eyes again.

"Satan made him do it," Nikki was saying. "Plus he was probably on LSD."

Abby imagined peeling the skin from Gretchen, pulling off her flesh like a damp glove, exposing her bones. But it didn't work. In her mind, she couldn't see what was inside Gretchen. She had no heart, no lungs, no stomach, no liver. She was full of bugs.

Gretchen and Glee waved.

Abby didn't wave back.

"I'm so sorry, Abby," Mrs. Spanelli said. She was dressed as a witch, holding a shopping bag that contained her turban and crystal ball. "They didn't tell me until I got here this morning."

Friday was a half day because of the Halloween carnival. It was sponsored by the parents, but the upper school clubs were expected to run the booths that filled the Lawn, and whichever club took in the most tickets got half the door money. Abby didn't belong to any clubs, so she'd agreed to help Mrs. Spanelli do the fortune-teller booth. Except this year, no fortune-teller.

"They don't want anything that might be, you know, occult," Mrs. Spanelli said. "Especially after Geraldo."

"That's okay," Abby said. "I might go home early."

Instead she went to the downtown library.

"I'm trying to find out where this area code is," she asked the librarian, showing her Andy's number. Abby felt very mature asking for help tracking down a phone number.

"Eight-one-three is Tampa," the librarian said.

"Do you have any Tampa phone books?" Abby asked.

The librarian jerked her thumb over her shoulder.

"Back wall," she said.

Abby walked over to a a dimly lit section of shelves that stank of newsprint and found a broken-spined Tampa phone book on top of a pile of worn directories. It felt greasy and used. She flopped it onto a table and flipped through until she found three Solomons. She wrote down their names, street addresses, and phone numbers, and that night she closed herself in her room and started dialing.

No one answered at the first Solomon household. The second one was an answering machine. The third was registered to Francis Solomon. Abby knew it was the right one. It was only two digits different from the number in Gretchen's daybook. Someone picked up on the fifth ring.

"Hello?" the woman said and then hacked out a smoker's cough. "Sorry. Hello?"

"Is Andy there?" Abby asked, fighting the instinct to hang up.

"Andy!" she heard the woman scream. "There's a little girl for you!"

There was a long pause, then a *click*.

"I got it, Mom. Hang up!" a whiny voice shouted. Abby heard another *click* and then a boy was breathing in her ear. "Tiffany?"

"This is Abby." A confused silence followed. "I'm Gretchen's friend." More confused silence. "Her best friend." The silence lengthened. "Gretchen Lang? From camp?"

"Oh," the boy said. "What?"

It was Abby's turn to be confused.

"I wanted to ask you . . ." She didn't know how to get into it. "Has Gretchen seemed weird to you? Or said anything about me?"

"What do you mean?" he asked. "At camp?"

"Or on the phone," Abby said.

"Why?" he asked.

"Because I'm her best friend," Abby said, hating how childish it sounded. "And I think something might be wrong with her."

"How would I know?" he asked. "I haven't talked to her since camp ended. She never called me. I have to go. We don't have call waiting."

After he hung up, Abby sat on the phone for a minute. None of it made sense. She vowed that on Monday she would risk being humiliated and confront Gretchen about Andy and figure out what was going on. But that weekend it was Halloween. And by Monday it was too late.

UNION OF THE SNAKE

"I appreciate you taking the time to be here today," Major rumbled. "I would like to discuss with you Abigail's future at Albemarle Academy. It is my opinion that she does not have one."

Abby sat across from Major. To her left was her dad, jammed uncomfortably into a hard wooden chair. He was all sharp angles and bony knees, awkward elbows, jutting shoulder blades. He'd shaved but missed the spot beneath his lower lip. His palms rested on his thighs, and unconsciously he rubbed them over his worn khakis, back and forth, back and forth. It was making Abby crazy.

On her right sat her mom, leaning forward, keyed up, jaw clenched, ready for a fight; she blinked her eyes rapidly to stay awake. Mrs. Rivers had worked double shifts over the long Halloween weekend, and she was not prepared for a parents' meeting on Tuesday after school. She clutched her purse in her lap and hadn't taken off her puffy winter coat. It was overkill for Charleston, but Abby's mom was always cold.

Major placed a manila folder in the middle of his desk and flipped it open, then he put on his reading glasses and made them wait while he scanned its contents. Once finished, he looked up again.

"Several incidents occurred over the Halloween weekend," he said. "And I have it on good authority that Abigail was involved in at least one of them. She has also been accused of theft. And while her grades have been excellent up to this point, I do not believe that past progress is indicative of future performance. At least one parent has called and asked me to ensure that Abigail does not interact with her child because she believes, as do I, that she is using and selling narcotics."

"Are you on drugs?" Abby's mother snapped, turning on her. "Are you selling drugs?"

Abby was shaking her head.

"No, Mom," she said. "I promise."

"You swear to me?" her mother demanded.

"I promise," Abby said. "I don't even do drugs."

Mrs. Rivers turned to Major.

"Who said that about my daughter?" she asked.

"I'm not at liberty to discuss names," Major said. "But it comes from an unimpeachable source. As does the information that Abigail was involved in the distribution and consumption of alcohol on campus Friday night."

On Friday night, while Abby worked the closing shift at TCBY, the Albemarle football team suited up and trotted onto home field to battle Bishop England for last place in the division. It was the final game of the season, rescheduled from the homecoming rain-out, and tensions were high.

Ten minutes to game time and Coach Toole was freaking out because Wallace Stoney, his star quarterback, wasn't there. Someone said he was making out with a girl in his truck, but no one could find him. Then Wallace strolled onto the sidelines, cool as a cucumber, right after the coin toss; Coach Toole was so relieved, he put him in the game immediately. By the end of the first quarter, Wallace was on his hands and knees at Albemarle's thirty-yard line, spraying vomit out his helmet. Medics rushed onto the field, thinking he was concussed. It took one whiff to convince them otherwise.

"Get your player off the grass" the ref told Coach Toole. "He's drunk."

The game collapsed into chaos, ending only when Major made his way down from the bleachers and ordered Coach Toole to forfeit. Albemarle Academy was officially the worst football team in South Carolina. And it was all Wallace's fault. His house was egged on Halloween and someone threw a rock through the back window of his truck. He hadn't shown up for school that morning.

"What happened at that game was a humiliation for this school," Major said. "And although Abigail was not present, I have it on good authority that she was the individual who purchased alcohol and provided it to this student."

"I didn't—" Abby said before Major raised his hand to silence her. She turned to her mother. "Mom . . . ?"

"Miss Rivers," Major said, "if you cannot control yourself, you may leave and I'll discuss the matter with your parents alone."

Trapped in Major's overheated office, Abby felt a trickle of sweat dribble down her chest. Even without touching the skin on her face, she knew grease had started oozing through her makeup. Her empty stomach rumbled embarrassingly. Her dad kept rubbing his hands on his thighs. Shk . . . shk . . . shk . . .

"More importantly, a student has come to me and accused Abigail of theft," Major rumbled on, mellow and unstoppable. "The stolen item is of great emotional value to this student. Stealing is an honor code violation, subject to immediate expulsion. I will ask at this point: Abigail, do you have it with you?"

Abby knew he meant Gretchen's daybook. Gretchen knew Abby had it and she had gone to Major. He looked at her from underneath hooded eyes, and Abby stared straight ahead at a crack in one of the cinderblocks.

"Abigail?" Major repeated.

"I didn't steal anything," Abby said.

Major stared at her for another moment and then sighed.

"It is our considered opinion," he said, "that you should remove Abigail to a less academically strenuous environment where she can receive the help and guidance that she needs."

There was creaking from the right as Abby's mom adjusted herself.

"Where's that?" she asked.

"Not here," Major said.

"Are you expelling her?" Mrs. Rivers asked.

"No one would benefit from Abigail being expelled," Major said. "Which is why I have called you here this afternoon so that you may voluntarily withdraw her. In which case I would certainly be prepared to overlook the reports of her behavior I have received and write her a letter of recommendation that would guarantee her admittance to one of the many fine public schools in the Charleston area."

Major's eyes darted to his left, and Abby saw that a button on his phone was blinking. Instantly, his gray tongue slicked his lips, his head retreated to his shoulders, his voice went up an octave.

"Excuse me," he said, picking up the receiver.

"Yes," he said and then sat in silence, listening intently.

Abby's parents didn't have a clue, but Abby did. It was the hospital. Nikki Bull had told her what happened in first period that morning.

"Someone stole a baby," she'd said.

"What?" Abby had asked.

"A dead one," Nikki had said. "At the gross anatomy lab. They had babies in a bucket, and when we were there someone took one. I guess they counted them over the weekend and came up short. Mrs. Paul has been in Major's office all morning. That's sick, right?"

To Abby, it sounded like more Nikki Bullshit. But administration had conducted a search of Hunter Prioleaux's locker during fourth-period break, and a substitute was teaching Mrs. Paul's class. Abby couldn't believe it. Someone had touched one of those sad, boneless things, shoved it in a bookbag, hidden it on the bus. It made her want to cry.

Major hung up the phone. He looked at it for a long minute, then returned his attention to Abby and her parents. "So, we are agreed?" he asked. "You will withdraw Abigail from Albemarle Academy and I will write her a letter of recommendation. You should have no trouble placing her in one of Charleston's public schools. I feel this is best for everyone."

He reached into the paper tray in front of him, took out a blank sheet, and uncapped his pen. Abby waited for someone to say something, but nobody said anything. Major began to draft his letter. Abby's dad started rubbing his thighs faster: shk-shk-shk-shk . . .

Abby was being thrown out of school and no one was going to do anything. Her throat closed to the size of a straw and pressure built up behind her eyes. She dug her fingernails into the inside of her wrist, hiding it in her lap, trying to keep herself from crying. Whatever happened, she would not give them the satisfaction.

"There," Major said, pushing the sheet of paper across his desk. "If you would read that and approve it, I'll have Miss Toné type it up on letterhead, and you can take it with you when you leave. We'll send Abigail's transcript to whichever school you decide is best."

He leaned back and folded his hands across his stomach, satisfied that his work was done. Abby's mom didn't pick up the letter. They all sat like that for a long moment, and then Major sighed.

"In light of Abigail's troubles," he said patiently, "this is the least disruptive course of action. She cannot continue at Albemarle, and if you force us to resort to expulsion, there will be no letter. Any school that takes her as a transfer student is going to call and ask me for my recommendation, and I will have no choice but to share my suspicions regarding her involvement with narcotics, providing alcohol to an underage student on campus, and this theft."

"My daughter doesn't do drugs," Abby's mother said. "She doesn't drink."

"Mrs. Rivers," Major rumbled, "any parent would say the same thing, but I suggest that you might not know your daughter as well as you think. Abigail—"

"I asked her," Mrs. Rivers said. "You saw me, and you heard her answer. She says she doesn't do drugs. And while my daughter is a lot of things, she is not a liar."

"Well . . . ," Major began.

"What was that you said she made on her PSATs?" Abby's mom said. "Oh, you didn't. Well, I saw her scores. They were 1520. Now I haven't seen the scores for your other students, but I'm betting that's a darn sight higher than some of these Middletons and Tigners whose parents' names are all over your buildings. And I know it's Grace Lang who called you, because she called me, too. If anyone's doing drugs, it's that little girl of hers, but I understand why you're being nice to the Langs. You're going to squeeze a damn sight more money out of them than you'll ever get from the Rivers. I don't judge you for it. It's your job."

"I do not appreciate the accusation," Major protested.

Abby had never heard Major sound weak before.

"Not an accusation, Julius," Abby's mom said. "Just stating

facts. I'll be damned if you're going to kick my daughter out of school for being poor and talking back. And I'll be double damned if you're going to rope me into doing your dirty work for you. If you want to throw my little girl out, you'll have to do it yourself. And know this: the minute, the very second, that you write a letter saying she's not suitable for Albemarle Academy, I'm going to be at the next PTA meeting questioning every single decision you've ever made. So you'd better have your ass covered or it's going to be grass, and I'm going to be the lawn mower."

Abby didn't even know it was possible to talk to Major this way. Incandescent rage was radiating from her mother, but her voice wasn't raised; she wasn't yelling or carrying on. She was simply taking Major apart and glowing with a white-hot fury.

"Now, Mary," Major said, "getting angry and blowing off steam in my office is all fine and good, but it's not helping Abigail."

"Save it, you puffed-up gym teacher," Abby's mom snarled. And, unbelievably, Major's mouth snapped shut. "How a degree in physical education makes you qualified to run this monkey farm, I'll never know, but that's not up to me. Even back at the Citadel I didn't like you. You always kissed up and kicked down."

"Martin," Major said, appealing to Abby's dad, "out of respect for our friendship, I'm asking—"

"Oh, can it," Abby's mom said. "Martin never liked you, either."

Abby's dad stopped rubbing his pants for a moment and shrugged his bony shoulders.

"Now that's not entirely true," he said. "I just never thought about you long enough to develop an opinion."

Major started to say something, but again Abby's mother was on him.

"I know there are parents here who are sick and tired of the little club you run," Mrs. Rivers continued. "I bet every single one of them would be only too eager to hear about my daughter being made a scapegoat for your incompetence. I bet they all have stories of their own. I bet if we all started talking, we could really make your job a whole lot harder."

A long silence took hold while her threat settled.

"Mary . . . ," Major began.

"We're through here," Abby's mom said, standing up and hitching her purse over one shoulder. "I don't want to hear any more about Abby moving to another school or having any more difficulties with you, and I don't expect to be dragged into another waste-of-time session like this. My daughter flunks out or my daughter drops out, we'll deal with her then—and trust me, I will tear up her hide. But this conversation right here? It is over."

To Abby's amazement, her dad stood up and her mom opened the door and they walked right out of Major's office. Abby kept expecting Major to call her back or give them all Saturday School, but he didn't make a peep. Abby was the last one out the door; she turned around to see him still sitting, bent over his desk, with his fingertips rubbing his forehead. She almost said she was sorry, but then her mother was pulling her through the little hallway, past Miss Toné, and outside.

The wind was blasting out of the marsh, scouring the Lawn, howling through the breezeway. No one said a word until they were standing by Abby's mom's car parked in the faculty lot, their hair and coats being tossed around. The only sound was the flag snapping in the sky behind them. For once, Abby was actually excited about going to her shift at TCBY. "Mom," she said, "thank you. You were totally awesome and—"

Abby's mom whirled; her face was such a mask of fury, it snatched the words right out of Abby's mouth.

"Damn you for ever putting me in this position, Abigail," she hissed. "How dare you have us called in here like a bunch of white trash. I have sacrificed so much for you, and this is how you repay me?"

Abby tried to put a sentence together.

"I—but I didn't do anything," she said. "You even said I didn't."

"I'm giving you the benefit of the doubt because you're my daughter," her mother spat. "But God help you if you make a liar out of me. How far do you think your scholarship goes? When's the last time you looked at the bills? Your father and I scrape to keep you here, and this is how you act?"

Abby knew she looked stupid, mouth flapping open, trying to form words, but this wasn't fair. None of it was fair.

"He said all that because he hates me," she said. "He's blaming me for what other people did."

"Your job is to make that man like you," her mother came right back at her. "He should speak your name one time in your life, and that's at graduation when he hands you your diploma. He's blaming you for what other people did? I wonder who those people are. I wonder why I heard Gretchen Lang's name in there?"

Abby wanted to lie, but she was too raw.

"It's not the way you think," she began.

"I'm sure I can't possibly understand anything about your wonderful friends," Mrs. Rivers said. "I warned you those girls would take you down this path, and you thought I couldn't possibly understand anything about your life. Oh, no, you're too smart for me. So you ignored everything I said and here we are. Well, I hope you feel clever now."

"I—" Abby began.

"Enough," her mother snapped. "I have put up with enough

from you today. I have to get to work."

With that, she slammed into her car. Her dad walked slowly to the passenger door and got in. Abby watched as they pulled on their seatbelts, backed out, and drove away. Behind her, the halyard banged against the metal flagpole like an idiot trapped inside a cage, causing the metal to echo as the wind lifted impossibly higher. A sheet of white paper skirled across the sky, riding a crashing ocean of air currents over Abby's head.

Abby watched her mom's car brake at the stop sign, then turn onto Albemarle, chased by another sheet of paper snapping at its rear bumper. She looked back toward school and saw, framed in the breezeway, a blizzard of paper rolling and tumbling across the Lawn. Thin shouts reached her, and she started walking, then running, toward campus, her heart iced over with dread.

It was 4:05 and the sounds of volleyball practice were sucked from the open gymnasium door and torn to scraps by the wind. Afterschool detention was in full effect in Mr. Barlow's computer room. Rehearsals for the Founders Day concert were under way in the auditorium. And a girl stood half naked on top of the bell tower, throwing papers into the sky.

One cartwheeled past Abby and she snatched it up. It was a photocopy of a handwritten note that began, "Dearest One, like a lily among thorns is my darling among the young women . . ." She let her eyes fall down the page to the signature: Bruce. There was only one Bruce on campus—Father Bruce Morgan—and she looked up and realized why the silhouette of the girl looked familiar, with her tan arms and white breasts.

A few students and teachers had stopped to stare, and more were drawn from their offices and classrooms; the girl on the tower was stumbling close to the edge. The ground lurched and rocked beneath Abby's feet as the figure waved her arms, shouting, the wind pulling away her words and draping her hair over her face. Abby started to walk toward the bell tower. Now the box of photocopies was empty and the girl tossed it, but the wind didn't lift it anywhere. It just fell straight down and hit the bricks, a dress rehearsal for what Abby knew would happen next.

Maintenance staff wrestled with the tower door as the girl teetered on the lip, set against the sky, the wind swaying her back and forth. Abby stopped because she didn't want to hear what was about to happen. She knew that if she got too close, the sound would be something she would never stop hearing.

The girl prepared herself: She bowed her head, raised her arms to the sky, then stretched out one leg and stepped forward into the void just as two arms wrapped around her from behind and lifted her out of the air. A man pulled her against his chest, her legs kicking into empty space; he heaved himself backward, staggering out of sight with the girl in his arms.

Abby ran for the bell tower. Her feet kicked at swirling papers, and the noise of shouting became clearer as the auditorium blocked the wind screaming off the marsh. The door at the base of the tower banged open and a circle of maintenance men backed out, holding the girl thrashing in their hands.

"I want to die! I want to die! Let meeee!" Glee shrieked.

Calm, reasonable, boring Glee was screeching and howling, clawing at the men who carried her. Glee, who refused to fight because she was a "no drama mama," kicked at their thighs, scratched their arms, spat in their faces. The girl who had once proclaimed that nothing in the world was worth getting upset about, really, who said crying was the way boring people showed off, began to scream and sob. Her black stirrup pants had been pulled low in the struggle and her soft belly hung out; Abby noticed Glee wasn't wearing a top, and someone brushed past her holding a blanket.

Across Glee's breasts was written "For you" in black marker.

"Let me die. Let me go, please, let me go," she wailed.

A sharp odor tickled Abby's nose. Glee reeked of vodka. Her entire body was now wracked with sobs, jerking in time to her heaving chest as "For you" twisted and swayed. While the maintenance men wrapped Glee in the blanket, her rescuer hung back in the bell tower's doorframe, obscured in darkness, afraid to step into the light. It was Father Morgan.

"I love him, I love him, I love him," Glee sobbed, turning around, reaching for him. Glee's voice was hoarse and full of passion, and Abby didn't recognize her anymore.

LIKE A PRAYER

The exorcist loved corn dogs. He sat across from Abby at a plastic table bolted to the floor of Citadel Mall and inhaled the steam rising from his order of six. He picked up the first one, pulled out the stick, dunked it in ketchup, and chowed it down in two bites. As his enormous jaws worked up and down, he leaned back and closed his eyes. His huge neck flexed as he swallowed the wad of meat and breading.

"Corn dogs," the exorcist said, "are all the proof I need that there is a God."

Then he picked up another one.

Big bands of muscle flexed as he swallowed his second corn dog. While he chewed, Abby tried to think of how to start this conversation, but he saved her the trouble.

"So," the exorcist said, blotting his lips with a teeny paper napkin, "you're friends with that girl who's possessed by Satan?"

This is not what Abby had expected when she'd called the number on the Lemon Brothers Faith and Fitness Ministry pamphlet. She'd dialed, a finger resting on the cradle, ready to hang up if things got uncomfortable. Her finger relaxed when Christian himself had answered the phone.

At first he'd agreed to meet her at Waffle House in West Ashley, but he called back five minutes later and changed the location to the Hot Dog on a Stick at Citadel Mall. Apparently, he loved corn dogs. When she arrived, he gave her a firm handshake and then placed his order. Abby got a lemonade she didn't want.

The exorcist was huge. Far bigger in person than he had been onstage, and the plastic table stretched across his lap like a napkin. He wore a gray sweatshirt that he'd cut the sleeves off himself, and his pants sported a busy neon-green and pink pattern and an elastic waistband. A hot-pink fanny pack was strapped around his waist and a pair of Aloha Surfer sunglasses hung from a strap around his neck.

"I don't know what's wrong with her, Mr. Lemon," Abby said, unwilling to use a crazy Bible word like *possession* out loud.

"Call me Brother Lemon," the exorcist said. "Mr. Lemon is my dad. My parents call me Chris, but I don't know. They named me Christian because we all have Bible names, but I was a whoopsy-baby. So by the time I popped out, they were short on inspiration. Ha! I probably shouldn't say that around you. Do you know where babies come from yet?"

"I'm sixteen," Abby said.

"Rad!" Chris Lemon beamed, swallowing his final corn dog.

Carefully, he folded up his garbage, tucking one item into another, then into another, then another. When it had all been reduced to fit into his large Coke cup, he reached into his fanny pack and pulled out a wet wipe, then cleaned off his spatula-sized fingertips. "I don't want to shock you. What do you know about demons?"

"Demons?" Abby asked.

"Demons, devils, unclean spirits," he said. "Incubuses, succubi, creatures from the pit. They have many names."

Abby looked around to make sure no one was overhearing this craziness. All around her, Citadel Mall shoppers continued about their business, totally oblivious to the discussion at the corner table of Hot Dog on a Stick.

"Why do you think Gretchen has one?" Abby asked.

"Because I've got the gift of discernment," Brother Lemon said, and grinned. "Well, my brothers say it's Elijah who can discern demonic entities, but I can do it, too. I see them all the time. There's not a day goes by that I don't see at least three or four. My brothers give me a hard time because, well, that's how brothers are. They rail on you, ride you; it's their job, I guess. Do you have any brothers?"

"No," Abby said.

"I love my brothers," he said. "Don't get me wrong, but I'm the baby so they treat me like I don't know anything. But you know what? Our show relies on me. They're all strong guys, but none of them has the muscle definition that I do. I'm one buff specimen and they're just jealous I've got all this."

He curled one arm and popped his biceps. It quivered next to his face, the size of a football.

"I think I made a mistake," Abby said, and she stood up and slid her purse off the back of her chair.

"Oh, wait a minute," Brother Lemon said. "You came all the way out to the mall, at least tell me if I'm right." He grinned and leaned in close, lowering his voice. "She is possessed by Satan, isn't she?"

Abby blushed.

"There's no shame in asking for help," Brother Lemon said. "I've been there. You come up against something that's bigger than you are, bigger than anything you've ever experienced before, and you're lost and you need help. You want to turn to someone who understands spiritual warfare with the Enemy, am I right?"

Abby stood still, holding her purse, and nodded. Brother Lemon patted the table.

"I'm a good listener," he smiled.

Slowly, Abby sat down.

"I don't really know why I called you," she said. "But when you said you saw something, it kind of clicked with me. And then I found your pamphlet, and I guess I was upset and gave you a call. I almost didn't come but I thought, because I called, it'd be rude not to show up."

Brother Lemon squeezed her arm reassuringly. It left a bruise.

"You did the right thing," he said. "Now the first order of business is, we've got to be sure she's really possessed. It's easy to get it wrong, you know. A lot of people think someone's possessed, but they're actually being misled by the Enemy."

"Well," Abby said, "Gretchen's changed a lot. She used to be nice and we were best friends. But now she's really horrible."

She felt a pang of disloyalty saying this kind of thing out loud about Gretchen. Brother Lemon leaned across the table, way too eager to hear what she had to say, and it made Abby self-conscious. She looked down and traced patterns on the yellow plastic.

"You're scared because the Enemy doesn't want us to be open with each other," Brother Lemon said. "He wants to make us feel ashamed and alone. Will you let me help you? Will you let me ask you some questions?"

Abby nodded.

"Okay," he said. "All you need to do is answer truthfully, okay?"

Abby nodded again. Her throat was dry and she'd lost the ability to form words. He was taking her seriously, and she felt like she'd set foot on a road that couldn't be untraveled. Her heart was fluttering against her rib cage; she couldn't breathe deep.

"Did your friend get sick?" Brother Lemon asked. "Real sick? Like, physically she got all grotesque and horrible?"

Abby nodded.

"And then what happened?" he continued. "Did she talk about suicide and depressing things? Maybe try to hurt herself?"

Abby thought about Gretchen in her bedroom, she thought about the gouges down Gretchen's arms, about Gretchen grabbing the wheel, and she nodded.

"Did she get obsessed with death and violence? Maybe obsessed with talking about religious stuff, like Hell?" Brother Lemon asked.

Abby remembered Gretchen's daybook and her obsession with Molly Ravenel. She nodded again.

"Then, all of a sudden, she got better, right?" Brother Lemon asked. "In fact, she looked better than before. She seemed alive again?"

Abby's eyes widened. All she could do was nod.

"She's better in body," he continued, "but not in spirit."

Abby didn't understand that one.

"She looks copacetic," he explained, then tapped his skull. "But up here she's coo-coo for Cocoa Puffs."

Abby took a sip of her lemonade. It coated her throat with citrus-flavored chalk.

"Yeah," she croaked.

"Is she committing sins?" Brother Lemon asked.

Abby thought about Wallace, and Glee, and Margaret and the German milkshakes, and she wondered how many of the Ten Commandments Gretchen had broken by now.

"Yeah," she said again.

"Is she grouchy? PMS-ing all the time?" Brother Lemon asked. "You know what that means?"

"I know," Abby said, nodding.

"Has she committed desecrations of holy ground?" Brother Lemon asked. "Vandalism of churches and graveyards? Burning the American flag?"

Abby paused.

"Maybe," she whispered.

"Is she leading others into sin?" Brother Lemon asked. "Tempting them? Causing them to do bad things?"

"Yes," Abby said, and she thought about Glee screaming, stinking of vodka. "A lot."

"And did her eyes turn black, so there's no more pupil?" he asked. "Like a shark or an alien?"

Abby caught herself and shook her head.

"No," she said, confused. "Her eyes are fine."

"Oh," Brother Lemon said, disappointed. Then he brightened. "Even without the eyes, it sounds like demonic possession to me."

Abby was embarrassed to be talking about something so crazy at Hot Dog on a Stick. She looked around again to see if anyone was listening to Brother Lemon's booming voice. He saw what she was doing.

"Don't stress," he said. "Demonic possession is a lot more common than people think."

"It is?" Abby asked.

"If I'm lying, I'm dying," Brother Lemon said. "My brothers and my daddy have been doing deliverance ministry for years, and there's more of them all the time. You won't read about it in the paper, but at Columbia Hospital, where they keep the crazies, they'll sometimes clear the rooms, close off a floor, and my daddy'll perform a deliverance after-hours. The Health Department just puts 'irregular procedures' on the medical chart. Right there in black and white. Everyone knows it's a code word."

"How many have you done?" Abby asked.

Brother Lemon leaned back and looked out the window onto the mall concourse for a moment.

"Well," he said, "I've assisted on a few, you know, with my brothers and my daddy."

"You've seen it?" Abby asked. "For real?"

"Oh, sure," Brother Lemon said. "I've seen some real blast-'em-out deliverance ministers do their thing, and I tell you, it is a privilege to see those fellas work. These are real hour-of-power-type deliverances, you know, with screaming and fighting and howling and vomiting all over the place."

"So you've fought a demon?" Abby asked.

Brother Lemon stretched his arms wide, then scratched the back of his neck and tried very hard to look casual.

"As an assistant," he said. "You know, helping out. I've seen demonic influences, and I've met plenty of people who have."

"Maybe I should find one of them?" Abby asked. "Like, an expert?"

Brother Lemon looked alarmed and lowered his voice.

"Come on now," he said. "There aren't any experts in the field of deliverance. Most people kind of make it up as they go along. Which means I'm as good as the next guy."

"Maybe I should talk to your dad," Abby said.

"You don't want to do that," Brother Lemon said. "He's getting old. I'm young and strong, and that's what you need. You've got to blast the demons out of your friend, have a good old-fashioned power encounter. We went up to a puke and rebuke in Spartanburg a couple of months ago, my daddy got so winded he had to take a breather in the middle. That's not going to happen with me. Plus, I've picked up things. Like, you never wear a tie during a deliverance. Do that and you'll wind up getting strangled, guaranteed. Happens every time."

Abby nodded. That sounded like the voice of experience.

"So what do you do?" she asked.

"Well," he said, "do you think she'd go somewhere with you? Like on a trip?"

"Maybe?" Abby said.

"Okay," he said. "So we'd have to find somewhere to go."

"Like where?" Abby asked.

"Somewhere private," Brother Lemon said. "With a way to tie her down so she doesn't hurt herself. Or us. And then we're there for a few hours, praying over her. I've got some holy oil I can bring. Really, we just get in there and pry the demon out of her. It's better not to use a hotel. People can get the wrong idea. Oh, shoot, there I go again!"

He laughed nervously.

"I think I know a place," Abby said.

"Great," Brother Lemon said. "We just have to get her there. There are all kinds of demons. There are demons of confusion, and nihilism, and self-harm, and anger, and pride. There's demons of infant baptism, Roman Catholicism, Jewish mysticism. They all know different things, like some know about theology, and some know about nuclear missiles, and some know a whole lot about science. But the one thing they all have in common is that they're sort of wily creatures. So we have to have a backup plan for what to do if the demoniac—that's your friend—says yes, she'll get in the car with you, then at the last sec she changes her mind."

"Like, trick her?" Abby asked.

"Or drug her," Brother Lemon said casually, looking off into the distance behind Abby.

"This is a bad idea," Abby said. "I'm sorry, I—forget I came."

"What?" Brother Lemon said, leaning forward and waving his hands. "It's not a big deal. Sometimes, you know, you have to break a few eggs."

"She's my best friend," Abby said.

"Not anymore," Brother Lemon said, staring at her. His eyes were green and beautiful. "She's a demoniac. One possessed by a demon. She's a creature of Andras now."

"What?" Abby asked.

Brother Lemon enveloped her wrist in an enormous hand and pressed it to the table, lightly but firmly. "You know why I'm talking to you like this? Being so open and up-front? Because I've seen who's inside of your friend, and I'm scared for you. This demon wants to isolate you. It wants to drive everyone else away. Then, when the time comes, it'll make the demoniac wipe herself out and take you with it. You won't have anyone left to help you when that hour is upon thee."

It sounded crazy, nuts, insane. But also very close to what was really happening.

"Demons are ideas made flesh," Brother Lemon said. "Bad ideas. The one inside your friend is discord, anger, and rage. He is the bringer of storms with a smile like lightning, brother of owls and giver of nightborn intelligence. He is the cleaving that can never be healed."

Abby didn't dare to breathe.

"Have you seen a lot of owls around?" Brother Lemon asked. "Heard them calling at night? They sense their master is near. You think I'm lying? Then tell me, is your friend trying to sow discord? Is her goal to turn friend against friend, family against family? Does she spread lies and deceit that bring down punishment and wrath on the innocent while the guilty go free?"

Abby thought about Margaret. She thought about Glee. She thought about Gretchen reporting her daybook stolen. She thought about the notes Gretchen had brought Glee, and she knew that Gretchen had written them. She didn't want to nod, but it was the truth.

"You are not alone, Abby," Brother Lemon said. "I'll be your listening ear, your strong shoulder, and at any time, you can walk away. But don't let Andras make you silent. Talk to me."

Tears slipped down Abby's nose but she was determined to speak. It took fifteen minutes for her to tell Brother Lemon everything.

"Yeah," Brother Lemon said when she had finished, handing her a tissue from his fanny pack. "That totally makes sense. All those things happened over Halloween, which is the number one day of power for Satan. Andras often pretends to be a good guy as a smokescreen for his own agenda. The whole communist hunts in the fifties? Those were Andras. He uses chaos and anarchy for his own ends."

"He sounds bad," Abby said in agreement, balling up the soaked tissue and trying to figure out how ruined her makeup was.

"Abby," Brother Lemon said, "do you know how this ends?"

Abby shook her head.

"It ends when your friend is crazy and in Columbia State Mental Hospital," he said. "It ends with her smearing poop on the walls to make occult symbols of devil worship. Or it ends when she takes pills and dies, or eats a shotgun. And she will take people down with her. You told me a little bit about this Gretchen, and it sounds like she was a good friend. Well, if you're her good friend, you can't abandon her now. I know all the stuff I'm saying sounds pretty gnarly, but your friend is no longer in that body. She is somewhere else, lost and scared and alone. It's up to us to save her."

"How do we get her to the place?" Abby asked after a moment. "You know, if she won't come?"

"GHB," Brother Lemon said. "Weightlifters use it all the time. It's a dietary supplement, but it knocks you right out if you take too much. Hard to get, though, and tricky to use. Demons may be evil little suckers, but they have to eat and drink just like the rest of us. Slip some in her drink, then we'll take her to the car and convey her to the site of deliverance."

"I don't know . . . ," Abby said.

"Well," Brother Lemon said, shrugging his massive shoulders, "you think about it, and when you do know, you give me a call. But don't wait too long. Your friend is probably still alive somewhere, but who knows for how long."

They walked out to the parking lot together, and on the way Brother Lemon said:

"Want to see something?"

Abby hesitated.

"Come on," he said. "I want to show you something in my car."

Abby followed but hung a few steps behind, remembering all the stories about men in white vans stealing girls from mall parking lots who were never seen again.

Sure enough, Brother Lemon drove a white minivan, which set off alarm bells inside Abby's brain. She looked around to see if anyone was watching as she followed him around to the back. He opened the door, and she checked to make sure she had a clear escape route. Just in case.

"I thought you might have your friend here with you," he said. "When you called? So I got all loaded up and ready to rock and roll if needed."

He unzipped two electric blue surfboard bags. Inside were nylon straps, handcuffs, a straitjacket, duct tape, ball gags, chains, collars, a leash and muzzle, a leather hood, shackles.

"It's for our safety, of course," he said. And then he laughed and clapped his hands. "Hot darn, I'm excited," he said, hopping from one foot to the other.

BEDS ARE BURNING

"I'm ruined," Glee sobbed.

It was later that evening, and Abby had just answered the phone.

"I can only talk for a minute," Glee continued, her voice drunk with tears. "You have to know it wasn't me."

That "me" turned into a keening whine and more crying.

"It's going to be okay, Glee," Abby said.

"No," Glee said, suddenly clear-headed. "It's never going to be okay again. We're leaving. But someone has to know it wasn't my fault."

"What happened?" Abby asked.

"He sent me those letters," Glee said. "All those letters saying he loved me and he'd never felt this way before and that he'd wait until I graduated and then quit his job and move to be near me wherever I went to college. He said that. And she said I had to talk to him, and when I did, he acted like he'd never noticed me before."

"Who said?" Abby asked.

"I was humiliated," Glee said, not stopping. "And I remember drinking orange juice and she said she'd put a little virtue in it, and then I remember being at the copy shop and then the sky was spinning all around me and then this."

"Who said?" Abby repeated. But she knew.

"You know exactly who it was," Glee said. "It wasn't my fault. It wasn't . . . I have to go."

Abby called back but the phone was off the hook, and the next day Glee had disappeared; her family swept her out of sight and swallowed her up. But Abby knew she was broken in a way that might never be repaired.

Of course she knew the name that Glee didn't say. It was Gretchen.

Abby couldn't stop her alone, but who was going to help? Not Brother Lemon. No one carrying handcuffs and duct tape in their trunk was a real solution. Not Glee. Not Father Morgan, because he was gone, too. So Abby went to the toughest person she knew: Margaret.

Margaret had been out of school for weeks; probably being treated for anorexia privately in her home, where the Middletons could keep an eye on her. Before going to her house, Abby stopped by the Market and picked up a bunch of red carnations. On the way out, she spotted a pint of Frusen Glädjé pralines and cream—Margaret's favorite, but was that the sort of thing you took someone with anorexia? Abby wasn't sure but decided to get it anyway. By now Margaret was probably bouncing back; nothing kept her down for long.

The Middletons had houses all over Charleston, but their downtown house was an enormous wooden pile on Church Street with the roots of a live oak busting up the sidewalk out front, cracking the first two brick steps that led to the door. It was an old Charleston single house, so it had two columned porches stacked up on the side, pulling the massive wooden wreck slowly to the right, collapsing gracefully in a two-hundred-year swoon.

Abby parked on the street and rang the doorbell, heard the

chimes echo deep inside the house, and then waited, scanning up and down the street to make sure no one spotted her. She didn't know why, but she felt like she was doing something wrong. She rang again. Somewhere inside, an Irish setter barked. Finally she heard the front door crack open and a man yell:

"Beau, no! Stay, dummy."

Heavy footsteps tromped across the porch, making the house shake, and then the door opened.

Riley stood in the doorway, looking down at Abby. He was too cool to admit he remembered her, if he even did.

"Hey," Abby said, trying to sound cool. "I'm friends with Margaret. I came to see her?"

Riley slumped one shoulder against the door jamb and picked something from between his back teeth with a finger.

"She's sick," he said.

"I brought her Frusen Glädjé," Abby said, holding up the plastic bag. "It's better when it's soft, but I don't want it to melt everywhere. And I got her flowers?"

Riley studied the tip of his spit-slicked forefinger for a minute, then threw the door wide and walked back into the house, the porch boards cracking and popping beneath his feet.

"Close the door," he called over his shoulder as he disappeared inside.

Abby followed and closed the street door as best she could, but it was so warped by humidity and layers of old paint that it barely fit in its frame. Then she followed Riley into the dim interior.

Old Charleston houses were everything you didn't want in a coastal home: they were big, they were uninsulated, and they were made of wood. They cost a fortune to maintain, but if you owned one you cared more about living south of Broad than you did about money. Besides, shabby chic was the order of the day. Every downtown house's exterior looked exactly the same: neatly painted white columns, shining coats of fresh paint on the exterior walls, glossy black shutters pinned back from the windows, scrolled wrought-iron fences and gates enclosing microscopic front yards. But every interior, hidden from public view, was its own secret study in decay. Ceilings sagged, walls cracked, paint blistered, plaster peeled, sometimes down to the lath, but the owners just shrugged and walked around the holes in their floors, or ate in the kitchen if the dining room ceiling had collapsed. Families of humans coexisted peacefully with families of raccoons living in the walls, and when fires were lit for the first time in winter, the pigeons living in the chimneys asphyxiated and dropped down the flues in swirls of sooty feathers. The help constantly swept the floors to pick up the flakes of lead paint that rained from the ceilings. Plaster dust showered onto plates at dinner parties when someone walked across the floor upstairs. Doors couldn't be opened because the keys had been lost years ago or the locks had rusted shut. The right kind of people endured these inconveniences without complaint because, if they didn't, it was a sure sign they had no business owning a real Charleston house after all.

Abby entered the dark front hall, just as Riley's broad back disappeared toward the kitchen. She stepped over a rolled-up carpet and followed him into the dining room. A hole in the ceiling over the mahogany table showed the raw cedar joists holding up the second floor, and the china and crystal in its breakfront rattled and chimed as she walked across the uneven floor. Then she was pushing through the swinging doors and entering the bright back kitchen.

The light hurt her eyes. This was the one renovated part of the house, along with a rear addition that had central air. Riley was sitting at the sleek white island, eating a banana and a jar of peanut butter with a knife. A copy of *Hustler* was open on the counter in front of him.

"What?" he asked.

"Spoons," Abby said. She clanked open the overloaded drawer next to the buzzing refrigerator, yanked it past the point where it stuck, and grabbed two mismatched spoons. She threw them in the bag with the Frusen Glädjé, then slammed the drawer closed with her hip.

"Don't be long," Riley said, studying his *Hustler* with peanut-butter-sticky fingers. "I'm not supposed to let anyone see her."

"When's your mom coming back?" Abby asked.

Riley shrugged and turned another page, revealing a woman in too much makeup displaying her vagina. Abby went out of her way not to look. She walked past Beau's pillow, where the Irish setter looked up at her, shivering, and headed up the servants' stairs at the back of the house, balancing her bag and the flowers, the spoons clinking against each other as she went.

The stairs were steep, dark, and narrow; a long-ago fire had caused smoke damage that scaled the avocado-green walls. Abby emerged in the high-ceilinged upstairs hall and walked toward the front of the house, the wood floors creaking all the way; finally, she pushed open the massive door to Margaret's room.

The curtains were shut, the room was dark, and it was dank with the humid smell of sickness.

"Margaret?" Abby called into the shadows.

The bed was an enormous pile of blankets and tangled sheets, slept in but empty, glowing white in the dimness. Abby picked her way toward the bathroom, where a nightlight was burning, and then jumped when the bedsheets spoke:

"M'Riley?"

Abby froze.

"Margaret?" she asked.

"Abby?" Margaret sounded as surprised as she could muster with her weak voice.

"I brought Frusen Glädjé," Abby said, holding up the bag in the darkness, hoping that Margaret could see her from wherever she was. "And spoons. We have one mission: to eat all this ice cream." Then she told a merciful lie, one she hoped would put Margaret in a receptive mood: "Wallace asked me to bring you flowers. They're carnations, of course, which is exactly what he would pick."

"Why're y'here?" Margaret moaned, and the sheets thrashed.

"Because you've been out of school for weeks." Abby walked over to the bed and reached under the tasseled shade of a bedside lamp. "And even though you're mad at me, you're still my friend."

She clicked on the light and immediately wished she hadn't.

"Oh," Abby said. When she couldn't think of anything else to say, she said it again. "Oh."

Margaret was a yellowed bone buried in dirty sheets. A withered thing, lying weak and helpless, eyes E.T.-sized, face gaunt. Her hair was as colorless as her eyes, and it was thin and started high on her forehead; Abby could see too much scalp. Thick foam was caked in the corners of Margaret's mouth. She blinked in the light, and greasy tears slid from her eyes.

"Wallace didn't . . . give you anything," Margaret rasped. "Quit being . . . so fucking nice . . . all the time . . ."

When Margaret spoke, Abby saw a gray fuzz coating her tongue. She looked away, trying to focus on something—anything—else.

"I got poisoned . . . ," Margaret rasped. Then she dragged a skeleton's claw from beneath the blanket, the bones barely covered with skin, fingernails growing into calcified talons as her cuticles retreated. "Someone . . . poisoned me . . ."

In Abby's mind, the pieces slot-machined into place. She set down the carnations and took one of Margaret's ice-cold hands.

"Was it the German milkshake?" she asked.

Margaret gagged and Abby saw every tendon in her cheeks flex.

"Don't talk . . . ," Margaret gasped as her throat spasmed. ". . . about food . . ."

"But you have to eat," Abby said. "You look like an Ethiopian."

Margaret's watery eyes focused on the plastic capsule of Frusen Glädjé. Her tongue snaked out and slid over chapped lips. Her shoulders hunched, her skull lifted, and for a second it looked like she was going to sit up, but then she flopped her enormous, fragile head back down onto her pillows. Fecal air puffed out from beneath the pile of blankets.

"They want it to . . . pass through my system," Margaret said. "But I'm . . . hungry . . ."

"And here I am with Frusen Glädjé," Abby said, smiling. "It was meant to be. Just a spoonful."

Margaret was too weak to nod, so Abby went to the vanity and dragged the frilly white piano bench to the side of the bed and sat down. She cracked the top of the plastic pint and then peeled back the white film, setting it faceup on the bedside table. Instantly, the cold, snowy smell of ice cream filled the sweaty room.

Margaret's lips slid up to reveal her teeth. They looked huge compared to the rest of her sunken face, and Abby realized she was trying to smile.

"Good?" Abby asked.

"Lemme jus' . . . smell it first," Margaret said.

Abby held the ice cream underneath Margaret's skull nose and watched as she closed her eyes and seemed to fall asleep. Margaret's nostrils flexed slowly as she got stoned on the scent of frozen, whipped sugar. None for Abby, though. Even though her mouth was watering, she didn't think she could keep anything down in this room.

"You want to try a spoonful?" she asked.

Margaret, nodded, eyes flickering behind closed lids. Abby put the softening ice cream in her lap and dug down with the spoon, scraping off half. It was better to start with tiny bites. She extended the spoon to Margaret, who didn't open her eyes. Maybe she'd fallen asleep, Abby thought, but then she saw her gullet heave; her forehead slide translucently over the bony ridges of her brow.

"Hurts?" Abby asked.

Margaret nodded, bloodless lips pinched tight, and Abby knew that look: she was going to puke. She stuck the spoon back in the ice cream and set the container on the bedside table while she looked for a wastebasket. There was one by the vanity, so she ran over, got it, and came back.

"Margaret?" she asked. "Can you roll over on your side a little? You can't throw up on your back."

The sound of the words "throw up" made Margaret wince again. Abby pulled down the covers and saw that Margaret's chest was a bony plate beneath her Rockville Regatta T-shirt. Her shoulders were sticks lashed to other sticks. A puff of stale air wafted out, but Abby didn't care. Margaret was in pain, squirming softly and slowly. The blankets looked too heavy for her, so Abby pulled them lower and then stopped.

Margaret's stomach was swollen into a hard mound. Abby couldn't believe how big it was, and for a second she thought Margaret was pregnant. But you didn't get nine months pregnant after missing school for a couple of weeks. Margaret made a gasping noise and her bony claws scrabbled at her swollen belly, scratching and caressing the bulge.

"Are you okay?" Abby asked again.

Margaret opened her mouth to scream but out came a loud gurgle—a wet, sucking, gagging sound that made Abby's stomach flex in sympathy. Margaret twisted, her spine bending backward into a C, head toward heels. Then she twisted the other way, doubled over, curling herself into a protective ball around her distended belly. The sheets slid off the bed and onto the floor.

"Uh! Uh! Uh! Uh!" she chanted.

Abby was scared that Margaret might bite off her tongue or go to the bathroom in her bed. *What do I do? What do I do? What do I do?* The question ran on a loop inside her brain, but she didn't have any answers.

The door flew open.

"What'd you do to her?" Riley bellowed. Peanut butter was smeared across his knuckles, and he left streaks of it around the doorknob. Abby could smell it all the way over by the bed. The scent seemed to send Margaret into a new seizure, and she clawed feebly at her frail throat, letting out a long moan.

"Guuuuuuuuuuhhhhh," she said.

Beau, the Irish setter, came around Riley's legs and stared into the room at Abby, at Margaret, and then trotted over to stand by the side of the bed, snuffling at the blankets.

"She's sick," Abby said. "I didn't touch her."

"I shouldn't have let you in," Riley said. But he wasn't moving past the door, as if he was scared to get too close to his sister's spasming, half-naked body, with her boxer shorts rucked up to show one mottled thigh.

"What do we do?" Abby asked.

"We're going to be in so much trouble," Riley said.

"We have to help her," Abby said.

Riley shook his head. Then he snapped his fingers at the dog.

"Come on, Beau," he said. "Let's go."

"We need to call an ambulance," Abby said. "Does she have a doctor?"

Suddenly, Margaret stopped writhing. Her body lay completely still, stiff as a board, toes pointed down, knees locked, arms rigid at her sides, neck straining, tears leaking.

"She's fine," Riley said. "See? She's okay. Is she okay?"

Abby had no clue.

"I really think we need to call somebody," she said. "Or give her CPR or something."

"She's still breathing," Riley said.

That's when Beau took two steps back from the bed, locked his legs, and started to growl low in his throat. Margaret's jaws flew open, exposing a deep black cavern that extended all the way down to her stomach, and she started to beg.

"Oh, gawd," she moaned. "Make it stop, Abby, please make it stop. I want my mom . . . please make it stop . . . Mommmyyyy!!!"

The last word became a scream so loud that Abby felt it in the soles of her feet. So loud that Beau started to bark. It went on and on and on and just when Abby thought she couldn't take another second, it became muffled, like something was clogging Margaret's throat. Then the muffled noises started to sound wet and sticky, and Abby saw something pale and white squirming in the blackness of Margaret's gullet, curling around her tonsils.

Abby leaned forward for a better look, and the thing inside moved. She jerked back, smacking into Riley, who'd crept closer to investigate. The thing kept coming, oozing up out of Margaret's throat, rising to the surface. Tears were spilling down Margaret's sallow cheeks and her throat and chest kept spasming; her bony hands scratched and clawed uselessly at the tight skin on her neck. But the thing kept slithering out.

It slid over the root of Margaret's tongue, and then Margaret gave three explosive, throat-clearing coughs, each one pushing it out farther. It was sticky, gelatinous, and alive—a blind white worm, thick as a garden hose, and it was hauling itself out of Margaret's stomach with single-minded intent.

"What. The. Fuck." Riley said.

"I don't know, I don't know, I don't know," Abby chanted softly, backing away from the bed.

The worm kept coming, hauling more and more of its slick body out of Margaret's stomach, moving over her trembling lips and spilling onto her chin, where it stuck for a moment and sensed the air with its blunt, blind snout. Then it turned toward the Frusen Glädjé, forgotten on the bedside table, and dragged its long, rippling, white body another half inch toward the container, moving across Margaret's cheek. Exhausted after its journey, it lay still for a moment. Margaret breathed fast through her nose, panicking, wanting to scream but unable to; the worm's heavy body kept her vocal cords from moving.

That's when Beau leapt onto the bed, barking furiously. With no regard for anything but his fury, he ran up Margaret's body, stomping her swollen stomach with his paws, sending Abby grabbing for his collar as he barked and snapped in Margaret's face. Abby thought he was trying to bite her, and she got one hand on the scruff of his neck.

"Beau!" she yelled. "No!"

But when she pulled back Beau's head, he had the end of the worm clenched between his jaws. Margaret let out a muffled hiss of a scream as Beau yanked the worm out of her gullet. Abby pulled her hand away from his fur and the dog gave the worm a few hard chews right in Margaret's face, but it was tough like jerky and his teeth couldn't sever it. Now it was squirming back and forth, hauling more of its body out of Margaret's throat as Beau gnawed a better hold and began pacing backward.

The worm looped over Beau's muzzle, wrapping itself around his face. The dog growled low and deep, shaking his head from side to side, and the worm kept coming. Margaret gagged, trying to suck in enough air while Abby and Riley stood there, unable to do anything but watch.

Beau reached the end of the bed, with almost six feet of worm extended from Margaret's mouth, slimed with saliva and dripping with stomach juices. Then he jumped off, the worm still clamped in his jaws, and Margaret moaned in alarm and pain. The dog landed on the hardwood floor and kept backing away. Abby and Riley stared in horror as the worm stretched to eight feet, then ten, then fifteen.

It finally snapped when Beau reached the door.

They found twenty-three pounds of tapeworm in Margaret's stomach. The longest measured thirty-three feet. Her doctor had never suspected tapeworms to be the cause of her illness, so while Margaret had been screened for everything from leukemia to anorexia, they'd been missed. The creatures had been feeding off her for weeks, reproducing in her guts, which were now a seething nest of *Taennia saginata*.

Riley's license was suspended, so Abby had driven them to the hospital. In the churn of parents, and doctors, and purgatives, and consultants, and nurses swirling through Margaret's tenth-floor room, they sort of forgot about her in the corner. Which meant that Abby was still there, along with Mr. and Mrs. Middleton,

Riley, and Margaret's other three brothers, Hoyt, Ashley, and Saluda, when the doctor told them what had happened.

Margaret had eaten tapeworm eggs. A lot of them. It was a common weight loss scheme. Advertisements in the backs of magazines called them a "fast and natural solution to your slimming needs." You sent the company a check or money order, and they would mail you a plastic canister of eggs. They looked like chalky powder. You mixed it with water to form a thick milkshake. Then you drank it down. You were supposed to drink one milkshake and give it time to work. If Margaret had drunk more than one, it could be dangerous. Even two could be life-threatening.

The doctors wanted to know how many she'd consumed. And where she had gotten the idea. Did she know how dangerous it was? Did she know she could have died? But they couldn't ask Margaret anything because she'd been sedated the minute she arrived at the hospital. It was the only way to make her stop screaming.

But Abby knew.

TONIGHT SHE COMES

Abby drove home, rising and falling over the bridges, and locked herself in her bedroom. She pulled the daybook from the back of her closet, where she'd hidden it, and turned the pages. Everything was there. Passages from *The Song of Solomon* ("Like a lily among the thorns, So is my darling among the maidens. Like an apple tree among the trees of the forest . . ."). Father Morgan's signature written in long columns, the forgery getting sharper with each line. Pictures slashed with red and black markers showing a nude figure on top of the bell tower, a girl with worms coming from her mouth, dogs surrounding another girl and tearing her to shreds.

She hunted through her desk, found the faculty directory, and dialed Father Morgan's number. It rang ten times, eleven, twelve. Finally, a man answered.

"Father Morgan?" Abby said.

"Who is this?" the man asked.

"I'm one of his students," Abby said. "I need to speak to him."

"That's not possible."

"Please," Abby said. "Tell him I'm Abby Rivers. Ask him if he'll talk to me. Just ask him."

A thunk as the phone was set down, followed by a long silence. Finally, someone picked up the receiver.

"Abby," Father Morgan said, and he sounded very tired. "I'm

no longer teaching at Albemarle, but I have the number for the chaplain who's filling in for me."

"Something's wrong with Gretchen," Abby said.

"That's not something I can help you with," he said. "I'm sorry, but I can't have any contact with students."

"I have her daybook," Abby raced ahead. "She practiced forging your name. I saw her giving those notes to Glee. She did it."

There was a pause and then Father Morgan spoke, sounding even more exhausted.

"I'm sorry, Abby," he said. "But I think it's best if I just move on."

"This has to stop!" Abby said. "She gave tapeworm eggs to Margaret, she got Wallace Stoney drunk, she forged those notes to Glee. All of it's written down in her daybook. She's been planning this for weeks, and unless you stop her she's going to keep doing more things. Worse things."

"Abby . . . ," Father Morgan began.

"Please believe me," Abby said. "You have to give it to someone. Major will think I made it up. But you could give it to someone in charge."

"Hold on a minute," Father Morgan said. "Don't hang up."

Abby heard fabric scraping as he pressed the receiver to his sweater and spoke to someone in the room. Their voices rose and then grew louder, talking over each other, but they were too muffled for Abby to make out what they were saying. When Father Morgan returned to the phone, his voice sounded stronger.

"This is all in Gretchen Lang's daybook?" he asked. "You're sure it's hers?"

Abby nodded, and then realized she was on the phone.

"Yes, sir," she said.

"I need to look at it," Father Morgan said. "And I think it

should be with your parents. Is your mother home now?"

"She's back in the morning," Abby said.

"All right," Father Morgan said. "First thing in the morning I'll be at your house, and I'm bringing a friend. He'll look at the book, and if it is what you say it is, then you'll need to call in sick from school, and we'll need to go to the police."

"The police?" Abby said, and she couldn't help feeling like she'd betrayed Gretchen. She had to remind herself that Gretchen was no longer her friend.

"These are serious crimes," Father Morgan said. "There will be serious consequences."

After they hung up, Abby couldn't sleep. She turned on the TV, but *Moonlighting* felt loud and coarse and obvious, so she switched it off and put on *No Jacket Required*, letting Phil Collins's soft, reassuring voice fill the room while she sat on her bed, the daybook at the other end. She was exhausted and relieved and scared, and her veins hummed with adrenaline, and then they ran empty and she pulled Geoffrey the Giraffe and Cabbage Head into her lap and laid her head against the wall and slept.

In her dream she wasn't alone anymore. In her dream, nothing had happened that couldn't be fixed. In her dream, everything was back to the way it was and she and Gretchen were driving out to Wadmalaw to go waterskiing with Margaret and Glee, and they had a case of Busch in the Bunny's trunk, and George Michael was on the radio, and the wind was in their hair and nothing smelled like United Colors of Benetton and she looked over and smiled and Gretchen smiled back, but there was a roach on her face, sitting on one cheek, and when Gretchen opened her mouth she said, "Hi! I'm Mickey!" and Abby told her to stop doing that, and Gretchen did it again and again until Abby opened her eyes and her light was still on and her phone was ringing.

"Hi! I'm Mickey!" it chirped. "Hi! I'm Mickey!"

She looked at her digital clock: 11:06. Abby snatched the phone off the cradle and heard a great, roaring wall of black static.

"Abby?" Gretchen said over the long-distance lines.

"Gretchen!" Abby shouted. "I'm doing it. Tomorrow. I'm going to make it stop."

The static cut out and the phone line was a vast gulf of darkness.

"You shouldn't have done that," Gretchen said, her voice swimming up out of the void. "You shouldn't have told."

"This has to stop," Abby said. "She's hurting everyone!"

"You'd better lock up all your windows and close all your doors," Gretchen echoed on the line. "She's coming."

The urgency in Gretchen's staticky voice alarmed Abby but she shook her head.

"No one's coming," she said.

"You don't understand . . . ," Gretchen began.

"I'm sick and tired of people telling me what I don't understand," Abby yelled at the phone. "This is over! It's ending!"

"It's over," Gretchen moaned down the phone line. "It's too late."

Abby's bedroom door swung open to reveal Gretchen standing there holding a shopping bag and grinning.

"Hi, Abby-Normal," she said.

"It's too late, it's too late, it's too late," sing-songed the voice on the phone.

"Is that little ghost still talking?" Gretchen asked.

She set her brown paper shopping bag next to the door, then she took the phone from Abby and hung it back on Mickey's arm with a terminal, plastic *clack*. Instinctively, Abby slid off her bed and stood up.

"I think it's bad luck to talk to yourself, don't you?" Gretchen asked.

Then she punched Abby in the stomach.

Abby had never been hit, and it took her by surprise. All the air whooshed out of her lungs, and she dropped to her hands and knees on the carpet. Gretchen kicked her in the stomach, digging the toe of her sneaker deep into Abby's solar plexus. Abby whimpered. Gretchen kicked her again in the side. Abby's body reflexively curled around itself.

Gretchen crouched down, grabbed a handful of Abby's moussed hair, and yanked her head up.

"You've been begging for this for ages," Gretchen said. "Okay, well, now you have my full and undivided attention. Do you like it? Does this feel good?"

Abby wept. Gretchen snaked her fingers tighter into Abby's hair and twisted.

"Stay out of my way," she said. "You're finished."

She gave Abby's head a final, furious shake, then bounced it off the carpet and straightened up. She put the sole of her shoe against Abby's cheek and ground it into the floor.

"Stay down," she said. "Play dead. Good dog."

Then she picked her daybook up off the bed and strolled out of Abby's room, taking her shopping bag with her. There was the sound of opening and closing doors in the hall, then something fell over in the living room, and after a minute Abby heard the front door slam.

Abby leapt to her feet and ran to the front door and shot the deadbolt home. Then she ran into her bedroom, slammed her door, and moved her desk chair under the handle. She felt so sick, she wanted to laugh. From the photographs around her mirror, Gretchen grinned at her, braces shining, Gretchen laughed at her, Gretchen stuck out her tongue at her and Abby looked at the clock and the time said 11:11 and in eight hours Father Morgan would arrive and she didn't have the daybook. She didn't have anything. She couldn't save Margaret, she couldn't save Glee, she couldn't stop Gretchen, she couldn't save herself.

She looked around her room and wanted to scream. How did she ever think she could do this? This was a little girl's room, this wasn't the room of a grown-up. This was the room of a child.

She ripped down her *E.T.* poster, yanking the brittle paper off the wall and pulling it to pieces; then she took Tommy Cox's Coke and pegged it into the corner. She clawed the photos out from around her mirror, shredding Gretchen's face and her face, screaming profanities as she reduced their years together to glossy confetti on the floor. She yanked *No Jacket Required* out of her tape deck, the black magnetic ribbon spilling like streamers, then she unspooled one mix tape after another: *Awesome Summer Mix 88*, *Halley Comet Beach Party*, *From Gretchen to Abby IV*.

It wasn't enough. The sight of her stuffed animals made her want to puke. They belonged to a stupid little girl. She turned her nails into claws and dug them into Geoffrey the Giraffe's face and tore out his shiny black eyes, then split the stitching down his back and turned him inside out. She twisted off Cabbage Head's skull and took a pair of scissors and slashed open Wrinkles the Pound Puppy's belly. She felt sick because she knew what she was doing was wrong, but she couldn't stop herself. She was tired of being stupid, she was tired of Gretchen laughing at her, she was tired of losing. She was so tired.

When Abby woke up, full sunlight was flooding through her window, and someone had just stopped screaming. Abby sat bolt upright in the wreckage of her room, heart pounding, scalp prickling. She'd overslept. The house was silent. Abby listened, hoping it had all been a bad dream.

The woman screamed again. It was her mother.

Abby threw her desk chair aside and opened the bedroom door. Three enormous police officers were waiting in the hallway. Abby's mom was down at the other end of the hall, crying, held back by a female officer.

"Mom?" Abby shouted. "What's wrong?"

"You need to come with us," the larger officer said.

"Why?" Abby asked.

"We need to know what you can tell us about this," he said, holding up a brown paper bag.

It was Gretchen's bag. The one she'd had the night before.

"What is it?" she asked.

"You tell us," a shorter cop said.

Before they could stop her, Abby snatched the bag and it tore open. Something boneless slithered to the floor with a meaty thump. It was gray, like a skinned cat. Its eyes were closed, its mouth was open, and its hands were balled into little fists. It landed on the tips of the shorter cop's feet. He covered his mouth and nose and turned away.

They'd found the missing baby.

HARDEN MY HEART

After Abby was taken into custody, identified, advised of her rights, questioned, given an intake screening, interviewed again by a member of the Department of Juvenile Justice, and assigned a date for a detention hearing forty-eight hours away, it was made clear that she could be released to her parents or spend the next two days in the juvenile detention center. Mr. Rivers wanted to leave her there to teach her a lesson, but Mrs. Rivers wasn't about to let her daughter spend the night in juvie, so they brought her home.

Abby would have had an easier time in the detention center. Her dad drove, staring straight ahead through the windshield, not saying a word. Her mom wept the entire time. Whenever it seemed like she was about to stop, she started up again. When they got home, she went to her bedroom and slammed the door. Abby could hear her crying through the walls.

Her dad poured himself a Diet Pepsi over ice, then sat down carefully at the kitchen table, sipping it and staring at the wall.

"Dad?" Abby said, getting up off the sofa and creeping toward him. "You know I didn't do that, right? You know I would never do anything like that. Someone put that here to make me look bad. You believe me, don't you?"

He turned and looked at her, blinking calmly.

"I don't know what I believe," he said.

Abby backed away from him, stumbled down the hall, and locked herself in her bedroom. She had forgotten she'd destroyed it and wasn't prepared for the wreckage. Her stomach hollowed out when she stepped on one of Geoffrey's black eyes, which she'd ripped from his face. She wanted to cry. She didn't even have a past anymore.

They had already taken the keys to the Dust Bunny, but that was all right. It would mean that her parents couldn't be blamed for what was about to happen. It wasn't much, but it gave Abby some small comfort. Because she was about to break their hearts.

She took a shower and put on her face. It took forever because her skin was a suppurating mess. When she finally finished, she put her makeup in her gym bag along with a change of underwear and socks, a clean bra, a sweatshirt, and another pair of pants; then she turned on her TV and sat on her bed, watching through the back window as the sun went down.

She wished there was another way, but she was out of options. Maybe if she were smarter, she could have come up with a better solution, but this was all she could think of right now, and she had to do something. She looked out the back window and watched the light turn the long grass and abandoned lawn mowers first golden, then orange, then lavender, and finally black.

Abby listened for sounds of movement in the house. Hearing none, she slid her window open and popped the screen. Something caught her eye in the ocean of garbage strewn across her bedroom floor, one piece of her past that had escaped destruction: Tommy Cox's can of Coke from the fifth grade. She picked it up and slid it into her gym bag, then zipped it up and snuck out of the house.

When she reached the Kangaroo gas station, she made a call on the payphone. Then she waited inside as if she was browsing magazines until the white van pulled up to the pumps. She ran outside and knocked on the passenger side window. Brother Lemon opened the door.

"Do you have it?" she asked, getting in.

He opened the glove compartment and showed her a plastic sandwich bag wrapped around a few tablespoons of gray powder. Right next to it was an identical baggie.

"Why two bags?" she asked.

"Always bring a backup, just in case," he said. "Like astronauts in NASA."

"Let's go," she said. "Straight through the light across Coleman Boulevard."

As he pulled out and they drove into the Old Village, Abby slumped low in her seat.

"Do you have the number of the pay phone?" she asked.

"It's taped to the baggie," he said.

She opened the glove compartment and took both bags.

"I don't know why I can't park there and wait," he said.

"Because in this part of town, they call the police when they see a strange car," she said. "Pull over here."

A wedding reception was being held at Alhambra Hall, and cars were parked all the way down the street. Abby stuffed both baggies in her pockets and got out of the minivan. Brother Lemon cruised away, brake lights flaring at the corner, and then he was gone.

Abby walked up the line of cars toward Pierates Cruze. Inside Alhambra a band was playing a beach version of "Don't Worry, Be Happy," and the guy doing the whistling wasn't bad. Abby let the noise fade behind her in the dark as she walked past the park, beneath the live oaks, and onto the Cruze.

When she got to Gretchen's house, she noticed Mrs. Lang's

Volvo in the driveway, but not Mr. Lang's Mercedes. She hoped that meant they'd gone to a friend's house to watch the Clemson/Carolina game, along with everyone else in the Old Village. Mr. Lang was a Clemson grad, and for a game this big, Abby knew that parents liked to hole up together somewhere; the men would get drunk while the women fluttered around the kitchen.

Abby slipped around the side of the house and snuck into the backyard. The upstairs was lit up, but downstairs was dark. She could see light all through the second story, shining in every window, throwing big bright rectangles across the yard. It made the harbor look blacker in comparison.

Abby watched the windows of the house, trying to see if anyone besides Gretchen was home. A cold wind cut through her jacket, and she started to shiver. Somewhere in the dark, she heard an owl. After a while she crept to the front door, expecting yard lights to pop on at any minute and pin her to the grass.

Nothing happened, and she made it to the door. Slowly, she pressed down the handle and felt the latch turn, then click open. She pushed the door, breaking the seal as quietly as she could, and then slipped inside, closing the door behind her.

It was cold inside, colder than it had been before. Abby didn't know how anyone could live like this. Almost immediately, she started shivering.

She slipped into the dark living room and advanced toward the kitchen, where she hoped to find a bottle of Diet Coke in the refrigerator. Gretchen was constantly drinking Diet Coke, and Abby planned to empty the contents of one baggie into a two-liter bottle. Then maybe Gretchen would drink enough and pass out. And then *maybe* Abby could get her out of the house before Gretchen's parents came home and drank the drugged Diet Coke themselves.

It was a terrible plan, but Abby was all out of clever.

Something barked behind her. Abby jumped and her nerves caught on fire. Silhouetted in the light from the hall was Max, staring into the living room, his eyes fixed on Abby. While she watched, he barked again.

"Max," she whispered, "it's me."

She squatted down and held out one hand, trembling from the cold. Max cocked his head.

"Max," she whispered. "Good dog. Good dog, Max."

He barked again, but it was a qualified bark this time. More of a "whuf?"

Upstairs, she heard footsteps. Abby froze.

"Max?" Gretchen called down. "Who's there?"

"Max," Abby whispered, "come here, Max. Shhh . . ."

More footsteps as Gretchen walked to the head of the stairs. Abby crept backward, retreating into the darkness of the living room, squeezing between the end of the sofa and the wall, ducking down.

"Who's here, Max?" Gretchen called. Abby could hear her coming down the stairs. She pressed herself tighter into the corner. Gretchen wouldn't see her if she stayed out of the living room. Max's collar jingled as he trotted toward Abby, pressing his muzzle into her face, licking her lips.

"Go away, Max," she whispered. "Go, go, go."

The dog stuck his snuffling nose into her chest.

"Please, Max," Abby whispered. "Go."

"Who's down here, Max?" Gretchen said from the bottom of the stairs.

Abby made meaningful eye contact with Max, holding his head, and she stared deep into his eyes and channeled everything she had into conveying to him how very important it was that he go away.

"Go," she whispered into his ear.

"Come here, Max," Gretchen called. Max whipped his head around, as if hearing her for the first time, and raced out of the living room. "Good dog, Max. Come with me."

There was the sound of something clicking, a rattle and a jangle of Max's dog tags, and then Gretchen and Max were running up the stairs together. Abby sagged, then she heaved herself up out of the crack and raced to the kitchen. The light over the sink was on. She opened the fridge.

Everything was rotten. The food had decayed into mush or dried into brown scraps. The only intact items were six two-liter bottles of Diet Coke, the first one cloudy with greasy handprints. She was reaching for it when she heard Gretchen's bare feet come galloping downstairs again. Abby closed the fridge and spun, taking three long steps and slipping into the dark doorway of the TV room, just as Gretchen entered the kitchen through the living room.

Backing up into darkness, Abby bumped into the ottoman where the Langs kept all their magazines and fell backward. Tightening her legs, she managed to fall in slow motion, catching herself and a copy of *European Travel & Life* before it hit the floor. Frozen, bent over backward, she listened.

In the kitchen, Gretchen opened the fridge door, then a cabinet. The ice maker growled and Abby used its noise for cover, sinking slowly onto the leather ottoman as Gretchen finished plinking ice into her glass. Abby crept to the door.

Gretchen was standing at the counter, her back to Abby, wearing shorts and a tank top. She had a glass out, full of ice, and the bottle of Diet Coke stood next to it. She pulled out a wrinkled dried lemon from a line of rotting fruit on the window ledge, then rattled open a drawer and slid out a broad, gleaming butcher's knife.

Holding the dried lemon steady on the counter, Gretchen started to saw through it, but then her head snapped up and she sniffed the air. Turning, she looked directly at Abby, then she turned the other way and looked into the dark living room.

"Who's here?" she asked. "I can smell you."

She padded toward the dark living room, butcher knife gripped in one hand, and disappeared. Quickly, Abby tiptoed to the sink, pulling the baggie of powder out of her waistband. She dumped the entire packet into the glass. It was supposed to have been enough for two liters of Coke, but Abby didn't care, she just wanted to get it in. She stirred the clumped powder with one finger, and ice tinkled gently against the glass.

"Abby?"

The footsteps were coming back, padding quickly, and Abby started for the TV room.

"Are you here, Abby?" Gretchen called from the TV room.

Abby backtracked so fast her shoes almost slipped out from underneath her. Six quick steps and she was in the dark living room as she heard Gretchen coming through the kitchen, right on her heels. Abby kept going, moving as fast and quiet as she could, slipping into the front hall just as Gretchen snapped on the lights in the living room behind her.

It was close. She might not make it out the front door before Gretchen, but she had to get outside, get out of this freezing house, get away from Gretchen. She turned the handle. The door was locked. The deadbolt needed a key. Abby spun around to search the hall table.

Gretchen was standing in the doorway to the living room, butcher knife in one hand, glass of Diet Coke in the other.

"You really are gay for me, aren't you?" Gretchen said, taking a sip.

Abby thought about smashing through the glass door and running, but she couldn't move her legs.

"I can't believe you were dumb enough to come here. Especially after you were arrested," Gretchen said, sighing. "Come on. If you're here, you might as well see something cool."

Gretchen trudged up the stairs to the second floor. Abby hesitated, then followed. She found Gretchen in her bedroom standing in front of her closet, pulling on a baby blue raincoat.

"What are you doing?" Abby asked.

Gretchen took a deep pull of her Diet Coke and set it down on her desk.

"You'll see," she said.

Gretchen lifted the enormous butcher's knife from her desk. Its blade caught the light in the room and sent silver shards dancing across the walls.

"Come on," she said, then she beckoned to Abby with the knife. "I'm not going to hurt you."

Gretchen walked into her bathroom. Abby knew it was stupid to go into a small room with a crazy girl holding a knife, but Gretchen didn't feel dangerous right now. She felt like Abby had interrupted her in the middle of an extra-credit project and Gretchen wanted to finish it up before starting anything new.

Abby entered the bathroom. Gretchen was waiting for her, leaning against the sinks, the knife lying on the counter. In her hand was the black pistol from her parents' bedside table. In the shower was Good Dog Max. His leash was looped over the faucet and he was dancing from one foot to the other, his claws clicking on the fiberglass tub. When he saw Abby, his tail began to wag.

"See," Gretchen said, "he likes you."

Max let his tongue fall out, then the wastebasket next to the tub caught his interest and he stuck his head inside and started rooting around.

"It's because he likes you so much that I got this idea," Gretchen said. "So in a way, what's happening to him is all your fault."

Gretchen pulled up the hood of her raincoat and stood at the edge of the tub.

"Good dog, Max," she said. "Who's a good dog?"

Gretchen took Max's collar and pulled his head out of the garbage. Good Dog Max tried to lick Gretchen's hand that was holding the gun; then she had his chin in her hand, lifting his head, and she pressed the gun to the base of his neck.

"You don't have to hurt him," Abby said. "You don't have to do any of this."

"You don't know who you're talking to anymore," Gretchen said.

Max whined, his claws tapping at the fiberglass, trying to twist his head to get back in the garbage.

"I know who you are," Abby said.

Without hesitation, Gretchen released Max, stepped away from the tub, and backhanded Abby. Caught off guard, Abby spun to her side, hit the wall, and fell to the floor. Gretchen was straddling her, yanking her head back by the hair, the cold metal gun pressed to the underside of Abby's chin. Abby had never been on the wrong end of a gun before, and ice blossomed inside her guts.

"Lesson learned," Gretchen said. "Don't talk shit."

Then Gretchen was standing, and she kicked Abby in the stomach. Watery spit flooded Abby's mouth. Through blurry eyes she saw Gretchen standing at the side of the tub, and Good Dog Max's feet were thundering on the hollow fiberglass.

Unable to catch her breath, Abby crawled into the bedroom and dragged herself to the far wall by the door. A moment later the air cracked in half and slapped her in both ears as a flash lit the room. In the silence that followed, gunsmoke and the stink of cordite wafted from the bathroom door. Through the ringing in her ears, Abby heard something moving, thumping against the tub, and then Gretchen came out.

"Whew," she said. "Thirsty work."

She chugged the rest of her Diet Coke, gulping it down, her throat moving as she drained the glass. Abby stared at her. Half of Gretchen's face was misted in blood, and in one hand she held the gun. Blood dripped from the raincoat and pattered to the floor. Gretchen finished the Coke and set down the glass, then she leaned back through the bathroom door and checked on her work. She looked back at Abby, whose eyes were swimming in tears.

"Don't cry, Abby," Gretchen said. "Dogs are like cars. They're cheap in the country."

She grinned. And at that moment Abby knew something was broken that could never be fixed.

"Now, here's what you're going to do," Gretchen said. "We have to toss this mutt over Dr. Bennett's fence, because can you imagine what kind of drama is going to break out when Pony Lang discovers the remains of his beloved family pet in the next door neighbor's yard. I wouldn't be surprised if some seriously gratuitous violence broke out. I mean, they both own guns."

She set the pistol on her desk and picked up the knife.

"But that's a whole lot of dog," Gretchen said. "So I want you to take this knife and give me—oh, I don't know?—just his head? Don't give me that look, Abby. You and I both know you'll do it. You always do what you're told, especially when I'm the one telling you."

Abby couldn't face what was in the bathroom: that lifeless bag of wet fur slung in the corner of the tub. She started to panic. Gretchen picked up the knife and stepped toward Abby. Her leg buckled and Gretchen caught herself against the wall. She leaned there for a moment, breathing hard, her hand gripping the door-frame. She swayed again. Then she raised her head and looked at Abby with hatred.

"Oh," she said. "You bitch . . ."

Then someone unplugged Gretchen and she hit the floor in a boneless heap. Abby didn't move for a few minutes, not until she heard deep, regular breathing coming from Gretchen. She went to the phone in the Langs' bedroom and dialed.

"Hurry," Abby said when Chris Lemon answered. "It's number eight. The modern one."

She hung up and, careful not to look in the bathroom, dragged Gretchen downstairs in her bloody raincoat, not caring as Gretchen's head bumped hard against each carpeted step. She left her slumped in the hall while she went to the living room and grabbed two woolly throw blankets off the sofa; she pulled off Gretchen's raincoat and rolled her in the blankets.

Then she waited.

The grandfather clock tocked next to her. The cooling system blew soft air through the vents. The house was cold. The house was quiet.

Something flashed outside the window and Abby leapt to her feet. She heard thrashing and movement, and then a barn owl was standing on the limb of a live oak, staring in at Abby as if it knew her name.

Headlights lit the downstairs hall, then went dark. A car door slammed and Brother Lemon was there. Abby opened the front door and let him inside.

"Holy cow," he said. "What did you do to her?"

"It's not her blood," Abby said. "She killed her dog."

"She what?" he said.

Abby thought about Good Dog Max, so sweet and stupid, sticking his head in every trash can he could find, and she almost cried. Then she dug her fingernails into her wrist until the pain made the image go away.

"Forget it," Abby said. "Let's hurry."

Brother Lemon tied nylon straps around Gretchen's blankets so she couldn't move, and together they carried her out of the house and laid her in the back of his van and drove away. The owl watched them the entire time.

DON'T STOP 'TIL YOU GET ENOUGH

"Promise me she won't get hurt," Abby begged.

Brother Lemon leaned back in the wicker chair he'd commandeered from the living room of the Langs' beach house. He spread his legs wide, cracked his knuckles, and rested his elbows on his knees.

"That's up to her," he said. Even seated, he was taller than Abby. "An exorcism is a contest of wills between the demon and the exorcist. Now, I'm a pretty strong guy, but I'm going up against the forces of darkness, so there're no guarantees. As Jesus Christ once said: by any means necessary."

Brother Lemon paused and looked around the dark living room.

"You sure her parents don't have a video camera? I'd love to get this on tape."

All the way over, Abby imagined blue lights flickering silently in the rearview mirror. Some cop at the base of the Ben Sawyer Bridge was going to stop them for going seven miles over the speed limit, and when he gave them the ticket he'd hear Gretchen struggling in the back. Were her parents already looking for her? Had the Langs come home and called the police? Abby's guts were so full of stomach acid, her burps could etch steel.

Her stomach kept twisting as they drove over the short bridge from Sullivan's Island to the Isle of Palms, headed north on Palm Boulevard, and pulled up outside the empty beach house. Why hadn't anyone stopped them? Why were they being allowed to do this?

"Here we are," Brother Lemon said, putting the van in park. "Now what?"

The Langs' beach house sat high on stilts, a wooden trellis enclosing the unpaved first floor and a long flight of steps leading up to the front porch on the second. Abby forced herself out of her seat, walked across the crushed oyster-shell driveway, unlatched the gates that led to the parking space beneath the house, and swung them wide. Brother Lemon cut the headlights and slowly rolled forward until he was under the house, then the pilings flared red and he cut the engine. There was no sound but a wall of crickets and the ocean.

While Abby found the key hanging from a nail on the back of the stairs, Brother Lemon pulled the tube of blankets containing Gretchen out of the van and slung her over one massive shoulder. Then they clomped upstairs.

Standing in the living room, breathing hard, Brother Lemon decided on the extra guest bedroom for the exorcism because it didn't have any windows. They went into the room and switched on the single overhead light. The walls were bare wood paneling, the plank floor was covered with a rag carpet. The only furnishings were a plain metal bed frame with a bare mattress and a flimsy white wicker headboard. A matching white wicker dresser stood in the corner.

Brother Lemon went downstairs and bounded back up, panting, carrying his two surf bags and a cooler; he dumped them in the living room. Then he went into the guest bedroom, unwrapped Gretchen, laid her on the bed, and pulled out a wide selection of black nylon straps and handcuffs. All of them were too short.

"Are you sure you've done this before?" Abby asked.

"Get me an old sheet," he said.

Abby came back from the linen closet with two sheets, which Brother Lemon tore into strips and used to tie Gretchen's wrists and ankles to the bed frame. He left her hands down by her sides.

"It's less pornographic this way," he explained.

Leaving the door open, he and Abby went into the living room and waited for Gretchen to wake up. It was winter on the Isle of Palms, so no tourists were renting houses, only year-round people. Even so, Abby made Brother Lemon turn out the guest room light, and she wouldn't let him turn on any others, so the two of them sat in the dark and went over the plan.

"Mostly we're going to wing it," Brother Lemon said.

"Wing it?" Abby repeated.

"Expertise, plans, strategies," Brother Lemon said. "None of those are any use in an intense exorcism-type situation. You have to enter the arena of diabolic battle armed only with faith, love, and the power of Jesus Christ. Oh, shoot, I can't believe I didn't ask this before. You are baptized, aren't you?"

"Sure," Abby said, who actually wasn't very sure at all.

"It'll be dangerous in there for an unbaptized soul," Brother Lemon said. "I'll be doing some serious blasting of prayer and if you're not girded with the full Armor of God, you might not make it through with your soul intact."

Beach houses on the Isle of Palms weren't supposed to be occupied in the winter. None of them had insulation, and none of them had heat. It was so cold that Abby's fingernails ached. Wind whistled through the cracks around the windows and pressed hard against the walls.

"I want you to know what we're walking into," Brother Lemon

said. "I need you in the room as my auxiliary, but you're cherry, so I need you to follow my lead. Do exactly what I tell you to do, nothing more or less. Can you handle that?"

Abby nodded.

"There are four stages of an exorcism," Brother Lemon said. "Although we're not doing this the Catholic way, so technically it's a deliverance. The first stage is Pretense. The demon hiding inside your friend wants us to give up. It wants us to doubt ourselves. So it's going to pretend it isn't there. I can see it, but you can't, so you're going to think I'm crazy. But you have to trust me. I've got some tricks up my sleeve, but it might take some time. Check?"

Abby felt ridiculous saying the word.

"Check," she said.

"Once I get the demon to reveal itself," Brother Lemon continued, "we move to the second stage. That's the Breakpoint. That's when things might get a little weird. The demon will stop pretending to be your friend, and it will begin conversing with us directly. No matter what happens, do not converse with the demon, do not engage with the demon, do not speak to the demon. It'll try to trick us and draw us deeper into its traps and snares. Check?"

"Check," Abby said.

"Then comes the Clash," Brother Lemon said. "This is like the Breakpoint, only much, much worse. It'll be full-on spiritual battle. Demons command the powers of darkness, so all kinds of funky stuff might happen. My daddy once saw a glass of water boil. I'll do everything I can to protect you, but you have to follow my lead without question, check?"

"Check," Abby said.

"Finally," Brother Lemon said, "comes the Expulsion. This is when I'll banish the demon and drive it from your friend's body. When that happens, be ready for anything. It might attempt to enter one of us, it might take out this whole house. Who knows what it's capable of, so stay frosty. You got all that?"

Abby nodded.

"How long do you think it'll take?" she asked. Even in the dark, she could see her breath puff out of her mouth.

Brother Lemon blew into his hands and rubbed his palms.

"Deliverance can take anywhere from fifteen minutes to, oh, about an hour," he said. "Maybe four or five, but that's rare."

It didn't sound too bad, Abby thought. Maybe they could even return Gretchen before her parents came home.

"Abby?" a voice called in the dark. "Where am I?"

Brother Lemon and Abby looked at each other, eyes gleaming in the shadows, and then he stood up. Rummaging in one of his duffel bags, he pulled out an athletic cup and slid it down the front of his pants. He caught Abby staring.

"First place they go for," he explained. Then he adjusted himself and picked up a well-worn Bible. "Let's do the Lord's work," he said and headed for the bedroom, walking slightly bow-legged.

Inside, he snapped on the overhead light. The glare blinded Abby for a moment, but then her eyes adjusted and she saw Gretchen squirming on the bed, turning her head away from the light, pulling on the strips of sheet holding her down.

"This isn't funny," she said.

Abby closed the door behind them. Brother Lemon stood at the foot of the bed while Abby stayed near the door. Gretchen studied Brother Lemon.

"Saint Michael the Archangel, defend us in battle," Brother Lemon prayed. "Be our protection against the wickedness and snares of the Devil. May God rebuke him, we humbly pray. And do thou, O Prince of the Heavenly Host, by God's power, thrust into hell Satan and all evil spirits who wander the world seeking the ruin of souls. Ay-men."

"What the hell is this?" Gretchen asked. She turned wide eyes to Abby. "What're you doing with this guy? You're scaring me."

Brother Lemon began to recite the Lord's Prayer.

"Our Father, who art in heaven, hallowed be thy name . . ."

"Why are you doing this to me?" Gretchen asked. "I want to go home. Please, my parents will do anything. Abby, why are you doing this?"

". . . Give us this day our daily bread, and deliver us from evil. For thine is the kingdom, the power, and the glory, forever and ever. Ay-men."

He repeated the prayer a second time, and then a third. It was so cold, Abby was shivering. She watched Gretchen, waiting for her to smoke, or scream, or vomit, or something. But Gretchen just kept talking.

"Are you mad at me, Abby?" she asked. "Is that why you're doing this? I know I've been weird lately, and I'm so, so sorry. There's a lot going on at home. Things are . . . really bad. I think my parents are getting divorced and you've seen how my mom treats me. But that's no excuse. I've been a bad friend. I've been shitty to you and Glee and Margaret. I just got so angry at them, and I probably overreacted, but you know how it is, right? I'm sorry. I screwed up, and I'm not good to you, and I know that. I'm really sorry. But you have to let me out. Look at this, it's not right. You know it's not right."

Brother Lemon braced his legs and squared off against the bed, as if he was getting ready for a fistfight.

"I command you, unclean spirit!" he boomed. "Along with all your minions now attacking this servant of God, by the mysteries of the incarnation, passion, resurrection, and ascension of our Lord Jesus Christ, reveal to me your name. Tell me your name!"

Gretchen kept talking to Abby.

"This is crazy," she said. "You can't keep me tied up like this."

"I command you, unclean spirit," Brother Lemon repeated. "Along with all your minions now attacking this servant of God, by the mysteries of the incarnation, passion, resurrection, and ascension of our Lord Jesus Christ, that you reveal to me your name. Tell me your name!"

"Please, Abby," Gretchen said. "Let's get out of here. I won't tell anyone what happened. I promise."

"I command you, unclean spirit," Brother Lemon started for a third time, even louder. "Reveal to me your name!"

Gretchen turned her head on the bare mattress to look at him.

"Gretchen Lang," she said. "That's my name, okay? You could have asked Abby."

"That's not your real name," Brother Lemon said. "Once more, by the power of my Lord and Savior Jesus Christ, I command you to tell me your name!"

"I just told you my name!" Gretchen said.

"Your true name, demon!" Brother Lemon said.

There was a long pause. Gretchen started to laugh.

"I'm sorry," she said. "I just realized what you think you're doing. The two of you standing there like it's *The Exorcist*, asking me my name over and over. You think I'm possessed. Oh my God! Abby, this is bizarre."

She kept giggling, eyes closed, rolling her head from side to side, grinning.

"Demon," Brother Lemon said. "I command you to tell me your name!"

"Andras," Abby said quietly.

"What?" Brother Lemon looked at her, startled.

"Andras," Abby said, embarrassed. "His name is Andras. You

said so before."

There was a long silence. The air pressure dropped and the walls and ceiling in the beach house gave off a crack.

"Ander Ass?" Gretchen asked from the bed, still giggling. "Is he in Menudo?"

"Come here," Brother Lemon said, grabbing Abby and leading her out of the room, slamming the door behind him.

They stood in the darkness and Abby could feel anger vibrating off Brother Lemon's body. Then he lit his face with a squeeze flashlight he had on his keychain.

"What did I tell you?" he asked. "What is the *one* thing I told you *not* to do?"

"She's laughing at us," Abby said.

"I said 'Do not talk to the demon.' I said, 'Do not engage with the demon.' And what's the first thing you do? We haven't even been there an hour."

"It's taking a long time," Abby said.

"Longer than I anticipated," Brother Lemon admitted. "But it is vitally important that I show this demon who's king of the ring. It has to understand that I'm top dog. By forcing it to reveal its name, I bend it to my will. This is called harnessing the demon and it's very, very important. Now if I let you back in there, do you promise not to talk?"

Abby nodded.

"Yes, sir."

"Good," Brother Lemon said, and then he softened. "I'm only trying to protect your immortal soul."

He let the flashlight go out and together they reentered the room. Gretchen was watching the door.

"Is your exorcism still okay?" she asked. "I don't want to mess up your hot date."

Brother Lemon took up his position at the foot of the bed, and Abby stayed by the door.

"I command you once more," he began. "I command you, unclean spirit . . ."

"I command yew onthce more, I co-co-command you un-un-uncwean spiwit," Gretchen repeated, doing Porky Pig.

"Whoever you are, along with all your minions now attacking this servant of God," Brother Lemon continued.

"Who-who-uh-whoever yew are, awong wit all yer minyunth now athwacking thwis serwant of Gawd," Gretchen Porky Pigged.

It threw Brother Lemon off his script.

"By the, uh, the mysteries of the passion, and uh, the passion and the resurrection of Jesus Savior," he stumbled.

"Enh, what's up, Doc?" Gretchen said, doing a perfect Bugs Bunny.

Brother Lemon's face got tight, his jaw clenched, his joints got stiff. Then he pulled a prayer sheet from his Bible and read from it, using a finger to keep his place. This time Gretchen repeated him, but just a second behind. The time after that, she spoke in an English accent. She threw him off the time after that, and the time after that, and the time after that.

The exorcist prayed for so long and so hard that he blew out his voice. Abby's kneecaps creaked. Her feet were swollen. She leaned her back against the doorframe, then shifted from one foot to the other, stretched, touched her toes, cracked her knees. Her shoulders ached. From time to time, Brother Lemon would shoot her an annoyed look, but mostly he concentrated on reading from his paper, again and again and again.

Finally, Brother Lemon stormed out of the room. Abby turned to follow.

"Wait!" Gretchen hissed. Her throat sounded sore.

Abby turned around. Gretchen was looking at her.

"I'm scared," Gretchen said. "I'm really, really scared. This guy is crazy, and I've been here for a long time. Tell him I'm not possessed."

Abby looked down at her watch. It was past two in the morning. By now Gretchen's parents would be home. They'd have seen Max in the shower, they'd have realized their daughter was missing. The police would be looking for them.

"Come on, this is crazy," Gretchen whispered. "You have to know this is crazy. This is how people get killed."

Abby looked through the doorway into the dark living room but didn't see Brother Lemon.

"Are you scared of him?" Gretchen asked. "Is he making you do this?"

Abby turned back to Gretchen.

"I'm scared of *you*," she said.

She got out before Gretchen could say anything else and found Brother Lemon in the kitchen, slamming through the cabinets.

"What's happening?" she asked.

"What's happening," he said, his voice constricted, "is that we need a provocation to draw out the demon. Things are escalating, Abby. We are at DEFCON 3."

He picked up a dark blue canister of Morton's iodized salt and gave it a shake. It was almost full.

"What does that mean?" Abby asked.

"It means," he said, setting the salt on the counter, "that I need you to join hands and pray with me over this salt. Our Father, who art in heaven, hallowed be thy name . . ."

They said the Lord's Prayer over the salt three times and then went back to the bedroom. Gretchen was squirming on the bed.

"I've never done anything to hurt you," she said. "Please,

please, please, think about—"

Brother Lemon filled his hand with salt.

"In the name of Jesus, I remove you," he proclaimed. "Spirit of discord and disharmony, I send you to the cross."

With that, he dashed the fistful of salt in Gretchen's face. She recoiled and sputtered. He poured another handful.

"In the name of Jesus, I remove you," he repeated. "Spirit of discord and disharmony, I send you to the cross."

This time he threw the salt so hard, it left a mark on Gretchen's right cheek. Then he did it again. Salt was in Gretchen's nose, stuck to the spit on her chin and in the folds of her neck. It was in her hair, collecting in the wet corners of her eyes.

"In the name of Jesus, I remove you," Brother Lemon said again. "Spirit of discord and disharmony, I send you to the cross."

He smashed another handful of salt into Gretchen's face. She began to weep. The next time Brother Lemon drew back his arm to hurl more salt into Gretchen's face, Abby touched it. He whirled on her.

"You're hurting her," Abby whispered. "I don't understand why we're hurting her."

"It is right to mortify the flesh of the demoniac to draw out the demon," Brother Lemon said.

He lashed the fistful of salt onto Gretchen's face as she rolled from side to side, trying to protect herself. Her lips moved and she said something, but it was so faint Abby couldn't hear.

"You're so smart?" Brother Lemon shouted, his face inches from Gretchen's. "If you're so smart, why are you tied to a bed and I'm standing up here?"

Something broke behind Gretchen's face and she crumbled into tears, blowing spit bubbles, her body shaking, her face blotchy.

"That's right!" Brother Lemon shouted, smashing another fistful of salt into her face. "Tell me your name, truth to God, tell me your name, demon! Tell me your name!"

There was the sound of a faucet turning on, of hissing from a leak, and the front of Gretchen's shorts turned dark. A rivulet of urine raced from her crotch, down her right leg, pooling at her knee. Its briny tang filled the cold room. Abby was ashamed for her.

"She's going to the bathroom," she said.

Brother Lemon turned to her.

"Get a towel and run warm water on it," he said.

Abby went to the kitchen and found a dish towel. When she turned on the tap, the pipes vibrated in the walls and the spigot spat rusty water, then ice water, then a lukewarm trickle. She soaked the towel and rushed back into the room.

Brother Lemon was praying, holding his hands over Gretchen.

"Go on now," Brother Lemon said. "Clean her up."

"Me?" Abby asked stupidly.

"I must avoid touching any areas of the demoniac that might open the doorway to lust," he said.

Nervously, Abby stepped toward the bed and mopped at Gretchen's leg. Brother Lemon found a plastic bucket and Abby wrung the cloth into it. At first, touching Gretchen's urine disgusted her; then she started regarding Gretchen not as her friend, or even as a person, but as a thing to be cleaned, a car to be washed, and the task became easier.

"Abby?" Gretchen sobbed. "Why are you doing this to me?"

This time, Abby didn't have an answer.

Brother Lemon left the room briefly but then came striding back, brushing past Abby. He marched to the head of the bed, poured salt into his hands, and bent over Gretchen, who began to struggle.

"No!" she shouted. "No, get off me. Get off me! Abby!

ABBYYYY!!!! Help! Heeeelp!"

Brother Lemon smashed another handful of salt into her face.

"Step back, Satan," he commanded.

Another blast of salt.

"Tempt me not with vain things," he said.

Another fistful of salt. Gretchen's body was shaking helplessly.

"What you offer is evil, Satan," Brother Lemon shouted.

More salt blasted Gretchen's face.

"Tell me your name, unholy one," Brother Lemon shouted, his neck swollen and strained. "Truth before God. Tell me your name."

Gretchen had given up struggling, her eyes were closed, her chest heaved. Brother Lemon pressed on her sternum, right below her throat, and Gretchen began to hiccup convulsively, unable to draw a deep breath.

"Andras."

At first Abby wasn't sure where the whispered word had come from, but then she saw Gretchen's lips move as she said it again.

"Andras," she whispered. "Its name is Andras."

Gretchen opened her red shimmering eyes, and tears rolled down her temples.

"No," a deeper male voice said with Gretchen's mouth. "No crying, pig!"

"Abby," Gretchen pleaded. "Get it out of me. Please, get it out."

Two people were fighting to be visible on Gretchen's face.

"Help me," she choked. "Please, help me."

Brother Lemon slapped his Bible against one of his palms.

"Hot damn!" he shouted. "We got ourselves a demon!"

I THINK WE'RE ALONE NOW

The living room was dark and wind whistled through the windows, making the walls creak. The cold shrank Abby inside her clothes. Brother Lemon pulled out a baggie containing a chicken breast from his cooler and sat in a chair, eating it like a Popsicle.

"Sorry about this," he said, his massive jaws grinding the meat. "Andras is the sixty-third entity in the Lesser Key of Solomon, a grand marquis of hell and commander of thirty legions of demons, known as the sower of discord and bringer of ruin. I need to protein-load."

The back wall of the Langs' beach house was all windows, looking out across a screened-in porch to the Atlantic Ocean. Barely visible beyond were the waves, gray and angry, capped with white chop. To the far left, a wound sliced across the horizon and orange light was bleeding through. It was just after five a.m.

"We've been here all night," Abby said. "What if you can't do it?"

"Listen, Abby," he said. "When you came to me and said your friend had a demon from hell nesting in her soul, did I say you were crazy? Did I make fun of you? Nuh-uh. I believed you. Now you need to believe me."

"But what if you can't do it?" Abby repeated. "You barely even got it to tell you its name."

Brother Lemon brought his chair over and set it down in front of her.

"An exorcism is a harrowing," he said. "Do you know what that means? It's a test of the exorcist, a trial for his soul. You know why we can't just ask the demon to leave? After all, the Lord's strong right arm is by our side, and through God all things are possible. Christ the Savior could blast that demon out of your friend like that," he said, snapping his thick fingers in the cold air.

"But an exorcism tests us. It asks, 'How strong is your faith? How deep is your belief?' The exorcist must be willing to lose everything—all dignity, all safety, all illusions—everything is burned away in the fire of the exorcism, and what's left is the core of who you are. It's like lifting—when you're deep in a set, your arms are shaking and you're a melting candle of pain that's burned down to zero; you got nothing left to give. And in that darkest moment you cry out, 'Lord, I can't!' and a voice comes out of the darkness and says, 'But I can.' That's the still, small voice that comes in the night. That's the sound of something bigger than yourself. That's God talking. And he says, 'You are not alone,' and enfolds you in wings of the eagle, and he carries you up. But first you have to burn away everything that doesn't matter. You have to burn away leg warmers and New Age crystals, and Madonna, and aerobics, and New Kids on the Block, and the boy you're sweet on in school. You burn away your parents, and your friends, and everything you ever cared about, and you burn away personal safety, conventional morality. And when all that is gone, when everything is swept away in the fire and everything around you is ash, what you have left is just a tiny nugget, a little kernel of something that is good, and pure, and true. And you pick that pebble up, and you throw it at the fortress this demon has built in your friend's soul, this leviathan of hatred and fear and oppression, and you throw this tiny pebble and it hits that wall and it goes *ping* . . . and nothing happens. That's when you'll have the hardest doubts you ever had in your life. But never doubt the truth. Never underestimate it. Because a second later, if you've been through the fire, you'll hear the cracks start to spread, and all those mighty walls and iron gates will collapse like a house of cards because you have harrowed yourself until all that's left is truth. That's what that pebble is, Abby. It's our core. Few things are true in this life, and nothing can stand against them. The truth slices through the armies of the Enemy like the sword of righteousness. But to get there, to find the truth, we go through this trial, we submit ourselves to this exorcism. Do you understand what I'm saying?"

He leaned back and regarded Abby.

"But," she said, "what if we get arrested?"

Brother Lemon sighed.

"Think on what I said," he told her, standing up. "And in the meantime, do what I do and say what I tell you to say. Can you do that? Just for a little while longer? We've come this far."

Abby nodded. She was in too deep to quit now.

"Good," Brother Lemon said. "Now let's blast this demon back to hell."

Gretchen watched them from the bed, grains of salt crusted around her eyes and mouth, salt in her hair, salt in her ears. Brother Lemon raised a glass of water that he'd prayed over in the living room.

"Thirsty?" he asked.

Gretchen's tongue snaked out of her mouth and ran around her chapped lips. It was coated with a thick, white film. Brother

Lemon knelt by the head of the bed, holding the glass so she could sip from it. At the first taste, she threw herself back, thrashing and howling. Brother Lemon dashed the water into her face.

"Blessed water!" he said triumphantly. "I drown you in God's holy love!"

Foam spilled from Gretchen's lips as her eyes rolled back into her head, leaving only the bloodshot whites exposed.

"Gut, head, heart, groin!" Brother Lemon shouted, pressing his Bible against each part of Gretchen's body as he named them. "Face me, liar. Don't you hide. Face me!"

A deep rumble emerged from Gretchen's lips, a sound driven from the bottom of her stomach. The room filled with a dusty stench that Abby couldn't place. "Get it out," she gasped, her voice weak. "It's going deeper. It hurts. It huuurts . . ."

Her voice disappeared in a hiss of pain. Brother Lemon sniffed the air.

"Cinnamon," he said, smiling, and turned to Abby. "Smell that? Olfactory discernment. The unnatural odor of a supernatural presence."

"There's not much of me left," Gretchen gasped, her throat spasming. "I'm drowning . . . he's drowning me . . ."

Brother Lemon brushed past Abby, hurrying out of the room. He returned a moment later carrying a yellow plastic funnel and a gallon jug of Heinz distilled white vinegar. He used his massive hands to bend Gretchen's head backward and forced the funnel between her teeth. She released great, angry whooping moans around it.

"Hold her legs!" Brother Lemon shouted.

Using one hand, he twisted the top off the jug. He used his teeth to pull off the white paper disk and spat it onto the bed. Upending the bottle, he sloshed a third of the liquid down the funnel.

Gretchen choked, gagged, kicked her heels against the mattress. The vinegar sting burned Abby's eyes. Brother Lemon pulled out the funnel and held Gretchen's mouth closed.

"Bucket!" he roared, as Gretchen thrashed beneath him.

Abby grabbed the bucket from where it was lying on the floor and held it out to him.

"Closer!" he yelled. "By her head!"

Abby got there just as he released Gretchen's mouth, and she threw up all over her shirt. Brother Lemon twisted her to the side and she vomited thin yellow liquid. Then he repeated the process while Abby stood there, holding the bucket. This time, a gout of vomit sprayed the bucket in a high-pressure blast.

"I take up the sword of God's spirit," Brother Lemon said, forcing the funnel between Gretchen's teeth. "I pierce you, driving away your lies."

"It's hiding," Gretchen gasped. "Down deep, it's going. . . . Do you think this hurts me?" Her voice dropped lower, her vocal cords rasped and scraped. "You're damning your souls, both of you. You're throwing away your salvation by torturing this pig. What would your God say?"

Gretchen's head snapped back on her neck, and she bit her tongue. Her eyes opened, unclouded.

"Don't listen," she said. "Do it. Get it out. Get it out of me."

Brother Lemon stood up and turned to Abby.

"I want you to go into the kitchen," he said. "See if you can find some ammonia under the sink. We're going to have a real fight now."

Abby found half a bottle of ammonia under the sink, but she lied and said she didn't, so Brother Lemon kept using the vinegar. The struggle went on for hours. Abby's role was limited to saying "Christ have mercy on us" when Brother Lemon cued her, emptying the bucket as Gretchen filled it with progressively thinner and smaller amounts of bile, and holding down Gretchen's legs. The guest bedroom warmed from their body heat until it felt like a sauna and condensation trickled down the walls. When they finally stepped out for a break, the sunlight burned their eyes.

They sat in the living room and Brother Lemon chugged water from a gallon jug. He sucked down half and poured the rest over his head and shook it, spraying cold water.

"Brrr!" he exclaimed. "Want some of this? It wakes you up."

"There has to be another way," Abby said.

"Don't you worry," Brother Lemon said. "Andras thinks he's in the catbird seat, but he's about to feel the boot of the Lord in his ass. Go fill the tub."

Abby's heart sank. "Why?"

"Full-immersion baptism," Brother Lemon said, and he wasn't smiling anymore. "The more we mortify the flesh, the harder we sanctify the spirit, the tougher it is for the demon to hide."

Abby imagined him lowering a bound Gretchen into the bathtub as she kicked and screamed, pressing her to the bottom of the tub, bubbles rising from her mouth.

"No," she said. "It's too much."

Brother Lemon pointed a beefy finger at her.

"Don't coward out on me now," he said. "You heard her. She wants it out."

Abby shook her head.

"What good is the exorcism if she's dead?"

The exorcist considered Abby for a moment. Then he headed for the kitchen, shaking his head. "I'll just do it myself," he said. "Lonely are those who serve the Lord."

Abby heard him clanging around, followed by the sound of the sink running. Then it was quiet. She crept back into the guest bedroom. It smelled like rancid piss and sour vomit. Gretchen had stopped shaking and her skin was grainy with goosebumps. Her breathing was shallow. Her face was raw and wet, her lips swollen and bruised, cracked and chapped from the vinegar. Salt was in her hair, and her eyes were swollen and pink. She raised a bound hand as much as she could and beckoned for Abby to come closer.

Abby knelt beside the mattress. Gretchen opened one bloodshot eye.

"Let him do it," she whispered.

"He's killing you," Abby said.

Gretchen shook her head violently.

"It has to come out of me," she said. "Cut it out, burn it out, drown it out. I can't live like this."

Abby took her hand. It was icy and stiff.

"I'll talk to him," she said. "We can do something else. I can't keep hurting you."

"Andras showed me what I did," Gretchen said. "To you, to Margaret. To Glee. To Father Morgan. To Max . . ."

Her voice cracked on the last one.

"That wasn't you," Abby said.

"It was!" Gretchen said. "It was all me! Me and this—this thing inside of me. It has to come out. Before it destroys everything."

Far off in the house, a teakettle whistled.

"I won't let him hurt you," Abby said. "We can still fix this."

The door swung open and Abby turned to see Brother Lemon approaching the bed. In one hand was a steaming teakettle. In the other was the funnel.

That's when Abby realized that no one was going to stop him. No parent, no teacher, no friend, no cop. There was no one here who could make him listen. It was the most terrifying feeling in the world. She had uncaged a monster that she couldn't control.

"Ready for more?" Brother Lemon said, striding into the room. "We're going to DEFCON 2. Know what this is?"

He raised the kettle over the bed, steam roiling out the spout, and Gretchen's eyes widened with fear. Then she set her jaw.

"Do it," she said. "Get it out of me . . ." Her voice dropped back into its hoarse rasp. "I dare you."

"Get out of the way, Abby," Brother Lemon said. "Feel the word of God, like a hammer of righteousness, blasting you out."

"Stop!" Abby screamed. She stood up between Brother Lemon and Gretchen, arms spread to either side, shielding Gretchen from the exorcist. "You'll kill her!"

"No!" Gretchen shrieked. "Do it!"

"I have to kill the demon," Brother Lemon said, stepping forward.

Abby felt the heat from the kettle warming the left side of her face, starting to cook it. She grabbed at the funnel.

"Look at her," she begged. "Look at what you're doing."

Brother Lemon held the funnel out of reach, hands shaking.

"The Enemy seeks to humiliate me," he said. "The Enemy wants to make me small."

"She's just a girl," Abby said, backing away from him. The bed caught the backs of her knees, forcing her to sit on Gretchen's arm. "You can't take this back!"

"I will mortify her flesh until she gives up the demon," Brother Lemon shouted. "I'm not screwing up again!"

He was a wall of muscle squeezing Abby between himself and Gretchen, looming over her, blocking the light. He shoved Abby to one side and she slid off the bed, knees cracking against the floor. He forced the funnel between Gretchen's teeth as she nodded feverishly.

"Yes! Yes! Yeth!" she moaned in ecstasy as the funnel entered her mouth.

Brother Lemon lifted the kettle and started to pour. Abby threw herself toward it, arms outstretched, feeling nothing at first but then her hands burned where they hit the kettle. Boiling water splattered the length of her arms, and Brother Lemon roared and yanked back. The water burned him, too, and he lost his grip and the kettle clanged to the ground, spinning into the corner, disgorging gouts of steaming water across the floor.

Behind her, Gretchen shrieked in disappointment as Brother Lemon drew himself to his full height. He grabbed Abby by the neck, his face contorted with rage. She was so terrified, she wasn't scared anymore.

"When do you stop?" she shouted. "When she's dead?"

Brother Lemon froze. He looked down at this girl, crying in front of him, arms livid from the boiling water; then he looked behind her at the other girl, tied to the bed, soaking wet, covered with salt and urine, lying in her own vomit. Weakly she turned her head from side to side, chanting, "Kill me, kill me, kill me, kill me . . ."

The light in the room changed. A film dropped from Brother Lemon's eyes.

"I can't see it anymore," he said. "I can't see the demon."

He turned and left the room. Abby followed and found him in the living room, sitting in the big wicker chair, clutching his head.

"I saw the demon," he said to his lap. "I swear I saw it."

"We can fix this," Abby said.

He looked up at her.

"What have I done?" he said. Tears ran down his face.

Abby didn't know how to comfort him. He picked up his Bible and threw himself onto his knees, praying, pressing it to his lips. From the bedroom, Abby could hear Gretchen chanting over and over, "Kill me, kill me, kill me."

Finally, Brother Lemon raised his eyes.

"I need to get my daddy," he said. Then he repeated it, more sure of himself. "I need to go get my daddy."

He got up and started hunting for his keys.

"Why?" Abby asked. "What's he going to do?"

"This is just a trial," Brother Lemon said, convincing himself. "It's a test of our faith. I'm in over my head, but my daddy will know what to do. He deals with worse demons than this all the time. He'll fix this. He'll make it right."

"You can't leave me," Abby said.

Brother Lemon snatched his keys off the coffee table and then turned to Abby. She didn't like the way he wouldn't meet her eyes.

"I'm not leaving you," Brother Lemon said. "I'm going to go get my daddy, and then I'll come back and we'll beat that thing. You wait. I'll be right back. I promise."

And then he was out the door, banging down the stairs underneath the house. She heard a car door slam, an engine spark, and she watched from the front window as he reversed into the street, put the van in drive, and took off.

It was late afternoon, and the world was already getting dark. The house was quiet. Abby walked into the guest bedroom to check on Gretchen. She was lying on the bed, completely still. Abby leaned over to check on her.

"Please . . ." Gretchen moaned. "Make it stop . . ."

"It's going to be okay," Abby said. "He's getting someone who can help."

"Make it stop . . . make it stop . . . make it stop . . ." Gretchen moaned.

Abby went to hug her and Gretchen suddenly burst out laughing.

"It's so easy," she said, smiling cruelly, and Abby felt a rock sinking slowly from her chest to her gut. "Did you think Gretchen was still here? She's been gone for a long time, and you two stand there and pompously intone prayers to a God you don't even believe in and—what? You expected my head to spin around? You have the imagination of children. I barely had to reveal one-tenth of my majesty to dispense with that poser. Some silly voices here, a push there, a nudge, a wiggle, and now it's just you and me. As it was in the beginning, so it shall be in the end."

Gretchen smiled up at Abby, humming a little tune.

"I think we're alone now," she sang softly, eyes locked on Abby's. "There doesn't seem to be anyone aroun-ound. I think we're alone now, the beating of our hearts is the only sou-ound . . ."

I WOULD DIE 4 U

"You know what's going to happen," Gretchen said. "My parents are already looking for me. Can you imagine the choice tantrum my mom threw when she came home from the game, all full of crab dip and fried chicken, only to find her precious perfect baby girl missing? Beloved family pet dead? Blood all over her clean white carpets? I mean, those will definitely have to be replaced. They're going to call the police and the first person they're going to wonder about is that girl—what's her name?"

Abby crouched down and pressed the heels of her hands against her temples. *This isn't Gretchen*, she told herself. *Gretchen is someplace else.*

"That girl," Gretchen continued. "You know, the one dealing drugs? The one who almost got expelled? The one who stole the dead baby from the hospital for some kind of sick sex orgy? Oh, right, Abigail Rivers. Is she home? Ring-ring! Hello, Mrs. Rivers, at some point in the last twenty-four hours while you were being total white trash, did you notice anything different about your daughter? She's gone? Now, I know we're only the Mount Pleasant Police Department and we don't have two brain cells to rub together, but this might be a clue. Hey, Cletus? Do you think the crazy pizza-faced girl might have something to do with the abduction and possible murder of this nice, sweet, upstanding, and—dare I say—smoking-hot girl? Well, Retus, I think it's worth a look."

Abby began to rock back and forth. *This isn't Gretchen*, she told herself over and over. *This isn't Gretchen.*

"They're going to come for you," Gretchen said, and she didn't look cold anymore. In fact, she looked like she was exactly where she'd wanted to be all along. "They're going to find you here with me tied to the bed, and they're going to put you in a facility. Your parents will be the most hated people in Charleston. You're such a schizo it's going to be legendary. People are going to remember the dead-baby-stealing, kidnapping druggie from Albemarle Academy forever. Even after they finally let you out, even after you're old and dried up and thirty—even then, you'll never get to be anyone else. You're always going to be the same tainted, pathetic spaz you are today."

Abby leapt to her feet and ran for the living room. The thing using Gretchen's voice had wormed its way into her head and squeezed Abby's brain, making it pulse blood. She needed quiet. She went to the front window and watched the street grow dark. A man in a red raincoat passed by, walking his dog. A plane left contrails in the violet sky. Time passed. Eventually the streetlights blinked on and that's when Abby had to face facts: the exorcist wasn't coming back. She was all alone. A demon was waiting in the next room, and no one was going to help her.

"Abby," the Gretchen-Thing called out. "Can you hear me, Abby?"

Abby rested her forehead against the glass. There was no way out. She had ruined everything.

"What if I let you go?" she called desperately. "I'll let you go, and we'll just leave. We'll go to a neighbor and call the cops and you promise to tell them you took the baby. And then we'll go our separate ways, and you won't hear from me ever again."

"Oh, we're way beyond that now, Abby," Andras said. "You know why? Because you've truly pissed me off. I'm tied to this Christing bed, but you're the one who's trapped."

Abby shook her head, trying to wish everything back the way it was before she screwed it all up so badly.

"They're going to be here soon," Andras continued. "Are you ready to go far, far away? I think you're way past Southern Pines now. And once you're gone, I'm going to have so much fun. I think Margaret might become another teen tragedy. I've barely even started on Wallace Stoney. Maybe Nikki Bull can be the first girl at your school to get AIDS."

Abby looked down at the coffee table. Sitting on a pile of out-of-date *National Geographics* was Brother Lemon's Bible. She picked it up. His cheat sheet was shoved into its pages. She pulled it out.

It was the exorcism. All the prayers, all the rituals, all the rites, all written down, with directions. Abby took out the pages and looked at these useless prayers and incantations. She was going to jail, she knew she was going to jail, but Andras would keep going and going and going. There was no end to it.

"Do you know what I think, Abby?" Andras called. "I think it's time that Dereck White got tired of the way those football players treat him. I think maybe it's time he brought his gun to school. Can't you see it? He's walking down the hall, going from room to room, and for once no one can tell him to shut up. After you're gone, I'm going to have so much fun."

There was no more Margaret. No more Glee. No more Wallace Stoney. No more Father Morgan. Soon there would be no more Brother Lemon. When did it stop? How much misery did there have to be? Abby knew the suffering would be infinite. It would spread from person to person to person and go on and on until there was nothing else. Until everyone felt the way she did right now.

It had to stop. It didn't matter what happened to her anymore: this had to stop.

Abby turned out the lights in the living room and checked all the doors to make sure they were locked. She got a glass of water and walked into the guest bedroom, carrying Brother Lemon's Bible and instructions.

"Saint Michael the Archangel, defend me in battle," Abby read off the sheet. "Be my protection against the wickedness and snares of the devil. May God rebuke him, I humbly pray. Amen."

The paper trembled in her hands, but she told herself it was because of the cold. Abby stood at the foot of the bed and her voice sounded too loud, too theatrical, too much like she was pretending. The overhead fixture made everything look cheap and shoddy.

"Our Father, who art in heaven, hallowed be thy name," she prayed. "Thy kingdom come, thy will be done . . ."

"Seriously?" Andras asked, raising Gretchen's head. "You're seriously doing this?"

". . . as we forgive those who trespass against us. And lead us not into temptation . . ."

"It won't work," Andras said. "An exorcist has to be pure and honest, and that's the one thing you've never been. You're arrogant, Abby. You think you're the only person who works hard, you think no one suffers but you . . ."

". . . forever and ever. Amen," Abby breathed deeply. "Our Father, who art in heaven, hallowed be thy name . . ."

She repeated the Lord's Prayer three times.

"Ask yourself, Abby," Andras said, talking over her. "If you're so wonderful, if you are truly this selfless giving tree, why are you only friends with rich girls? You used to be friends with Lanie Ott and Tradd Huger, but they're not rich like me and Margaret and Glee. I bet you wouldn't even talk to your parents if you didn't have to live with them. They've done nothing but sacrifice for you and you're humiliated by them. You think they're trash."

Abby's hands were shaking harder now, and she raised her voice to drown out Andras.

"I command you, unclean spirit," she said, her voice quavering. "Along with all your minions now attacking this servant of God, be gone."

Andras laughed at her.

"Once more, by the power of my Lord and Savior Jesus Christ, I command you to depart this servant of God."

"You know, Abby," Andras said in Gretchen's voice, "this is one of those things that's broken, and it's not getting fixed. Some mistakes are forever, and you committed one. Welcome to the rest of your long, lonely life."

They went on this way for an hour. After a while, Abby couldn't remember how long she'd been in the room; Gretchen's body was exhausted, her hair sweaty and matted, wrists and ankles chafed raw by the sheets, the mattress cold and wet.

Abby's voice was shot, but she took another sip of water and kept reading. Her glass was almost empty, but she knew she couldn't leave this room.

"Depart, transgressor," Abby read. "Depart, seducer, full of lies and cunning, foe of virtue, persecutor of the innocent. Give way, you monster, give way to Christ, in whom you found none of your works!"

Andras blew an exhausted raspberry.

"The power of Christ compels you, demon," Abby said. "Leave this servant of God."

Andras let out a fake snore.

"I cast you out," Abby droned. "I cast you out, unclean spirit, along with every satanic power of the enemy, every specter from hell, and all your fell companions; in the name of our Lord Jesus Christ. Begone and stay far from this child of God."

Andras stared up at the ceiling with dead eyes. Abby stopped, and the silence rushed in and crushed her. She was so tired. This was so stupid.

"I cast . . ." Abby began, but her throat was so dry it croaked.

She looked over at the dresser and her heart leapt when she realized that her glass was still half full. She took a long gulp. It tasted sweet. Then she gagged and spat the water onto the floor. The liquid in her glass was cloudy and yellow and it reeked of sulfur. She was drinking urine. Tiny multilegged bugs swam in it, paddling toward the surface. Abby let the glass drop and it bounced and rolled, showering her pants with warm pee.

"Who said there were rules here?" Andras laughed from the bed. "What made you think I would be bound by your expectations?"

Gretchen yawned, and a roach crawled out of her mouth, brushed her nostrils with its antenna, crawled up her cheek, over her temple, and disappeared into her hair. She yawned wider and a swarm of roaches exploded from her mouth, scuttling off in different directions. Some of them ran up the wall, occasionally losing their grip and plopping to the floor; others scurried down the mattress, and still more blanketed her face and body, burrowing into her tank top, crawling into the legs of her shorts.

Abby raced to the bed and swatted them away, sweeping the bugs off her friend's belly and hips and chest as fast as she could. Andras made Gretchen grin and chew. She crunched roaches, their yellow creamy mash squeezing between her teeth.

"Stop!" Abby said, slapping roaches off Gretchen's cheeks. "Stop it!"

Then Gretchen's left eye twitched, and a bloodworm squirmed out of her tear duct, curling itself over the bridge of her nose. Bugs were clittering, chattering, twitching, rustling, hissing, latching onto Abby, seething around her feet, clinging to her fingers and the sides of her palms, swarming up her arms and legs. She jerked backward, screaming, and her back smashed into the wall.

Andras started to laugh as Abby ran from the guest bedroom crying and babbling, sweeping roaches from her hair, swiping them from her body, running for the bathroom. She crashed through the door and turned on the light, ready to leap into the shower, then she looked in the mirror and froze.

No bugs. They were all gone. Abby even checked down her pants and inside her shirt, but there wasn't a single bug to be found.

She went back into the bedroom, where Andras was waiting. No bugs there, either.

"Do you think you stand a chance?" Andras said. "You're not getting out of this alive."

Without hesitation, Abby marched to the dresser and picked up the Bible and Brother Lemon's paper.

"Your name is Andras," Abby said, reading from Brother Lemon's notes. "You have a smile like fire and eyes like thunder, and you make servants kill their masters and children kill their parents. You are the devourer of stars, the destroyer of time, the rash solution, the cleaving that can never be rejoined, giver of dooming rage."

"So you've heard of me," Andras said. "So fucking what?"

"You are one of the most powerful demons in hell," Abby continued, rolling over the interruption. "You start wars and slaughter millions. You're the bomb, the MX missile, the mushroom cloud that covers the world."

"And you're just a stupid little girl!" Andras shouted.

"And I'm just a stupid little girl!" Abby shouted back. "But I will not stop because you have my best friend and I am coming for her! Do you hear me? I am coming for her and there is nothing you can do, because I will not stop, I will never stop, I will never give up because I want my friend back!"

As Abby screamed, Andras laughed in a voice that came from deep inside Gretchen. The next time Andras spoke, she was speaking two languages simultaneously. One was German, the other was something much older.

> ***"Ich** Ils **werde** viv **dich** malpirgi **zu** salman **Tode** de **ficken** Donasdogamatatastos **wirst** ds **du** Acroodzi **sterben** bvsd, **und** bliorax **sterben** balit **und** Ds **sterben** insi **allein** caosg **schreien** lusdan **immer** pvrgel **und** Micalzo **in** chis **Angst** Satan **vor** od **Gott** fafen **ist** Zacare **tot** ca **Gott** od **sei** zamran **tot** Odo **ist** cicle **alles** qaa! **tot** Zorge **in dir meine schwarze Krallen** Zir **ziehen** noco! **das** Hoath **Herz** Satan **in** Bvfd **Stücke** lonsh **wie** londoh **faules** babage **Obst** Chirlan! **und** A **ich** bvsd **am** de **Fest** vovim **der** Ar **Schmerzen** i **aller** homtoh **gebrochenen** od **Stellen** gohed! **in** Irgil **dir** chis **alle** ds **Enttäuschungen** paaox **alles** i **Leben** bvsd **Sie** De caosgo **alle** ds **Leute,** chis **die** od ip Vran **Sie** teloah **verraten** cacrg iad gnai loncho"*

Abby fell to her knees, clapping her palms to the sides of her head as warm fluid leaked from her ears. Then the impossible sound stopped and there was just Gretchen's voice again, grunting in agony, panting and wheezing.

"Help me . . . oh God, help me, Abby, help me . . ."

With great big meaty pops of cartilage, Gretchen's hands began to stretch. Abby scrabbled for the paper and read as loudly as she could.

"Demon," she said over the sound of cracking knuckles, "I command you once more, I command you, unclean spirit, tell me the hour and time of your departure—"

Gretchen's arms were stretching, too. Her elbows dislocated, then her shoulders. Her kneecaps popped loose as her legs began to stretch, her toes dislocating, one by one.

"The power of Christ compels you!" Abby shouted, trying to sound strong. "Leave this woman! Begone!"

Gretchen whimpered like Good Dog Max, and now her palms stretched down to her knees and her feet were hanging off the end of the bed. With a gristly rip, her neck began to stretch.

"The light of God surrounds me," Abby read. "The love of God enfolds me. The power of God protects me. The presence of God watches over me. Wherever I am, God is. And all is well. And all is well. And all is well."

"Make it stop, Abby," Gretchen cried. "Stop . . . stop . . . stop. . ."

Her neck stretched another inch. Abby hoped it was an illusion, like the roaches. Abby prayed it was an illusion.

"Gek!" Gretchen gasped as her vocal cords went tight.

An icy wind kicked up and blew through the room, stinking of manure. The overhead light dimmed to brown, then flared, then flickered.

"In the name and authority of the Lord Jesus Christ," Abby shouted into the wind, "I renounce all the power of darkness which exists in Gretchen Lang. I bind all evil spirits assigned to Gretchen Lang and forbid you to operate in any way, Andras. The power of Christ compels you!"

Gretchen screamed louder. And then her body retracted, limbs snapping back into place in a flurry of popping joints and grinding cartilage. The cold wind continued to blow. Abby used two hands to hold the paper flat so she could read it.

"I command you, unclean spirit," she read. "along with all your minions now attacking this servant of God, by the mysteries of the incarnation, passion, resurrection, and ascension of our Lord Jesus Christ, that you cease your attack on this child of God and begone."

The walls of the room fell away, the wind was stronger, and Abby and Gretchen were no longer in the beach house; they were somewhere ancient and dead. Far off in the distance, Abby saw a man standing with his head on fire, his skull completely engulfed in flames that burned but did not consume. Behind a half-open door, a shape was watching her, hungry for her body.

Then Gretchen began to gabble, began to scream.

"The power of Christ compels you!" Abby attempted.

"Stop!" Gretchen cried over the wind. "Abby, he won't stop until you stop. Please!"

"The power of Christ compels you, Andras!" Abby shouted. "Leave this girl alone!"

Gretchen's screams were cut off as fingertips emerged from her mouth, crowned with dirty nails. The hand pushed out of Gretchen's mouth, slick with spit, her lips working helplessly against its knuckles.

"I command you, unclean spirit," Abby shrieked into the wind. "The power of Christ compels you!"

Gretchen's face was stretched tight. A hairy wrist followed the hand, then a thick forearm. Gretchen's shoulders heaved as, inch by inch, the hairy arm forced its way out, stretching her lips wider and wider. Gretchen's jaws locked at their maximum width, and still it pushed on.

"Leave this girl!" Abby screamed. "The power of Christ compels you!"

The arm kept coming, and now the skin around Gretchen's

mouth was splitting. Gretchen sobbed and gagged. The arm was almost exposed to its elbow, and now it bent and placed its palm flat against Gretchen's chest and it began to push itself out, tearing Gretchen's face in half.

"I can't!" Abby shouted, and she felt all the strength drain from her legs. "I can't. I'm sorry, Gretchen, I can't . . . I quit, I quit, I promise, I quit."

She collapsed onto her butt, and the second she hit the floor the wind stopped, the light quit flickering and the arm retreated inside Gretchen. And Gretchen finally, mercifully, lay still. It was quiet. The room was a room again, with bare walls again, a wooden floor again, a wicker headboard and wicker dresser again, and Abby dragged her broken body against the wall and slumped there.

Defeated.

They lay like that for a long time. Gretchen's breath rasping, Abby's shoulders shaking as she cried. She had failed. She had failed, and soon they would come for her and there were no more chances. It was over.

After a while she was aware of breathing in her left ear, very close, wet and thick, and with it came a guttural whispering that only she could hear. It was the greedy sound of triumph and victory, and the words polluted her brain and covered her skin in filth, and they pushed out her own thoughts until her mind was swimming in pus.

Invisible hands touched her, running possessively over her body—strong, bony hands, plucking at her hair, picking at the scabs on her face. Humiliated, she lifted her head and saw Gretchen's limp body on the bed; the invisible hands were fondling her, too. Gretchen's clothing moved as the hands ran over her breasts and between her legs, pulled at her shorts, and the breathing in Abby's ear grew hungry.

Abby wanted to fight, she wanted to resist, but the spark inside her was dead. They both belonged to Andras now. Abby gave up and let the hands do what they wanted. The whispering in her ear got greedier. She had failed. There was no more Abby, only a body that was pinched, and squeezed, and mashed, and violated.

That's when the drums started, deep down inside Abby's head. Deep, deep down—so deep that at first she couldn't hear them over the obscene whispers. But then they were there, faintly, and something in Abby's heart kicked over. Inside her skull, a piano and a guitar were banging, and her heart began to beat with the sound of hundreds of roller skates.

". . . freedom people . . ." she whispered through her cracked lips.

The hissing voices grew louder, angry and vile in her ear. Something slithered across her lips. The hands squeezed her breasts so hard they left bruises.

". . . marching on their feet . . ." Abby mumbled. ". . . Stallone time . . . just walking down the street . . ."

The voices paused, just for a second, and the drums got louder.

". . . we got the beat . . ." Abby whispered, then louder. ". . . we got the beat . . . we got the beat . . ."

The voices stopped. The touching stopped, but then it resumed with a vengeance, more painful than before, twisting and punishing her flesh.

Abby slapped one hand up on the wall, higher than her head, and she pushed off the floor with all her strength. The entire planet was holding her down, something heavier than the universe forced her back, and she felt a bone snap in her left shoulder. But still she rose until she was standing, swaying, on her feet. And in her head, the whispering voices were drowned out by the same four words again and again, the same nonsense chorus:

". . . we got the beat . . . we got the beat . . . we got the beat . . ."

She took a step toward the bed and a wind blew, slashing her to ribbons, pain exploding inside her broken shoulder. Abby bent her head down and walked toward the bed, one foot in front of the other. The hands twisted and tore at her flesh, and an invisible spike hammered between her eyes, but still she walked on.

"Tommy Cox," Abby said. "Tommy Cox, defend me in battle. Be my protection against the wickedness and snares of this world. May Tommy Cox and his holy can of Coca-Cola rebuke you, Satan, and all your works, I pray in his name."

She reached the foot of the bed and now the wind was howling, forcing her backward so violently that she grabbed the sheets holding Gretchen's feet and clung to them. She looked down at Gretchen's broken, ragged, bloody body, and she saw the invisible hands scratching and befouling her friend. She spoke in a loud clear voice.

"By the power of Phil Collins, I rebuke you!" she said. "By the power of Phil Collins, who knows that you coming back to me is against all odds, in his name I command you to leave this servant of Genesis alone."

The wind was screaming and the house shook as the wicker chest flew into the far wall. She held on to Gretchen's feet with one hand and kept reciting.

"By the power of *The Thorn Birds*," she cried, "by the sacred strength of *My Sweet Audrina* and *Forever* . . . I deny and rebuke you, Andras. By the power of lost retainers and Jamaica and bad cornrows and fireflies and Madonna, by all these things I rebuke you."

The wicker headboard was snatched by the wind and flew at Abby, glancing off the side of her head before hitting the wall. Blood poured from her torn ear. The wind was screaming now.

"By the mysteries and the power of Good Dog Max, and E.T. the Extra-terrible, and Geraldine Ferraro the first lady vice president ever, by the Eye of the Tiger, the Love Cry of the Koala Bear, by the passion and redemption of Bad Mama Jama, who will always have supper in the oven. In the name of Glee and Margaret and Lanie Ott, I command you to depart. By the power of the Dust Bunny and in the name of the Go-Go's I compel you, begone!"

The wind was shaking the room and the walls were rattling, the floor was heaving, the bed was vibrating. Gretchen lay limp, shaking bonelessly.

"I love you," Abby shouted into the storm. "I love you, Gretchen Lang. You are my reflection and my shadow and I will not let you go. We are bound together forever and ever! Until Halley's Comet comes around again. I love you dearly and I love you queerly and no demon is bigger than this! I throw my pebble and its name is Gretchen Lang and in the name of our love, BEGONE!!!"

Everything stopped. The wind, the storm, the voices, the hands. And then Gretchen bolted upright, sitting straight up in bed, eyes snapping open, and she screamed a scream she'd been saving since birth, a scream made out of everything that had ever hurt her, a scream so shrill and so loud that the walls split, and the ceiling cracked, and paint chips rained down as Abby held on to the bed. Vile fluid poured out of Gretchen's mouth and black tears drained from her eyes.

All over Charleston, phones started ringing and Gretchen's scream became unbearable. Abby felt a storm of evil ideas rush through her: hollow-eyed men standing behind wire, human lampshades, the pain in Good Dog Max's eyes because he didn't understand what was happening to him, Gretchen stumbling naked out of the blockhouse, Mrs. Lang beating her daughter, the smell of Margaret's bedroom, the silence at dinner tables, Glee screaming and thrashing as she was carried out of the bell tower, men laughing and cutting out a woman's tongue, carving out her heart, burying her alive in an unmarked grave—and there was so much of it and it all hurt so badly and Abby felt it all . . . And then it was gone.

The room was a wreck. Abby's shoulder throbbed. Gretchen lay on the mattress, covered in paint dust from the ceiling, head to one side, immobile. Then her chest rose and she inhaled, and her chest fell and she let out a gentle snore. Abby realized she was asleep.

And she was smiling.

Abby pulled her hand off the bottom of the bed and stumbled out of the room on legs made of wood; she winced. Full sunlight flooded the house and the ocean sparkled through the windows. They had been there all night. Abby heard muffled voices from far away, and she turned toward the front of the house. She heard a car door slam. She limped to the window.

Three police cars had pulled up in the yard, along with Mr. Lang's Mercedes, and everyone was pouring out of the cars. And then Mrs. Lang looked up and saw Abby and pointed, and the police were running for the house.

Abby hobbled back to the guest bedroom.

"Gretchen!" she whispered. "Gretchen! They're coming!"

She was kneeling by the bed, cutting the sheets off Gretchen's wrists, and Gretchen was waking up. She saw Abby and smiled, and it was Gretchen again.

"Abby?" she said.

Heavy feet were pounding up the wooden stairs outside the house and everything was shaking.

"Gretchen," Abby said. She cut the last knot and tore off the sheets.

"I could hear you," Gretchen said. "You were the only thing I could hear and I was drowning, and you reached down and you pulled me out."

Someone kicked in the front door, and then they were in the house, shoes thundering across the floor, shaking the walls, heading for the bedroom, voices shouting.

"I love you," Abby said.

And she was hugging Gretchen, and Gretchen's arms were around her.

"What about Max?" Gretchen whispered in her ear. "What did I do to Max?"

"It wasn't you," Abby said. "Max knows it wasn't you."

And that's what Abby was saying when arms grabbed her from behind and yanked her away. She was in the air, her feet kicking, and Gretchen held on as long as she could. But then cops were pulling her arms away, and Gretchen screamed and reached for Abby.

"Abby!" she shouted as her mom hugged her.

"Get her out," said a man's voice, and the Langs' beach house was full of men in blue uniforms. "Get her out of here!"

"Gretchen!" Abby shouted, reaching for her friend.

Abby was being hauled out of the bedroom backward, and the police were between them, and Mr. and Mrs. Lang were there, and the last thing Abby saw was Gretchen reaching for her over her mom's shoulders. And then they had her out of the house, and down the stairs in the cold, and they were slamming her into the back of a squad car; the engine was starting and the beach house was disappearing behind them.

She heard a faint cry: "Abby!"

Abby twisted around in her seat and pressed herself to the back window and saw that Gretchen had gotten away. She was running down the front stairs and through the yard, and they were all trying to catch her but she was pounding up the street in bloody bare feet, in her shorts and filthy tank top, her face a stricken mass of grief, and she screamed one last time.

"Abby!"

Abby pressed her good hand against the back window, and the car picked up speed, and it was going faster and taking her away and she couldn't see Gretchen anymore. She couldn't see her best friend, her reflection, her mirror, her shadow, herself.

"Gretchen," Abby whispered.

Gretchen was gone.

FAST CAR

They said it was a closed courtroom, but for Abby it might as well have been the middle of Marion Square: a pair of lawyers representing the Langs, two State Law Enforcement Division agents, the city prosecutor and his assistant, two bailiffs, the court reporter, and a consulting psychologist who specialized in satanism and ritual crime. The only person not in the room was Gretchen.

Abby sat on the hard wooden bench that smelled like furniture polish, her shoulder aching, her arm in a sling, stitches in her left ear, and she listened as the judge tore her parents apart. They were unfit, they were irresponsible, they should be ashamed of themselves. And they were. Abby's mom had done her hair like she was going to a party, which made Abby extremely sad, and she chewed the inside of her cheek and stayed silent while her dad rubbed his thighs and his eyes shimmered. Then the Langs were brought in and Abby was sent out in the hall with a female SLED agent. But she could hear every shouted word, even through the closed door: the judge, the lawyers, the Langs, but never her parents. They just sat there and took it.

"Sounds pretty crazy in there, huh?" the agent said.

The special juvenile hearing happened one week after they found Gretchen and Abby at the beach house. Abby had wanted to sneak out and see Gretchen and find out if the exorcism had worked, but her dad had nailed her window shut and padlocked her door. When she wanted to go to the bathroom, she rang a bell and her mom left the bathroom door open and waited outside.

An investigator from SLED came to their house and sat in the living room and asked Abby questions: How did they get to the beach house? Where did she get the GHB? Who else was involved? He pretended to be concerned about her, he pretended that it was all for her own good, but Abby remembered what happened when she tried to tell the truth to Major, and Father Morgan, and the Langs, and she didn't say a word. After half an hour of her silence, he stopped acting like her friend. He took her parents aside and, speaking loudly enough for Abby to hear, told them how she was going to ruin her future if she didn't start cooperating.

Too late, Abby thought.

When they finally let Abby back inside the courtroom, her parents looked harrowed. Abby thought the judge was going to let her say something, but it quickly became clear that no one expected her to say anything. They were going to make all the decisions about her life and she would never even get a chance to speak.

The lawyer for the Langs was talking about a residential treatment facility for at-risk teens in Delaware, he was saying something about a restraining order, he was talking about how many years Abby would have to live on a locked ward, when a man who looked like an accountant came in and whispered something in the judge's ear. The judge held a quick conference in his chambers for everyone except the Rivers family. Abby sat next to her parents, numb and cold, the courtroom empty except for the three of them and a bailiff, waiting for everyone else to come back and pack her away and ship her up north, and her shoulder hurt and her ear ached and she was glad because at least she could still feel something.

The judge returned and said there was someone who needed to speak, and the Langs' lawyer looked exasperated and made a big show of slapping down his legal pad; Gretchen's mom was crying and Mrs. Lang's jaw was clenched, and a few minutes later the rear doors opened and the exorcist was led in by three cops. He wouldn't meet Abby's eyes. Abby felt it all end. Now he'd tell everyone about Andras, and Abby approaching him, and how they planned it, and she would sound crazy. Now they were going to put her on drugs. They would send her to Southern Pines. He was going to make it all so much worse.

And then the exorcist saved her life.

He confessed to everything. He said Abby was at the beach house trying to save Gretchen. He said he'd forced her to steal the fetus for his own satanic rituals. He said he'd abducted Gretchen. He'd shot Max. He'd bought alcohol for minors. He'd coerced Abby into the whole thing. She was under his influence. He was an acolyte of Satan. He was out of control.

A conference was held in front of the judge's bench for everyone but Abby, and then it was all over. They had to send someone downstairs to get shackles in the exorcist's size.

When Abby and her parents got home, someone had broken two of their windows and sprayed "Babykiller" on the front door. Abby's name hadn't appeared in the papers, but everyone knew what she'd done. A week later, her mom told her they were moving to New Jersey. There was a shortage of nurses there. Her dad sold the Dust Bunny without even telling Abby he'd put an ad in the paper. And then Charleston was gone, like it never happened.

They got her a therapist in New Jersey, but Abby refused to talk to him. She knew that the longer she stayed silent, the more she was worrying everyone—but what good would talking do? Nothing she could say would change what had happened. They ate in the only booth of a Chinese take-out place on Christmas Day, and she slept through New Year's. January came. It was the first time Abby had seen snow. Her parents managed to rent a condo and sold their house at a loss. Abby thought about calling Gretchen. She wanted to know if her life was normal again, she wanted to know if she was okay, she wanted to know if anything good had come out of all this, but she was forbidden from contacting the Langs and so she didn't talk to anyone, and every day was the same as the day before.

February. The longer she didn't talk, the easier it became to stay silent. She tried to write Gretchen a letter, but it sounded thin and fake. She wrote a letter to Glee and another one to Margaret; both came back marked "Return to Sender." She had gone to the library and looked up the Charleston papers. The case against the exorcist was falling apart because no one would testify. Glee and her family couldn't be located, and Gretchen's parents just wanted everything to be over. He was sitting in jail, but eventually they'd have to figure out what to do with him.

Abby's parents were eager to move on. They had gotten Abby into Cherry Hill West. She could make up tenth grade in summer school and start as a junior in the fall.

"I know you're smart enough to do that," her mom said when they got home.

Abby didn't say anything.

Both her parents were working now. Her dad had found a job in the Garden Center at Wal-Mart and her mom worked in an old folks' home. Every day, they went to work and Abby stayed behind. They talked about making her see a new therapist, but they were so busy rebuilding their lives that they never got around to it.

Every day, Abby had assignments to get her up to speed for summer school, but the work didn't take her long. There was a neighbor who made sure she didn't leave the house, so mostly she watched TV. Before noon, there was *Family Feud*, *Wheel of Fortune*, and *The Price Is Right*. In the afternoons she lost herself in *All My Children*, *The Bold and the Beautiful*, *Santa Barbara*, and *Another World*. But more and more mornings, she missed *The Price Is Right* altogether and only dragged herself out of bed in time for the afternoon shows.

She was lying in bed one March morning, staring at the ceiling and trying not to think about anything at all, when a horn honked outside. She heard it beep once, then twice, then a third time. Abby ignored it, but it kept on blaring, eating into her brain, *bleeep bleeeeep bleeeeeeep*, refusing to leave her alone. Finally, she trudged into the living room and knelt on the sofa to look out the window and see who the hell was out there. Her heart gave a single, low kick.

Mrs. Lang's white Volvo was idling out front.

Thick billows of exhaust plumed from its dripping tailpipe and the rising sun hit its fogged-over windows and made them burn gold. In a trance, Abby dragged on her jacket, stuck her feet in a pair of sneakers, and opened the front door, fully expecting the car to have disappeared.

It was still there. She shuffled down the sidewalk on numb feet; the closer she got, the more real it became. She could hear its engine idling. She could see a vague shape behind the wheel. She could feel the frozen handle underneath her fingers. She heard the door clunk open. Warm air swirled out and she smelled hibiscus and rose.

"Hey!" Gretchen said. "Want a ride?"

Abby's brain couldn't put the pieces together.

"You always drove me everywhere," Gretchen said. "I figured it was time to return the favor."

Behind Abby, a condo door opened.

"Abby?" Mrs. Momier, their next-door neighbor, called. She was standing on her front porch, arms wrapped around herself, looking worried. "You're not supposed to be outside."

"Come on," Gretchen said. "I'm wanted in, like, at least two states by now. Get in."

Abby slid into the Volvo and slammed the door. The heaters were on high, drying the skin on her face and pulling it tight. Gretchen ground gears as she shifted from neutral into first, and the Volvo shuddered and jerked, then the smell of burning motor oil came through the vents as she pulled onto the street and shredded into second gear.

"I called but they wouldn't let you come to the phone," Gretchen said. "I wrote but I never heard back. I couldn't wait anymore, so I borrowed my mom's car and here I am."

Abby looked at her. Gretchen's face was greasy and a pimple was forming next to her nose. Her hair was sticking up in the back and the car smelled like she'd slept in it. But her eyes were clear and her chin was up as she overhanded the steering wheel to the left and they pulled out of the condo parking lot.

"I'm not sure how long we have," Gretchen said. "I called from the road to let them know I was all right, but I'm sure they're spazzing. Because when I say I borrowed my mom's car, I guess the technical term is that I stole it."

She pulled into a Blockbuster Video parking lot and the Volvo jerked to a stop. The engine gave a death rattle as they rolled into an empty space. Gretchen yanked the emergency brake, then turned in her seat to face Abby.

"Someone else was living my life," Gretchen said. "And all I could do was watch. I saw myself getting my friends drunk and telling them lies, and sleeping with Wallace, and feeding Margaret poison, and I can't remember much of anything except flashes."

A Blockbusters employee in a bright blue and gold shirt walked past to unlock the store, giving them a bored glance through the windshield.

"I'd wake up and have no idea where I was or how I got there," Gretchen said. "Where the cuts and bruises came from. I remember your face, and smearing something across it, and I remember listening to you cry and feeling happy, and I remember Good Dog Max . . ."

Gretchen's voice cracked.

"All winter," Gretchen said, "after the beach house, everything hurt so bad and I felt like it would never stop. Something was wrong inside of me. I was empty and ashamed and I knew I was broken in a way that could never be fixed. I needed to hit the reset button and start over. So a couple of days before Christmas I went into my parents' bedroom and got my dad's gun, and I carried it with me all day until it was warm; and I taught myself how to turn the safety on and off, and how to open it and put in the bullets, and how to pull back the hammer. And then I sat on my bed for a long time, and finally I just couldn't think of any reason not to do it, you know?"

Abby couldn't move. Outside, a customer walked up and dumped videotapes into the Blockbuster return slot, sending them rattling down the chute.

"I put it in my mouth," Gretchen said. "It tasted like poison, and I was so scared, and I had to pee so bad, and I had my finger on the trigger and I could feel exactly how much pressure I needed so I could stop feeling this way all the time. Then I realized you'd think it was all your fault, because you always think everything is all your fault, and I knew I had to explain to you that I was pulling the trigger because I was a fuck-up, not because of anything you'd done. So I decided to write a note telling you that it wasn't your fault, and then the note turned into a letter, and somewhere between pages five and eight I didn't want to kill myself anymore."

Gretchen shoved her hands into Abby's. They were warm and wet.

"You keep rescuing me and I don't know why," Gretchen said. "But every day I tell myself my life must be worth something because you keep saving it. They can't keep us apart. I don't care what happens. You never stopped trying to save me.

"I love you, Abby. You're my best friend, and my mirror, and my reflection, and you are me, and you are everything I love and everything I hate, and I will never give up on you."

Behind them, a police car cruised by slow. Gretchen stopped talking while they watched it pass.

"Do you remember fourth grade?" Abby asked. The words felt awkward in her mouth. "My birthday party at Redwing Rollerway?"

Gretchen thought for a minute.

"My mom made me give you a Bible," she said.

"No one came," Abby said. "I was so humiliated. Then you showed up at the last minute and saved the day."

The cop made a second pass and this time stopped behind them, his engine idling.

"What happened in the beach house?" Abby asked. "It all feels so real, but everyone keeps saying I made it up. I need to know if it really happened or if it was all just unicorns."

Gretchen put a hand on either side of Abby's face and pulled them together until their foreheads were touching.

"It wasn't unicorns," Gretchen said. "I need you to tell me everything. Because you're the only person I can hear it from without going insane. I need to know it all."

Abby started to talk. She was still talking when a second police car showed up, and she didn't stop when they put the two of them in the backseat. She kept on talking while they waited for her mom to show up at the police station, and she was still talking when they got home.

After some arguing, Abby's mom called the Langs, and Mr. Lang bought a ticket to fly up the next day. That night Abby and Gretchen slept in Abby's bedroom and kept talking all night.

They stopped briefly when an exhausted Mr. Lang arrived the next morning and launched into a tirade about what was going to happen to Gretchen and Abby if he had anything to say about it. Abby's dad waited until he ran out of steam and said:

"I think enough harm's been done, Pony. Why don't we leave it here. Let the girls write. If they can pay the bill, let them call. Can't you see this is tearing them up inside?"

Abby and Gretchen kept talking all the way to the airport, and then Abby went home and wrote Gretchen a letter, and that night at 11:06 her phone rang. They kept on calling, and writing letters, and making each other mix tapes with ornate covers they drew in silver and gold paint pens or made out of wrapping paper, recording messages to each other between the songs, mailing each other their high school yearbooks to sign, mailing each other rolls of toilet paper with stamps on the wrappers to see if the postal service would deliver them (they did), sending each other giant birthday cards, collages, weird candy, squirt bottles of Bartender's Friend artificial foam, ridiculous keychains, inappropriate Hallmark condolence cards for no good reason, and Abby sent Gretchen a corny postcard whenever the Cherry Hill West volleyball team went out of town.

They kept talking for years.

AND SHE WAS

The exorcist wound up sitting in jail for eight months, but ultimately no one would testify, so they threw a bunch of minor charges at him and commuted his sentence to time served. He walked out and disappeared. Abby always meant to write him a letter. She started a few, but she never knew where to send them; and after a while, like it always does, life happened, and the fall of 1988 began to fade.

It was little things at first. Abby missed a phone call because she had an away game. Then one time Gretchen didn't write back and never made up for the missing letter. They got busy with SATs and college applications, and even though they both applied to Georgetown, Gretchen didn't get in, and Abby wound up going to George Washington anyways.

At college they went to their computer labs and sent each other emails, sitting in front of black and green CRT screens and pecking them out one letter at a time. And they still wrote, but calling became a once-a-week thing. Gretchen was Abby's maid of honor at her tiny courthouse wedding, but sometimes a month would go by and they wouldn't speak.

Then two months.

Then three.

They went through periods when they both made an effort to write more, but after a while that usually faded. It wasn't anything serious, it was just life. The dance recitals, making the rent, first real jobs, pickups, dropoffs, the fights that seemed so important, the laundry, the promotions, the vacations taken, shoes bought, movies watched, lunches packed. It was a haze of the everyday that blurred the big things and made them feel distant and small.

Abby returned to Charleston only one time. The year she landed her first real job, she got the call everyone gets twice in their lives, and she packed a dress and drove out to New Jersey and sat in the church and stood in the graveyard and wished that she felt something besides tired.

The plan was to stay with her dad for a couple of days, but the first night she woke up from a dream she couldn't remember, and she knew she had to see Charleston again. She bought a ticket before her dad was even out of bed.

It wasn't until she was checking into the Omni downtown (now called Charleston Place) that she realized why she'd come. From there it was just a couple of phone calls before she was pulling her rental car up in front of the Franke Home visitors entrance, and a perky girl was telling her that he was leading a tai chi class in the Wellness Center. Abby walked over and looked through the window and waited for the exorcist to finish teaching repulse monkey pose to a roomful of eighty-somethings.

After class he helped his elderly students pick their bones up off the floor and then he was standing in front of Abby again for the first time in over ten years. He looked the same, only now he sported a hard little pot belly and wore a baseball cap to hide that he was balding. He was wearing baggy Joey Buttafuoco pants and a tank top.

Abby stepped forward and stuck out her hand.

"Hi, Chris," she said. "I don't know if you remember me."

Reflexively he stuck out his hand, but clearly he didn't.

"Did I teach one of your parents?" he asked.

"I'm Abby Rivers," she said. "I came here to apologize for ruining your life."

He looked confused for a minute, and just as she was about to fill him in, he remembered.

"I was the—" she began.

"Exorcism girl," he finished.

Now they were both nodding. Abby was prepared for him to storm away, chew her out; to drop her hand and disappear.

"Come on," he said. "I have a break until Low Impact Aqua Dynamics at four. Let's get a smoothie."

That's how she found herself sitting at Tasti Bites and Blends while the exorcist drank a large Green Dragon Juice with a double wheatgrass shot and she sipped a bottled water.

"I came to say thank you," Abby said. "For what you did. The way you came forward. You don't know how good your timing was. They were about to ship me away to Southern Pines."

"Your folks wouldn't have let that happen," he said. "Besides, it was the right thing to do. How's your friend?"

"Gretchen," Abby said. "She's good. It . . . worked. Not the way I thought it would, but it worked."

"That's good," he said.

The exorcist took a long pull on his straw.

"I don't think you'll be too happy though," Abby said, filling the pause. "She doesn't go to church or anything. I don't either, really."

"Who cares where you sit on Sunday mornings?" Brother Lemon said, and smiled. "I tried to come see you, after I got out, but I heard you'd moved. And with everything that went on, it didn't seem like a good idea to write you. But it's a blessing to see you again. To see that you've moved on, grown up. Where do you live now?"

"New York," she said.

"My life partner can't get enough of that Broadway," he said. "We saw *Phantom* when it came through here, and *The Lion King*. They're only the road companies, but they're still pretty good. Still waiting for *Mamma Mia!* Have you seen it?"

"The music's great," Abby said, not quite sure why she was sitting here talking about ABBA with Chris Lemon.

"Well," he said. "Maybe Barbara and I will get up there someday."

"I'm sorry," Abby said. "I'm so sorry you went to jail. I'm sorry I never said thank-you."

Brother Lemon met her eyes for a moment, then bowed his head, took a long sad drag of his juice, and lifted his face to hers.

"The reason it's a blessing to see you again," he said, "is that I owe you an apology. I am sorry for what I did, what I said to you, how I acted, the choices I made. . . . I'm sorry for all of it. I think about us in that house, and the way I lost control and laid hands on your friend. I trained for two years to place third at the Myrtle Beach Perfect Muscle competition, and I can't even remember what song was playing when I posed. But I close my eyes and I can remember exactly how it felt, standing over that bed, hurling salt at that girl like I was some kind of tough guy, thinking I was a vessel of God's wrath. Those six months I spent in Sheriff Al Cannon's detention center were no man's idea of a party, but they were my atonement for being possessed by the demons of pride, and vanity, and egotism. And seeing you now, sitting here, I know I did the right thing."

"How did it happen?" Abby asked. "I'm a nice girl, you're into musicals, Gretchen ran our school's recycling club. So how did we all end up in that room? How did we end up almost killing one another? How did that happen?"

"I honestly don't know," he said. "But what I do know is that we don't get to choose our lives. I've got Aqua Dynamics in fifteen; let me give you a ride back to your car."

They wheeled out in his pickup truck, and on the way back he made banal chitchat about New York and Abby gave banal answers. As they stood saying their goodbyes in the Franke Home parking lot, Abby tried one last time.

"You don't hate me?" she asked. "For getting you sent to jail?"

"If you forgive me, I forgive you," he said.

"That's it?" she asked. "It's kind of . . . anticlimactic. I was hoping you'd yell at me or something."

Brother Lemon stepped in close, his shadow blocking the sun.

"Abby," he said, "it wasn't a coinicidence that my brothers and I performed at your school that day. It is no coincidence that you and Gretchen love each other. And it was no coincidence that my daddy and I chose the moment we did to turn myself in at the city courthouse. The devil is loud and brash and full of drama. God, he's like a sparrow."

They stood for a minute in the early afternoon sun.

"You go on home now," Brother Lemon said. "They dock my pay if my students drown. I'll see you in New York sometime."

Abby watched him go, and when she turned around she saw a brown VW Rabbit parked at the end of the row of cars. Her heart didn't leap, she didn't scream excitedly, she just had a single practical thought:

"The poor Dust Bunny really needs a bath."

Then sunlight flashed off the rearview mirror of a closing car door, and it wasn't the Dust Bunny after all. It was just somebody's Subaru. She never told Gretchen about the trip.

Abby and Gretchen still kept up, but it was phone calls and letters, then postcards and voicemail, and finally emails and Facebook likes. There was no falling-out, no great tragedy, just a hundred thousand trivial moments they didn't share, each one an inch of distance between them, and eventually those inches added up to miles.

But there were moments when they had no time for distance. When Gretchen's dad had a stroke and she got the call to come home. When Abby's daughter was born and she named her Mary after her mom, and Abby's dad and Gretchen were the only two people who knew that whatever war the two of them had been fighting had finally ended in surrender. When Gretchen had her first solo exhibition. When Glee reappeared in their lives and things got messy for a while. When Abby filed for divorce. When those things happened, they learned that although those inches may add up to miles, sometimes those miles were only inches after all.

After Abby's divorce, no matter how hard she tried to hold everything together, it all kept falling apart. Mary wouldn't sleep and kept pulling out her hair and Abby couldn't get her to stop, and in the middle of everything Gretchen showed up at her front door a couple weeks before Christmas and moved in. That didn't fix everything, but now there were two of them, and Abby thought it was better to be miserable together than to be miserable alone.

On Christmas Eve, after Mary had screamed herself to sleep yet again, Gretchen poured them water glasses of wine and they sat in the living room feeling broken, knowing they had to wrap Mary's presents, lacking the energy to move.

"I hope you don't take this personally," Gretchen said after a while, "but I really hate your kid."

Abby was too exhausted even to turn her head. "Will you call the police if I murder her?"

"I've been saving something for you," Gretchen said.

Abby sat watching the Christmas tree lights while Gretchen went into the kitchen and came back with a can of Coke and two glasses.

"You left it in your gym bag," Gretchen said. "At the beach house way back when. My parents threw it out, but I snagged it from the trash. It's the one Tommy Cox gave you, isn't it?"

Abby's eyes focused on the red and white can, frosted with condensation, sitting on her coffee table—an artifact washed up from some ancient shipwreck.

"I can't believe it," Abby said. "You've been saving it?"

"Merry Christmas," Gretchen said, and popped the top.

It gave a crisp hiss and she poured it into two glasses, raising hers in a toast.

"To 1982," she said.

Abby picked up her glass and they clinked them together. She took a sip and was a little disappointed. She'd expected it to taste like magic, but it only tasted like Coke.

"Sometimes I wonder what keeps us together," said Gretchen, considering her glass. "Do you? Like when it got hard, there were times we didn't talk, and I always wondered why we kept on trying."

Abby took a long sip from her glass. She didn't want to say anything, but she had thought the same thing, too.

"I think for me," Gretchen said, "it's Max."

Her comment caught Abby off guard.

"The dog?" she asked. "Good Dog Max?"

"Max is still what hurts most," Gretchen said. "Isn't that crazy? He was just a dog, and not even a very smart one—and I've been engaged, almost had a baby, I've had friends die, and the few times I've run into Margaret, she's made it pretty clear that we're never going to be okay again. But I actually have dreams about Max, and you're the only person who knows that wasn't me. Everyone else thinks I killed my dog, even my parents, and the one person who knows I didn't do it is you."

Abby thought for a moment. "That's why I don't go back to Charleston," she said. "Everybody remembers me as the devil worshipper who stole the fetus from the medical university. I didn't tell Devin about it, and I don't know if I'll ever tell Mary."

They were quiet for a few minutes, watching the lights change on the Christmas tree.

"Halley's Comet is coming around again in forty-six years," Gretchen said. "Do you think we'll still be friends?"

Abby watched the red lights fade to green to yellow to blue.

"We'll be almost ninety years old," she said. "I can't think that far ahead."

Because in her heart, Abby didn't want to give the real answer. She loved Gretchen, but what really lasted? Nothing was strong enough to stand against the passage of time.

But Abby was wrong.

When she died at the age of eighty-four, there was one person holding her hand. There was one person who sat with her every day. Who made Glee leave when she got too loud and who made Devin, Abby's ex-husband, visit even though he hated sickness with a phobic intensity. There was one person who read to her when she could no longer see the pages of her book, who fed her pumpkin soup when she got too weak to feed herself, who held up a glass of apple juice when she could no longer raise it to her mouth, and who moistened her lips with a sponge when she lost the ability to swallow. There was one person who stayed by her side even after Mary got too upset and had to leave the room. There was one person with her, all the way down the line.

Abby Rivers and Gretchen Lang were best friends, on and off, for seventy-five years, and there aren't many people who can say that. They weren't perfect. They didn't always get along. They screwed up. They acted like assholes. They fought, they fell out, they patched things up, they drove each other crazy, and they didn't make it to Halley's Comet.

But they tried.

My Best Friend's EXORCISM

A NOVEL BY GRADY HENDRIX

Cast (in order of appearance):

Peter Mansfield

Alex Shortridge

Matthew Gibson

Adam Richards

Ralph Moore

Katie Crouch

Allen Hutcheson

Ryan Deussing

Kevin Hauck

Johnny Krell

Shannon Flynn

Jessica Hardin

Sean Anderson

Caroline Oakley

Ellen Middaugh

The Producers also wish to thank:

The citizens of Quirk Books

The PRHPS Sales Team

Dogs Unlimited Stunt Camp for Canines

ABOUT THE AUTHOR

Grady Hendrix's first novel, *Horrorstör*, was named one of the best books of 2014 by National Public Radio. He is also the author of the nonfiction book *Paperbacks from Hell: The Twisted History of '70s and '80s Horror Fiction*. He lives in New York City.

OTHER BOOKS BY
GRADY HENDRIX

Horrorstör

A Novel

ISBN 978-1-59474-526-3

Something strange is happening at the Orsk furniture superstore in Cleveland, Ohio. Every morning, employees arrive to find broken Kjërring bookshelves, shattered Glans water goblets, and smashed Liripip wardrobes. Sales are down, security cameras reveal nothing, and store managers are panicking. To unravel the mystery, three employees volunteer to work a nine-hour dusk-till-dawn shift. In the dead of night, they'll patrol the empty showroom floor, investigate strange sights and sounds, and encounter horrors that defy the imagination.

Paperbacks from Hell

The Twisted History of '70s and '80s Horror Fiction

ISBN 978-1-59474-981-0

Take a tour through the horror paperback novels of the 1970s and '80s . . . if you dare. Page through dozens of amazing book covers featuring well-dressed skeletons, evil dolls, and knife-wielding killer crabs. Read shocking plot summaries that invoke devil worship, satanic children, and haunted real estate. Filled with glorious full-color reproductions of hundreds of book covers, *Paperbacks from Hell* is an affectionate and funny celebration of your favorite novels—plus many, many forgotten treasures that you've never heard of.